The Storm Before
the CALM

America & Israel at the End of Days

K. R. Smith

WestBow
PRESS

WestBow Press books may be ordered through booksellers or by contacting:

WestBow Press
A Division of Thomas Nelson
1663 Liberty Drive
Bloomington, IN 47403
www.westbowpress.com
1-(866) 928-1240

ISBN: 978-1-4497-0250-2 (sc)
ISBN: 978-1-4497-0251-9 (hc)
ISBN: 978-1-4497-0249-6 (e)

Library of Congress Control Number: 2010929966

Printed in the United States of America

WestBow Press rev. date: 9/28/2010

[God] Who makes the clouds His chariot, Who walks on the wings of the wind, Who makes His angels spirits, His ministers a flame of fire . . . . said to me, "Do not seal the words of the prophecy of this book, for the time is at hand; behold, I am coming quickly, and My reward is with Me, to give to every one according to his work." Therefore . . . since we are surrounded by so great a cloud of witnesses, let us lay aside every weight, and the sin which so easily ensnares us, and let us run with endurance the race that is set before us—Amen[1]

To all who love the real America and Israel

Contents

Acknowledgements

I am deeply indebted, first, to my wife, VonDean, for her encouragement (and the patience of Job) in supporting a husband who often 'burned the midnight oil' while 'married' to a computer keyboard during the many months spent in the research and writing of this book.

I am further deeply indebted to the unstinting help, encouragement, and friendship of my neighbors, Becky Blocker, and Cyndii Sellers. Becky obeyed the prompting of God's Spirit and came to my rescue at exactly the right moment. Cyndii generously offered her literary expertise through many hours of poring over the text, critiquing and editing the first editions of the manuscript.

Without the support and encouragement of all three of these remarkable ladies, this book would never have seen the light of day.

I would also like to thank my friend, Bill Cyganovich, who carefully read and critiqued the final edition of the manuscript.

A 'thank you' and 'God bless you' to each and every one of these!—The Author

INTRODUCTION

On July 7, 1775, John Adams expressed his great concern for America in part of a letter to his wife, Abigail, saying, "Our consolation must be this, my dear, that cities may be rebuilt, and a people, reduced to poverty, may acquire fresh property. But a constitution of government, once changed from freedom, can never be restored. Liberty once lost, is lost forever. When the people once surrender their share in the Legislature, and their right of defending the limitations upon the Government, and of resisting every encroachment upon them, they can never regain it."

Having just addressed the assembled legislators at the opening joint session of the Connecticut Legislature of 1803, the Reverend Mathias Burnet turned to address the visitors' gallery and the common citizens of Connecticut thundering, "To God, and your posterity, you are accountable for your rights and your rulers. Let not your children have reason to curse you for giving up these rights and prostrating those institutions which your fathers delivered to you."

The world is presently sitting on a keg of blasting powder with a lit fuse, my friends. No matter what the personal cost, it is time for each of us to get our own houses in order and stand up to be counted while there is yet hope to preserve America's freedom—our great Representative Republic, unique Constitution and wonderful Bill of Rights—before Leftists, Secularists, Progressives, Socialists, Communists, Religious Leftists and other enemies of freedom succeed in subjecting our nation to the tyrannical rule of the New World Order and One World

Government. America is already in grave danger with far too many godless people in positions of power.

This is a plea to the American people: WAKE UP, STAND UP AND SPEAK UP, OR BE FOREVER SILENCED! — The Author

☆ 1 ☆

THE VISITATION

The morning dawned cloudy and cold near the eastern seaboard. A bone-chilling wind howled through the leafless trees. By early afternoon, a foot of new-fallen snow buried the area in a mantle of white. Neither man nor beast stirred in the forest or among the rows of huts at the Army's winter encampment on the farm of Isaac Potts.

It was one of those days when folks normally love to snuggle deeper into warm blankets and dream. But inside the huts, there was no snuggling in warm blankets—there were very few to be had. Most of the men were gaunt and haggard, some without shoes and many wearing only threadbare clothing. For some, only tattered blankets covered their bodies. Food and fuel were scarce. Some had died of disease, exposure and malnutrition. The Isaac Potts family had graciously allowed the troops to winter on their farm ground and done what they could to help them through the bitter winter but there was only so much a poor farmer could afford. The soldiers' misery had reached the point where many a man had finally reached the end of his endurance, reluctantly quit the army until spring, and gone home while he was still able.

On this wintry day, in the front yard of the Potts' farmhouse, a group of several dozen stalwart knights, unseen by the naked eye, stood quietly, huddled in a tight group, gathered around a central, blonde-haired figure who towered above the rest. None of these were ordinary men. Appearing young, each yet bore an almost imperceptible air of extreme age. Clad in body armor from head to foot, each wore a helmet and tunic; broadswords hung from heavy belts about their waists. All stood mute as the drifting snow swirled about them, while none shivered with cold or shielded himself from the cruel wind.

At length, a huge black warrior broke the silence to address the taller, flaxen-haired figure in golden armor. "What is the holdup, Michael? Why haven't we begun the mission we were sent here to carry out?"

"Patience, Tal, patience! Orders from headquarters!" replied Michael, "I was told to wait until 'someone special' arrives to run the show."

"Someone 'special'? Now who could that be, anyway?"

"We'll all know who it is when the 'special party' arrives, Tal. You know the Boss usually doesn't tell us everything up front! He's seldom early but He's never late! When I get the word, you'll be the first to know, my friend! And now you'll all be happy to know that help's on the way for the courageous men existing in these hovels. Even now, several of our comrades are accompanying a large wagon train of supplies from back east headed in this direction over bad roads through deep snow. They'll be here tomorrow before sundown."

Shifting his stance slightly, the big blonde folded his arms, leaned against a fence post and grinned at his comrades. "As members of the 'upper echelon,' you already know we've been sent here on an urgent mission to encourage a man who's indispensable to the Boss' program. We currently have four legions of warriors in place around the perimeter to protect the conduct of our mission but I still want you all to be alert and stay close to me."

Their conversation was suddenly interrupted as a shout arose from the ranks of the western legion. "On your guard, gentlemen!" shouted Michael, drawing his sword. The cold winter air rang as hundreds of warriors unlimbered their weapons. Swords at the ready, Michael's companions peered intently in the direction of the disturbance, expecting attack at any moment. But instead of a throng of enemy warriors ready to engage them in battle, there appeared only a slight figure dressed in a brown, hooded robe approaching on foot from the western tree line. Puzzled, the assembled knights gathered around Michael looked on, intent upon the interloper. At length, Michael gave a cry of recognition, reversed his hold on the hilt of his sword and swung the blade down, placing the tip on the ground. The others unquestioningly followed their commander's example as he dropped to one knee.

"My Lady!" exclaimed Michael, as the newcomer came within earshot, "To what do we owe the honor of your presence?"

Their newly-arrived companion proved to be a petite young woman. She pushed back her hood revealing a radiantly beautiful olive-skinned face with an aquiline nose and flashing brown eyes framed by a profusion of long, dark, curly hair. Around her neck hung an ornate silver cross on a scarlet cord.

Gazing about her at the kneeling knights, she smiled and exclaimed in lilting tones, "I am honored, gentlemen, but please do not bend the knee to me, for I am but a fellow-servant with you all. Rise mighty ones! Put up your weapons! I am the 'special someone' for whom you have waited, sent by the Master to deliver a vital message to our dear brother. His earnest prayers and days of fasting have been observed before the Father's throne. He is under intense attack by friend and foe alike and we must try to set his heart at rest in this time of his greatest trial. You all know your roles. Within a few moments, he'll be allowed to see us briefly to arouse his curiosity. Come, let us prepare for the task at hand."

Moments later, George gazed out the front windows of the Potts' farm house at the heavily falling snow, sighed and turned to consult his calendar.

December 22 already! My men freeze and starve! Congress twiddles its collective thumbs. . . .and Christmas . . . what will Christmas be like this year?

Light complexioned, standing about 6'-4" tall, with prominent nose and powdered hair, George towered over most of his contemporaries. A man of reserved but resolute demeanor, he cut a fine figure in uniform.

George turned again to the front room windows of the Potts' farm house, which served as his makeshift headquarters office, to view the front yard that had been so green only weeks before. Now everything bore a mantle of white and more was rapidly accumulating. With a sigh, he paused as he faced the stack of paperwork that confronted him.

Tea! Phooey! I cannot abide it! I need a cup of that coffee Mrs. Potts has cooking on her stove. I hope she doesn't mind.

Arising from his chair and grabbing his cup, he stepped around his desk intending to make his way to the kitchen. Glancing out the window again, a flash of color in the swirling snow caught his eye. Taking a closer look, he could barely make out a group of men that he had not seen only moments before, standing in the blowing snow out near the gate in the front fence.

Now why on earth would anyone in his right mind stand around in the open in this howling blizzard? Besides, those men are dressed neither in uniform nor homespun. In fact, it appears that they are dressed in medieval garb— each is wearing a helmet and what appears to be full body armor with a cloth over-garment. And each seems to bear a broadsword on his belt. How strange! And now that I look at them more closely, they seem inordinately tall. But knights? In armor? In this day and age? And there appears to be a monk or some such in a brown habit there among them. What in the world . .? This has got my curiosity up. I must investigate! I cannot tolerate practical jokers, so if this is someone perpetrating a prank for my benefit, I will have their heads. But. . . what if. . . what if what I'm seeing is real?. . . . . I'd better just be a bit cautious in any case!

All thought of coffee faded. Setting down his cup and rubbing his eyes just to be sure, he looked again. Sure enough, there they were, apparently oblivious to the blowing snow, bone-chilling cold and howling wind. Removing his house shoes and pulling on his boots, he quickly donned his overcoat and, sticking a pair of pistols in his belt, he glanced out the window again. Yes, they were still standing there in a huddled group, apparently visiting. Without further rational consideration for his personal safety, he quickly passed the dozing sentry sitting in the hall outside his office door.

No point alerting Sergeant Johnson; he just might get excited and open fire prematurely with that cannon of his and hit me, or someone else, with a wild shot.

George stepped out the back door of the farmhouse into the storm intending to approach the group from behind the house. But as he rounded the front corner of the building and started into the front yard, with both hands on the butts of his pistols, there was no sign of the unusual gathering he had seen only moments before. There was nothing but the whirling snow before his eyes.

What is this? Gone in an instant? What's happening to me, anyway! I must be losing my mind! I wonder if I'm suffering from battle fatigue or something.

George mushed through the snow out to where he thought he had seen the men standing and stood looking about for a few moments hoping to locate his quarry once more—but to no avail. They had simply vanished in a moment of time. Not even footprints in the snow. With a shrug, he scratched his head, and then turned back toward the house, entering by the front door. Stomping the snow off his boots in the entry, the startled sentry snapped a bit groggily to attention. Retrieving his coffee mug from his office, George cajoled Mrs. Potts into filling it at the kitchen stove, adding a dollop of cream and sugar from the pantry, and finally returned to his office. As he hung up his coat, he glanced out the window once again and sighed.

No one out there now. Perhaps the strain of the past months is beginning to tell—must get some rest tonight. How else can I explain seeing a medieval army that . . . that isn't there?

George called out to the sentry from behind his desk, "Sergeant Johnson, see to it that I am not disturbed this afternoon for any reason."

"I'll see to it, Sir," answered the aging sentry, closing the door to George's office.

Returning to his paperwork, George glanced at the clock.

I'm tired and it's only 3:00pm. Let's see. Hmm . . The Potts' will have supper around 6:00pm; I'll read until eight and retire for the evening.

Soon, he was so intent on his work that he was unaware of the silent, cowled figure that entered his office through the wall and approached the front of his desk.

Looking up startled from the dispatch he was writing at the young, dark-complexioned beauty standing just at the front of his desk, George croaked, "Wh . . . . wha. . . who are you, madam . . . and how did you get in here? Sergeant Johnson, front and center on the double," shouted George, a bit frightened at this breach in security and equally perturbed at this intrusion on his privacy.

Sergeant Johnson somehow failed to respond to George's order. The young woman did not reply either but simply raised her eyes a bit to look at George. It was as though he and his unwelcome visitor were encapsulated together in a sound-proof bubble, shut off from the world around them. George questioned her several more times with no perceptible response. Finally, it seemed as though his tongue was becoming paralyzed. As he was about to stand and personally usher her out of his office, he began to feel strange sensations spreading through his body and he felt weak in the knees, unable to stand.

What's happening to me? Everything around me is becoming rarified and luminous. This woman looks more airy and yet more distinct—like a ghost. I . . I don't understand. . . . I can't think or reason or even move. It seems as though I can only look, straight at her. I must look like a total idiot. I wonder if I'm dying! Oh well, if I am, I'm ready to go, Lord!

Suddenly, George heard a voice saying, "It is for you, Son of Liberty, to understand that your nation will become a great Republic. Son of the Republic, look and learn." George's mysterious visitor raised her arm toward the east as a heavy white vapor seemed to rise and roll, fold upon fold, some distance away, which gradually dissipated revealing a strange scene: From a vantage point high above Central America, George observed the North American Continent from Atlantic to Pacific. And all the countries of the world—Europe, Africa, Asia and the Americas—were spread out in one vast plain. The billows of the Atlantic Ocean were rolling and tossing between Europe and America. Between Asia and America lay the Pacific Ocean.

"Son of the Republic, look and learn," repeated the mysterious voice. George then saw a dark, shadowy angel floating in mid-air between Europe and America. The angel dipped water out of the ocean in each hand, sprinkling some on America with his right hand and some on Europe with his left. Instantly, clouds arose from the two countries and joined together in mid-ocean where it seemed to remain stationary for a while before it slowly drifted westward engulfing America in its folds. There were occasional flashes of lightning from it and George could hear what sounded like the smothered groans and cries of the American people. A second time, the shadowy angel dipped water from the Atlantic and sprinkled it out as before. The dark cloud was then drawn back to the ocean where it sank from view. A third time, George heard the mysterious voice intone, "Son of the Republic, look and learn." As he watched, villages, towns and cities sprang up, one after another, until the entire land from the Atlantic coast to the Pacific coast was dotted with them.

Then as George watched, fascinated, the mysterious voice came again, "Son of the Republic, look and learn." At this, the dark angel turned his face south, toward Africa, and a dark, ill-omened specter approached America flitting slowly over the entire land. Eventually, Americans set themselves in battle array against each other. As he watched, a bright angel who was wearing a crown of light bearing the word "Union," placed the American flag between the battle lines of the divided nation saying, "Remember, you are brothers." At this, the citizens of the land cast aside their weapons and united once again around the National Standard.

Once again, the mysterious voice said, "Son of the Republic, look and learn." At this, the dark, shadowy angel placed a trumpet to his mouth and blew three long blasts. Then, taking water from the oceans, he sprinkled it upon Europe, Asia, Africa and South America. Then George recoiled at a terrifying scene: From each of these land masses arose thick black clouds that joined into one. Throughout the mass of clouds, there gleamed a dark red light by which he could see hordes of armed men moving with the cloud, marching by land and sailing by sea to America. The whole country was soon enveloped in the cloud and he could see the vast armies devastate the land, burning the villages, towns and cities he had seen springing up before. As he listened to the thunder of artillery, the clashing of weaponry and the shouts and cries of millions engaged in mortal combat, George once again heard the mysterious voice saying, "Son of the Republic, look and learn." When the voice ceased, the dark, shadowy angel blew one long and powerful blast upon his trumpet.

Instantly, a brilliant light from above, like a thousand suns, shone down upon the dark cloud that had enveloped America, breaking it into fragments. At that moment, the bright angel wearing the crown engraved with the word "Union," carrying our National Standard in one hand and a great sword in the other, descended from the heavens accompanied by legions of other bright spirits. These immediately joined the inhabitants of America who were very nearly beaten. Renewing their courage, the

Americans closed their ranks and renewed the battle. Amid the fearful noise of the conflict, the mysterious voice once again said, "Son of the Republic, look and learn." For the last time, the shadowy angel dipped water from the oceans and sprinkled it upon America. Instantly, the dark cloud rolled away with the armies it had brought, leaving the inhabitants of the land victorious.

Once more, George saw the villages, towns and cities springing up where he had seen them before. The bright angel then stepped forward and planted the National Standard in the midst of the people crying with a loud voice, "While the stars remain and the heavens send down dew upon the earth, so long shall the Union last." Taking from his head the crown upon which was emblazoned the word 'Union,' he placed it upon the staff of the National Standard as all the people knelt and said, "Amen."

The scene began to fade and dissolve and George finally saw nothing but the rising, curling vapor he had seen at the first. Finally, even that disappeared and he was once again alone with his mysterious feminine visitor who, in the same voice he had heard before said, "Son of the Republic, what you have seen is thus interpreted: Three great perils will come upon the American Republic. The most fearful is the third, but in this greatest conflict, the entire world united shall not prevail against her. Let every child of the Republic learn to live for his God, his land and the Union." With that, the vision and the visitor vanished and it seemed as though he was awakening from a deep dream.

Once again aware of familiar surroundings, George bolted from his chair, as though propelled by a spring; he stood frozen for a moment trying to collect his wits. The last thing he remembered clearly, it had been 3:00pm, dark and stormy, but the storm had abated and the sun had even appeared. Confused, he glanced at the clock noting that the time was then 5:00pm.

It's nearly sundown. I've been occupied for two hours. But where was I? And who was that woman who surprised me? And how did she get in here past Sergeant Johnson, anyway? What a terrifying experience this has been!

He sat down for a moment to let his mind clear.

"Sergeant Johnson? Report, on the double!" ordered the bewildered officer.

8

"What is it, Sir?" inquired the alarmed sergeant as he rushed in and saluted.

"Sergeant, did you see anyone in a brown garment near my office door or my outside windows around 3:00pm?" George demanded.

"Well, Sir, I think I did see a woman in a brown cloak in the rear hallway around 3:00. . . . but . . .but I'm sure it was the Potts' daughter, Mildred. Begging the general's pardon, Sir, is something wrong?" inquired the alarmed old man.

George stroked his chin thoughtfully for a moment and then replied, "Hmmm . . oh . . it was nothing important, I guess! Forget it, sergeant. Return to your post. Dismissed!"

He's never let anyone get past him before and I've never known him to lie. Apparently, something else is going on. The experience seemed so real. I must inquire of the Lord.

George called out to the sentry, "Sergeant, have my horse saddled immediately and bring him around to the front door."

"YES, SIR!" replied the grizzled old sentry, as he scurried out the door towards the barn.

I'm sure many wonder why I go into the woods to pray instead of remaining in the comfort of my quarters in the Potts' household. Frankly, I can't explain it myself! Somehow, I seem most comfortable seeking the Lord out in the woods in that special cove. Ah, well . .here comes my horse. I'd best get dressed.

Donning boots and overcoat, George stepped out once again into the wintry landscape, mounted up and rode to a dense willow thicket among a few large old oak trees in an inner area of the camp. But today, as he sought the Lord, he found he could not concentrate—his mind was still reeling from the vision. After some time he stood up, shook the snow from his trousers, swung back into the saddle and headed home. Entering the house, George called to the sentry, "Sergeant, have my horse taken care of, please, and summon my aide, Colonel Sherman."

"I'll see to it at once, Sir."

George suddenly felt the urge to pray so he closed the door and dropped to his knees on his office floor.

9

"Lord, what is it? Was that a vision from You or was it something else? I don't know what to make of it!" asked George.

Immediately, a still but forceful voice seemed to speak in his mind, "You've asked a strange question: 'Can this possibly be so?' I will give you an answer and cause you to know of a surety that what you just experienced was from Me. Record it for posterity, for it is a true prophesy of the destiny of the nation you are about to birth. So let it be written, so let it be done!"

Shaken by the force of the answer, George arose and sat in his desk chair until his pulse returned to normal.

Fifteen minutes later, a tall, light-complexioned young man with dark, wavy hair and bright blue eyes, wearing the rank of a full colonel, knocked on the door and stepped in.

"You wanted to see me, Sir?" he queried.

"Yes, Colonel Sherman, come in! Come in and sit down, please," George responded warmly, rising from his hard desk chair and moving to one of two upholstered chairs in front of his desk.

Colonel Anthony Sherman, a very successful Virginia businessman, had volunteered early on as an officer in the ranks of the fledgling Army and was immediately appointed to the rank of colonel. Sherman stood 6'-2' tall and was a powerfully built, handsome young man. He had caught George's eye during a staff meeting at a local pub and been invited to dine at the general's table. After being formally introduced, the two had conversed at length concerning the prosecution of the war. George had been so impressed by Sherman's understanding of tactics that he had made the colonel his aide-de-camp.

As he approached George's chair, the newcomer looked intently at his superior. "Sir, you appear rather pale today. Are you feeling well?" he queried.

"As a matter of fact, I'm a bit out of sorts, Anthony," George began, "Something very unusual happened to me this afternoon. I'd like to discuss it with you in strictest confidence. There are so few I can trust with impunity these days."

"Of course, Sir, whatever we discuss will be held in the strictest of confidence as always," replied the young man.

"Anthony, since the day we met, you have become like a son to me. I cannot explain the bond between us but I have so appreciated your friendship, your discretion, and faithful service. I know this has unsettled some of my general staff but I hope they know that I mean them no disrespect or harm."

"The feeling is mutual, Sir. You are rather like a father to me and I am honored to serve you and our great country," retorted the colonel.

At that point, George looked askance at his companion, took a long swallow of coffee, leaned back in his chair and closed his eyes. Taking a deep breath, he began, "Anthony, I don't know if it is owing to the constant anxiety of command or what it is, but this afternoon, around 2:30pm, I was on my way to pour myself a cup of coffee when I looked out the window at the front yard and saw something most unusual—a large group of what appeared to be medieval knights in armor standing in that blizzard with no ill effect. So amazed was I that I decided to investigate, but when I exited the back door of the house and rounded the front, thinking to surprise some jokesters, they had disappeared. There were not even footprints in the snow. At that point, I wondered if I were seeing things. Then, a few minutes later, at about 3:00pm, as I was sitting at this desk engrossed in preparing a dispatch, something disturbed me.

"Looking up, I beheld standing opposite me a gorgeous young woman. So astonished was I, for I had given strict orders not to be disturbed, that it was some moments before I was able to inquire as to her identity and the reason for her presence. Several times I repeated my question, but received no answer from her except a slight raising of her eyes.

"By this time, I felt strange sensations spreading through me. I would have risen but the riveted gaze of this being before me rendered volition impossible. I tried once more to address her, but my tongue had become useless, as though it were paralyzed.

"A new influence, mysterious, potent, irresistible, took possession of me. All I could do was to gaze steadily, vacantly at my unknown visitor. Gradually the surrounding atmosphere seemed as if it had become luminous and filled with strange sensations. Everything around me seemed to rarify, the mysterious visitor herself becoming more airy and yet more distinct to my sight than before. I now began to feel as one dying, or rather to experience the sensations that I have sometimes imagined accompany dissolution. I did not think, I did not reason, I did not move; all were alike impossible. I was only conscious of gazing fixedly, vacantly at my companion.

"And then what happened, Sir?" inquired Colonel Sherman, intrigued.

For the next hour, George and his young companion shared the details of his earth-shaking experience during the vision.

Concluding his account, George said, "I seem to have received an answer from the Lord that it was from Him, Anthony, but I need a bit of human confirmation. How do you see it? I desperately need to settle in my mind whether this was the result of battle fatigue, a dream or a divine visitation."

By this time, Colonel Sherman noted that his companion's face was almost ashen. Concern for his superior flooded his mind and he said, "Sir, from your description of the events, I am absolutely convinced that this has indeed been a divine visitation. But, come now, this has been at once both a most glorious and a most terrifying day for you. Please, do relax a bit and get some rest tonight and we'll discuss it again later. Let's both pray about it and, if you wish, we can meet again at your convenience. For now, with your leave, Sir, I will return to my duties."

"Yes, by all means, Anthony. Let's plan to meet tomorrow afternoon at 4:00pm. And thank you for coming so quickly, my friend."

As Colonel Sherman departed, George's big frame slumped wearily in his chair.

Must get this dispatch finished. I'll eat supper with the Potts' and retire early this evening. Ah, let's see . . . . .good, it's all finished except for the address, date and signature.

Picking up his pen, George dipped it in the ink well and signed the document, dating it:

Valley Forge, Pennsylvania, December 22, 1777.

George signed it:

G. Washington, General
Commander In Chief

☆ 2 ☆
Back To The Future: July 2015

> "But you, Daniel, conceal and seal the words of this book until the end time when men shall run frantically back and forth on the earth and knowledge will increase[2]

"Excuse me, Sir! There's an urgent call for you on a secure satellite channel," Frank Samuelson called over his shoulder from the copilot's seat of the sleek biz-jet.

As Jim Black put down his magazine and picked up the handset by his seat, a familiar voice greeted him. "General Black, this is George Wing at Black Eagle Ranch—you probably don't remember me."

Jim laughed, "George, are you trying to make me feel guilty about not coming home more often? What's up, my friend? Is Grandfather giving you a hard time these days?"

George replied, "Yeah, as a matter of fact, he's been driving me nuts, Jim. I know you're super busy these days and I'm sorry to bother you, but Grandfather asked me to contact you ASAP—says he has something of the utmost urgency to discuss with you. He won't say what it is but you know that he is never insistent unless it's really important. By the way, where are you anyway?"

Jim laughed again, "We're at 45,000 feet over the Pacific Ocean, bound for Japan. Let me talk to Grandfather."

"Nope, he says he's 'not going to discuss anything over whatever that contraption is you talk over,' as he puts it. He says 'only face time will do,'" explained the voice on the other end.

"Well, okay, is the old codger sick or something?" inquired Jim.

"No, he seems fine physically—but of course at 85, he has good days and bad days. But you know him—once he gets something in his head, he won't lay it down. Do you suppose, for the sake of my sanity, you could stop by and see him sometime soon?" pleaded the voice on the other end.

"Now, George, don't apologize; when Grandfather says something is urgent, I always make it a point to listen. I should have come home for a visit a long time ago! Hold on a second and let me see what I can do."

Jim called forward to his expatriate Israeli pilot, Samuel Baruch, "Sam, have we reached the 'Point of No Return' yet?"

"No, Sir, that's still an hour up ahead. What's up?" replied the pilot.

"Turn us around and head back to Portland. We're going to Montana, *poste haste*. My Grandfather is having some sort of fit and I've got to find out what is going on!"

"Aye aye, Sir! Roger, WILCO! Hold onto your hats back there, ladies and gents, 'cause we're gonna pull a killer 180 turn," Sam yelped over his shoulder with a sly twinkle in his eye.

The trim biz-jet banked sharply in a tight, nearly 90 degree bank.

Jim yelled, "Sam, ease up, we're not wearing G-suits back here."

"Oops, sorry, Sir! Old habits are a bit hard to break," Sam grinned, "Has everybody kept their lunches down?"

"Barely," retorted a grim feminine voice.

"Sorry, Maryann, I'll try to drive more carefully in the future," teased the Israeli.

Jim merely smiled and returned to his phone conversation, "Listen, George, we've just reversed course. If Baruch doesn't kill us first, we'll probably arrive at the ranch some time tomorrow morning because I don't particularly relish making a night approach to the ranch's mountain runway again. The last time we did that we nearly took the top out those big ponderosas at the east end of the runway. Baruch spent all the next day picking pine needles out of my airplane. So, will tomorrow morning be soon enough for 'His Eminence'? "

"Gosh, I hate to interrupt your business, Jim, but maybe it would be best if you came home at that, if you can spare the time. Actually, we cut down those ponderosas, bark beetles and all, but the weather really is a little dicey here at the moment anyway, so I don't blame you. I'm sure whatever it is Grandfather wants can wait until tomorrow, Jim."

"By the way, George, are you still squiring Grandfather around in that old Lockheed Electra of his? That thing should have been in a museum years ago," quipped Jim.

Nah! Grandfather finally spent some of his moldy money and purchased a pretty little Learjet 40. I fly it for him but turbine equipment just goes against my grain—if it doesn't have propellers, it's just not cool for me. Well, anyway, we're all anxious to see you again, *mi amigo*. It's been a long time."

"You're right, George, it has that. I'll try to remedy that in the future. We'll see you tomorrow."

Jim dialed a number in Japan and a man with a heavy Japanese accent answered on the other end.

"Mr. Tanaga? This is General Black. Listen, I just learned of a family emergency in Montana. We have just reversed course and are headed back to Portland. I'm sorry to put our meeting on hold but I'll get back to you just as soon as I can. Will you give the Secretary my apologies?"

"Ah, no problem, General Black, in fact it's probably the best thing. Mr. Yoshiida is actually undergoing some unexpected tests for chest pains at the hospital this morning. We can all get together when things return to normal on both sides of the Pacific. Have a safe trip, Sir."

Some hours later, Jim's corporate jet touched down in Portland, Oregon, and taxied up to the fuel pumps. Sam hovered over the ramp attendants as they refueled the plane.

Sam's a case, but I'm sure glad I hired him. He's forgotten more than a lot of pilots ever knew.

Jim called out the door, "Sam, find a tie-down for our mount, here. I'll get us a cab and three rooms at the Marriot Downtown Waterfront. We'll sleep over tonight and be off after breakfast."

"Sir, the Fixed Base Operator here is an acquaintance of mine; says he has just the ticket for us on down the flight line—large hangar inside a fenced compound with 24 hour security. Why don't you and Maryann go on ahead? Frank and I will roll this bird on down there and tuck her in bed. We'll catch a cab and be along shortly."

"Okay, but don't tarry too long, we'll eat supper as soon as you arrive at the hotel," advised Jim.

The next morning, liftoff came at 9:07am into a baby blue sky on one of those rare windless, cloudless days on the Oregon coast. As Sam brought the ship level at 41,000 feet, it seemed you could see through the haze a thousand miles in any direction.

"Sam, how long you figure it'll be to the ranch?" Jim called from the back of the cabin.

"Oh, letdown should commence in about an hour, Sir."

Jim sighed, "Okay, guess I'll grab a cat nap before we get to the old homestead. Somebody wake me when we begin letdown."

At 10:15am, Frank Samuelson arose from the right seat and approached his dozing employer.

"Sir? Sir?" he said gently shaking Jim's shoulder, "We're beginning letdown now. We'll be landing at Black Eagle Ranch in about 20 minutes."

As the ship's engines changed pitch and the nose dropped slightly, Jim, yawned, stretched and gazed out the window just as the starboard wingtip dipped below the Montana skyline. The vista was breathtaking. The late morning sun shone on the big timber of the Bitterroot Mountains as the sleek little craft screamed in over the rocky spine of the North American continent toward the valleys and mountain ranges beyond.

It had been months since he'd been back—too many months. His roots were here. His grandmother and parents, along with a list of forbears reaching back into the nineteenth century, were buried in the family cemetery near the ranch house. Soon his grandfather would sleep with his ancestors. Ezra J. Black Eagle, known to everyone simply as 'Grandfather,' was descended from a long line of Apsáalooke, or Crow, chieftains that had possessed the opportunity and foresight to found Black Eagle Ranch in the late 19th century. Over the years, the astute businessmen of the family had parlayed the original tract of land into many thousands of acres and a fortune the exact extent of which Jim could only guess. The more he thought about home, the more he realized how much he missed his family.

I should visit more often; can't imagine what has Grandfather so fired up. But the old man could die anytime and there's too much left unsaid between us. We Americans are too often careless when it comes to those we love. Ah, Black Eagle ranch! It'll be good to be home for a while!

In the seat beside him, his wife, Maryann, the light of his life, began to stir from a nap. Blonde, blue-eyed Maryann Olson from Minneapolis, Minnesota, was a computer technology major finishing her master's degree when they met on campus at Cal-Tech—her professional expertise had pulled the couple through some lean times. She knew relatively little of Jim's family. He had kept it that way.

The fact was that at a tender age, a very rebellious James Black Eagle could hardly wait to leave Montana many moons ago to seek his fortune elsewhere—anywhere but in 'hayseed country,' as he put it. Eventually, he had officially shortened his name to Black to remove what he perceived to be the 'stigma of his Native American heritage,' a move he later regretted. At 6'-1", Jim was ramrod straight and light-complexioned with black wavy hair and penetrating blue eyes. Jim's parents had died in a traffic accident when he was three years old and his wealthy grandfather, the patriarch of the family, had raised him and paid his expenses through six years at Cal-Tech and three years at Massachusetts Institute of Technology.

After finishing their Masters degrees at Cal-Tech, Jim and Maryann moved to MIT for his Ph.D. in Aerospace Engineering and hers in Computer Science. In the meantime, Jim received a commission in the U.S. Air Force and flew fighters for six years, then he subsequently spent several years commanding first one unit, then another and eventually was promoted and assigned to the office of the Air Force Chief of Staff at the Pentagon. After 30 years in the Air Force, he had retired as a Major General, hung up his twin stars and became a partner in a small but successful aerospace firm in Houston, Texas.

Jim had acquired the company following the founder's untimely death in a plane crash. Renaming the company Black Defense Enterprises, International, Jim quickly gathered a staff of outstanding experts and rapidly built the company into a large corporation, eventually partnering with a former Israeli IDF fighter pilot, Colonel Ariel Ben-Yehudah, who had been at the time a relative upstart in the Israeli defense industry. With this impetus, the partners again renamed the company Etzion Defense Enterprises, International, quickly diversifying in several innovative high-tech defense and commercial ventures. Jim's personal fortune had grown into the billions by his 56th birthday.

"Fasten your seat belts, boys and girls, we're on approach to Black Eagle International Airport and there are some thunder-bumpers in the neighborhood," announced the pilot as the muffled whine of the engines changed pitch and the gear came down, locking into place. As they turned on final approach to the runway, the flaps lowered to 40° and the aircraft seemed to hang suspended in mid-air. Jim could see some of the Black Eagle staff waiting on the tarmac ahead. The gear settled onto the runway with a soft "chorf, chorf. . . .chorf" and it seemed as though a weight lifted from Jim's shoulders.

Ah, Black Eagle Ranch!! Home at last!!

The massive 20,000 square foot ranch house at Black Eagle Ranch was more like a mountain lodge than a house. Built in the late 1920's with huge native timber from the surrounding forests, many of the rough-hewn logs were two feet or more in diameter. The roof was constructed of fired clay tiles reminiscent of a Spanish *hacienda*. The interior was always cool in the summer and warm in the winter. There was nothing in Jim's mind that could compare with curling up on an over-stuffed leather sofa on a snowy winter's day in front of a roaring fire in one of the big fireplaces or relaxing in the cool, dark, great room on a hot summer's day. Yes, this was home at its best, something he had sorely missed in Houston's steamy heat. As Jim strode into the entry hall with Maryann on his arm, his old

Native American friend and head household manager, George Wing, ran up to give them both a big bear-hug and motioned Jim toward the master bedroom.

"How is he?" asked Jim.

"Can't be too bad, he's been driving me crazy asking when you were gonna arrive."

"Okay, here goes, pal! See y'all later," said Jim as he took a deep breath and strode quickly down the dark hallway to the old man's *boudoir*.

The elder Black Eagle was dressed in a lounging robe and slippers. As Jim walked in, he turned to greet him with a broad smile. "Ho, my grandson! You came at last! Praise the Lord!"

HUH?!! PRAISE THE LORD?!! WHAT?!! GRANDFATHER? THE NATIVE AMERICAN MEDICINE MAN? YOU GOTTA BE KIDDING ME!!

"What has happened to you, Old One? I came because I thought perhaps you were not well, but you look like a cat that has just swallowed a mouse," Jim laughed in spite of himself.

"Some day, I will go the way of all the earth my son. But I'm not dead yet—not even close! My health is not the reason I summoned you here. Come, sit with me. I have something important to discuss with you."

Jim settled cautiously into one of Grandfather's favorite, but rickety, cane-backed chairs facing the old man as he sat on the edge of the bed.

I used to sit on these things when I was a kid. You'd think we could afford some new furniture around here—this chair has got to be at least a hundred years old.

"Tell me, what is this 'Praise the Lord' business, Grandfather? I thought you were into the old ways," chided Jim.

"You are correct, Jim—many years ago I became bored with the lifeless humdrum I experienced in the spiritual deadness of our church and so I left what I mistakenly considered the 'white man's religion.' I studied the old religion of my ancestors and became an akbaalia, or medicine man—a shaman—and practiced all the ancient spiritual craft of our people," the old man responded.

"So, what changed your mind?"

"Six months ago, I received an unexpected visitor in the wee hours of the morning. That night, I snapped wide awake at exactly 3:00am. As I lay in bed, I could hear footsteps coming down the hall. Assuming it was George on some urgent matter, I got out of bed and was putting on my robe just as the door opened.'

"And?"

"And, who should walk in? Not George, but the King of the Universe, of all people, robe, sandals and all!"

"You mean Jesus appeared to you? Wow! What did you do? What was He like? What did He say?" Jim stammered excitedly.

"Well, when He looked at me, the glory of God just radiated from His face. Man, is He handsome! His robes sparkled like diamonds! But the first thing I did was fall on my face in front of Him. When you are in His holy presence, you can't stand up. All the strength leaves your body and there's not a thing you can do about it. His holiness just permeates your being. You remember what John related in Revelation:

> 'And when I saw Him, I fell at His feet as dead. But He laid His right hand on me, saying to me, 'Do not be afraid; I am the First and the Last. I *am* He who lives, and was dead, and behold, I am alive forevermore. And I have the keys of Hades and of Death.'[3]

"Just as John wrote, He laid His hand on my shoulder and said, 'Get up, My child, and sit with me for I have strengthened you.' He smiled at me and graciously asked me if I believed in Him and would serve Him. Of course I said 'Yes.' You know, there is a huge difference between true Christianity and religion—when you come face to face with the 'Real McCoy,' all doubt is erased and religion goes out the window. He talked with me for well over an hour and gave me some very specific instructions pertaining to myself, to you and your family in particular and many other things in general. I can tell you that you are a very, very important man to Him, my son."

"Me? Why should I be so important to Him? I'm just an old ex-soldier and an entrepreneur. Uh . . . . Gosh, why didn't you let us know about this earlier?" Jim asked, flabbergasted.

"For some reason known only to Him, He forbade me to tell you until now, Jim. Yesterday, He spoke to me and said 'TELL JIM NOW'," responded the old man, "And I said 'YES SIR!' That's why I had George call you in mid-Pacific."

Thunderstruck, Jim croaked, "What is going on?"

"Jim, there are dark days immediately ahead for America. We are fast approaching the time known as the 'End of Days.' For months, I have been troubled by dreams of the night. Every night, it is the same thing."

"Such as . . . .?"

"Traitors in our government at the highest levels. Americans have made the mistake of looking to politicians to solve their problems instead of God. I saw atomic bombs exploding in our cities, hordes of evil men invading America by sea, air and land, stripping it bare of everything they can carry away, wantonly burning our towns and cities, raping our women and murdering our people. Only those who are prepared will escape the wrath of the invaders with the blue helmets."

"Nukes in America? Yeah, that possibility has haunted me for a long time now! But invaders with blue helmets? Hmm . . .the only outfit I know that fits that bill is the United Nations," Jim mused. Jim dug into his brief and pulled out a color newspaper article with a photo of helmeted U.N. troops. "Is this the insignia you saw?"

"Yes! Exactly! They were among the invaders I saw, but not the only ones. There were other soldiers too, some carrying flags with a crescent moon and star as well as flags I did not recognize. I saw them come by the hundreds of thousands swarming over the land like locusts from coast to coast. Several groups first came to help us, or so they said, but then they seized power and began to carry off people, especially Christians and Jews, to prison camps and burn everything to the ground wherever they went—homes, hospitals, churches, businesses, nothing was exempt. Our military fought against them, despite the orders of the government to surrender, but there was only so much they could do with limited manpower and resources.

"You, my son, must be prepared to take refuge in the Eagle's Lair very soon now. The Lord directed me to prepare the place as a City of Refuge for our family, friends and associates. There is a large lodge there with guest rooms and cottages enough for at least two hundred people. I know you have about a hundred in your church in Houston, and they are all welcome to come.

"But . . . but Grandfather, if the country is invaded what will prevent the invaders from finding us in the Eagle's Lair?" sputtered Jim.

"I asked Him that very question and He assured me that the Lair will be secure—that all the people there will be protected from the enemy. No one who is unworthy will be able to find it. Our household and yours, as well as your friends, will be safe there," declared the old man.

"Soon, we will finish the remodeling there and get it stocked with everything needed for 300 people to survive for several years. The water, sewage and power systems have already been revamped to run with minimal maintenance. The runways are still in excellent shape and the old Instrument Landing System we put in years ago has been updated. I'll stock a commissary there from my pharmacy in Billings and there's a dentist and a family physician setting up satellite offices there for me. We're installing chicken and turkey brooders and moving several thousand head of Black Angus cattle into a fenced area on the far side of the preserve to provide fresh meat. But there's something else there that's important for you to find and I don't know what it is—the Lord would not reveal it to me. He said you'll find it yourself at the right time.

"And just so you'll know that all of this isn't the wild imagination of a senile old man, the Lord said to ask you about that new, secret, uh . . . let me find my notes. . . Ah yes! The ACGSX-22RV aircraft weapons system you completed along with your Israeli partners a week ago. And now, I am tired—leave me until this afternoon. I will rest and we will talk later."

Stunned, Jim walked slowly into the great room in a daze and sat on his favorite sofa, forgetting all about Maryann and the rest of his party.

That ACGSX-22RV system is ultra top secret. No one without the highest-level government security clearance could have known about its existence. It hasn't even been delivered to the Pentagon yet. As wild as it sounds, the old man really has received a divine visitation. Sends a chill up my back.

The Eagle's Lair . . .hmm?

Jim had been to the Lair several times as a child and teenager. Located some miles east of the ranch house in a large box canyon in a high valley, the Eagle's Lair was surrounded by heavy forest. The place had always been an awesome and mysterious place to Jim. There had never been even a road into the place while he was living at home. It was an abandoned World War II era airbase—beyond that, his knowledge of the place was spotty.

Grandfather finally emerged from his bedroom in jeans, western shirt and boots around 2:00pm and sat down in front of the huge stone fireplace alongside Jim on the big leather sofa.

"Tell me about the Eagle's Lair, Grandfather. I really never knew that much about it," said Jim.

"Well, it's a unique place, Jim," began the old man, "As a young boy, I vividly remember the day in early 1942 when an official olive drab Ford War Department car with a white star on the side drove up in front of the house and two agents came to the door. I stood beside my father, your great grandfather Jedediah Black Eagle, as he met with them in this very room. They said that the war effort needed a restricted military installation to be located in the Eagle's Lair box canyon and asked if we would be willing to give the government a long-term lease. They said the base would be built self-contained—that everything would be brought in by air and that they would not even require a road into the site. Jedediah thought that was a bit strange but, being patriotic, consented and signed the lease. The agents left and the base was indeed built just as they had said; how they did it is still a mystery. By late 1943, we began hearing and seeing military aircraft of all kinds flying in and out of the place—heavy bombers like the B-29 and even some early jets towards the end of the war. We assumed the base was being used as a secret research site, but we never knew for what exactly. We tried to sneak in through the forest and get a look at what went on there but the perimeter guards caught us. The base commander warned us not to come back or we would be arrested. So, we had to content ourselves with catching glimpses of aircraft flying in and out.

"After the war, in 1946, the same two government agents came to the house and met with Jedediah again; they said the base was being deactivated. The War Department had signed the lease back to our family and everything there was now ours to do with as we wished, which we thought was most unusual. They handed Jedediah a large ring of keys, a roll of maps, plans and other drawings, thanked us for our cooperation and left.

"We rode in on horseback a few days later to look the place over and what a layout it was! The place had beautiful 8,500 by 250 foot wide concrete runways of glass-hard concrete, a commissary, hospital, and a full complement of officer's quarters and enlisted men's barracks, everything you'd find on any normal military post. The place had two deep water wells, a natural gas well and a hydro power generator fed by a concrete dam on the nearby lake.

"Man, we were elated—the place seemed perfect for an all-year-around vacation spot and tourist attraction. By 1952, we laid plans to make it into a grand place. We remodeled some of the buildings, built a lodge, twenty-five guest cottages and began advertising in some national publications.

"We received a number of inquiries and soon reservations were starting to come in. But then the trouble began. Only part of the people who sent in reservations showed up, quite a number made angry phone calls or sent us nasty letters complaining that they had followed our directions, drove or flew in to the area but never could find the place. After several years of this, we finally closed the operation. It was then that some of the elders of the Crow Nation told us that this was the area that our forefathers called, in our native tongue, 'The-valley-that-is-not-there.' The traditions say that this is a mystical place that only worthy people are allowed to find—you may know exactly where it should be and walk right through it but never find it. Since then, we've used it mostly as our own private hunting and fishing preserve."

"Almost sounds like the mythical village of Brigadoon in the Scottish highlands that disappeared into the mists and only reappears for one day each century," opined Jim.

"Exactly! You've doubtless heard of people disappearing in the Devil's Triangle area off the Florida coast and the Dragon's Triangle east of the Sea of Japan—I'm thinking the Eagle's Lair must be a similar place. Anyway, it doesn't surprise me that the Lord would establish a City of Refuge in such a place. In fact, truth be known, He may very well have created the place for the sole purpose of shielding us from harm there today," the old man concluded.

"Well, tomorrow, let's visit the place and get the lay of the land, Grandfather. Can you come and give us the fifty-cent tour?"

"Absolutely—wouldn't miss it for the world."

That evening, the entire party was briefed on the situation during dinner. There were looks of incredulity on the faces of Maryann and the rest of Jim's companions but none was willing to express reservations out of respect for their host.

The next morning, Grandfather joined the group in the cabin of the Citation. Jim sat down in the pilot's seat, lit off the engines and taxied out to the runway. "This may be overkill, but I thought we should do this from the air instead of driving over since we'll undoubtedly come by air in the event we ever have to use this place for real some day," he explained.

Sam Baruch sat in the copilot's seat with his charts on his lap and a frown on his face. "Sir, have you noticed that there isn't any airfield, or anything else, shown on the sectional navigation charts where this Eagle's Lair is supposed to be?"

"Nope! Never has been, never will be, Sam," laughed Jim, "It's just simply not officially there."

As the biz-jet approached the old airbase, the party observed a ring of high cliffs and heavy forest surrounding the canyon and an azure blue lake near the north rim. Clearing the cliffs and forest, Jim made a high-speed pass down the main runway twenty feet off the deck.

"Yup, runway looks clean as a whistle! Let's drop in for coffee!" he joked as he brought the ship around to land.

The little craft touched down softly on the ancient runway and rolled to a stop on the tarmac near the lodge. As the turbines wound to a stop, everyone exited the ship and stood gaping at their surroundings, awed by its verdant beauty and quietude. The only sounds to be heard were the wind swishing through the trees and tall grass and the occasional chirp of a bird.

"This is an awesome place!" someone murmured quietly, almost reverently.

Grandfather shattered their reverie as he piped up, "Do you notice anything unusual about this place, Jim?"

Carefully surveying the landscape with an analytical eye, Jim finally said at length, "Yes, as a matter of fact, I don't see any hangars. Never saw an airfield without hangars."

Grandfather handed Jim an instrument that looked very much like an antique three-button radio control with a telescoping antenna and stepped back with a smug look on his face.

"What's this?" Jim demanded.

"Try pushing either one of those buttons marked '1' or '2' and see what happens," the old man exclaimed, his eyes twinkling with excitement.

Jim pushed the button marked "1". In the near distance, there came the low rumble of hidden machinery as the side of one of the cliffs started to open.

"What the. . .?" Jim exclaimed, awestruck.

"Hidden hangars built right into the mountain side. Push the other button," chortled Grandfather.

As Jim pushed the button marked "2," a second hangar door began to open.

Jim gazed at the sight with awe, "Those hangars are just enormous," he exclaimed, "Wonder why they built them into the side of a mountain. My whole menagerie of war birds could fit in just one corner of one of them. What's this third button do, Grandfather?"

"Third button doesn't do anything—must've been meant for a future expansion that didn't happen," replied the old man. "Let's go look at them and the rest of the physical plant up close—I think you'll like what you see. We do have a pretty decent road into the place nowadays so we brought this old bus over for hauling folks around. Everybody get aboard and let's go have a look around."

After several hours of inspecting the premises, the group returned to their aircraft to take stock of what they'd seen. As they all sat in the cabin, Jim summed up the place: "Let's see now. We have a beautiful log lodge with fifty furnished rooms, a library, fully equipped multi-media lecture hall and a communications center. We have twenty five modern, fully furnished three-bedroom log family guest-houses. We also have a medical and dental clinic that will soon be fully equipped and a pharmacy that will be fully stocked from Grandfather's pharmacy in Billings. And we will soon have a food store and warehouse that will be stocked with enough food and other products to last 300 people three years, teen-agers notwithstanding. Plus, the place is equipped to handle our needs for natural gas, water, sewage and electricity, to say nothing of those two enormous hangars. Pretty awesome, I'd say, Grandfather!!"

"It would never have been possible but for Him, my son," replied the elder Black Hawk, pointing skyward.

"Well, my friends, I have a delayed appointment with the Japanese government and we've got to get on the road—big defense contract pending. And after that, I have to get back to Houston as fast as this bird can fly! I have a list of meetings as long as my arm scheduled for the next six weeks. I'll leave the completion of this place in the capable hands of George and Grandfather. Grandfather, be assured that I will fund whatever remains to be done to bring it swiftly to completion. Send me the invoices at the plant. Keep me informed on the secure channels and no arguments about calling me on my 'newfangled contraptions,' Grandfather, this is no time for games," chided Jim, as he turned in the pilot's seat and started the engines.

ARIEL BEN-YEHUDAH

For behold, your enemies make a tumult; And those who hate You have lifted up their head. They have taken crafty counsel against Your people, And consulted together against Your sheltered ones. They have said, "Come, and let us cut them off from *being* a nation, That the name of Israel may be remembered no more." For they have consulted together with one consent; They form a confederacy against You: The tents of Edom and the Ishmaelites; Moab and the Hagrites; Gebal, Ammon, and Amalek; Philistia with the inhabitants of Tyre; Assyria also has joined with them; They have helped the children of Lot. Selah [4]

At 8:00pm, Israel time, retired IDF Colonel Ariel Ben-Yehudah arose from his lounging chair in the modest Tel Aviv home he shared with his wife and three young sons. Standing in his stocking feet, he glanced at his comely, raven-haired wife, Sarah, fast asleep on the sofa. Silently, he praised God for her and all the blessings He had so prolifically showered on them, especially his three young sons growing up in *Aretz Yisrael*—the Land of Israel.

Swarthy, with brown eyes and dark curly hair, Ariel was ruggedly handsome and athletic at 6'-2". 'Arie,' as he was known to friends and family, was a fourth-generation *sabra*—a native Israeli. His great-grandfather had been a freedom-fighter who immigrated to Palestine in the late 1930's and fought British and Arab alike during the 1948 establishment of the State of Israel. His father and grandfather had both become high-ranking officers in the IDF, the Israel Defense Forces. Arie had served his own term as a fighter pilot, rising to the rank of Alúf mishné—a full 'Bird' Colonel. Although their parents were observant orthodox Jews, Arie and Sarah believed that Yeshua [Jesus] was the Meshiach [Messiah]. Arie's young family attended a small Messianic Christian assembly in Tel Aviv.

At nearly 6'-0", Sarah was a vivacious, dark-complexioned third-generation *sabra* whose grandparents had made *aliyah*, emigrating from New York City many years before. Her father had been a Professor of Physics at Technion until his untimely death in an auto accident. Arie's soul-mate was born and raised in her early years in beautiful Kibbutz Ketura, 50 kilometers north of Eilat in the Arava Rift valley. A graduate of Georgia Tech, she had earned a PhD in Electronic Engineering from MIT where she met Arie. Sarah worked with Arie in the Etzion Defense Enterprises, International corporate offices in Tel Aviv as corporate secretary and technical innovator on the project design teams. Sarah's genius was responsible for many of the technical breakthroughs that Etzion had achieved.

Arie had met Jim Black some years before at MIT in the Aerospace Engineering curriculum. Both had graduated with highest honors and the two had formed a fast friendship, which later coalesced into the partnership that became known as Etzion Defense Enterprises, International. Etzion had created many military defense and weapons systems over the years but their crowning achievement was the creation and launch of a set of virtually impregnable, high powered armored observation, communications and navigation satellites which covered every square foot of the globe; these were the envy of the free world and an unblinking 24/7 'Eye-In-The–Sky' which was the bane of rogue nations.

Responding to the quiet, but insistent, alarms coming from his home office, Arie slipped into his house slippers, flip-flopped into his special room, sat down in his favorite leather swivel chair and switched on the satellite equipment. While waiting for his video equipment to poll the satellites, he punched a communications switch on the console that linked him to Etzion's nerve center across town in Tel Aviv hoping that Uri Asimov, his Mid-East surveillance chief, would still be on the job late today as usual.

Uri Asimov was an immigrant from Belarus who had been educated in America at Cal Tech before making aliyah to Israel. As a former Russian military intelligence officer, Uri was well-versed in the inner workings of eastern European espionage. Short and dark complexioned with curly black hair and green eyes, Uri was a natural addition to Etzion's Middle East operations.

"Uri? Are you there?"

"I'm here Boss."

"Uri, what's going on with the alarms?"

"Something's gotta be brewing, Sir! The U.S. military just jumped from DEFCON 4 to DEFCON 1 and NATO has gone on full alert. And the IDF is gearing up for something like mad, exactly what it is I don't have a clue. Of course, I'm pretty sure it has something to do with 'Iran and Company' but I'm canvassing the globe to see what I can pick up on the satellites. This whole scenario gives me the creeps! I just checked with our people in IDF headquarters and they seem to have contracted lockjaw. My close confidant in the U.S. military essentially told me he was busy and to mind my own business—that's not like him. No one will talk to me—me, the great Uri Asimov—it's a downright insult! I just know that something big is going to blow any minute and I hate nasty surprises."

"Okay, keep at it, Uri; I'm bringing up my home equipment now. I'll talk to you a bit later. Let me know if you see or hear anything more unusual than usual."

As he adjusted the satellite equipment, Arie began to rehearse the plight of Israel:

Tiny Israel has bent over backwards to live at peace with Muslim neighbors whose only acceptable idea of Middle East 'peace' is the complete eradication of the State of Israel and the annihilation of every Jew in the Middle East— neighbors who hate them simply for being there and being Jewish "infidels."

To make matters worse, the U.S. Congress, the American State Department and the Whitehouse continue to meddle in Israel's affairs using monetary and military aid as a club to push Israel around as they have for years. The onerous idea of a "Two-State Solution," giving away part of Jerusalem and the East Bank to a "Palestinian State" ruled by those who are not interested in living peacefully with Israelis in any case, is just more of the same old same-old Progressive political correctness. It makes no sense that America conducts military operations against Muslim radicals elsewhere, but turns around bowing and scraping to the Palestinians' every complaint against Israel, beating the drum for more and more political concessions and land giveaways that would ultimately reduce Israel to little more than a postage stamp. Such arrogance and stupidity! And to add insult to injury, Israel's own government sometimes seems to be acting as if it were in a fog, frequently considering caving in to the demands of certain world governments to accede to the demands of the terrorists. Even though the Roman government may have originally coined the name, there's no doubt that the name 'Palestine' is really nothing more than a corruption of the word 'Philistine,' Israel's ancient enemy. It's no mystery why neighboring Muslim countries refuse to absorb the Palestinians themselves and grant them a homeland in their own domains; after all, why would anyone in their right mind knowingly welcome a flock of troublemakers into their own backyard?

Because of the Muslims' virulent hatred of the Jews, Israel is considered by radical Middle East elements to be occupiers—squatters, if you will—in a land that is not rightfully theirs. But the inconvenient truth is that God gave the entire ancient Land of Israel, to the sons of Isaac and Jacob, not the Ishmaelites or the descendants of Jacob's brother, Esau. Israel's King David established Jerusalem as his capitol over 3,000 years ago, 1,600 years before Islam was ever thought of. Solomon, his son, built the first Temple around 1,000 B.C. on the Temple Mount where the Dome of the Rock and Al Aqsa mosques sit today. Despite this known history, the Muslims insist that Israel has no claim on Jerusalem or the Land and that the Jews never occupied the Temple Mount—never mind that the Dome of the Rock Mosque sits astraddle the location of the Holy of Holies of the First Temple where the indentations carved into the rock are still readily visible. As Adolf Hitler knew, if you tell a big enough lie often enough some will begin to believe it. The fact is that it is Islam that has no rightful claim to anything within the borders of Aretz Yisrael. During the centuries that the Saracen occupied the Land of Israel, the land degenerated from a fruitful garden to a barren, rocky wasteland interspersed with mosquito-filled swamps and treeless hills. Since the return of the Jews to their promised land in 1948, the swamps have been cleared, forests planted and the desert once again literally 'blooms like a rose.' In fact, Israeli agriculture feeds much of Western Europe today.

In Genesis, God speaks very specifically to Abraham: "I will establish My covenant between Me and you and your descendants after you in their generations, for an everlasting covenant, to be God to you and your descendants after you. Also I give to you and your descendants after you the land in which you are a stranger, all the land of Canaan, as an everlasting possession; and I will be their God . . . . . Sarah your wife shall bear you a son, and you shall call his name Isaac; I will establish My covenant with him for an everlasting covenant, and with his descendants after him. And as for Ishmael . . . behold, I have blessed him, and will make him fruitful, and will multiply him exceedingly. He shall beget twelve princes, and I will make him a great nation. But My covenant I will establish with Isaac, whom Sarah shall bear to you at this set time next year." Then He finished talking with him, and God went up from Abraham. [5]

Yup! In other words, God was saying, "Sorry to disappoint you Abraham, but Ishmael is not in my chosen line of descent, but rather your as-yet-unborn son, Isaac, is the one I have chosen. Ishmael will be blessed in many ways, but his hand will be against all his relatives and neighbors,[6] so I have not chosen his bloodline to inherit the Land and that is all I have to say about that!"

People in the West, and even in Israel, do not always totally understand the real roots of the conflict. Many people tend to regard the accounts in the Old Testament as dusty stories of people long dead which have no bearing on their everyday lives. But those accounts really have everything to do with all our lives, particularly the modern Middle East conflict. At the end of the day, the current Middle East situation is primarily the result of an ancient family feud.

Because of God's gifts to Jacob's children, the descendants of Esau and Ishmael as well as the spiritual forces behind Islam, hate the God of the Bible as well as the people of God—both Jew and Christian. Rejecting the Holy Bible, Muslims are firmly convinced that their Quran is superior to the Bible. In their view, Israel is nothing but an occupier in a land that really belongs solely to them; they have repeated this claim so often, even they have begun to believe it. Truly, the hatred between Abraham's offspring, Isaac and Ishmael, Jews and Muslims, to say nothing of the animosity between Isaac's descendants, Jacob, called Israel, and his other son, Esau—is still very much alive after thousands of years. The Ishmaelites and the children of Esau today have made common cause in their hatred of their Israeli enemy. Yet Jerusalem is mentioned 822 times in the Old and New Testaments of the Bible but never in the Quran, but like a child jealous of a cousin's toys, Islam has made Jerusalem a bone of contention claiming it as one of their "Most Holy Cities" which now simply must, in their view, be the capitol of their much-ballyhooed worldwide caliphate.

It all started when Jacob cheated Esau out of his birthright, as well as the patriarch's blessing, and had to flee for his life. Although the Bible is silent on this part of the matter, Jewish tradition says that Esau never really forgave Jacob and before his death charged his son Eliphaz, and his grandson Amalek, to dedicate themselves and their posterity to the destruction of Israel. Additionally, Esau married the daughter of Ishmael to spite his father Isaac, and so we have the modern alliance of Esau and Ishmael. Predictably, years later Amalek treacherously attacked the people of Israel as they traversed the desert before entering the Promised Land. Some 900 years later, when Israel, under King Saul, was told by God to utterly destroy the tribe of Amalek including every one of their animals, Saul and the people disobeyed the Lord and saved the Amalekite king, Agag, and apparently a few other Amalekite people as well, and some of the best of the animals. Furious, the Prophet Samuel announced that God was removing Saul from the throne of Israel over this incident.[7] Apparently, Agag was informed that on the morrow he was going to die and Jewish tradition says that he raped the servant girl who brought him his last meal. The next day, Samuel sliced Agag in small pieces but apparently a few other Amalekites had already escaped before. What was the result of Saul's disobedience? Fast forward some centuries to the Babylonian Captivity where Persian King Ahasuerus took 'Esther,' a beautiful little Jewish girl named Hadassah, as his queen. Ahasuerus' right hand man, Haman, was plotting to destroy all the Jews in the kingdom. Now Haman is described in the Bible as an 'Agagite,' which meant he was an Amalekite. Ultimately, Haman tried to rape queen Esther in his last moments and ended up much like his forbearer, Agag, dead on a gallows. But the story doesn't end there. There are still any number of Agagites, and their relatives the Ishmaelites, roaming around that are infected with Esau's pathological hatred of Israel.

Fast forwarding again to the twentieth century and World War II, Adolf Hitler had determined that his mission in life was to destroy the Jews. Der Fuhrer had formed an alliance with the Grand Mufti of Jerusalem. He and his new ally planned the creation of a Muslim army in the Middle East to make the Middle East free of Jews. Hitler would also insanely rant that New York City was the center of world Jewry and, just six months before the Normandy invasion, had begun building a fleet of long range suicide bombers capable of crossing the Atlantic Ocean as flying bombs, planning to fly them into the tall buildings of New York 'to teach the Jews a lesson.' None of these plans were realized in

1945 before the end of WWII. But radical Muslims recently discovered the Nazi library in Germany and apparently got the idea to fly airplanes into the Twin Towers as a modern extension of Hitler's delayed WWII plans.

We know that Jerusalem will someday be the capitol city of God's earthly kingdom when Jesus returns to earth. Jesus will enter Jerusalem through the closed and sealed Eastern Gate of the walled city—known as the 'Messiah Gate' or 'Golden Gate'—to set up His throne on the Temple Mount. In a last-ditch effort to delay or prevent the return of the Lord, Satan has inspired his servants to seal up the Eastern Gate and occupy Mount Moriah, building mosques over the spot where the Holy of Holies of the First and Second Jewish Temples once stood upon the Temple Mount.

Syria, the descendant of the ancient House of Esau, in cooperation with the descendants of Ishmael, is spoiling for a fight and Israel is ready, reluctantly, to oblige them. Islamic doctrine holds that once a country has been conquered by Islam, it can never rightfully reside under any other regime. But no one is immune to God's anger when it comes to Israel and Jerusalem, be he Gentile or Jew. It is extremely hazardous to trifle with the God of Israel and God's land. Dividing up His land is something that ought never be contemplated by anyone who wishes to live to a ripe old age. Only the foolhardy tread that path, but apparently their name is Legion, regardless.

Abandoning his reverie and once again focusing his attention on the satellite monitors, Arie was shocked at the massive troop movements in Israel, Syria and the Bekaa Valley of eastern Lebanon. It looked as if major trouble was brewing. Many of the defense systems that Etzion produces are lynch-pins in the Israeli defense system. Arie prayed they had covered every possible contingency.

Hezbollah's leadership allegedly resides in Damascus and takes their orders from Iran. The fanatical Iranian mullahs and politicians have threatened for years to wipe Israel off the map. As Arie watched the scenes unfolding beneath the satellite camera's gaze, claxons sounded and a message scrolled across the screen "THREE STRATEGIC WEAPONS LAUNCHED, TARGET ISRAEL, SOURCE: IRAN—PREPARING COUNTERMEASURES." The satellite was abuzz with activity as the computers tracked the offending weapons, computing their trajectories, then scrolling another message across the screen, "WEAPONS TARGETED ON TEL AVIV, HAIFA, TEL MEGGIDO. AWAITING INSTRUCTIONS." As Arie considered his options, the IDF launched three Arrow missiles from several locations in Israel, disintegrating the incoming missiles over the western Iraqi and Jordanian deserts. Arie issued an instruction to the satellite: "SUSPEND COUNTERMEASURES."

Things seemed to be spinning out of control as another alarm sounded and across the screen scrolled the message: "TWO STRATEGIC WEAPONS LAUNCHED. SOURCE: IRAN. TARGET: SAUDI ARABIA, DIEGO GARCIA. INITIATING TARGET DESTRUCTION SEQUENCE. This time, an anti-missile missile was fired from a U.S. aircraft carrier in the Arabian Sea, taking out the Iranian weapon as it flew towards Diego Garcia. The satellite's powerful energy beam took out the missile intended for the Saudi capitol.

Now perspiring in spite of the air conditioning, Arie shifted back to the movements of Israeli and Muslim military units below. He was newly startled by an alarm from the satellite itself. Across the screen scrolled the words: SATELLITE #1—MISSILE LOCK—ACTIVATING DEFENSIVE SYSTEMS.

What in the world. . . . ? What now . . . ?

Searching frantically for the threat, he finally spotted a thin plume of rocket exhaust arcing up toward the satellite from the Bekaa Valley. Hezbollah was trying to silence Etzion's Middle East satellite. The satellite's computers targeted the incoming weapon and traced its launch point. There was a flash of light as the satellite fired a missile targeted on the missile's launch site. As the incoming weapon approached half way to the satellite, there was another brilliant flash of light as it was destroyed by one of the satellite's energy beam weapons. Arie watched in awe through the onboard television camera as the satellite's return missile unerringly homed on the mobile launcher and destroyed it and the personnel around it so quickly they did not have time to pick up and move. Somehow, the very thing he himself had helped create still amazed him.

Arie's senses were again rapidly assaulted as across the screen came an announcement from IDF headquarters: WEAPON DETONATION, HAIFA.

That wasn't a missile-delivered weapon. Must have been trucked or packed in by some mule. Hezbollah apparently thought it was time to turn up the heat.

At that point, another general alarm sounded: MULTIPLE MISSILES LAUNCHED, SOURCE LEBANON—INITIATING TARGET DESTRUCTION SEQUENCE. The satellite lit up as its powerful energy beam weapons destroyed the airborne vehicles before they could impact in Israel.

Minutes later, Uri came back over the intercom. "Arie, guess what Washington just did. The Pentagon ordered the American military to hold their fire, break contact and head south away from Iran. And do you know what the supreme American commander answered back?"

"I'm not sure I want to know," came Ariel's reply.

"He said 'NUTS! We are under fire and are returning same!'" yelped Uri.

Refocusing the satellite's cameras on the American naval armada in the Arabian Sea at the mouth of the Gulf of Oman, Arie was horrified to see Iran's Revolutionary Guards launch a swarm of anti-ship missiles at the fleet. The 20-millimeter MK 15 Phalanx Close-In Weapons Systems opened fire, as well as the fleet's other anti-missile defenses. But, there were so many incoming menaces that they overwhelmed some of the fleet's perimeter vessels. The carriers remained safe behind their massive defensive envelopes but, in the end, an American destroyer slipped beneath the waves. Retaliation to this aggression would doubtless be swift. The fall of the Houses of Persia and Esau—Iran and Syria—were alike inevitable.

Arie again focused one of the satellite's cameras on the Chagos Archipelago, zooming in on the U.S. military base on the tiny spit of real estate known as Diego Garcia. Bat-like B-2 stealth bombers were preparing for launch. Their bomb bays were being stuffed with something that looked about the size of a small automobile. B-1 and B-52 strategic bombers were also preparing for launch. Some were still being loaded on the tarmac with what appeared to be 1,000 or 1,250 pound bombs. Over the Arabian Sea, just off the coast of Oman, a dozen aerial tankers circled in a wide-spaced pattern flanked by F-22 and F-16 fighter escorts. Several other gaggles of airborne tankers, with fighter escorts, were circling over the Iraqi desert.

Looks like some of the B-2s are carrying those 30,000 pound bunker-buster bombs.

Arie again shifted the gaze of the satellite's video cameras to the American carrier groups in the Indian Ocean and the Gulf of Aqaba. Predictably, the carriers were turning into the wind and their aircraft elevators were busily populating the flight decks with the deadly F-35 JSF, Joint Strike Force, fighters. The magnetic catapults were preparing to launch Navy aircraft. Marine Corps F-35s were already taking off vertically from the deck while the Navy's standard aircraft awaited their turn at the catapults.

My God, my God, here we go!

Swinging the cameras back to Israel, his attention was drawn to movements around the main IDF airfields. Residing behind individual blast-proof revetments, Israel's tactical air force was as impregnable as it was humanly possible to make it. Zooming the video in on the most sensitive and secret areas, it was obvious that something big was in progress there also. Usually the fighters would launch straight out of the hangars during an alert, but today Israeli-modified F-22 Raptor stealth fighters, F-16 "Soufas" which are the newest American-built F-16I, and Israeli-customized F-15 fighters were taxiing out and lining up in formation around the heads of the runways. The equipment mounted on the aircraft's hard points was something Arie had not seen before. The satellite's scanners revealed that some of the weapons were 5,000 pound GBU bunker-penetrating bombs, but some others were new. As he watched, at least five dozen of the craft became airborne from several airfields and headed northeast over Iraq—toward Iran. Arie scanned the trailing aircraft with the satellite's special equipment.

Just as I thought—tactical nukes!

Pressing another intercom button on his console, Arie waited for his American partners to answer.

"Yo, Arie, this is Eli. What's up my friend?"

"What's up? Don't you guys ever monitor our network? We've got big trouble, man! The whole Middle East has just gone postal. Switch to Satellite #1 and take a look."

Resembling an old-west cowpoke, Elijah Walton was a wiry, leather-faced, 50-something, Texan with steel-grey eyes and salt-and-pepper hair. Calling El Paso in West Texas home, he possessed a slow Texas drawl and razor-keen wit. Characteristically dressed in blue jeans, western boots, Stetson hat and western shirt, the casual observer would never guess he was a first-rate fighter pilot and the chief operating officer of a major corporation. Retired from the U.S. Marine Corps, Eli had earned Lt. Colonel's oak leaves during the early stages of the Iraq war. As Jim Black's right-hand man, Eli was the individual who handled most of the day-to-day operations at the Houston, Texas, branch of Etzion Enterprises.

Eli came back on the intercom exclaiming, "Woof! Sorry, man! I see what you mean, Arie. I'll notify Jim immediately. This does not look good at all!"

"Okay, I'm going back to work. I'll call Jim myself a bit later, Eli."

Arie again watched, enthralled, as the combined flights of American and Israeli aircraft closed on Iran in an obviously pre-planned sequence. The sky was crisscrossed by errant missiles and the con-trails of dogfights between American, Israeli and Iranian fighters. As the bunker-buster bombs and nuclear weapons struck their targets, the evening sky lit up like an early dawn.

A few moments later, there was another satellite alarm: METEORITES APPROACHING SATELLITE #1— ACTIVATING SHIELDS.

As Arie watched awestruck, a swarm of space rocks whizzed past the satellite at incredible velocity and rocketed toward the earth below. The satellite's computers clocked their speed at nearly eight miles per second.

Wow! Something is going to get smacked when those things hit! I wonder what?

Within seconds, Arie's question was answered. There were fiery plumes as the meteorites entered the dense lower atmosphere and plummeted to the earth, followed by brilliant flashes of light and mushroom clouds rising over Mecca, Medina, Damascus, southern Beirut, the Gaza Strip and the Bekaa Valley. The earth rumbled under Arie's chair and there were tremors in his coffee cup.

Wow!! Bullseye!! This can be nothing but the hand of God!!

Finally, to add amazement to amazement, Arie spotted something he never imagined he would ever see: American B-52 bombers closing on Israel. As the former IAF pilot watched, the formation split into several parts, one heading for southern Lebanon, another for the Gaza Strip and another for the West Bank area.

"Hello, what have we here?"

Arie's curiosity was rewarded shortly as the 'BUFFs' turned to appropriate headings, opened their bomb bay doors and laid long strings of 1,000 pound bombs on Hezbollah and Hamas military installations and troop concentrations. Once again, although miles away, Israel's shallow bedrock telegraphed the shocks of the immense, mind-numbing impact of the carpet-bombing. The china and glassware in the cupboards tinkled and vibrated.

Perhaps it was the earth tremors, or maybe it was that he had unconsciously voiced aloud his amazement at the panorama of destruction he had been watching, but Sarah walked into the room drowsily scratching herself and asked, "Arie, what is going on? Is there an earthquake or something? The china has been rattling like crazy!"

"Sarah, something is getting socked but it's not a soccer game." Arie crowed, "Iran just initiated their long-threatened attack on Israel and tried to make a move on the Emirates, the Saudi oil fields, the American fleet and their land base in the Indian Ocean. Bad idea! The IAF and the Americans have just rewarded Iran for their misbegotten efforts: huge holes in their nuclear establishment and nuclear suntans all around. Then Hezbollah hit Haifa with a major packed-in weapon. Almost immediately, some meteorites whizzed past our satellite from deep space and wiped out Damascus and Hezbollah in both Beirut and the Bekaa Valley to say nothing of Mecca, Medina and Hamas in the Gaza Strip. Those places are now nothing but huge glassed-over holes for the 'Jihadis' to walk around. And to top it all off, American B-52s carpet bombed enemy positions all around Israel's borders."

As Arie and Sarah conversed, Uri called over the intercom from the control center. "Boss, have you noticed the Temple Mount?"

"The Temple Mount? No, what about the Temple Mount?"

"Focus on the Old City and check out the Temple Mount, man. See if you see anything different."

Zooming in on the area, Arie gasped, "Sarah, look at this! This is incredible! The Al Aqsa and Dome of the Rock mosques on the Temple Mount were demolished by something—must have been those space rocks! There is nothing left of them but tiny pieces strewn all over the place. God made direct hits on all the important sites. Looks like He used His own weapons inventory so mankind would have no room to boast—or argue. You mess with God's people and God's land, you're eventually going to pay the price—big time!

"The 'Jihadists' have been yearning for their Mahdi, or Twelfth Imam, to come and take over the world. If he's climbed out of that well in Iran, he'd better be wearing asbestos and lead underwear because if he isn't, he is going to glow in the dark tonight," said Arie darkly.

"Oh, my goodness!" replied Sarah, "What do you think will happen now, Arie?"

"That remains to be seen. Whatever happens, it will not be pleasant. I'm afraid things are going to get worse for Israel and America before they get better."

"What about Egypt, Arie? Are they not likely to attack us or aid the Palestinians?"

"I don't think Egypt would be enthusiastic about getting actively involved even if they were so inclined. Think about it. The Aswan High Dam on the Upper Nile River is one of the largest man-made lakes in the world and is hundreds of feet deep. One or two carefully placed bombs could take out the dam and the resulting wall of water coming down the Nile Valley would wipe out everything of value in Egypt from the Upper Nile to the Mediterranean. They could forestall that scenario by draining down the lake but it would take a long time and that would cut off their supply of hydro power—Egypt would go dark. Egypt and her Soviet allies unwittingly built a Sword of Damocles over Egypt's head."

"Arie, I remember our Rabbi talking recently. He was discussing something in the Prophets concerning an unfulfilled prophecy about Damascus being destroyed."

"Yes, that's right, sweetheart," said Arie, "Isaiah 17 reads 'Behold, Damascus will cease from being a city, And it will be a ruinous heap"[8] and in Obadiah, God chastises Syria, the House of Esau, for helping to pillage Israel centuries ago saying:

> "Oh, how Esau shall be searched out! How his hidden treasures shall be sought after! All the men in your confederacy shall force you to the border; the men at peace with you shall deceive you *and* prevail against you. *Those who eat* your bread shall lay a trap for you. No one is aware of it. 'Will I not in that day,' says the LORD, 'Even destroy the wise *men* from Edom, and understanding from the mountains of Esau? Then your mighty men, O Teman, shall be dismayed, to the end that everyone from the mountains of Esau may be cut off by slaughter. 'For violence against your brother Jacob, shame shall cover you, and you shall be cut off forever. In the day that you stood on the other side—in the day that stranger carried captive his forces, when foreigners entered his gates and cast lots for Jerusalem—even you were as one of them. But you should not have gazed on the day of your brother in the day of his captivity; nor should you have rejoiced over the children of Judah in the day of their destruction; nor should you have spoken proudly in the day of distress. You should not have entered the gate of my people in the day of their calamity. Indeed, you should not have gazed on their affliction in the day of their calamity, nor laid *hands* on their substance in the day of their calamity. You should not have stood at the crossroads to cut off those among them who escaped; nor should you have delivered up those among them who remained in the day of distress. For the day of the LORD upon all the nations *is* near; as you have done, it shall be done to you; your reprisal shall return upon your own head."[9]

"In other words, God is saying that in the past, the people of Esau—Syria—had aided and abetted the destruction of Israel by Israel's enemies, and God has not forgotten—or forgiven. Sarah, we have just witnessed scripture being fulfilled. With those meteor strikes just now, the place is undoubtedly covered with molten glass. When space rocks come in at that velocity, they release as much energy as a hydrogen bomb. God grabbed the ball and ran with it Himself. Those meteor strikes were just too precise to be accidental," chuckled Arie.

Arie continued thumbing through his Bible until he came to the Book of Ezekiel. "Listen to this, Sarah. God spoke prophetically through the

Prophet Ezekiel some 2,600 years ago exactly what would happen to the enemies of Israel in the last days when they would come up against the Land of Israel—and here it is in plain language:

"Now the word of the LORD came to me, saying, 'Son of man, set your face against Gog, of the land of Magog, the chief prince of Rosh, Meshech, and Tubal, and prophesy against him, and say, 'Thus says the Lord GOD: Behold, I *am* against you, O Gog, the prince of Rosh, Meshech, and Tubal. I will turn you around, put hooks into your jaws, and lead you out, with all your army . . . Persia, Ethiopia, and Libya are with them, . . . Gomer and all its troops; the house of Togarmah from the far north and all its troops—many people are with you. Prepare yourself and . . . all that are gathered about you . . . In the latter years you will come into the land of those brought back from the sword and gathered from many people on the mountains of Israel, which had long been desolate; they were brought out of the nations, and now all of them dwell safely. You will come up. . like a storm, covering the land like a cloud, you and all your troops and many peoples with you. . .On that day it shall come to pass that thoughts will come to your mind, and you will devise an evil plan: You will say, 'I will go up against the land of unprotected villages . . a peaceful people, who are living in safety . . without walls, and having neither bars nor gates to take plunder and to take booty, to stretch out your hand against the waste places that are again inhabited, and against a people gathered from the nations, who have acquired livestock and goods, who dwell in the midst of the land. Sheba, Dedan, the merchants of Tarshish, and all their young lions will say to you, 'Have you come to take plunder? Have you gathered your army to take booty and . . great plunder? Therefore, Ezekiel, prophesy to Gog, 'Thus says the Lord GOD: "On that day when My people Israel dwell safely . . . . you will come from your place out of the far north, you and many peoples with you. . a great company and a mighty army. You will come up against My people Israel like a cloud, to cover the land. . . In the latter days I will bring you against My land, so that the nations may know Me, when I am hallowed because of you, O Gog, before their eyes. Thus says the Lord GOD: 'Are you not he of whom I have spoken in former days by My servants the prophets of Israel, who prophesied for years in those days that I would bring you against them? And it will come to pass at the same time, when Gog comes against the land of Israel. .that My fury will show in My face. For in My jealousy and the fire of My wrath I have spoken: 'Surely in that day there shall be a great earthquake in the land of Israel, so that . . . all men who *are* on the face of the earth shall shake at My presence. The mountains shall be thrown down, the steep places shall fall, and every wall shall fall to the ground. I will bring a sword against Gog throughout all My mountains. Every man's sword will be against his brother. And I will bring him to judgment with pestilence and bloodshed; I will rain down on him, on his troops, and on the many peoples who are with him, flooding rain, great hailstones, fire, and brimstone. Thus I will magnify Myself and sanctify Myself, and I will be known in the eyes of many nations. Then they shall know that I *am* the LORD.'" [10]

"The Lord isn't half done yet and goes on in Ezekiel 39:

'Son of man, prophesy against Gog, and say, "Thus says the Lord GOD: 'Behold, I am against you, O Gog, the chief prince of Rosh, Meshech, and Tubal; and I will spin you around and drag you . . up from the lands of the far north . . against the mountains of Israel. I will strike the weapons from your hands. You shall fall dead upon the mountains of Israel, you and all your troops and the peoples who are with you; I will give your dead bodies to the birds of prey and the beasts of the field to be devoured . . .And I will send fire on Magog and on those who live in security in the coastlands. Then they shall know that I am the LORD. So I will make My holy name known in the midst of My people Israel, and they will not profane My holy name anymore. Then the nations shall know that I am the LORD, the Holy One in Israel. Surely it is coming, and it shall be done," says the Lord GOD. This is the day of which I have spoken. Then those who dwell in the cities of Israel . . . will plunder those who plundered them, and pillage those who pillaged them . . . It will come to pass in that day that I will give Gog a burial place there in Israel, the Valley of the Travelers, and it will fill up the valley, because there they will bury the millions of bodies of Gog and all his multitude. For seven months the house of Israel will be burying the dead, in order to cleanse the land. . .They will set apart men specifically employed, with the help of search parties, to search throughout the land and bury any bodies remaining unburied, in order to cleanse it. . .The search party will pass through the land; and when anyone sees a human bone, he shall set up a marker by it, till the buriers have buried it in the Valley of Hamon Gog. Thus they shall cleanse the land. And as for you, son of man, speak to every sort of bird and to every beast of the field: "Assemble yourselves and . . gather together from all sides to My sacrificial meal which I am sacrificing for you, a great sacrificial meal on the mountains of Israel, that you may eat . . . the flesh of the mighty and drink the blood of the princes of the earth. You shall eat fat till you are full and drink blood till you are drunk, at My sacrificial meal which I am sacrificing for you. You shall be filled at My table . . with all the mighty men of war." I will set My glory among the nations; the nations shall see My judgment which I have executed, and My hand which I have laid on them. So the house of Israel shall know that I am the LORD their God from that day forward. The Gentiles shall know that the house of Israel went into captivity for their iniquity; because they were unfaithful to Me, therefore I hid My face from them. I gave them into the hand of their enemies, and they all fell by the sword. According to their uncleanness and according to their transgressions I have dealt with them, and hidden My face from them . .Now I will bring back the captives of Jacob, and have mercy on the whole house of Israel; and I will be jealous for My holy name … and I will not hide My face from them anymore; for I shall have poured out My Spirit on the house of Israel," says the Lord GOD.' [11]

"You see, Sarah, Ezekiel speaks of Gog and Magog, the chief prince of Meshech and Tubal, coming down out of the lands of the north, which is Russia or 'Rosh.' As you know, in the Bible Jerusalem is considered the center of the earth and so all directions are measured from the City of God. If you draw a line due north from Jerusalem to the North Pole, it passes almost exactly through modern Moscow, which is undoubtedly biblical 'Meshech,' and passes a bit to the west of the modern oil city of Tobolsk which is biblical 'Tubal.' So there's no doubt that Ezekiel was speaking of modern Russia long before Russia, as such, ever existed. What is the traditional symbol of Russia? The 'Russian Bear,' of course. When he speaks of putting hooks in their jaws and spinning them around to attack Israel, well, that's a definite allusion to the old Russian pastime of 'bear-baiting' still practiced in parts of the former Soviet Union today, in which they catch a wild bear and torment it by putting hooks in its jaws attached to ropes and jerking it around violently first one way and then another to taunt it and make it angry. Looks like God is going to do some bear-baiting of his own. Now how could Ezekiel have known about the 'Russian Bear' thousands of years in the future unless he actually heard it from God? Now, we don't have a clue as to the identity of Gog. Gog may be a person or group or he may be the demonic prince over Russia—I'm not sure it matters that much. We only know he and his allies are Satan's minions."

"I've got to discuss this mess with Jim Black; all this will have dire ramifications for America. You can bet that all the bad guys will come unglued when they see that their friends in Iran and Syria are no more.

☆ 4 ☆

OUT OF THE FRYING PAN

"If God does not judge America, He will have to apologize to Sodom and Gomorrah." --Billy Graham

As Jim Black arose wearily from his favorite chair, preparing to retire late at night—or maybe it was the wee hours of the morning, he wasn't sure—the secure phone rang with a call from Israel.

"Houston, we have a problem. Everything has just hit the fan over here, Jim. Iran launched three nukes against Israel; they were destroyed over Iraq. Then they tried to whack Saudi Arabia and the Emirates as well as the American Fleet and the U.S base on Diego Garcia. It wasn't long before Israel and the U.S. carrier groups launched tactical aircraft which were joined by strategic bombers from Diego Garcia and Iraqi bases. The whole map of Iran just lit up like a Christmas tree. The Iranian Mullahs are getting a nuclear suntan. Now, our satellites are observing troop and naval movements all over the E.U., Russia, Eastern Europe, China and most of the Middle East and a bunch of them were already sitting on Israel's doorstep. The American fleet is currently repositioning into the Indian Ocean to await further developments.

"About a half hour ago, someone detonated a major weapon in Haifa. Probably one of Saddam Hussein's old weapons of mass destruction that he squirreled away in Syria. It was apparently packed in overland and detonated in Haifa. We haven't assessed its nature as yet, nor do we have any idea of casualties. In any case, the IDF would have had no choice but to uncork our nukes on Syria and Hezbollah."

"Arie, what do you mean 'The IDF WOULD have had no choice?' What prevented them?" replied Jim, half afraid of the answer.

"Well, at that point some space rocks whizzed past our Middle East satellite from deep space headed for the earth below, setting off the satellite's alarms and firing up its protective shields. Anyhow, our bird clocked the rocks at a velocity of nearly eight miles per second as they went by. Jim, Mecca, Medina, Damascus, southern Beirut and the Bekaa Valley are all toast! There were mushroom clouds all over the place. And last, but by no means least, something totally destroyed the Al Aqsa and Dome of the Rock Mosques on the Temple Mount in Jerusalem. It was a sovereign act of God—the Houses of Esau, Persia and Ishmael just received their just desserts after some thirty centuries. Anyway, the fat is now in the fire, my friend!"

"Arie, you better believe that most of the ruling class around the globe hates America, Israel and the God of Abraham, Isaac and Jacob. You can bet that everything that lives under a rock will capitalize on this as an excuse to wipe both of our countries off the map, if they can. We have also been monitoring the general situation and we certainly don't like the looks of it, although I hadn't been notified of this latest development until just a few hours ago. We're very concerned about the presence of 'Jihadists' with nukes all over America. With this latest situation, I look for them to retaliate very soon. If they start touching off atom bombs in our cities, it's going to be 'Katie bar the door.' In fact, we are presently preparing to evacuate Houston ourselves. Let's stay in very close contact."

"Evacuate? Where will you go, Jim? If America is attacked there won't be any place for you to hide," inquired the Israeli, incredulously.

"I can't go into detail right at the moment, but we have had a divine visitation in which we were instructed to go to my family's wilderness 'City of Refuge' in the wilds of Montana. I wish there were some way to get you and your people over here. But it's a long way from Tel Aviv to Montana—7,000 miles as the crow flies. I'll send you the coordinates of our destination so you'll know where we are," explained Jim.

"Don't worry about us, Jim, God will provide for us somehow. We'll be in touch, my friend. Shalom for now," declared Arie.

After signing off with Arie, Jim hurriedly summoned Eli to his plant office. Jim leaned back in his chair and began, "Have a seat, Eli. Listen, I've been feeling especially uneasy about the world situation ever since I visited Black Eagle Ranch a few weeks ago and spoke with my grandfather. Now, Arie reports massive events in the Middle East. Our enemies are threatening to put both America and Israel out of commission. I think it's time to close up shop here for a while. I want to begin preparations to fold our tent and move to Montana immediately—I don't think putting it off is wise or we may get blind-sided."

"Yep, I agree. I've been watching the satellite monitors worldwide since Arie called—don't like what I'm seeing. I'd like to look all those bums in the eye and discuss my opinion of their canine ancestry," snarled Eli.

"Okay, Eli, Okay, I get the picture!" Jim laughed, "Here's what I want you to do immediately: Contact Pastor Nelson and have him summon our church congregation to an emergency meeting at 7:00pm at my home tonight. Get our pilots prepared to ferry my menagerie of WWII aircraft up to the Eagle's Lair as soon as possible. I want my babies in safe storage. Tell whoever flies the 'Black Knight' to check with me before he shoves off; she's a mean bird. Furthermore, go wake up 'Connie' and get her primed to travel.

"Get the department heads busy assembling our records, technical data and inventory of parts and finished projects into the 18-wheelers. If there are some things too large to transport, destroy them. Don't leave behind anything an enemy could use. I want all our rolling stock ready to get on the road by day after tomorrow. We're shipping everything up to the Lair. I especially want our three military Humvees sent up on a transporter. Oh, and Eli, furlough all employees with six month's salary as of the end of the month, except those of the critical staff who will be going with us."

"Whew! OK, boss. I'll git right on it! Anything else?" responded Eli.

"Don't neglect your own household—pack everything you can't live without."

"Will do, Chief!"

As Eli walked out, the phone rang. "Jim, this is Bob Dalton" chirped an upbeat voice on the other end, "Hey, how's about dropping in and we'll take in that Philly's game on the 5th?"

Hey, I'd love it, Bob. I'll let you know how my schedule is as soon as possible. Let me get back to you."

Senator Dalton hates baseball. That's our prearranged distress signal. Must get a flight out to location number 5 and pick him up tonight.

Robert Dalton was a tall, white-haired, blue-eyed U.S. Air Force Lt. Colonel and who was the senior U.S. Senator from Texas. A born-again evangelical Christian minister, he was a staunch conservative patriot who had no use for the crooked power politics he had faced for so many years on 'The Hill.' With the ever-increasing liberalization of America, he stood with only a handful of others in Congress, against a landslide of moral and physical decay in the nation he loved. His stand had earned him many enemies both domestic and foreign.

That evening, as nearly 80 members of Jim's church assembled on the back patio of the Black mansion at 7:00pm, Jim stepped out of the house to address the group.

"Folks, this will be rather brief. I've called this special meeting because we have a very grave world situation rapidly developing that threatens the freedom of the United States and Israel. As you are undoubtedly aware, we are now in a state of war with Iran and Syria. Just hours ago, the State of Israel and our military in the Persian Gulf were attacked by Syrian and Iranian forces. We have retaliated with devastating results. But, the United States is now pretty much isolated from the rest of the world by our enemies both foreign and domestic. As you know, I manufacture a number of highly technical lines of defense products; my sources of materials have been totally shut down. Presumably, the Progressive establishment means to make good on their threats to bring the U.S. and Israel to its knees and force us to knuckle under to them. And if American 'Jihadist' groups have nukes as they claim, and start setting them off in our cities, things are going to go south in a hurry. My people who monitor our satellites, tell me that Russia, the E.U. and many of the Middle East nations are moving troops, aircraft and warships into position to march on Israel and probably the U.S. Since Israel has already employed nukes in Iran today, you can bet things will get very messy if they are pushed too far again. If

America is invaded, you can also bet that most of the U.S. military forces will never surrender and will resist with everything they have. However, we can't count on our devious politicians. More than likely, our group is going to be pretty much on its own if the worst happens. Although we've discussed the possibility of an invasion of America before, just in theory, I guess none of us ever thought it would actually happen."

"The bottom line is that everyone in this congregation has an open invitation to join us at our secluded Montana retreat center. If you'd like to come with us, pack the things you can't live without. Especially bring along indoor and outdoor clothing, outdoor gear and weapons, if you have them. Leave the kitchen sink but pack personal articles, medications, family photos and records—everything you'll need to reestablish your lives after it's all over. We'll fly you to Montana in my recently restored Lockheed Super Constellation airliner as soon as we get everything arranged, possibly as early as day-after tomorrow. Any excess items will be shipped up either by truck, in the Connie or our three C-47 'Gooney Birds.' I know that walking away from everything you've worked for all your lives is a bitter pill to swallow, but staying alive and free is more important than houses, cars and jobs. Now, we have an excellent cross-section of professionals in this church—many experienced pilots, a dentist, several qualified preachers, a pharmacist, several physicians, engineers of different disciplines, etc. We have the necessary manpower to cover just about every contingency we'll face in a survival situation and my personal staff will also be joining us. The retreat center remodeling is presently coming to completion and the place is being stocked with supplies. We'll have enough food and goods to last at least three years. We've done our best to provide first-class living accommodations—I think you'll be pleased.

"I am guessing that someone, either the enemy or our own government, will impose martial law throughout the country if we are invaded so no one will be able to travel openly then, therefore we need to try to stay ahead of the curve on this situation and get to our new home before things get to that point. I've been assured by the Lord that we'll be safe in Montana. So, go home tonight my friends and pray about what you should do. Then notify Eli Walton as soon as possible, regardless of what you decide, so we will know how to plan. PLEASE, don't mention what we are planning to do to anyone, not even your closest friends and relatives. Remember that Noah nearly had to repel uninvited boarders from the Ark. We definitely don't need any trouble like that. Thanks for coming on such short notice.

Please partake of the refreshments and visit as long as you wish," concluded Jim.

Jim excused himself, walked back into the house and sat down in his private study with his satellite phone in hand. George Wing answered the phone at Black Eagle Ranch. "George, Jim here. How is it going at the Eagle's Lair? Things are rapidly heating up on the international front. Arie tells me the bad guys are on the prowl so we may be coming up there in short order," said Jim.

"Yeah, we've been watching the news, too. Things don't look good at all. We're moving as fast as we can and things are almost ready at the Lair. Everything from the ranch house has been transported to the Lair and we should be finished by noon tomorrow," George answered.

"That's just great, George! How's Grandfather doing?" laughed Jim.

"Ornery as ever," chortled the Native American manager.

"Okay, I'll be sending up my war birds tomorrow and as much freight as we can put on the road in our 18-wheelers, so expect visitors shortly. I'll talk to you soon," said Jim.

As the congregation on the patio slowly dispersed, Jim sat alone in the gathering gloom of his home study, uneasily contemplating the world situation.

William Burgoyne, was recently crowned Emperor of the E.U. and popularly— no, cynically— dubbed "Kaiser Bill" by the public in a sardonic play on words likening him to Kaiser Wilhelm, the German Emperor and King of Prussia of WWI infamy.

With somewhat questionable Jewish heritage, Burgoyne approached a beleaguered Israel "selling" himself as an ethnic Jew. He proposed supplying 75,000 combat troops complete with armor and air support, as well as another 250,000 on standby in Europe. He offered this protection gratis, if Israel would guarantee a continued flow of agricultural products to Europe, along with the right to buy at wholesale prices certain minerals found in abundance around the Dead Sea. Of course, there's little doubt that Bill is even more concerned about control of the Middle East's oil fields. He cannot afford the opportunity for China, Russia and Iran to hold Europe hostage. Were it not for the fact that America had just elected, an administration which promises to essentially abandon Israel and the Middle East, Bill doubtless could not have succeeded with such a larcenous arrangement. Israel's Knesset and Prime Minister, weary from years of war, threats and suicide bombers, finally agreed. The majority of Israelis, however, especially the ultraconservative Hasidim, are unhappy with this new arrangement and consider the E.U.'s presence as nothing less than a new 'Pax Romana'—something Israel has not endured for millennia. An underground movement has subsequently arisen to rid Israel of the E.U.'s influence and rely solely on the IDF, regardless of the danger from their Muslim neighbors. Several assassination attempts by unidentified parties against the Israeli prime minister have already been made.

Both Israel and the Muslim nations know that the entire world, including America, will soon turn against Israel. The vast majority of Americans know that something is radically wrong in their government but are powerless, at the moment, to do anything about it. Few can scarcely believe that their elected representatives would intentionally orchestrate the subversion of their nation's sovereignty. But the Progressive Left's labor of love, the New World Order, intends to pull America into its reeking maw partly through the ministrations of its other love-child, the United Nations, eventually melding America, her neighbors and Europe into one huge conglomerate under their iron-fisted control.

The way has now been effectively opened for the absolute destruction of America's strength by first destroying her economy and the value of her currency, completely disarming the citizenry, then utterly surrendering her sovereignty to World Government. Their plan involved engineering a sudden economic crash, immediately nationalizing the banks and as much of our major industry as possible, then quietly drawing Mexico, Canada and the United States into one huge country

Several states have elected Muslims to the U.S. Senate and House of Representatives, some of whom have questionable backgrounds, and the administration in Washington is openly friendly toward Islamic radicals. The Politically Correct 'hate America first' wing of the liberal Progressive establishment has quietly decided to neglect the sealing of America's borders and promoted building a NAFTA super highway through the Midwest from Mexico to Canada, with a port of entry in Kansas City, of all places. Muslim 'jihadists' present in the American population are thought to possess suitcase size nuclear weapons. The nuclear weaponry has simply been carried in through

Mexico and Canada by human 'mules.' The 'jihadis' undoubtedly intend to use these weapons at the optimum moment for the maximum terror effect.

The President, and his unelected 'czars', have succeeded in establishing a 'Civilian Law Enforcement Corps' and mandated that all American young people between the ages of 18 and 25 must train for 'public service' in a 90 day training camp. This is actually an opportunity to brain-wash these young people into accepting Marxist-socialist doctrine. Since most of these children have already been indoctrinated in public school systems, they have never been taught the true nature and character of our Founding Fathers, the whole background of the American War For Independence or of Communism and hard-core Socialism. No one has pointed out that this organization is an almost exact parallel with Adolf Hitler's 'Brown Shirts' and the SS, the elite private army within the German government that answered only to Hitler himself. Because most young people below the age of 30 are not generally mature enough to recognize false doctrines taught by the Progressive propagandists, they are vulnerable and readily succumb. Such was the technique employed by Vladimir Lenin with his own civilian corps of what he derisively called 'Useful Idiots' to precipitate his diabolical 1917 Russian Communist revolution. Once the revolution was solidly established, most of these 'Useful Idiots' were deemed too dangerous to have around so Lenin either had them executed or shipped them off to slave labor camps.

The First Amendment of the Bill of Rights has now been effectively hamstrung by Leftists with Ivy League law degrees and is now only for the privileged few of the Progressive persuasion; they had to find a way shut up the citizen patriots from being heard by the public. Speaking out against the government or the threat of radical Islam is now classified as a 'hate crime.' The 'Civilian Law Enforcers,' just like Hitler's Brown Shirts, have been showing up at any and all political meetings everywhere; if anything is said they don't like, they wade in with night sticks and ear-splitting sound devices, then start cracking heads and arresting the speakers. If night sticks are not enough, they send in the guys with machineguns.

And then radical Islam is deftly manipulating our own legal system against us by using the 'hate-speech' laws to jail and sue Christian ministers and others who criticize it, with the complicity of activist judges. They have been demanding and getting more and more concessions in their program for the Islamization of America.

Progressives in Congress and the Whitehouse have also done an end-run around the Constitution, trying to disable the Second Amendment, and attempting to confiscate most types of privately owned firearms, to place America and Americans at the mercy of any and all enemies, domestic or foreign. Fortunately, their efforts have not met with universal success; many of the various states have banded together and filed suit with the Supreme Court and enacted state laws that prohibit abrogation of the Second Amendment. Much to the consternation of the 'inside-the-beltway gang', the Supreme Court, observing precedent, has declared the federal laws unconstitutional.

Doubtless, the axe will fall on America at some critical moment by decree of the shadow government of the New World Order, or whatever they call themselves. At that point, the government will openly seize absolute power under some pretense of 'restoring order.' Most likely it will occur during some contrived disturbance during the public's legitimate protest against the government's own treacherous policies and actions. Many in the know say the government is actively planning to utilize American combat troops who are being retrained to 'control' domestic protests—a clear violation of the Posse Comitatus Act of 1878. These battle-hardened veterans will have to be convinced by government propagandists to believe that angry groups of American people are their rabble-rousing enemy instead of what they really are: outraged citizens voicing legitimate demands for redress from the government under the rights enumerated in the Constitution. They've already arrested scads of citizens and shipped them off to prison. American citizens—particularly Christian, Jewish and secular patriots who legitimately oppose the government—will be rounded up by U.S. troops, branded 'enemies of the state,' and shipped off to FEMA prison camps. But then, laws are such a bore to dictators. The old saying, 'Power corrupts and absolute power corrupts absolutely' is spot on. Adolf Hitler would be just so proud of his Progressive sycophants!

America and her freedom is definitely on the chopping block!

Picking up the phone, Jim called his second-in-command, "Eli, send Baruch over here. I need to see him, stat."

"Sam's taken the airplane and gone to Hot Springs, Arkansas, today to visit family, Jim. He called in a minute ago—he's on his way back and should be here in about half an hour."

"Okay, tell him to report to me at my house as soon as he gets in."

Jim picked up the phone, dialed a Washington, D.C. number and left a voice message. "Bob, this is Jim. I would very much like to join you for that Philly's game. I will let you know details of my schedule ASAP. Give me a call," and hung up the phone.

Jim no sooner hung up the phone than it rang.

"Jim? Sam here. Eli said to call you. I'm almost home. What's up?" asked the Israeli expatriate.

"Get down here to my office at the house on the double. I can't discuss this even over a secure channel," exclaimed Jim.

Thirty minutes later, Sam walked into Jim's office and before he had a chance to sit down, Jim started to explain the situation.

"Sam, we have a very serious situation developing. I'm sure you know, in general, what El Presidente, Kaiser Bill and Hezbollah have been up to of late. The bottom line is that we must prepare to evacuate our people here in Houston very very soon. But we have something of utmost urgency to do first just as soon as we can pull it off. Are you up to a midnight ride to the east coast?"

"No problemo, boss! I'm fresh as a daisy; that airplane of yours flies like a dream. Where are we going?"

"We're going to pick up Senator Bob Dalton, from the Winchester, Virginia, airport just outside suburban Washington, D.C. I received a distress call from him earlier today. He has been on several organization's hit-lists for the past few months and apparently someone's goons are actively on his trail now that the devil is on the move—we've got to get him out of there tonight, preferably not in a body bag."

"Frank is topping off the tanks as we speak. We'll have the ship ready in 10 minutes, Sir.

"I want you and Frank to draw side arms and automatic rifles with 200 rounds apiece. Also, draw me a Squad Automatic Weapon and several canisters of ammo. I'll be right down to the airstrip."

Within moments, the phone rang. "Jim? Bob. I'm in the woods behind my house—hopefully alone. What's your schedule look like?"

"Bob, it's 11:00pm CST here. How does 2:00am EST strike you?"

"I'll be at 'Location 5' with bells on. Come ready for social trouble—I've got company but I'll try to shake them."

"Copy that. We'll do our best, Bob."

Neither Jim nor Frank detected a stealthy figure in the hallway, silently stealing away from Jim's office door into the night.

As the Citation climbed to cruise altitude under a brilliant moon, Jim relaxed a bit, bathed in the beauty of the night.

Lord, give us favor tonight. Let not your angels be transparent. Help Bob make it to the airport and let us extract him without any problems. And above all, keep us away from hostile military aircraft—this thing can't shoot back.

At 1:55am EST, Sam announced, "Sir, we're on short approach to Winchester Airport. My scanner's picking up Bob's tracer near the far end of the runway. Get ready for action! There's hardly any wind tonight and no air traffic around the airport. I'll spin us around at the end of the runway, Jim. You open the door and let Bob in and we'll just take right off the way we came in."

Jim loaded the light machinegun and checked his 9mm pistol.

Lord, here we go. Give us clear sailing.

The biz-jet crossed the threshold of the runway fast and Sam held off the touch-down until half way down the runway. As the gear settled onto the concrete, Sam stood on the brakes hard slowing the ship rapidly as the end of the runway barrier rushed toward them. In the brilliance of the landing lights, Senator Dalton could be seen running zig-zag toward the runway with a backpack and satchel in hand. Some distance away, Jim could see the muzzle flashes of weapons as he swung the boarding steps down. As the Senator neared the ship, Jim opened fire with the SAW in the direction of Dalton's pursuers. The Senator rushed breathlessly up the steps and collapsed on the floor of the cabin as Jim slammed the door shut and yelled, "Hit it Sam. Let's get out of here."

As the engines spooled up and the aircraft gathered speed, rotating off the runway, they could hear the *pop, pop, pop* of gunfire. Dalton's pursuers were apparently too far away for hand guns and nothing struck the ship.

Thank you, Lord. Now, get us safely to Houston.

As the little jet rocketed toward its eight-mile-high cruise altitude, Jim turned to the red-faced man sprawled on the cabin floor who was just recovering his breath and shedding his backpack.

"Senator Dalton, I presume? Fancy meeting you here! How the heck are you anyway?" Jim grinned extending his hand.

"Glad to be aboard and very glad to be alive, Sir. I thought I had shaken the bad guys for a while—rode my motorcycle out the back side of my property at half-past midnight. Don't know how they anticipated my every move. I'd been told there was a contract out on both of us. American patriots aren't too popular with a lot of nasty folks, my friend."

"What else is new, Bob? We're preparing our whole company to head up to a mountain retreat in Montana, Bob. Care to join us?"

"Can't think of a better place to be, than with my friends. With Marnie gone, I sure don't have a thing to hold me in Texas."

"I was just going to ask about your wife. You say she's gone? Gone where?"

"Uh . . . well . . . she died two weeks ago of a massive heart attack, Jim. Just keeled over at the dinner table. I administered CPR and the medics tried to save her, but she never regained consciousness," replied the Senator with tears in his eyes.

"I'm so sorry, Bob. You should have let me know; I'd have been there for you."

"Couldn't risk putting your neck in a noose, Jim. Our enemies are nasty customers. America is in a heap of trouble. And the terrible part is that some of our worst enemies are native-born Americans. The President has built up an army of civilian enforcers just like Hitler did in WWII. I found out that most of them are ex-cons and other 'pillars of society.' I've been seeing more and more of them around D.C. They are some of the thugs he recruited to go all over confiscating citizen's firearms and strong-arming government critics a while back. Real fine bunch of boys; kinda resemble Mafia enforcers. You know, Jim, George Mason IV who co-authored the Bill of Rights, wrote, 'To disarm the people is the best and most effective way to enslave them.' Looks like the President and his partners in crime agreed with Mason and tried to do just that.

"What do you mean, they 'Tried to do it?'" inquired Jim.

"They haven't had universal good luck in a many areas of the country; seems like a whole lot of Americans take a dim view of surrendering their guns and still cling tightly to them as well as their religion. But the Supreme Court recently decided in favor of the Constitution, anyway, after the states dug in their heels too. The administration kept it very quiet, but I heard around the corners the President lost a bunch of his hand-picked boys some place. I was never able to get full specifics as to where it was—guess it was a military secret or something. Seems they thought they were gonna drop in and surprise a bunch of what they called 'hillbillies' somewhere as an example to the whole country to kow-tow. They parachuted and choppered in about 500 of their 'storm troopers' in the south some place, in an area of forests, hills 'n hollers. Seems like I heard less than 80 of their people were finally able to walk out under their own power; lost three Blackhawk choppers in the process—those RPGs are bloody murder. The 'ignoramuses' they were planning to teach a lesson were ready for 'em and let 'em have it with both barrels. After that, they were a whole lot more careful and discreet," snickered the senator.

"How did he manage to get around the Second Amendment in the first place?"

"Jim, even some of the most liberal guys in Congress were squeamish about that one and opposed it forcefully to the point that when push came to shove, it seemed he wasn't going to get the votes to pass it. Subsequently, he and the Secretary of State managed to negotiate a treaty with the U.N. that bypassed and nullified the Second Amendment; he got it passed by the Senate through some unusual procedural maneuvers. Then the voters turned out the majority of incumbents at the next election cycle so the administration was really left high and dry. After that, congressional resistance to most of his agenda continued to grow and grow. So, the President finally said 'Okay, fine, I 'm the President and I'm going to do what I want, so I'll just do it my way' and he started issuing shady Executive Orders to get a lot of his dirty work done and let Congress clean up the mess as best they could. From that point on, he and Congress were on an inevitable collision course, to say nothing of the angry citizenry. Law is such an inconvenience to dictators, you know."

"What do you mean he was 'on an inevitable collision course'? asked Jim.

"Uh . . well, this morning in my prayer time, the Lord said, 'Don't go up to 'The Hill' today, there is danger afoot for you.' So I said 'Yes, Sir,' called in sick, loaded my illegal .45 automatic and stuck close to home.

"Just an hour before I called you the first time, I received a cell phone call from the freshman senator who sits at the desk to my right. He said, 'Bob, I don't know what's going on, but the President just suddenly called for a joint session of Congress and demanded the justices of the Supreme Court also attend. We're all in here and waiting but his enforcers are at all the doors—I have a bad feeling about this. You better stay away!' Then about a half-hour later, I got another call from him. He said, 'Bob, the President just walked in and announced he is suspending the Constitution, abolishing the Supreme Court, disbanding Congress and turning the government over to his czars and Cabinet secretaries. We were elected by the people; how can he just dismiss us like that?' I answered, 'He can do that on the slightest pretext by Executive Order—America has finally been had. He may now be addressed as "Comrade Caesar." If you can find a way to get out of there, do it— and run for your life.' Moments later, my friend screamed, 'My God, Bob, the civilian enforcers are pouring into the chamber with machineguns and the doors are being locked. They're gonna kill us for sure. Too late . . . ! "

"The phone went dead after I heard several long bursts of automatic weapons fire and heard a chorus of screams. I have no doubt that all of my colleagues, as well as the Supreme Court justices, are dead and America is now totally in the hands of Progressive Marxist revolutionaries. With that, I completed hurried preparations to bug out of D.C.; that's when I called you. I figured they'd nail me for sure if I tried driving to Texas."

"I threw away my cell phone thinking they wouldn't be able to track me, and rode my motorcycle out the back of my property onto the main highway. I rode ten miles before slipping into a heavily forested area to bide my time while I estimated my best ETA at the airport. As I rode up to the runway fence, I spotted you on final approach so I ditched the bike and cut a hole in the fence. As I ran through the tall grass toward the runway,

I spotted some goons crouching in the grass up ahead of me silhouetted in the lights and facing the runway. I shot three of them at a dead run. I surprised them and ran right through their area like crazy. I just can't figure out how they knew to get there ahead of me," pondered the Senator.

"Well, I'd ask you the same thing your late Senate friend asked you, Bob," said Jim, "I knew Washington was corrupt to the hilt but how can the President just usurp the government of the United States and seize power for no good reason? And murdering Congress? And the Supreme Court? Unbelievable! What a monster!"

"Jim, ever since World War II, various Presidential Executive Orders and such have been periodically generated that would one day enable the usurpation of our government by an unscrupulous President; whether this was an unintended consequence or was done with the full knowledge and cooperation of some of our most trusted politicians is an unanswered question. Then, back in the early to mid '70s there evolved a family of secret executive orders revolving around Executive Order 11490 which gives the President and the various departments the power to seize absolute control of the government on the pretext of 'civil disturbances.' That Executive Order can be used by an unscrupulous administration to essentially turn this country into a dictatorship in which the President and his sundry heads of government call all the shots—no pun intended—and the citizens lose all their rights under the Constitution and Bill of Rights. If you criticize the government, they just ship you off to a FEMA prison camp somewhere and you're never heard from again. And believe me, they have set aside prison camp areas many years ago all over the U.S. in preparation for all this. Most Americans would never have believed such a monstrous evil could happen here, but I'm afraid that is exactly what has occurred. I can hardly believe it myself."

"I know one thing: my defense industry is out of business, Bob. The enemies of America have cut off most of the strategic materials to the U.S. With the whole world coming down on us like they are, I wouldn't be surprised if we are going to be surrendered to our enemies without a shot being fired," lamented Jim.

"Oh, Jim, listen, many of the big shots in D.C. are essentially either shills of the U.N., the New World Order, Kaiser Bill or radical Islam. All those seemingly disparate groups are in bed together for their own varied reasons. This 'One World' globalist crowd's utopian world view considers nationalism to be a mental illness and the cause of all evil; if we could only dispense with nationalist attitudes and eliminate international boundaries and institutions, we would all live as brothers and war would be no more. In their minds, traditional American values are ignorant, arrogant and elitist and need to be replaced. They swoon in adoration of the European Union, the United Nations and the World Court. It is their fondest wish to remake America into a model of Europe and subject her to international governance and law—One World Government. Why, I will never know. Never mind that American's forbears came over here from Europe to escape the ills of European society. Never mind that it has been American exceptionalism and our faith in God that has made us the richest, most powerful, most blessed nation in the history of the world. You know, Thomas Jefferson wrote: "The comparisons of our government with those of Europe are like a comparison of heaven and hell."

"The Progressive 'Billionaires Club' has been buying power in Washington and it's obvious they own most all of D.C., and its inmates, lock, stock and barrel. These international super-rich behind-the-scenes, movers and shakers give the President and his minions their orders and call the shots like chess players. I personally think Al Qaeda and Hezbollah operatives sit on these guys' board of directors.

"This 'Billionaires Club,' and the rest of the Progressive herd, think that America is an evil imperialist nation that has ripped off the rest of the world and that we are actually to blame for causing terror attacks on our people. They believe that Israel has no right to exist so they hope to put both the America we've known, and Israel, out of business. These people have utopian dreams of turning all of North America into one huge country—sort of a 'Mexamericanada,' or some such—under their control, of course, which would at least encompass Mexico, America and Canada with no borders. So, it's no mystery why no one has been allowed to close the U.S. borders in years. They engineered the near-simultaneous American economic crash a few years back and the near collapse of the Mexican government through their boys in the banking establishment, Wall Street and the Mexican drug cartels. They now have a virtual lock on the election process of the American presidency, along with many senate and congressional seats. If you're a prospective candidate and you're not on their approved list, it's virtually impossible in most places to ever get the nod. Not too many years ago, the American electorate was presented with a Progressive Presidential candidate from each major party—kind of like being given a choice between being shot and hanged! The American politicians they own would sell their grandmothers for political and monetary gain and they'd jump at the chance to turn America over to our enemies—if the price is right. Secretly—or perhaps not so secretly—most Progressives despise Christians, Jews, the Constitution, the Bill of Rights and everything the Founding Fathers believed in. The Bible and the Constitution are both examples of absolute truth and Progressives hate absolutes because they have such a hard time twisting them to fit their views. That's why they will always refer to the Constitution as a "living document" so they can come up with specious arguments to justify twisting, misinterpreting and changing it to do whatever they want and no one should find fault with them.

"And now I hear Kaiser Bill is flying into New York City to meet with the U.N. as we speak. You can bet that whole crowd is up to no good! I'm not at all surprised the President ordered the liquidation of Congress. As I said before, law is such an inconvenience to dictators.

"The only thing that's going to save America and Israel right now is a return to God. God's people absolutely must cast aside denominational differences and stand together against the Devil's minions. I remember that one famous Founding Father said, "We must, indeed, all hang together, or most assuredly we shall all hang separately," concluded the senator.

In the midst of their conversation, the phone rang by Jim's seat. Eli's voice came over the receiver sounding very alarmed. "Jim! Jim! Are you there? Pick up, man, it's an emergency."

"Slow down, Eli, slow down! Chill, man! What's put the burr under your saddle?" answered Jim, looking at the phone as if it were a venomous snake.

"Jim, our American satellite just spotted five nuclear explosions in the continental U.S." cried Eli.

"Lord, NO!! . . . . . Where?" shouted Jim.

"Boston, Chicago, Miami, Phoenix and San Diego," said Eli.

"Were they delivered by missiles?" questioned Jim.

"Nope, apparently the Islamic 'sleeper cells' did the honors with their suitcase bombs!" answered Eli.

"Not only that, but the folks from south of the border are now streaming north in large numbers as if on cue," continued the lanky Texan, "And get this: The mushroom clouds haven't even dissipated yet and Kaiser Bill and a consortium of European, oriental, Middle East, South American and African nations have already announced they'll send in 'aid' for us—and contingents of troops 'to maintain order,' if you can believe that. And El Presidente has welcomed them in. Most all of these are no friend of America. Talk about the foxes guarding the henhouse. And I've just spotted a number of trains headed inland coming out of coastal port cities on both of the left coasts loaded with foreign military trucks, tanks and armored personnel carriers. The corpse isn't even cold yet and buzzards are already swarming the carcass. Kind of makes you wonder who is really behind this, doesn't it?"

"No, question about that one, Eli. By the way, Senator Dalton says that 'El Presidente' has just 'retired' Congress and the Supreme Court—at the business end of a gun barrel. He's declared himself the Grand Poobah of the land and seized absolute power. Look, man, we've got to move to the Eagle's Lair immediately, if not sooner!" warned Jim.

"Yeah, I know! By the way, our American satellite just destroyed two incoming missiles that were fired from ostensibly tramp steamers, one off the coast of Oregon and one off Nantucket Sound—probably those electro-magnetic pulse, or EMP, bombs to destroy electronics all over the country. Our satellite then sent each of them a nice white phosphorus bomb. Made spectacular fires! That stuff burns right through armor plate, y'know," chuckled Eli, "Yep, it looked like the crews were abandoning ship like rats right into the mouths of the sharks. And now both ships are on fire and slowly sinking. Serves 'em right!"

Their conversation was suddenly interrupted by a brilliant flash of light through the right cockpit portal. "What the . . ." yelled Sam and Frank in unison as their heads snapped to the right.

"What's going on . . .?" shouted Jim as he rushed to peer out a side portal. What he saw made his blood run cold.

"Oh, my God! 'Terror Incorporated' just hit Washington, D.C.," groaned Jim.

"Look at that mushroom cloud!" exclaimed Bob Dalton.

"Well, Eli, we have another small problem my friend: D.C. was just nuked. Makes me wonder if this is partly to cover the President's tracks. Contact everybody on our list of potential evacuees and tell them to be at the company airfield with all their stuff just as fast as they can get there—but no later than 8:00am today without fail—or they'll walk to Montana! We've got to get everyone in the air to the Lair before the Texas State Militia is overwhelmed, a bomb goes off in Houston or someone declares martial law."

"Get the A&P mechanics out of bed right now and get the Connie ready to go. Now, my warbirds will have to be our first line of defense. We may have to fight on our way up to Montana, Eli. I want the fighters and the B-25s armed with a full complement of Browning machineguns and a full load of ammo—just in case we run into social trouble on the way. I also want the 75mm howitzers loaded and ready to go on the B-25s and the 20mm cannon stocked on the P-38. The stock P51's and the P-38 have the range, with drop tanks, to escort the Constellation all the way to Montana. But the gas-guzzler fighters like Eli's P-47 Thunderbolt and my 'Black Knight' will probably have to refuel at our emergency strip in northwestern Kansas, if necessary. Oh, and make sure you triple the security around my house and the plant tonight. Tell the guards to shoot anything that walks, crawls or flies inside the fence without permission."

"Will do, boss. So, Washington's gone too, huh!? My God, you gotta be kidding!" Eli's shocked voice trailed off as he hung up the phone.

Jim turned to the senator, "Bob, bad news! The Muslim sleeper cells aren't sleeping anymore. They've just nuked six major cities, now, including Washington."

"I'm not surprised. I heard about the bombing raids on Iran just a few hours ago. I didn't think it'd be long before they retaliated," the senator answered ruefully.

"Why don't you stay at my house tonight and get a couple of hours of sleep. We can't do anything until daylight anyway since it will take our people some time to get their stuff together. Besides, flying by visual flight rules and the seat of our pants at night in antique airplanes is not a good way to live to a ripe old age. I'm not going to fly up like a king in this biz jet and abandon my people to their own devices. I'm going to fly the 'Black Knight' up myself. If they don't make it, neither will I. We'll just have to trust the good Lord that nothing happens in Houston over the next few hours. We can possibly get you to your Houston house in the morning with a chopper and a security detail if there's anything there you need," suggested Jim.

"Nope, we sold the Houston house a year ago, my friend. All my extra junk is in storage and I don't really need any of it. So, I'm looking forward to Montana."

☆ 5 ☆

THE EXODUS

Arie returned to his monitors after talking to Jim. There was no doubt about it. The unthinkable, prophesied centuries before, was coming to pass: A vast army was descending upon the land of Israel. The Russians were wasting no time in teaming up with what was left of Iran, Syria and a host of Israel's other Muslim neighbors. The only thing standing in their way was the small American presence, the IDF and advance units of Kaiser Bill's military.

The Tell of Megiddo is the location of one of Israel's most strategic and sensitive subterranean airbases and the launch-point for much of its air forces. The loss of this base would severely handicap the IDF. The question remains whether or not it could be adequately defended under the pressure of such a massive onslaught as appears to be forming up.

The intercom rang, snapping Arie out of his reverie. "General Ziv to see you, Sir," announced his secretary. "General Ziv? Oh, by all means please show him in, Miriam!" responded Arie.

In the face of unprecedented military straits, General Zechariah Z. Ziv had been advanced to the highest rank ever created in the Israeli military and granted the authority normally reserved only for the Defense Minister. To put it plainly, in matters of national security, General Ziv's word was now virtually law in Israel. Ziv, who had made *aliyah* to Israel as an adult, was an evangelical Christian and made no secret of it. Despite his Christian faith, his charisma and ability as a commander were unparalleled. The Knesset and the Prime Minister knew they could not place the defense of Israel in more capable hands.

Miriam came in with the distinguished, silver-haired warrior in tow. "General Ziv! So good to see you, Sir. Wish it were under better circumstances. Need I ask what's on your mind?" asked Arie.

"Greetings my friend! I suppose you're aware of the 'unfortunate' destruction on the Temple Mount?" grinned Ziv.

"Yes, General, a truly terrible tragedy," chuckled Arie.

"You'll be interested to know that when I went up there with a commando unit and some Merkava tanks, we were confronted by a belligerent group of Al Aqsa Martyrs Brigade people. We rounded them up and shipped them across the Jordan. I warned them that they would indeed become martyrs if I ever laid eyes on them again. I informed the Muslim *Wakf* that they are now essentially homeless. I warned them all that the Temple Mount, along with all of Jerusalem, is now totally under Israeli management and to keep their hides out of Israel or they'll be carried out in body bags. I certainly do not intend to leave any of them ensconced any longer as a fifth-column in Jerusalem. Nor do I intend to give away more of our country to our enemies. I have over 2,000 crack troops presently clearing the Mount and the rest of the Old City of David. There are people both here in Israel and worldwide who do not like me, Arie. They say I'm 'too harsh and intolerant.' But Israel has accommodated her enemies far too long. How can you be too harsh when dealing with the pit vipers of the world? I am determined to leave them not so much as a pit to hiss in. But enough of that!" said Ziv, changing the subject.

"You and your people are uppermost on my mind right now, Arie. Your company's technical expertise and creativity will figure greatly in what seems to be an inevitable exchange of unpleasantries with the hoodlums of the world. As you well know, much of the world appears to be preparing to attack us. Although we seem to have an uneasy ally in Kaiser Bill and the E.U., I personally do not trust him. The American people generally support us, but we cannot count on the American government, or anyone else for that matter, to fight our battles for us. While the U.S. has helped us neutralize Iran, I fear they will not be much help to us beyond this point. America is under threat and I am leery of their new regime. Besides, America will have its own problems to deal with. They have been infiltrated by fifth columnists crossing their borders with Mexico and Canada and their military is spread too thin to boot. We are prepared to go it alone, along with our supposed allies, in an all-out 'scorched earth' shootout. We will use every weapon at our disposal, many of which were created by your company. We will prevail, with God's help, and they will pay a terrible price for every drop of Israeli blood they spill. But I am concerned that we may lose you and your associates in the process. I want you to prepare to leave Israel immediately. You and your most prominent scientists along with wives and families, will be moved somewhere that is more secure than this postage-stamp-sized State of Israel," announced the general, the gold-braid on his uniform flashing under the high-intensity lighting.

"Where do you propose to send us, Sir?" Arie inquired.

"That is the entire crux of the matter. I'm open to suggestions," fumed Ziv, "Since the entire world hates us simply because we are Jews, there really is no place I can think of on the face of the planet that would be safe for a Jew, and don't even mention Antarctica!" Ziv chuckled wryly, "Most certainly, Israel is not the place for you to be at this time, my friend. Do you have even an inkling of where I could send you?"

"Greenland and Iceland are probably not really acceptable on the basis of accommodations and weather. Japan is a possibility but they are already in the cross-hairs of several rogue nations. My American partner, General James Black, is preparing to evacuate the American branch of our company from Houston to a wilderness redoubt in the state of Montana. I know him very well and any place he approves of is good enough for me. Black says he has been instructed to go there by divine visitation. That's about the best suggestion I can think of at the moment," said Arie.

"Yes, I am acquainted with General Black—a man of unimpeachable integrity and ability. Do you suppose there is an improved airstrip within two to three kilometer runways in the vicinity of his wilderness establishment?" questioned Ziv.

"Yes, I understand they have an excellent airstrip right within the refuge itself large enough to handle major aircraft. They also have lodging for over 200 people," answered Arie.

"Excellent! Excellent! All right, then, that's a relief. At least there is some realistic hope for your security," said Ziv. "I have just the thing to get you there too: a U.S. Airforce C5-B. It's the only aircraft at our disposal which is large enough to handle everything and everyone in your party and that has the range to fly the 11,000 kilometers to Montana with minimum refueling connections. I will make the necessary arrangements for refueling immediately," decided the General.

"Wh . . . where'd you get a C5?" stammered Arie.

"Don't ask, Colonel Yehudah!" the general grinned, "Let's just say it's 'on loan' from the U.S. Air Force. I'll send up a special detachment of troops today large enough to pack up all your company's sensitive records and equipment, as well as household items and vehicles for yourself and three or four of your most important scientists and get it all loaded into the one aircraft. You'll all have to ride together in the upper deck of the cargo hold. It won't be a plush trip, but I have two unmarried American-born transport pilots and a flight engineer whom I can spare to fly you there on a one way basis. They are excellent aviators and will get you there safely. The aircraft has classified countermeasures to fool an enemy as to its identity. You really couldn't have a much more secure ride. Well, with that settled, I must return to the next of my pressing duties, but I want you on your way to America by this evening. That's not a suggestion, that's an order, Arie. . . . .And may the God of All Comfort be with you all. Shalom, my beloved friend and God speed to all of you. Perhaps we will meet again this side of the veil, God willing." The two men embraced and wept together.

As the general exited his office, Arie picked up the phone and dialed the corporate headquarters. "Sarah, I need you to come to the lecture hall in the next half-hour, we have a major emergency." Arie pressed a button on the plant's intercom and announced, "All personnel, summon your spouses and report to the lecture hall in thirty minutes."

Soon, the entire staff and spouses of the Israeli branch of Etzion Defense Enterprises were assembled in the lecture hall. Arie strode to the podium and turned on the microphone. "My friends and colleagues, this will be a short and not-so-sweet meeting. Time is short. I have called you here to inform you that the company is shutting down for the duration of the impending war. You will be furloughed with six month's pay and, hopefully, we will be able to recall you soon. I am sorry to drop this on you on such short notice, but I am afraid there is no alternative. General Ziv has ordered my family and our three highest-ranking scientists to evacuate Israel immediately. When I dismiss you, I would like Benjamin Cohen, Samuel Koenig and Abraham Adelson and their wives to remain here. Thank you and Shalom." The room was abuzz with discussion as the stunned employees exited.

When the room was cleared of all the other employees, Arie addressed the small remaining group. "I have been ordered to dismantle the plant of all sensitive equipment, inventory and records in preparation to leave Israel. You will all be evacuated with myself and my family. General Ziv is sending up a special detachment of men to move all our possessions for us into a giant aircraft which will take us to a wilderness retreat center—a City of Refuge, if you will—in the state of Montana in America, where our American partners are heading."

"What if we'd rather not go?" asked one of the wives.

"Marah, we are considered vital to Israel's security. General Ziv has issued the order for us to leave immediately. As Secretary of Defense and senior commander of the IDF, his word is law. 'No' is not an optional position," replied Arie.

"But won't that be like jumping out of the frying pan into the fire? America is already in danger of being invaded by half the world!" questioned Sam Koenig.

"Well, as General Ziv said, he and I are both open to other suggestions. If you have a better one, let's hear it. I know my partner, General Black, who is a retired two-star general, and I know he is trustworthy. Jim Black would not lead anyone into a death trap, which is really where we sit here in Israel at this very moment. God has appeared to Black and told him to take his family and associates to this Montana enclave where they will be safe. So, I believe we are far more likely to die here than in Montana. The fact is that there is no place on planet earth right now that is anywhere near completely safe for Jews, or Christians for that matter," countered Arie.

There was a long silence followed by a buzz of discussion between husbands and wives. "We are agreed," announced Ben Cohen, "We will go along with this plan. It would appear that we really have no alternative."

"All right," concluded Arie, "you people need to go home and quickly determine how much of your household you want moved. Leave behind everything you can live without, but don't leave behind anything important either. Be prepared for a swarm of soldiers to come to your house to pack and move your vital belongings in one fell swoop. Your homes will be locked and secured behind you—hopefully, they will be alright until your return."

As the scientists and their wives were departing, a convoy of military vehicles pulled up in front of the corporate offices and an Israeli Colonel walked through the door.

"Dr. Yehudah? Colonel Abrahamson. I've been sent by General Ziv to move your things. Let's get started," exclaimed the colonel brusquely. Arie took a deep breath and led the way to the records room. This was going to be a very long and unpleasant day.

Twelve hours later, everything the four families owned, other than furniture, as well as everything of major value at Etzion Enterprises, was stored in the cargo bay of the gigantic transport and the cargo doors were closed. Arie entered the cockpit to talk with the crew. "Captain, what will be our itinerary and time of arrival in Montana?" Arie queried.

"We plan to depart around 1600 proceeding northwest on a course that will take us over Greenland and the Arctic Circle. That's the shortest route. General Ziv has made arrangements for aerial refueling over Sweden, Iceland and Canada's Hudson Bay. Although we are lightly loaded, this monster has only a reliable unrefueled range of 2,400 miles and I am not in the habit of stretching the tanks. We may still have to pamper them if we hit adverse headwinds. Our planned route is approximately 11,000 kilometers, or a bit less than 7,000 statute miles, to Montana so at our cruise speed of 500 knots we will be in the air for many hours. Depending on the winds aloft, we should arrive in Montana sometime around 0800 Mountain Standard Time. We have lunch and refreshments ready to go when needed. Try to make yourselves as comfortable as possible on the upper deck. That portion of the ship is heated and pressurized, but I'd suggest you have blankets and warm garments available anyway. It will be a long, cold ride, particularly over the polar icecap. I'm sorry we don't have better accommodations, especially for the families, but this is a sort of 'Noah's Ark' mission so we'll all have to suck up and get through it the best we can. By the way, we'll be navigating by our inertial guidance systems as well as Etzion's global satellites. They're the only friendly birds still on the air," said the pilot.

The enormous transport's takeoff roll began just after 4:00pm, Israel time. As Arie peered out toward the Sea of Galilee and the Golan, he involuntarily shivered as he wondered what lurked over the hills beyond the Golan Heights.

☆ 6 ☆

INTO THE FIRE

When you see the 'abomination of desolation,' spoken of by Daniel the prophet, standing in the holy place" . . . then let those who are in Judea flee to the mountains. Let him who is on the housetop not go down to take anything out of his house. And let him who is in the field not go back to get his clothes. . . . And pray that your flight may not be in winter . . . For then there will be great tribulation, such as has not been since the beginning of the world until this time, no, nor ever shall be. And unless those days were shortened, no flesh would be saved; but for the elect's sake those days will be shortened.[12]

Church members and Etzion staff were pouring into Etzion Enterprise's Houston airfield by 5:30am the next morning. The group assembled around the shiny 4-engine Lockheed Super Constellation airliner sitting on the ramp, as baggage was stowed and fuel trucks topped off the tanks with aromatic aviation gasoline.

"She's a beauty, Jim," remarked Bob Dalton, examining the old airliner. "I understand they were a luxury liner in their heyday, but were retired in the 1950's in deference to jets. I guess there aren't many airworthy Connies left anymore."

75

"That's right, Bob. I spent a bundle restoring her. She's even better than new, with new engines and our most advanced avionics. And she has the range and capacity to get everybody to the Lair without refueling. She carries over 100 passengers in luxury. Anybody left over can hop aboard my Citation, one of the 'Gooney Birds' or one of the B-25s. Come over here and have a look at my collection of WWII era aircraft we're bringing up to the Lair."

The two men were joined by Eli and a few other church members as they approached the assembled antique warbirds sitting on the tarmac. Three C-47 cargo planes sat beside two twin-engine B25-J bomber gunships, two P47-N Thunderbolts and three P51-D Mustang fighters and a twin engine P-38 Lightning fighter. Each of the B25 bombers, as well as the fighters, bristled with machine-guns and the B-25s had a tunnel in the lower nose housing through which peered the muzzle of a 75mm howitzer barrel.

Parked all by itself, was a dead black P51-D Mustang with twin, contra-rotating, three blade propellers. The black propellers sported white tips and spiral white striping on the propeller hub for ground safety. Nose art, in white relief, showing a mounted knight dubbed her the "Black Knight." The "Knight" was definitely possessed of a certain lethal, sinister, persona.

With obvious pride, Jim explained the uniqueness of the 'Black Knight.' "She has a custom-built engine and the custom contra-rotating 3-blade propellers were originally intended for pylon air-racing, but we never got around to finishing the customization or removing the military wiring harnesses. We painted her dead black with some of the special paints that were used on the stealth planes. Her blueprinted 12-cylinder fuel-injected Rolls-Royce 'Merlin' type engine burns 130 octane aviation gasoline, plus nitro-methane when extra power is called for. She produces nearly 4,000 horsepower as opposed to the stock Mustang's 1,675 horsepower. She can cruise at over 600 miles per hour if you're in a hurry. Consequently, her control surfaces have been enlarged a bit to help handle the engine's increased power. The special propellers cancel the normal Mustang torque problems on takeoff and landing. With 4,000 ponies stomping around in the engine compartment, we just had to get rid of the torque. More stock P-51s were lost during landing operations in WWII than were lost in combat. Anyway, I know all her tricks, so I'm generally the only one who flies her."

A man walking beside Eli said, "What's the purpose of mounting fake guns on these old crates? They're certainly not going to scare anyone. Seems like they'd just add weight. "

Eli snorted, "Listen, Bub, go over there and stick your finger in one of those gun barrels and tell me what you feel."

The man did as he was told and looked up startled, "Whoa! Cold steel and rifling! That's a real gun, isn't it? Where did you guys get real machine guns?"

"Don't ask," winked Eli.

"But what good are machine guns against modern weapons?"

In his best Texas drawl, Eli responded, "Well, ya know, my great grand-pappy was a west-Texas peace officer in his younger days. When I was a teen-ager and he was in his 80's, he and I were out behind our ranch house one day shooting handguns just for kicks. I made some ignorant remark about a .22 pistol we had just fired being a wimpy weapon. Boy, he let me have it with both barrels. He said, 'Listen, Boy, I was out fishing at a lake one day long after I retired and I had the strangest premonition that trouble was headed my way. I had neglected to wear my usual sidearm that day so I was kinda worried. Well, I fished out the little .22 revolver I always carried in my tackle box—in case I ever snagged a man-eating fish—and stuck it in my belt. About an hour later, an ex-con who had a beef with me emerged from the tree line and surprised me. He took several shots at me with a .45 and missed. I returned the compliment with my little .22 and ended his career. So remember, Boy, whenever you wander into a gunfight, any gun is better than no gun. If I hadn't been armed that day, that bozo would've killed me for sure.' So, my friend, never despise these .50 cal machine guns, they're powerful weapons. When 'Ma Deuce' speaks, you better listen."

"Ma Deuce? What's that?" inquired Eli's companion.

"That's what American soldiers call the Browning .50 caliber M2A2 Heavy Machinegun. This weapon has been around for over 100 years and it's still the finest heavy machinegun in the world. Airborne .50 cals can be adjusted to fire at about 1,000-1,200 rounds per minute per gun. These B25s over here have 14 of them under the control of the pilot, as well as a 75mm howitzer. They can fire nearly 17,000 rounds per minute, that makes the modern .30 cal mini-gun look puny by comparison. The P47s have eight .50s and the Mustangs carry six. The P-38 has four .50s and a 20mm cannon," explained Eli.

"Man, Eli, I never knew WWII airplanes had that kind of firepower," replied the man.

"General Black," called the pilot of the Constellation, "We're ready to go! Everybody is here, all the luggage and freight has been stowed and we're awaiting your order to depart, Sir."

"Has anyone seen Pastor Nelson and his family this morning?" wondered Jim.

"I'm right here, Jim," responded the preacher from the back of the crowd, "We've decided we're not going with you right now. We feel we are going to be needed by the people in this area—we just can't walk off and leave them to fend for themselves."

"I wish you'd reconsider, Steve, but I understand. You're a great pastor and it's your decision. I don't have time to argue. You know you're always welcome at the Lair."

"Okay! Gather 'round everybody," shouted Jim, "the stock P-51s have drop tanks which should get them to Montana without refueling. But don't assume anything. All you pilots will need to be aware of your fuel stores when you get near the Kansas checkpoint north of Sherman. Sherman is about half way to the Lair, so if you have less than 60% fuel at Sherman don't take chances—top off your tanks. The 'Black Knight' will undoubtedly need to refuel. If we have social trouble anywhere along the way, you B25 and fighter jocks will have to handle it the best you can. You're loaded for bear but keep your arming switches off, unless you're sure you need the guns. And conserve your ammo in a fire fight because those guns each eat it at 1,000 rounds per minute and you don't carry an awful lot of ammo. When I refuel in Kansas, I'll need you, Eli, to fly cover for me, just in case there is any opposition there. Eli, you can refuel along with me. Any questions? Alright, fighters, B-25s and transports will cruise at 20,000 feet. Everybody mount up and let's hit the trail! The C-47s go first, then the Connie, the Citation and then us warbird pilots—I'll be off last."

Jim sprinted across the tarmac with the other warbird pilots. Donning a flight suit, noise-limiting helmet, parachute and sidearm, he climbed into the cockpit of the 'Black Knight' and strapped in. Flipping the cockpit switches, Jim primed the engine and hit the starter, drowning out the sump pump whine of the electric fuel pump. The 'Black Knight' rocked from side to side on her gear as the big V-12 racing engine roared to life, then idled down into a rhythmic, reedy, galloping staccato from the un-muffled short stacks. Jim watched Eli taxi past in his P-47 dubbed "Howdy Hun" and his partner P-47, the "Berlin Bomber." Ahead, Jim watched the C-47s and the Constellation lift off the runway, followed by the other aircraft. After performing his own engine run-up, Jim taxied onto the runway, lined up on the centerline, took a last look at the plant, slid the canopy shut, and released the brakes, while slowly advancing the throttle to full stop. With flames from the rear exhaust stacks licking at the fuselage, Jim rotated off the runway, quickly retracting gear and flaps. The Knight's climb to 20,000 feet was fast, effortless and exhilarating.

Man! I've flown all kinds of jet fighters but I've never experienced anything to compare with flying a Mustang. General Chuck Yeager was right when he said 'They took all the romance out of airplanes when they removed the propellers.'

The trip across Texas, Oklahoma and most of Kansas went without incident. As the group neared the Kansas emergency airfield near Sherman, Jim keyed his mike, "All aircraft, we're coming up on our emergency fuel point at Sherman. How's your gas looking?"

One by one most reported better than 60% fuel left. The Black Knight, however hovered at a bit less than 55%.

It's just not safe to proceed with gas this low. I've got to refuel.

"Boys, I'm very close to 50% fuel. I'm not going to push my tanks so I'm going to refuel the 'Knight.' Eli, cover me," ordered Jim as he rolled his ship over into a 'falling leaf' dive.

"I'm right behind you, Chief," called Eli.

As they neared the emergency field, the men spotted two police cruisers, with flashing lights running, sitting at the locked gate to the property.

In the distance, several miles away, a small military truck convoy was approaching.

"Looks like trouble waiting for us, Eli. I'd hoped to do this peaceably, but we'll soon see what all these guys are up to."

"Roger that, I'll go reconnoiter the outfit coming down the road, Jim, and see what they have in mind," drawled Eli, as "Howdy Hun" rolled right and set out down the road.

The gate to the airstrip property was directly in line with the end of the runway. Jim lined up on the runway and dropped gear and flaps for a 'short approach.' As he neared the runway threshold, six men exited the police cruisers with long guns and pointed them in his direction. Jim immediately banked left, increasing power as he retracted the flaps and landing gear. When his airspeed was up to par, he fire-walled the throttle, climbed several thousand feet and circled back toward the air strip.

"Eli, the guys in the cop cars are not friendly. I'm going to have to take them out. Don't take any chances with that convoy, either. And you better gas up too before we go on." warned Jim

"Yeah, I just flew over the convoy. They took some pot-shots at me with a .50 cal. off the top of a light armored vehicle. Not only are they lousy shots, but I'll bet they don't think I'm armed either. I'm gonna turn around and introduce them to their worst nightmare—'The P-47 Jug.' "

Incredibly, the men who had exited the police cruisers were still standing beside their cars as Jim made his second approach to the field. With his gun sights lined up on the cruisers, Jim flipped the arming switches on, waited until he was about a quarter mile away, then pressed the gun trips on the stick sending out a hail of red-hot tracers from the six Browning machine guns. The men and the police cars disappeared in a huge cloud of dust and a ball of fire. The 'Black Knight' flew through the cloud of smoke and came around in a climbing 360° turn. Dropping gear and 40° of flaps as he made his third approach, Jim saw nothing moving near the gate. He landed and taxied to the end of the runway, kicking left rudder, spinning the mustang around as he slid the throttle to idle-cutoff. He pressed a button on the instrument panel that brought four hidden gasoline pumps up out of the ground. Checking his pistol, he clambered out of the cockpit. Sprinting to pumps on both sides of the tarmac, he dragged two fuel hoses over to the Knight and began filling the tanks. In the distance, he could hear the heavy pounding of the P47's guns accompanied by thunderous explosions and huge clouds of smoke down the road.

Looks like Eli's administering the coup de grace.

Moments later, "Howdy Hun" tore in over the field, did a victory roll, and dropped gear and flaps as he circled around to land. Taxiing up in front of the 'Black Knight', Eli quickly exited the cockpit and proceeded to fill his own tanks. Within a few short minutes, both fighters were refueled and in the air leaving Kansas mercifully far behind them as they rocketed to 20,000 feet.

"Whew, that was no fun, Eli. Glad I had your company back there. Can't figure out how they seem to know our every move. What was that outfit you hit anyway?"

"Have no idea, Jim. I can only guess at their pedigree. Some kind of rag-tag, quasi-military. As I approached them, they opened up on me with a single .50 cal. off the top of a vehicle. That wasn't very neighborly! I swung back around, approached them from the rear for a strafing run. These eight 'Ma Deuces' made mincemeat out of the whole convoy. I didn't see a single thing moving as I passed over again. If anybody is still alive in that mess, they're gonna be walking for sure. Too bad, so sad!"

"Hey, how're you fighter jocks doing back there?" called the Constellation pilot from many miles ahead.

"Oh, we had some unwelcome admirers, but they're on their way to the 'Court of No Appeals.' We're all gassed up and back in the air. How's the weather up your way?" responded Eli.

"Weather's okay, but we received an FAA broadcast, while you guys were target shooting back there, ordering all aircraft grounded within two hours. But we should make it to the Lair okay. I don't think they can enforce every square foot of North America on this short notice."

"Keep your eyes peeled. I think we'll make it okay. But it's funny they haven't tried to intercept us in the air if they know where we are and where we're headed," ruminated Jim.

"Oh, well, now that you mention fighters, two blow-torch jockeys with E.U. markings went past us a few minutes ago and they acted like they didn't even see us. Came so close they just about scraped the paint off us as a matter of fact. I thought for sure they'd circle back and let us have it but they just flew on out of sight instead. Apparently the angels are nontransparent today, Boss."

Twenty minutes later, Jim and Eli caught up with the slower aircraft in the rear of the formation. Up ahead, the lead aircraft spotted their destination. "Talley Ho!" crowed the Connie pilot, "We have the Lair's runway in sight."

"OK, run the ships into Hangar Number One and get everyone out and organized—we're about 30 minutes behind you," ordered Jim.

After what seemed an eternity, the runway at the Eagle's Lair hove into view. "Everybody down as fast as you can and taxi into Hangar Number One. Eli, you and I will sweep the area for a few minutes and I'll land last."

"Boss, I'm running on fumes, something's wrong with my fuel transfer valves and I've gotta land NOW," reported Eli.

"Okay, don't let me hold you up!" ordered Jim.

Jim watched as Eli made his approach and lowered the gear and flaps before he crossed the threshold of the runway but was horrified to see the P-47's propeller coast to a stop a moment before the gear hit the runway.

"You OK, Eli?" Jim asked anxiously.

"Yep! This thing glides like a suitcase when the fan quits. She bounced ten feet in the air when I smacked the concrete but she's a tough old bird and everything still seems to be in one piece. I had visions of being picked up with a stick and a spoon," laughed Eli, "If I'd waited any longer to land, me and this airplane would've been splattered all over the place."

Jim executed the fighter pilot's classic 360 degree overhead approach and landed half-way down the runway to stay clear of Eli's aircraft. As Jim pulled the throttle to idle, the 'Black Knight's' engine back-rapped and the craft settled onto the runway while he heaved a huge sigh of relief.

Thank you, Jesus! We all made it in one piece!

Jim taxied into the cavernous Hangar Number One and pulled the throttle to idle-cutoff. As the propellers slowed to a stop amid only the sound of the engine's valve tappets—tickety, tickety, tickety, tickety, tick.. . . . tick . . . tick . . . . .tick—Jim slid back the canopy and let loose a loud war-whoop. "Woohoo, we made it!!"

"Praise the Lord! Hallelujah!" everyone was shouting all at once.

"Hey, you mechanics get out there with a fuel truck and get Eli's 'Jug' started for him. He ran out of gas and he's sitting in the weeds part way down the runway."

"We're on it. We'll get him in here in nothing flat, General."

Momentarily, the old bus pulled into the hangar. Grandfather and George Wing stepped out.

"Welcome, everyone, to the Eagle's Lair. It's getting along toward sundown so you'll all bed down on the carpet in the Lodge tonight and we'll get everybody situated in the morning. Fill up the bus and we'll come right back for more. We'll get to your large luggage as soon as everyone is in the Lodge."

While the party was being transported, Jim found Maryann and, arm-in-arm, they stepped out of the hangar into the chill mountain air where snowflakes were starting to fall.

"Looks like we got here just in the nick of time, Honey. It's September and 'Old Man Winter' is already on the move."

"Sir? Sir!" came a breathless, insistent voice at Jim's elbow. "Ivan, your communications guy, says he just received an urgent call from somebody named Arie. Says you should call him back, ASAP" announced one of the teenagers.

Ivan Skvinsky Skvar, was chief of communications for Etzion. Ivan was a Jew of Russian heritage who had made *aliyah* to Israel as a child when his aunt and uncle with whom he had been living were allowed to emigrate from Mother Russia in the early 1990's. Graduating from Technion, the electronics genius was snapped up by Arie and eventually sent to Houston to run the corporation's far-flung electronic empire. He was charged with maintaining and operating all communications between the satellites as well as the secure telephones.

Jim drew the satellite phone from his belt and dialed Arie's number. Arie answered, "Hi, Jim. I tried to call you before but got no answer. Israel is under siege. Hope you have room for us because we're on our way to the Eagle's Lair—left Tel Aviv six hours ago. Our ride is no speed demon, but she does have capacity. Should arrive in about ten hours or so. How large is your runway there?"

"Runway's 8,500 feet by 250 feet wide but . . . . but what are you flying in on anyway?"

"USAF C5-B. It's the only thing available big enough to hold all our stuff and with the range to get to your place. Even so, we're just now being refueled."

"C5 . . . Where on earth did you commandeer one of those monsters?"

"Long story, my friend. Had to get the top people out of Israel by order of General Ziv. Oh, and I'm bringing my family . . . and those of three of my most prominent colleagues. Hope you can accommodate us."

"You bet, Arie, we can take care of all of you, no sweat—it's great that you're coming here, my friend. I just got here myself. Just so you'll know, the weather may be getting dicey here in Montana by tomorrow morning—snow, you know—and all civilian aircraft have been ordered grounded under martial law, but we'll have the lights and the ILS on for you. Do you have our coordinates and radio frequencies?"

"All of Etzion's satellites are still on the air. Just give us your exact coordinates and radio frequencies and we'll dial them into our navigation system. Our ship has ECM equipment to trick the enemy's radar and air control. These IAF pilots will get us there no problem."

"Arie, I'll have Eli call your captain in a few minutes with our data. Shalom, my friend. Stay warm."

"Okay, Jim, we'll see you soon. Pray for us! Shalom for now."

Jim quickly phoned Eli, "Eli, Arie is on his way here from Israel. Contact his aircraft commander on the satellite phone ASAP and give them the lowdown on our installation here."

"Roger, WILCO, Chief! Never expected to see him here, but, hey, the more the merrier," drawled the Texan.

Jim smiled at his spouse, "Well, Maryann, our Israeli partner and his family are on their way here with three of our top Israeli scientists and their families. They should be here sometime tomorrow morning."

"Wonderful!" Maryann beamed excitedly, "I haven't seen Sarah and the boys in such a long time. But I wonder how they'll get here with America under martial law?"

"They're coming in a late-model American C5 the IDF managed to scrounge up somewhere. It's about 7,000 miles from here to Israel. I'd guess they'll either fly in below the radar over the Canadian Shield or they'll employ ECM equipment to hide their identity. Probably the latter because they're pushing the envelope on their fuel tanks now and flying low eats more fuel," Jim opined.

At 8:35am the next morning, the Lair's aircraft intercom radio crackled to life with a heavy Hebrew accent, "Eagle's Lair, this is military N, six, four, niner, alpha, approximately five-zero clicks northeast of your position. We need up-to-date landing instructions for your aerodrome."

"Our runway is 8,500 feet long at elevation 3,558 feet above mean sea level, runways are one-two and three-zero, 200 foot barriers approximately 1000 feet from each threshold. Wind is presently northwest at 25mph, gusting to 35 with heavy snow. Suggest you use runway three-zero. Keep your power up during your approach and don't get low on the glide slope once you engage or you'll likely decapitate a pine tree or an elk," responded Eli with a grin.

"Roger that! We are picking up your radio beacons now. Ah, there! We are now engaged on the glide slope. We will be there shortly."

As he and Maryann climbed into his Humvee, Jim shouted to Eli, "Open Hangar Number Two, and tell the C5 pilot to just taxi right on into it. Get some maintenance guys out there to guide them in. I'm going out to meet them. Have someone bring the bus over too."

With the inmates staring out the windows in anticipation, the Lodge began to shake as a gigantic aircraft burst through the snowy overcast, like an enormous prehistoric bird, with snow sworls in the wingtip vortices.

"Man! That thingy is absolutely ginormous—looks like a battleship with wings," marveled Eli.

As the mammoth aircraft taxied into Hangar Number Two , she cleared the hangar doors with only three feet to spare on either wingtip and the vertical stabilizer cleared the top of the door by not more than a foot. The turbines were just coasting to a stop as Jim drove into the hangar to watch the nose hinge up and the other cargo portals open.

Shortly, a middle-aged, tall, swarthy, curly-haired man in a nylon jacket, aloha shirt and shorts emerged from the cargo hold, followed by a beautiful, raven-haired woman and three teenage boys similarly attired.

"Arie, my friend, welcome, welcome," shouted Jim as he grabbed the Israeli in a bear-hug. "And welcome to your boys and lovely lady, Sarah."

"Jim, these are my sons, Reuben, Joshua and Caleb. We are so glad to be safely here at last, but Israel is in grave danger. I could see the foreign armies on the monitors approaching the Golan north of the Sea of Galilee just as we left. The jihadists love death and welcome it because they think a special place in paradise awaits them. Only God can save Israel," sighed Arie.

"I know, Arie, we have been watching the situation and it looks pretty grim. But Israel is the apple of God's eye, my friend. God help the invaders. They will regret their decision to attack Israel. I know He will certainly save both Israel and America eventually, but things are going to get worse before they get better. You are probably aware that our own government has been seized by traitors. But . . . all that aside for now, I'm curious, my friend. How did you rate this aircraft, Arie? This is not exactly a biz-jet, you know!"

"Well, the airplane obviously belongs to the U.S. military, but how Israel acquired it I don't have the foggiest. My close friend, General Zechariah Ziv, who is now Israel's top military man, ordered us to leave the country immediately for our own safety. The catch was that he didn't know where to send us until I mentioned the Eagle's Lair. He seemed relieved and said that sounded like the best suggestion he'd heard all day and that he had just the thing to get us here, with two American-born heavy transport pilots and a flight engineer to fly it. Ziv sent up several hundred soldiers yesterday and in just hours they packed and loaded the company's inventory, sensitive files and equipment, as well as the entire households of all four families, into the cargo bay of this giant. We even brought our personal vehicles. And we were given several tons of equipment, food stuffs and clothing as well. We were refueled three times on the way by somebody's aerial tankers. I'll never know how Ziv managed to pull that one off, considering everything that is going on. " concluded Arie.

Maryann came up behind the little gathering and embraced Sarah. "Sarah, it's so wonderful to see you, Arie and your boys again. Wish it were under better circumstances." Then she poked Jim in the back, "Jim, you can talk later. These people are freezing in their light clothing."

"Yes, it's quite a change from Tel Aviv," shivered Arie.

"Oh, of course you're cold! Forgive my stupidity! It's only 20 degrees Fahrenheit here! Get your family into the Humvee; we have a bus coming over for the rest of your party. We'll get you and your associates settled in our family units just as soon as possible. The flight crew can room in the Lodge," declared Jim.

The next week was a blur of activity, as a mountain of belongings and cargo were off-loaded from all the assembled aircraft and the trucks that had arrived from Houston. Families with children were situated in family cabins, with singles and some couples settled in the Lodge.

"I know things are somewhat cramped for some of you, but I hope you'll all be relatively comfortable," remarked Jim at a gathering on Sunday morning in the Lodge's multi-media theatre. Arie shouted with a smile from the back of the room, "Jim, compared to our house in Israel, the place we're in here is a palace. Don't apologize! Trust me, we'll all manage handsomely. Besides, you can't beat the price of the rent!"

Jim continued, "I want you all to know that our staff has set up our portable satellite control equipment here and we are monitoring the situation around the world, especially in America and Israel. The invading armies have swarmed into America by the hundreds of thousands. Troops from nations all over the globe, most from nations who hate America, have landed on both coasts, marched in through Mexico or Canada, and flown in by airlift. Although ordered to surrender, most of our U.S. military is fighting with every resource at their command. The invasion of Israel has paused for some reason with the invaders drawn up all around the perimeter of the country. And there's been a further development. An unusually powerful solar storm has knocked out the power grids in most developed countries and fried the electronic innards of most satellites. Most significantly, it has knocked out all of the enemy's satellites. Our satellites are the only functioning birds on the air. The invader's surveillance network will be essentially blind for the foreseeable future and is going to have a hard time controlling the world for a good while. Our nuclear naval assets have run for cover to await an opportune time to strike in force. Most of the nuclear fleet is able to remain at sea for better than a year."

"How can you possibly monitor all this?" someone wanted to know.

"Our company has a string of extremely sophisticated satellites which span the globe," explained Jim.

"Who owns your satellites? You had to have had government involvement to get them launched, didn't you?" asked the same man again.

"Well, it's like this: The government paid us for the satellites and put them in orbit, however we retained an ace in the hole, so to speak, because we suspected they could someday be used for nefarious purposes. So, we built in a secret fail-safe interlock mechanism only we could control. How right we were! When we realized that Washington was about to use the birds in a manner that was deleterious to American interests, we seized sole control of the satellites. Washington likely would not have been happy but, since it happened in the period when the bombs went off, there was too much confusion for anyone to be able to lean on us to make us give them back. Today, we have 100 percent control of them, thank God."

"Can't the enemy knock them out?" the man continued.

"Nothing is totally immune," Arie volunteered, "but our high-power satellites are formidable entities. They are steerable and are not only armored and shielded against EMP attack, they have classified active and passive countermeasures which protect them from virtually everything, from space junk to missiles, to lasers or energy beam weapons. They can track the source of any attack and return tactical weapons to silence those sites. We can neutralize ballistic missiles in flight. This has already occurred in several instances, much to the consternation of the enemy. It's not really healthy to mess with our birds."

"What I wanna know," said one of the church members, "is why you can't use those energy beams, or whatever you called them, to clobber the invaders?"

"The energy beams were generally meant to be used in the vacuum of space. The problem with them is that, first of all, they require a considerable amount of electric power to operate and with the satellites having to conserve their power, these weapons can only be used sporadically while the batteries recharge. But the second reason we seldom use them in the atmosphere is that they are terribly ionizing to both the atmosphere and electronic equipment. Were we to uncork them in an uncontrolled manner, they could do a lot of damage to the population and the environment," explained Arie.

"We'll be monitoring the situation and keep you all informed. In the meantime, let's stay engaged. We have several certified teachers with us so we'll soon get all the children into school sessions, so they don't get too far behind in their learning," admonished Jim.

"Senator Dalton, could we impose upon you to be our chaplain?" inquired Jim.

"Certainly, Jim! I'd be delighted to go back to preaching again. I've missed the ministry since I've been ensconced in D.C.," replied the Senator.

"Okay, then, looks like we have things pretty well in hand already," concluded Jim.

"Uh . . . General, we have an incoming aircraft, a 4-place Cessna 172, asking permission to land" announced Ivan from the doorway of the auditorium.

"Tell him to come on in—the more the merrier," sighed Jim.

The little Cessna landed and taxied in toward the Lodge. As the Lycoming shuddered to a stop, out stepped a stocky, middle-aged man in a heavy wool tweed coat and hat.

Jim greeted the newcomer on the tarmac. "Who are you, Sir, and how did you happen to find us in this weather?"

In a mild Scottish brogue, the newcomer explained, "I am Angus MacLeod of Scotland. I was on my way by commercial air to Denver intending to travel from there to this area to locate a man who I understood lives somewhere in this vicinity. My airliner was forced down at Rapid City, South Dakota, by the invaders. I managed to sneak away from the other passengers and hide out. The next night, I was able to 'liberate' this pretty little Cessna in the wee hours when no one was looking, and flew out at tree-top altitude. The invaders are too busy and too few right now to pay attention to everything, thankfully, or I'd probably been in detention like everyone else there."

"Well, Mr. MacLeod, just whom is it you seek?" inquired Jim.

"A man named Alexander MacIntosh. Big fellow! Do you happen to know him?" the newcomer asked.

"No, I'm not acquainted with anyone by that name. But you are welcome to join us here, Angus. You were lucky to get here as it is—but you're not going to be able to leave safely for quite some time, I'm afraid," responded Jim.

"Well, if you can spare me some gasoline, I really must go on. I'll fly on to Great Falls where I have friends. Perhaps I will locate Mr. MacIntosh there," insisted the Scot.

"I think you're making a grave mistake by leaving. I'd advise you to stick around for awhile until we have a better idea of conditions on the outside," cautioned Jim.

"I thank you for your concern, Sir, but I really must be going if you don't mind," replied MacLeod.

"Well, you're certainly not a prisoner here; you may leave if you're bound and determined to do so. Pull your ship up to the pumps and we'll load you up with 100 octane."

As MacLeod's aircraft disappeared over the rim of the canyon, Jim asked Ivan to keep an eye on his progress if possible. "Let me know if he arrives in Great Falls. I fear for his safety."

THE ISLAND

Pastor Steve Nelson watched with dread as foreign military units made their way methodically through every neighborhood in Houston, pulling men, women and children out of their homes, separating them and sending them off to an uncertain fate in concentration camps. The screams of women being savaged and children being torn from their parent's arms were heart-rending. How he wished there were something—anything—that he could do, but alas he could only watch helplessly as the entire community was systematically pillaged of people and their belongings.

The day finally came when oriental units started down their street in the Nelsons' neighborhood. The invaders had imposed a 24 hour curfew on the neighborhood—anyone found outside their homes would be shot on sight.

At 5:00pm that day, the house next door was raided before the plunderers retired for the evening. While peeking out of his garage door at the Chinese soldiers, their commander looked over the fence at him and laughed. "Ho, Yankee preacher. You no worry! Tomorrow morning we come for you at 0800. Ha-ha-ha-ha!!! You sleep well tonight, yes? We have nice prison camp for you and your family," he leered in broken English.

Steve withdrew to his living room and sat with his head in his hands, praying. That night, he hardly slept. At midnight, he opened his gun case and loaded his Mini-14 rifle and the .45 automatic pistol he normally kept in his night-stand. For hours he agonized as to what was best to do. Should he stand and fight until he and his family were dead? Should he submit to the invaders and see his family torn apart, probably never to see each other again? No definite answer came to mind.

At 8:00am the next morning, there came an insistent knock at the front door just as George's family joined him in the front room. Steve grasped the stock of his rifle tightly.

"Who's there?" Steve asked, afraid of the answer.

"Marines! Gunnery Sergeant Sansone. Open up!" came the reply.

Still clutching his rifle, Steve slowly opened the door and was relieved to see American uniforms but at the same instant, anger arose in him at the thought that American military would be helping the invaders. But he simply could not bring himself to fire on fellow Americans, so as the soldiers rushed into the house, he laid down the rifle but kept the .45 concealed.

"Reverend Nelson, take your family and get into the back of that ¾ ton truck parked at the curb while we close things up here."

"But . . . . . ." hesitated Steve .

"MOVE!" barked Sansone.

Numb with fear, Steve herded his little family out the door towards the truck. As they walked across the lawn, he could see the Chinese soldiers at the house next door.

Huh, that's really odd—the foreign troops have leap-frogged over our house and gone to my other next-door neighbor. Wonder why this American unit showed up at our door instead? I feel like drawing my old 'punkin roller'.45 and shooting that leering Chinese colonel who's running the show next door. Nah, better not—too risky!

Steve helped his family into the back of the truck as directed. Parked behind the truck they had boarded was an olive-drab moving van with a large trailer. The Marines began moving the entirety of the Nelsons' possessions and furniture into the trailer. Once again, blinding anger arose in him as he watched the possessions that had taken them a lifetime to accumulate being ripped-off for the benefit of the invaders. Without thinking, he reached into his waistband and placed his hand on the butt of the .45 while trying to decide what to do. His wife, Martha, spotted the gun and the look in his eye and gave him a wifely "Don't-even-think-about-it-stupid!" look. With that, he gave up and began to weep. Little five-year-old Chloe came over to him and sat in his lap saying, "Don't cry, Daddy. Jesus just told me not to be afraid 'cause we'll be okay." Steve hugged her, kissed her forehead and dried his own tears.

Soon, the soldiers finished their task and the engines on both vehicles started. A Marine with an M-4 rifle climbed into the back of their truck holding Steve's Mini-14, lowered the canvas rear cover, smiled and sat down as the truck began to move.

They had driven for nearly an hour when Steve could hear the whine of jet engines. Peeking out through a gap in the canvas top of the truck, he could see that the truck was now driving up a ramp into the hold of an aircraft.

The soldier stood up, flipped back the end-flap, jumped to the floor of the hold and lowered the end-gate of the truck for them.

"You folks can get out and stretch your legs now," the marine announced.

After the Nelsons exited the truck, it drove out the other end of the hold and the moving van pulled into the hold behind the truck, unhitched the trailer and then also exited.

"What is going on?" asked Martha.

"You've got me," said Steve, "But I'm sure not gonna demand answers from a guy with a rifle."

Within minutes, another truck, similar to the one they had arrived in, backed into the hold, deposited another family who were in turn followed by another moving van. At that point, the cargo ramps on the aircraft began to close and the engines began to spool up. Another soldier came around and escorted the two families to a seating area in the upper floor of the hold, then disappeared into the bowels of the aircraft after instructing everyone to buckle up. Presently, the ship taxied out and was soon airborne. As the aircraft reached its cruise altitude, the soldier reappeared and informed them they could leave their seats and move around if they wished. Steve introduced himself to the husband of the other family.

"Do you have any idea where we're going?" asked Steve .

"Not a clue, my friend. I got a glimpse of this aircraft as we were backing into the hold—looks like an American C5 or maybe a 117. Anyway, I thought we'd be in a prison camp by now for sure but apparently our captors have something special in mind for us. I'm not sure I wanna know what it is," replied the other husband, ruefully.

For hours, the aircraft droned along, then one of the soldiers appeared and instructed everyone to strap into their seats. The engines throttled back and there came the sound of landing gear motors and flaps as the attitude of the ship changed and the engines spooled back up.

"We're flying on the backside of the power curve," observed the other husband, "we must be about to land."

Presently, the gear hit the runway and the engines went into thrust-reversal as the ship slowed and then turned onto a taxiway. Soon, all around them, the little band of refugees could hear the whine of jet engines.

One of the soldiers came through and announced "We've stopped to refuel. We're going to open the rear cargo hatch so you can get some fresh air in here. You folks can walk around inside the hold and stretch your legs but do not leave the ship. Do you understand?"

Everyone nodded as Steve walked cautiously toward the open cargo ramp. Peering out, he was surprised to see all sorts of foreign cargo and passenger aircraft sitting on the ramp or taxiing. There were U.N., Chinese, North Korean, E.U. and obviously a number of Muslim countries represented. The view of the expanse of terminal glass displayed the reflection of their own aircraft which sported the Stars and Stripes on its tailfin. Steve was scratching his head and trying to process it all when a rifle-toting North Korean soldier nearly walked across the ramp, stopped and appeared to look into the cargo hold right at Steve. The man did not appear to see Steve as his eyes seemed focused on something more distant. Presently, he re-shouldered his rifle and walked on.

That guy acted as though we weren't even here. What in the world is going on?

Minutes later, the Marine that had spoken with them announced, "We're refueled. Everyone back in your seats and strap in for takeoff."

Hours passed as the ship droned on its way. Suddenly, one of the marines approached Steve saying, "Reverend Nelson, the Captain wants to see you in the cockpit."

Reluctantly, Steve followed the guard to the door of the cockpit. As the Marine stepped aside, Steve entered a world of electronics and instruments.

"Come in and sit down in the jump-seat behind me, Reverend Nelson," said the pilot, "We are approaching your new home and I thought you might like to see it from the air."

Steve stared in disbelief at the beautiful isle just ahead. The island jutted out of the ocean with several mountain ranges at higher elevations that were shrouded in rain clouds. The coastline consisted of a wide, palm-covered plateau ringing the island several hundred feet above sea-level. Behind the plateau, the mountains rose precipitously with a high valley in between the ranges. Waterfalls could be seen splashing into beautiful clear lakes.

"Well, what do you think, Sir?" queried the pilot.

"Not too bad for a prison camp," muttered Steve.

The pilot seemed surprised by Steve's response and paused before he replied, "Well . . . . . . I guess you could call it that. Return to your seat now until we land, Sir."

As the cargo ramps opened on the tarmac, the perfumed trade winds of the island wafted through the hold. The two families stepped out into a scene of verdant tropical beauty. As they stood quietly contemplating their new surroundings, a Marine officer wearing the eagles of a full colonel greeted the party.

"I am Colonel Alejandro. Welcome to 'Aurora.' The men will take you to your new accommodations and get you settled. Tomorrow, we'll give you all a tour of the island."

"Tour? But . . . . . but . . . . I thought . . . . . . ", Steve stammered.

"That this is a prison camp?" laughed the Colonel, "No, no, no!! You're not the first to assume that! This is a place of refuge to shield you temporarily from the eye of the storm that has engulfed your country. Now, if you will follow the soldiers to the vehicles, we'll get you all settled. Your house's kitchen is stocked with food and there are towels and soap in your baths. We'll set up your furniture and help you get settled. Let us know if you need anything else. There will be a smorgasbord breakfast and orientation tomorrow morning for all new arrivals at the activity center—your driver will pick you up at 9:00am."

After the Nelsons were seated in the Humvee, a Marine sergeant got in and drove them several miles in the direction of the mountains before abruptly turning into a narrow, gravel drive flanked by manicured lawns. The vehicle pulled up in front of two beautiful tropical homes, complete with lanais, situated on the banks of a crystal clear lake typical of homes Steve had seen in the Hawaiian Islands several years before,.

"Welcome to your new home, folks," said the sergeant over his shoulder, "The men will have you unloaded and settled in no time. Mrs. Nelson, why don't you direct where you want your furniture placed and I'll ask the other lady to do the same."

"Steve, I just can't believe that God has so blessed us by bringing us here. I wish all our poor neighbors could have come here as well. What a terrible ordeal they will have to endure," said Martha.

"I know, dear. I don't know what we have done to deserve this blessing, but I praise God for His love. I wonder how General Black and the rest of our congregation are faring in Montana," ruminated Steve.

After breakfast the next morning, everyone boarded a bus for a tour of the island. For over an hour the bus traveled past vast plantations where every imaginable fruit and vegetable was being grown and harvested. Soon the bus began a gradual climb into a central valley. As the road leveled off, it was obvious that they had entered a more temperate zone where there were apple, cherry, pear and peach orchards, as well as cattle pastures. Midway through the valley, the bus stopped to allow the passengers to get out and walk along the shores of a beautiful lake that was fed by a rushing mountain stream from higher up the mountain peaks. The return trip brought them past residential neighborhoods and apartment housing, as well as what appeared to be a business district with a number of different store fronts.

Steve asked the driver, "How do we buy and sell here since we have no money?"

"Not a problem, Sir. If you have a need, it will be taken care of—just ask!" came the astonishing answer.

Turning to Martha, Steve grinned, "You know what? I think we're gonna like it here, Sweetheart."

☆ **8** ☆

THE MOUNTAIN MAN

Snow was falling heavily as a huge buckskin-clad figure on snow shoes mushed through the forests of central Montana.

This is certainly an unusual winter. So much snow on the ground so early! The elk should have come down out of the high country by now but so far, I haven't seen a thing. Hope I won't have to go up after them. I'll take anything right now—elk, deer, moose, buffalo. At this point, meat is meat! This is my third day out here and I haven't run across anything of value—not even a rabbit! Man, I am chilled to the bone but I know Mary and Tom are out of meat. There is no way this old Scotsman is going home empty-handed!!

Just then, ahead in a tangle of undergrowth amidst stately pines, he sighted his preferred quarry—a small herd of elk bedded down in a secluded clearing.

Aye, there y' are Wapiti. Caught ya in your bedroom, I did!

The rack of the dominant bull was readily identifiable through the tree line as Alex carefully maneuvered to position himself for a good shot. In all probability, he would only have a chance at one animal and he must be sure to bring home the largest animal possible. After considerable time and effort working quietly into position, he was satisfied that he had a sufficiently clear shot through the trees that would not be deflected by overhanging branches.

The large bull, sensing something was not quite right, arose from his bed to scan the forest for danger just as Alex drew a bead behind his front shoulder.

Great, he's a fine one! He'll feed us for a long time. Easy now Alex—squeeze the trigger, man, don't jerk it!

The muzzle blast of the powerful rifle reverberated among the trees, jarring snow from the drooping pine boughs. The cloud of gun smoke momentarily stung his nostrils. His aim was perfect. The bull dropped in his tracks as his harem scattered like rabbits.

Getting late! Got to work fast if I'm to be home before dark.

After replacing the rifle in a buckskin case across his back, Alexander MacIntosh retrieved a large freight sleigh and team of horses he'd tied up some distance away. Throwing a rope over the branch of a nearby tree, Alex hoisted his kill off the ground and, with the experience of many years, deftly field-dressed the animal in minutes. He manhandled the steaming carcass onto the bed of the sleigh and heaved his own considerable frame into the driver's seat behind his team of horses, Molly and Ben, and began the trip home through the forest with his prize.

Years of roaming the Montana wilderness had given Alex a healthy respect for the grizzly bear and mountain lion, so he constantly watched the horses for sign of bear or cat scent. Grizzlies are fast on their feet and do not tolerate interlopers in their domain. The heavy snows had come early this year but there was no guarantee that all the big predators would be hibernating yet.

Hope Ol' Griz is snoring away by now and the pussy cats are occupied elsewhere. Don't need any trouble.

As the forest trail wound towards a meadow ahead, the horses became increasingly skittish. Molly and Ben were big Belgian draft animals and veterans of the forest. Not much of anything spooked them except lions— and bears. Alex picked up a double-barreled weapon from a keeper by the seat, checked that it was loaded and cradled it in the crook of his left arm.

Don't like the way the horses are acting, better be ready for trouble!!

As the sleigh broke out of the trees into the clearing, the reason for the horses' nervousness became readily apparent. A huge male grizzly was not more than one hundred yards away, eyeing this intrusion on his magnificence with snorts and typical grizzly ill-temper. By this time the horses were rearing in fright as the bear decided to charge at a dead run. Trying to outrun an adult bear was not a good idea in their situation. Alex instinctively wrapped the reins around a seat fitting and brought the double-rifle to his shoulder. With the sleigh pitching violently, Alex swung the rifle as if he were shooting pheasants on the wing and pulled the front trigger. Because of the awkward position in which he was sitting, the gun butt smacked his shoulder like the kick of a mule and the trigger guard bit into his scarred fingers. The bear went down with a bullet through a front shoulder that apparently broke the leg bone, but he immediately got back up and charged again on three legs not fifty feet away. Alex took better aim this time and fired the left barrel. The bear shuddered visibly under the impact of the heavy bullet, rolled head-over-heels like a downed jack rabbit and expired with his muzzle resting near the sleigh's runner. In one fluid motion, Alex retrieved the reins and gave the frightened horses their head.

Gotta get these horses out of here before they wreck this rig and me.

With the clearing and the bear out of sight and out of mind, he managed to get the horses stopped to let them rest and calm their nerves. Alex took a swig of peppermint schnapps from a silver hip flask to calm his own nerves.

That was close, old man—too close! That bear was one tough puppy! You might say the grizzly practically died on my shoe laces—he would've come up in this sleigh in another second and killed me in the blink of an eye. Thank God for this 'whopper-stopper' of mine. Someday, I'd like to live some place where a man's life isn't constantly in danger from varmints big enough to have him for lunch. Ordinarily, I'd go back and get that bear, too, but I have enough bear-skin rugs and the meat is similar to a substandard hog, anyway. Nah! Let the wolves eat him, I'm going on home.

The remainder of the trip home was relatively uneventful until he turned the horses onto the trail along the creek about a quarter mile from the cabin. Over the breathing of the horses, Alex could hear an engine somewhere up ahead; he stopped the horses and strained to locate the direction of the sound. It seemed to be very near the cabin he shared with his wife, Mary, and his disabled brother-in-law, Colonel Tom Ryan.

Strange!! Wonder who that could be! No one ever comes around here in this howling wilderness in the summer, much less the winter!

Alex was abruptly shaken by the angry barking of Tom's .45 automatic pistol, followed by several rapid rifle shots, several long bursts of automatic weapons fire and then—silence.

Oh, my God! Don't tell me an enemy has found where we live—and my family has paid the price. If they've been hurt . .

Alex hurriedly tied the horses to a tree, grabbed the double rifle and slung the other weapon across his back. Hanging several ammunition belts across his chest, he set off at what approximated a dead run on snow shoes, toward the cabin.

Nearing the house-yard, he ditched the snow shoes and paused to let his heart-rate and breathing calm a bit. Then, edging up to the back wall of the cabin, he peered around the corner. There sat a snow cat with a U.N. insignia on the door and a man sitting in the driver's seat. Three uniform-clad bodies lay in the snow a short distance from the vehicle. Alex was puzzled by the fact that the men were dressed in Canadian uniforms. Something didn't make sense.

Looks like Sam and Mary gave 'em what-for, whoever they were.

Stepping to the other side of the cabin, he looked through the window and his knees nearly buckled. There on the floor lay his family, apparently dead. He observed three men in uniform busily ransacking the cabin. Fighting blinding anger, he was gripped by a terrible resolve. Alex worked his way back around the cabin and slipped up behind the snow cat, and quietly unscrewed its radio and GPS antennas. Stepping quickly to the driver's side, he grasped the door handle and wrenched the door open. The dozing driver gasped in surprised fright just before Alex's "Texas Toothpick" ended his career.

Moving quickly to the corner of the cabin nearest the door, Alex was calculating his next move when he heard the crunch of boots in the snow and a puff of cigarette smoke wafted around the corner. Apparently one of the soldiers had come out for a smoke to calm his nerves. The man made the fatal mistake of walking around the corner of the cabin without checking his surroundings. The blade of Alex's tomahawk turned off his lights.

Placing the tomahawk back in his belt, Alex stepped quickly to the open door of the cabin with the double-rifle. Drawing a bead on one of the soldiers who was facing the fireplace, he pulled the front trigger. The man fell face forward into the fire.

The other soldier spun around to face the angry Scot a fraction of a second too late. The second barrel of Alex's rifle sent him to the 'Promised Land.'

Stepping through the door, Alex let out a roar of anguish and frustration, jacked the empty cartridges out of the double-rifle and began to reload. Looking around, he was startled to see another soldier inside the cabin he hadn't noticed before. The man stared at Alex and, as their eyes met, the man blanched in terror, threw down his weapon and rushed out the door past the startled avenger. The soldier must have been a sprinter because by the time Alex finished reloading his weapon, the miscreant was fast disappearing, running down-slope toward the creek bank. Setting down the double rifle, Alex quickly drew a long-barreled rifle with a telescopic sight and side-hammer from the buckskin case slung across his back.

Sorry, Bud, you're not going anywhere.

Alex cocked the hammer, drew a careful bead on the fleeing soldier and touched off the shot amidst a billowing cloud of white smoke. In the stillness of the forest, the muzzle blast echoed among the trees and returned a resounding 'thud' as the heavy bullet struck its mark. The man pitched forward and lay still in the snow.

Alex quickly reconnoitered the area to be sure there were no more surprises. Satisfied that all the soldiers were *hors de combat*, he approached his wife's still form. Alex noted the pallor of her skin and the multiple gunshot wounds to her chest, he checked her carotid arteries for a pulse—there was none. Mary still clutched Alex's .30-06 rifle and he tenderly unwrapped her hands from it.

Looks like she killed some o' the devils 'afore she died.

Approaching Tom's body, there was no need to check further—still clutching his .45 automatic pistol, the old soldier had caught a bullet squarely between the eyes.

All those 30 years in the military as a Green Beret, through four tours of combat duty, he survived a landmine explosion in Afghanistan that crippled one leg—and now he dies like this at the hands of criminals.

With his entire family gone, Alex suddenly felt weak and sick to his stomach. He sat down on a broken chair, wept bitterly and vomited. Producing the silver hip flask, he took several long belts of schnapps.

Oh Mary, Mary, my beloved wife, what will I ever do without ya? And Tom, me best friend, how will I cope without your advice and friendship? Oh Lord, how could this have happened? And why?

There was no answer to his agonized questions. After what seemed an eternity, Alex regained his composure and retrieved the team and sleigh, off-loading the elk into the smoke house. He tenderly moved Mary and Tom's bodies into a secure out-building. Placing the corpses of the soldiers inside the snow-cat, he started the vehicle and ran it into a small shed.

No sense leaving this thing sit out where it can be spotted from the air. Better make sure the' GPS is totally disabled.

Finally, Alex unhitched, stabled, fed and watered Molly and Ben, made a sandwich from the fridge and wearily sank into his bed in the ransacked cabin.

The next morning, the temperature hovered at -20 degrees Fahrenheit and snow was still falling as Alex skinned the elk, butchered and boned-out the meat, storing it in plastic bags in the smoke house.

I'll bury Mary and Tom in that cave up on the hillside, then dump these other boys and their vehicle in that deep ravine about a half-mile from here—the forest critters will make quick work of them. By spring there won't even be bones left.

Up the hill behind the house was a small cave he'd found years before, just high enough to stand up in. First spreading throw rugs on the floor of the cave, Alex carried the bodies of his family in and tenderly placed them on the rugs. Taking a final look at the faces of his loved ones, he wept bitterly again.

Taking out a small Bible, he intoned, "Ashes to ashes, dust to dust, in the sure and certain hope of the resurrection of the dead. Lord, I commit my family into Your tender care. I know we'll meet again on the other side of the veil, but for now it's terribly painful and lonely. Please help me to live the rest of my days as Your man. Amen."

Alex set up a large flat stone across the entrance.

Hopefully, that'll keep the critters out.

Alex started the snow-cat and drove it to a deep, forested ravine a half mile from the cabin. Removing the soldier's bodies, he threw them into the ravine one by one. Putting the snow-cat in gear, he jumped out watching as it ran over the cliff and crashed to the bottom of the ravine.

Thank God there was no fire!

Taking out his Bible, he again intoned, "Ashes to ashes, dust to dust, in the sure and certain hope of the resurrection of the dead. Lord, I commit these men into Your tender care. I don't know who they are or where they're from, but I know You love them and I know their families loved them. I just hope some of them were Yours. Help me to forgive them for what they did to my family. Amen"

Well now, my enemies know where I live, so I think I'd better move on elsewhere—I certainly can't stay here or they'll come back and get me too. Maybe I can winter at the Eagle's Lair.

Alex loaded everything of value from the cabin and sheds on the sleigh. Returning to the cabin, he was going through its contents for the last time when a knock at the doorpost startled him. Leveling the big double-rifle on the doorway, he shouted, "Who's there? Show yourself with your hands up."

Slowly, an upraised arm appeared in the doorway.

"Don't shoot, Sir, we're friendly. Please, we came a long way to find you," exclaimed the male voice of the owner of the arm.

"Alright, lad, let's have a look at you then," replied Alex cautiously.

Slowly and carefully, two tall, obviously full-blood Native Americans entered the cabin with their hands raised. Seeing they were not armed, Alex lowered the rifle.

"Alright, you boys can relax. What can I do you for? "

The men stared wide-eyed at Alex. "Great Day! I mean, we saw you in our visions but we had no idea how you'd look in the flesh! You are awesome, man! Anyhow, we came looking for you, Sir. We had heard about you several months ago and we needed to find you as soon as possible," replied the nearest man, "I'm John Glass and this is Ed Swan."

"Pleased to know you gentlemen. What do you mean 'visions'? You been smoking peyote? You boys don't look like Crow, where are you from?" asked Alex.

"Very astute, Mr. MacIntosh! We're Lakota Sioux from the Pine Ridge Reservation in South Dakota. And, no, we don't smoke anything, Sir," replied Glass.

"I'm surprised that you know my name. To what do I owe the honor of your presence?" asked Alex warily.

The two men exchanged nervous glances as John Glass began, "You may find what I'm going to tell you a bit bizarre, Sir, but it's gospel truth. We're all Spirit-filled Christians and all eight of us had similar dreams some months ago. We all saw an eagle circling over a mountain man living in a cabin in the forests of Montana. Both he and the eagle were in dire need of help against an evil enemy and we heard a voice telling us to find you quickly. We saw your name and this cabin exactly as it is.

Usually, we take dreams with a grain of salt, but because of the similarity, consistency and detail of all our dreams, we decided to check it out with some friends who live in Bozeman. They said they thought they knew who you were and told us they thought you had moved into this area some time ago, but they weren't sure exactly where. We finally located your place through some of their local acquaintances in the Crow tribe. We managed to get here with six of our friends and twelve head of horses. We ran out of gas about three miles back so we abandoned our vehicles and horse trailers and came in on horseback."

"Och, laddies, these days I don't find much of anything too bizarre to believe—I've encountered a lot of unbelievable things lately. But tell me, what are your plans at this point?"

"We are all former Spec Ops—Marine Corp Scout Snipers, Navy SEALS, Army Rangers and US Army Special Forces. I was a USMC Senior Master Chief Gunnery Sergeant. Ed here was a Captain in the Army Rangers. Over the years after we mustered out and went home, we got a little bored so a group of us got together to organize a kind of informal 'Sioux Warrior Society' and began regaining knowledge of the way our forefathers had lived, hunted and fought. We mastered the art of horsemanship and learned how to make the traditional clothing of our people. We also learned how to make and use the ancient Sioux weapons—the flat bow and war arrows, the tomahawk, the lance, etc. Naturally, our military training has served us well in tracking and survival in all kinds of weather and terrain. Guess we're what some would call 'Snake Eaters.' We are armed with scoped 7.62mm National Match Grade M-14 type rifles but we also carry our traditional weapons. We can dress much as our ancestors did and can ride our horses bareback if necessary. We know we are to be involved in the resistance movement against the invaders. But our part of South Dakota is just too open and barren for guerrilla operations—nothing much to hide behind from aircraft in South Dakota's West River grasslands. We don't know exactly what you are involved in but we know we're supposed to help you any way we can. By the way, what happened here? This place is really trashed," said John Glass glancing about the cabin.

"My family was murdered here yesterday and the cabin ransacked by a group of eight U.N. goons who came in by snow cat while I was out hunting. Between my wife, my brother-in-law and myself, we killed every mother's son of them. I just buried my wife and brother-in-law and dumped the enemy vehicle and bodies in a local ravine," said Alex flatly.

"That's awful, man! We are so sorry for your loss, Mr. MacIntosh. How can we help you?" said Ed Swan sympathetically.

"Well, lads, I was just about to move on to a safer place I know about some twenty miles from here. As a matter of fact, I think the eagle you saw in your dreams stands for the place where I'm going—the Eagle's Lair. I'm so low right now you'd have to jack me up to bury me; I could surely use some friendly company. You're welcome to come with me. You boys and your *compadres* can mount up. I'm ready to roll right now!" announced Alex.

"We're ready when you are, Sir. Come on out and we'll introduce you to our buddies. They're all rearing to go," responded John Glass quickly.

"Alright, I'll lead the way to the new place. The trail ahead can get tricky if you don't know it so follow me closely. Be alert for grizzlies and cougars. They're still out and about an' we raise 'em big 'n mean here in Montana," warned Alex with a grin.

"Yeah, we know. On the way here, a bear growled and came toward us. We were ready to drop him but I guess he thought better of the idea and ambled off," laughed Ed Swan.

Alex hitched up Molly and Ben, dreading the trip ahead through the deep forests to the Eagle's Lair. With a heavy heart, he heaved himself into the driver's seat and gently tapped the horses' backs with the reins. "Giddy-up, my old friends. Let's be on our way."

Behind him rode an unusual procession of mounted riders and pack horses reminiscent of an 1880s Indian war party.

AND THERE WERE GIANTS IN THE LAND

With the Montana winter in full swing, the days seemed to drag by for the band of refugees at the Eagle's Lair. Thanksgiving was approaching but many days dawned gray and lowering, holding little appeal for most of the adults—only the children and teens were having fun in the snow. The cold and snow seemed to seep through the pores of the buildings.

Then one day, someone gazing out the plate glass windows of the Lodge yelled, "Hey, everybody, there's a huge man out there . . . with a horse-drawn sleigh. Looks a little like Santa or maybe Jeremiah Johnson," he grinned. "He's coming toward the Lodge. And it looks as if he has an Indian war party with him!" the man continued in amazement.

Jim quickly glanced out the window just in time to see a huge stranger walk up the front steps, stomp the snow off his boots and approach the front doors. The doors shook under the impact of an enormous fist.

Opening the door, Jim, open-mouthed, beheld an amazing sight. There stood a giant of a man dressed from head to foot in furs and beaded buckskins looking for all the world like a nineteenth century mountain man. He had a large sheathed knife on a beaded sash belt with a tomahawk stuck in the other side. Slung across his back, in a buckskin case, was some sort of large weapon. In the crook of his left arm was what appeared to be a double-barrel shotgun. Ammunition belts bearing enormous cartridges circled around his waist and diagonally across his chest. The man's fiery red bush of a beard spilled out of the wolf-fur trimmed parka hood which surrounded ruddy, rounded cheeks and twinkling, deep-set green eyes beneath shaggy eyebrows. Behind him, standing near a sleigh, were eight Native Americans with saddle horses and pack animals.

Jim could only stand there staring at a complete loss for words. Finally recovering his composure, Jim croaked "Come in, Sir, come in! And, . . uh . . tell your friends to come in too. It's cold out there!" Beckoning to his partners, the newcomer had to stoop noticeably to negotiate the doorway. Once inside, he straightened up to a height that was considerably above the top of the standard 6'- 8" high door frame.

This guy's some sort of giant. Must be a good seven foot-six.

As the newcomer pushed back the hood of his parka, long red hair spilled over his shoulders as he grinned and pulled off his gloves. With a thick Scottish burr, the voice behind the beard boomed, "Thanks for the hospitality. Who's in charge 'round 'ere, lads?"

Jim explained, "My Grandfather is in charge. I'm Jim Black and these are my friends, here for an, uh, extended vacation."

Grinning from ear to ear, proffering a hand the size of a Virginia ham, the big man replied, "Alexander MacIntosh at your service, Sir! And these gentlemen with me are South Dakota Sioux Indians—all U.S. military Special Operations veterans. This is Master Chief Gunnery Sergeant John Glass and Captain Ed Swan; these others are Aaron Red Shirt, George Standing Bear, Sam Red Eagle, Bob Walksahead, Ed Beal and Augustus Red Cloud."

"Glad to meet all you gentlemen. Take off your heavy clothing, get warmed up by the fire and make yourselves at home, we have food, hot coffee and plenty of room." said Jim shaking hands with first one then another of the men.

Turning to the awestruck faces around him, the Scottish giant chortled, "What're ye lads an' lasses starin' at? Ha' ye no' seen a Scotsman 'afore?"

"How big a boy are you anyway, 'Redbeard?'" asked the irrepressible Eli Walton.

"Och, Laddie, last I checked I stood 7'-9" an' weighed a trim 425 pounds," replied the Scot with a grin.

"I just wondered. I've never seen a man the size of a Bigfoot before!" Eli retorted.

The Scot's face darkened ominously "Och, Lad, you should never joke about Bigfoot! He's in these woods 'round here and he's no laughin' matter!" said the giant darkly.

"Uh, sorry, Sir. I . . . I didn't mean . . .uh" stammered an uncharacteristically cowed Walton.

"Ah, but of course you didn't," rebounded the newcomer smiling again, "Forgive me, Lad, I dinna mean ta brow-beat ye. But most people think that Bigfoot is a figment o' the imagination. But one of those 'figments' killed someone very near and dear t' me some years back."

"Whaaat . . . . ?" Eli spluttered.

"Aye, 'tis true. I'll tell you about it some time," winked the big man.

"So . . . . I did not expect to find a livin' soul 'round these parts, especially this time o' year. The owner of this place, Ezra Black Eagle, is a personal friend who gave me a key to this Lodge and a standin' invitation to make myself at home here if ever the need should arise. And, unfortunately, the need has arisen. My companions here say they saw a vision some time ago in which they saw me at my cabin and something about an eagle in trouble and were told by the Holy Spirit to find me—seems they came to Montana by revelation. Anyway, this place appeared to be occupied this mornin'. Not wantin' to be shot, I thought I'd best knock," concluded the mountain man.

"Well", began Jim, "Ezra Black Eagle is my grandfather and right now he's upstairs resting. Some time ago, in view of the present unpleasantness, he invited me to bring a group of my church congregation, friends and associates up here for the winter from Houston—or for however long we can stay without being discovered by the invaders."

"Aye, I've met some o' th' devils! There's eight of 'em won't be goin' home again!" announced the Scotsman darkly. Eyebrows shot up and everyone edged in closer to catch every word.

"Please tell us. What, exactly, happened?" someone began to beg.

Alex continued, "Well, my wife, Mary, myself and my partially disabled brother-in-law lived together in a large log cabin we'd built 'bout twenty miles from here, way back in the tall-an'-uncut, on land we'd purchased from Ezra. My brother-in-law, a U.S. Army Special Forces bird colonel, taught me much of what he knew about guerilla fighting and survival. I also learned a lot about the wilderness from the local Native Americans. Well, my two darlings were at home whilst I went hunting for fresh meat. Returnin' home with an elk on my sleigh about a quarter mile from the cabin, I could hear a vehicle approaching the yard. Then I heard several single gunshots followed by bursts of automatic weapons fire. Approaching the cabin carefully, I spied a U.N. snow-cat parked with a man inside. Looking in the window of the cabin I saw a sight that broke my heart; my wife and brother-in-law were dead on the floor and four foreign soldiers were ransacking the place."

"My goodness! What did you do?" a young wife asked breathlessly.

"Och, I killed the man inside the snow-cat with my 'Texas Toothpick' here," he said drawing the huge knife from its sheath. "I killed the next man outside the cabin when he came out for a smoke—he ran into my tomahawk blade. There were still three in the cabin, two of which I killed with the express rifle. The last one tried to run an' I took him out with Ol' Betsy here," he said.

"Express rifle? I thought that double-barrel was a shotgun. So what exactly is that cannon?" inquired one of the men.

With obvious pride, MacIntosh explained, "This is not a shotgun, Sir, it's a double-barrel rifle with a very large bore as you can see—it's a .600 Nitro Express rifle, to be exact. After several close calls with some of the dangerous denizens of these forests around here, I began to cast about for a weapon that would be the last word in any argument with a grizzly bear. I settled on one of these small artillery pieces which were developed 'bout 1900 for hunting dangerous African game. Few of them have been made in recent years so I sent to England a few years back and had this weapon and 3,000 cartridge cases custom built by one of England's premier gun makers. It cost me over $50,000 but it was worth every penny. It has saved my life more times than I can remember. I call her my 'whopper stopper'—a rifle that can stop a charging elephant or Cape buffalo with one shot. She fires a 900 grain jacketed bullet. It is more than adequate against the largest North American animals. I've killed many mountain lions, brown bears and grizzlies with it, while hunting in heavy timber and underbrush. I can easily reload the cartridges in the wild with hand tools. The only drawback to her is that she weighs twenty pounds and recoils like a small howitzer. Look at the scars on my trigger finger. This rifle has broken that finger several times. She's a relatively short-range weapon, since the barrel alignments converge at 250 yards; that's why I have 'Ol Betsy' for open country."

"And what is 'Ol Betsy'?" one of the women wanted to know.

The big Scot unlatched the buckskin case slung across his back and drew out a large antique-looking rifle with a long octagonal barrel, telescopic sight and exposed side hammer. "This is my constant companion. She's a special-built replica of the ultimate Buffalo rifle, an 1874 Long Range Sharps Express rifle. She's chambered in a wild-cat .50-170 caliber an' built right here in Montana," he grinned. "She's a single shot falling-block rifle with a 38" barrel developed for long range hunting. It's a very powerful black powder burner which shoots a 700 grain .50 caliber copper-jacketed bullet on top of 170 grains of FFg black powder, and has a removable range-finder telescopic sight. I've shot big game at nearly a half mile distance with her, but this type of rifle has killed men and animals at more than a mile back in the day. I paid $10,000 bucks for her and that, too, was well worth the price. Don't know just how many elk, moose, bear and deer I've gotten with this one. But she's surely saved my hide on many an accidental run-in with Ol' Griz out in the open country. Her recoil is heavy, but milder than the nitro and surprisingly low for the size of these cartridges. And you'd be surprised how fast you can reload a single shot when it's a matter of life and death. Again, the nice thing about all these weapons is that, in a pinch, the cartridges can be reloaded with simple hand tools in the field," concluded the mountain man grinning like a fox.

"Sir, who's 'Ol' Griz'?" a little girl wanted to know.

"Grizzly bear, little lassie! Quite a few of 'em in this area and they're as dangerous and unpredictable as any critter on earth. Their scientific name is *ursus horribilus* which means 'terrible bear,' an' terrible they are! If you ever see one, run in the opposite direction as fast as you can—never go near one on purpose! If one takes after you, try to get up in a tree or someplace else out of its reach if you can. They're ferocious and tough, with absolutely no fear of man and it takes a lot to stop them. But either of these rifles can 'shiver their timbers' with one shot. Now, some of you folks may think this is crude of me, but there's a further benefit to shooting a black powder weapon—no matter whether you're fighting man or beast. At less than 20 feet, the sparks from the burning black powder coming out of the barrel behind the bullet sets them on fire. I've left several grizzlies on fire!" grinned Alex mischievously.

"I also have the epitome of all sniper rifles out on the sleigh. Its a .50 cal Barrett with the Barrett Optical Ranging System scope sight. That one fires the extremely powerful .50 cal Browning machine gun cartridge and can hit a man-size target at nearly two miles. That one doesn't just wound you, it destroys you. Never shot any game with it and probably won't but since I knew the right people, I got it because I thought I might need it someday—and I guess this mess we find ourselves in just might be that day," chortled the bearded giant.

John Glass piped up, "Oh, man, the .50 Barrett was my weapon of choice as a Marine sniper. I'd give my eyeteeth for one of them right now."

"Och, Laddie, this is far from over, so you may get to use mine yet. And, if anything happens to me, it's all yours. Oh yes, last, but not least, I carry a .50 cal Smith & Wesson 6-shot revolver in a shoulder holster as back-up bear medicine," announced the Scot, reaching under his vest and withdrawing a large, long-barreled revolver.

"Man! You are literally loaded for bear, Big Guy," grinned Eli.

One of the older teen girls piped up, "Mr. MacIntosh, I think it's terrible to kill people and destroy wildlife like Grizzly bears and Elk and the like. Don't the Ten Commandments say 'Thou shalt not kill'?"

Alex's eyes blazed as he replied, "Little lassie, I have just lost my entire family to murderers and you lecture me about morality? You are very young and sadly misinformed. First off you should know that what the Ten

Commandments actually says in the Hebrew is 'Thou shalt not commit murder'; it does not say 'Thou shalt not kill, *per se*'. It certainly does not mean that killing another human being or an animal is never justified. Killing a human being or animal in defense of person, country or home is not murder. Murder, you see, is the unjustified, unlawful killing of a human being with malice aforethought, but God Himself ordered the killing of many people by the Israelites because of their evil ways. If He really forbade all killing, then He would have violated His own commandment. Furthermore, God ranks animals below human beings and when He put people in charge of this world, He gave certain of them to us as food. Animals somehow neglect to die on our doorstep so we can eat them so they must be killed one way or another. The beef and chicken you eat every day has been killed in some way. Of course, abusive or wanton destruction of animals for no good reason is very wrong, but killing them for food or in self-defense is certainly permitted by God. Like the Indians, true sportsmen and those of us who survive in the wilderness such as myself, never kill or maim anything not needed for food or survival," came his impassioned answer.

"In any case," Alex continued, "Where there is a choice between man and animal, in God's view, the human being is valued far above the animal. At the very least then, self-defense against man or beast isn't wrong. Whether I am eye to eye with an angry bear or an angry man, I have every right, every duty, to defend my life by deadly force if necessary. I never go looking for trouble, but if trouble comes looking for me, I am completely within my rights to deal with it appropriately—and grizzlies have a very nasty temperament!" Alex said.

"There is nothing evil about a gun. It is simply a machine, a tool, which can be used either for tremendous good or tremendous evil depending upon the character and intentions of the person using it. Some people think that taking away guns by passing anti-gun laws will solve all the problems of crime and violence in our society. In actuality, that is simply 'pie-in-the-sky' wishful, magical thinking by people who view life through rose-colored glasses with an inverted system of values. Where these practices have been carried to their ultimate end of outlawing guns or their use in self-defense, the criminal element has had a field day," Alex remarked angrily.

"Our War for Independence became a shooting war when the British government decided to take away the American colonist's guns. The exchange of gunfire at Lexington and Concord was the citizen's answer to the British: 'No way, King George! Tax us if you must but keep your hands off our guns!' The fact is that where guns are outlawed, only outlaws and tyrants have guns and the common person is at the mercy of criminals and worse—just ask any older Russian or Cuban citizen about that. Samuel Colt was right when he called his new frontier 'peacemaker' revolver 'the great equalizer.' Because with it, anyone who knew how to use it—a small man, a child or a woman—was equal in power to the largest man around. Billy the Kid reputedly killed his first man with a gun in self-defense at twelve years of age.

"Many tend to think of 19th century America as the 'wild west.' Although it was wild in many ways, it was also a polite society where most people were armed. A lot of those people carried a handgun on their hip and they knew how to use it. For the most part, folks knew better than to throw their weight around with deadly force because there was always someone who was better with a gun than they were and they never knew when they'd run up against that person. Nevertheless, the main difference between then and now was the moral climate of America. In those days, America was still truly a Christian nation and even the worst desperados generally came from families that had at least one praying parent, usually a praying mum. Most children were taken to church during their childhood and read the Bible at their mum's knee, so they knew what God expected of them. Many retained a degree of decency, even as outlaws. Take the most dangerous gunslinger of them all, John Wesley Hardin, who is said to have killed between 40 and 50 men in gunfights. His first and middle names indicate he was born and raised in a Methodist holiness family. Although he was a very efficient killer, like most gunfighters of the day, even Mr. Hardin had an innate decency which would not permit him to intentionally harm a woman, a child or an unarmed man. Actually, gunslingers dealt mostly with other gunslingers and lawmen, not common citizens. Truth be known, Mr. Hardin gave up gun slinging and became a prison warden in his latter years. But today, we have an ever increasing number of rabid, insane people who have neither ethics nor morals. They regard nothing as sacred, who kill and maim innocent people for no good reason at all. Well, I digress! Do you see what I mean, little miss?" concluded the big man.

"Yes, Sir. I apologize for my bad manners! I never thought of all that before. Please forgive me. What you just said makes a lot of sense when you explain it as you have," she replied sheepishly.

"You are certainly forgiven, lil' sweetheart. Unfortunately, you're not alone in your beliefs. There are far too many Americans who cling to the opinions you just expressed."

Alex continued, "Anyway, after I buried my family, I loaded all my possessions onto the sleigh out there and dumped the bodies of the soldiers and their snow-cat in a deep forest ravine. I was about to come here, when these Sioux gentlemen showed up. I was about as low as a man can get so, I invited them to come along with me as I really needed some friends who know a little something about dealing with bad guys. So, there ya' have it! Here we are in the flesh, folks! We all need a place to 'hang out.' Sooo . . . if ya'might be needin' a mountain man who knows his way around and some very elite soldiers, we're all available."

Just then, Grandfather came down the stairs and his face lit up when he spotted Alex. "I heard all the excitement down here. Alex, my old friend, so good to see you again! I never expected you here."

"Grandfather, the invaders murdered his wife and brother-in-law and he came here for shelter with these Sioux gentlemen," explained Jim.

"Oh, Alex, I'm so sorry to hear Mary's gone. She was one of my favorite people. I know you'll see her and her brother again on the other side of the veil. I've never met a more friendly man than Colonel Tom Ryan," said Grandfather sadly.

"Aye, I look forward to seeing both those darlin's again someday. Frankly, I can't wait," came Alex's choked reply.

Jim turned to the Native American newcomers and said, "Gentlemen, you can stable your mounts in the horse paddock, which is about three hundred yards west of here. There's plenty of room for the horses, as well as ample feed and water."

"Great! We'll take care of Molly and Ben for you, Alex. You get warmed up and we'll be back shortly," said John Glass on his way out the door with his companions.

"I don't know about you folks, but I'm really encouraged by the arrival of all this company. It never hurts to have giants and Spec Ops guys around to watch out for you," grinned Eli.

Grandfather turned and addressed the assembled company, "I want you all to know that Mr. MacIntosh here, is more than just a mountain man. He is actually Dr. MacIntosh, a distinguished scholar in his own right with a Masters degree in theology and a PhD in history who has taught at the university level. Go ahead, Alex, tell these folks more about yourself," urged Grandfather.

Alex continued, "Well, you've undoubtedly heard of the book and movie some years back entitled '*The Da Vinci Code*' by Dan Brown. Well, they were billed as fiction, but I'm here to tell you that there is more truth than fiction in them. That whole genre was based on an earlier book entitled '*Holy Blood, Holy Grail*' by Michael Baigent, Richard Leigh and Henry Lincoln which speaks of two ancient organizations, the Order of Knights Templar and the Prieure de Sion, or the Order of Zion, which I understand were formed during the First Crusade to the Holy Land in 1099 which deposed the Muslim Saracen.

"It was related to me as a young man that I am the descendant of one of the ancient Knights Templar, who managed to survive the purge by the Pope and the King of France on Friday, October 13, 1307. On that day, the Knights were betrayed by the Prieure de Sion, arrested, stripped of their property and tortured all over France. Their Grand Master, Jaques De Molay, was eventually burned alive over a roasting spit on an island in the Seine River in Paris. If you've ever wondered how Friday the 13th came to be an 'unlucky day,' now you know."

"My ancestor was said to have escaped to Scotland, where he married the daughter of a highland chieftain. I guess you'd say I come from a somewhat noble lineage of sorts, some of whom I have learned had a hand in defeating the British at the Battle of Bannockburn in 1314. I understand my large stature was inherited from my forbears.

"When I was but a wee *bairn*, there was something that threatened my family. I don't know what they were involved in, but I assume it must have been something of a political nature. I have been told that I was spirited out of Scotland to Canada, by persons unknown to me, and smuggled across the American border to Glasgow, Montana. There I was adopted and raised by friends of a distant relative and his wife named MacIntosh. My parents were also secretly removed from Scotland, but to another location. I have never learned what happened to them. My adoptive parents were sworn never to tell me much about my background, therefore, I have no idea whether my biological parents are alive or dead or where they might possibly have gone.

"In my teen years, I became a born-again Christian in an Assembly of God church. I rather dismissed some of the story about my background as a fairy-tale. When I graduated High School, I first decided to go to university to study theology at the Masters level, but ultimately ended up studying European history for my doctoral work. I eventually graduated from Yale with a PhD in European History and was offered a teaching position at the Sorbonne University in Paris where I taught for three years. I was able to carry on a great deal of first-hand research into the Templars and their reputed sister organization, the *Prieure de Sion* while there on the Continent.

I learned that the two supposedly 'Christian' Crusader organizations, the Knights Templar and the Order of Sion, were basically French Cathar Gnostics. Apparently, the two organizations consorted with minions of the Muslim Saracen known as the 'Hashishim,' or 'Assassins,' who were supposedly the Islamic equals of the Templars and reputed to be in the Templars' employ at some point. From their name—Hashishim—it is obvious they smoked something stronger than tobacco. Apparently these ostensibly desultory enemies 'cross-pollinated' each other theologically and culturally during their decades of intimate contact in the Holy Land. With this in mind, it is no mystery that the Templars were later accused of holding extremely heretical views of Christianity, if you could even call it Christianity. It was reported to the Inquisition, probably with good reason, that the Templars worshipped a severed head known as 'Baphomet' and that some of the Templar's ceremonies involved such niceties as urinating on the cross—not too surprising when you consider their Muslim friends' opinion of Christianity. I concluded that, as a Christian, I definitely wanted no part of the Crusader's ilk.

"But an unusual incident occurred while I was in France which really shook me. I met William Burgoyne, now popularly known as Emperor 'Kaiser Bill,' at a ritzy party on an estate outside of Paris. I had received a special invitation through Professor Henri Montsegur, a colleague and friend at the Sorbonne. At this party, I had occasion to meet a number of bureaucrats and diplomats within the E.U. government. When I was introduced to Burgoyne, who was at the time a garden variety E.U. official, he looked at me with a very strange expression and said 'Well, I'm glad to finally meet my long-lost first cousin.' I've never figured out how he knew who I was, when even I did not know my true identity or that we were even related in any way. I was completely blown away and spent about an hour with the man trying to pump him for particulars. He was not at all accommodating, at least nothing I could get a grip on. Frankly, there was just something about him that made my skin crawl. I saw something positively evil in his eyes which frightened me—and I'm not easily frightened! Cousin or no, I was glad to get away from him.

"At the end of my third academic year in France, I had had quite enough of French culture and decided to return to the good old US of A. I accepted a position at Montana State University in Bozeman where I later met and married my darlin' wife, Mary.

"However, during that summer before I moved back to Montana, I drove the 'Chunnel' to England and traveled to Edinburgh, Scotland, where I made an exhaustive search of the genealogical records in the General Register Office. I assumed my first name was more than likely correct but I had no earthly idea what my last name might have been. All I knew was the approximate date when I was born and that I was born into a highland family. Aware that Argyll was reputed to have been the traditional 'stomping grounds' of dispossessed Templars, I searched through those area records first. I finally came across the entry of an unusually large male child named Alexander Campbell, which seemed most likely, so I traveled to the tiny settlement of Kilmartin in Argyllshire."

"When I walked into the area's Constabulary Office, the head constable reacted as though he'd seen a ghost. Wherever I went, I received the same look. No one would tell me anything substantive. It was almost as though they were afraid to talk to me. After two days of nosing around, I returned to my room at the Kilmartin Hotel to find a note stuck to the door with a dagger which read 'If you value your health, get your giant hide out of Scotland.'"

Being a typically stubborn Scot, I decided that before I left, I would at least visit the rector of the local church, whose name I learned was MacLeod.

He was a bit more forthcoming and said he remembered my parents and that I was a dead-ringer for my father. As to what became of my parents, he had no idea. He only remembered that they, and I, had mysteriously disappeared overnight many years before."

"As we were talking, an obviously powerful automobile drove past the front of the church and I was completely startled to hear several long bursts of automatic weapons fire before the car sped away. Exiting the church, I was furious to find that they had shot my little French car full of holes with what appeared to have been a submachine gun. Well, that was enough for me! I was a stranger in a strange land, and obviously a sitting duck for someone who didn't want me there. Now, you must admit, a man my size is an easy target to hit. I quickly retrieved my belongings from the hotel and drove through the night back to Edinburgh in my, then, very breezy car. I sold the car for junk and immediately booked the first available airline reservation back to America. The strangest thing was that the junk yard proprietor never batted an eye at the condition of my car. I'll tell you, my friends, when that aircraft landed in New York City, I was never so glad to be back on American soil!"

"Now, I had always kept in close contact with my adoptive parents in Glasgow, Montana, since they were getting on in years. Then one day about two years after my return from Europe, I tried contacting them, but got no answer. For five straight days I phoned them with no results. I started to get worried so Mary and I decided to drive to Glasgow to check on them. We knocked on their front door but got no answer. Their front door proved to be unlocked so we went in. The house was a shambles—totally ransacked. There were signs of a disturbance but no sign of my parents. We immediately called the police to investigate. Soon the Montana State Police, and eventually the FBI, got involved but no trace of them has ever been found. Mum and Dad had warned me that all of us could be in danger some day, from whom or what, exactly, I never knew—I'm not sure even they knew. I'm certain the people who shot up my car in Scotland must have been members of the same organization that attacked my birth parents, my adoptive family and my own family, as well. The spooks in high places in this world are enough to give you the willies.

"But, I suspect Burgoyne had a hand in all this—somehow, I just know he was involved. But how do you prove something like that? And who would stand up for you against so powerful a man if you could? I'm sure it had something to do with his idea that I, or my family, are some sort of political threat to him and his precious European Establishment.

"Mary and I decided, right then and there, that it was not safe to live in town anymore. My wife was independently wealthy, so I resigned my position at MSU and we bought a remote tract of forest land out in the tall timber from Ezra here, built a log cabin and moved out there with her partially disabled brother. We lived more or less off the land there over the past several years with no problems."

"But when I walked into the carnage in our cabin yesterday, I knew in my heart that I was the one the assassins were really after, whoever they are. If I'd been home, I probably wouldn't be standing here now. My family paid the price for me. I knew that the killers would eventually be back and eliminate me too, if they could. I'd surprised them that day, but maybe they'd send a detachment of Spec Ops guys out to bushwhack me when I least expected it. Knowing that only certain worthy people can find this place, I decided to try to come to the Lair and figure out what to do from here. So, here we are!" concluded Alex.

"Well, it's truly a sad day we're living in, but we're very glad indeed to have you all here. You're a giant of a man in more ways than one, Alexander MacIntosh," smiled Grandfather affectionately.

☆ 10 ☆

THE MOLE

Late November saw a deepening snow cover at the Eagle's Lair. With the watchful eyes of Eli, Arie and Uri monitoring the satellites, it was evident that an avalanche of destruction and pillage was spreading across the United States; towns and cities were going up in flames as the invaders made their way across the continent. Men, women and children by the thousands were being slaughtered, driven from their homes and shipped off to prison camps. The highways were clogged with refugees moving toward the interior of the country.

Several weeks went by and Christmas was drawing near. The women were baking festive cakes and holiday cookies and making decorative candy. Christmas trees were being cut from the forest and set up all around the Lodge. The place smelled wonderfully of pine and cinnamon. Everyone was busily decorating the Lodge, as well as their personal quarters. Some of the men had gone hunting around the lake and had already brought in several dozen Canada geese and mallard ducks for the big Christmas feast.

Alex had cooked some of his elk meat and his new friends loved it. "It's actually better than beef and the only thing almost as good is bison. There are some of them around also, but the elk seem to be more plentiful right now," explained Alex.

Then one day, Ivan and Uri abruptly walked into Jim's office and announced, "Boss, we've got a mole in our midst."

Taken somewhat off guard, Jim responded, "Hunh? What are you talking about? I'm not following."

"I'm not talking about the furry kind, Sir. You mentioned during your extraction of Senator Dalton from Virginia as well as the incident with the welcoming party at the refueling stop in Kansas, it seemed as though the enemy knew your every move. Am I not right?" inquired Ivan.

"Well, yes, it did appear that way. But why are you bringing that up?" asked Jim, hesitantly, still uncertain of Ivan's point.

"Well, Sir, for some time now, we've been picking up continuous wave shortwave radio transmissions in International Morse code on the 20 meter ham band, every day from noon to 5:00pm. I never paid much attention to it. It just seemed to be so much 'normal ham band background noise.' But one day last week, for some reason, my attention was really drawn to it. It suddenly hit me that almost nobody uses Morse code on the 20 meter band, which is the premier long-distance voice band used exclusively by worldwide Amateur Radio.

"Uri and I sat down and began to copy the messages and, lo and behold, someone was transmitting coordinates and other bits of information pertaining to the Eagle's Lair. We wanted to be absolutely sure of what was going on, so earlier this week Uri and I took two directional radio antennas and a couple of field-strength meters, split up, and got a triangulation fix on the source. As nearly as we can tell, it's coming from Cabin 25, the one farthest out of the family units. We've checked and double-checked our findings from several different set-up points. We're 95 percent certain that's the source," concluded Ivan emphatically.

"Hmm! That's Jamal Khatibi's cabin. I saw him and his family leave for the lake a few minutes ago. Ivan, Uri, Eli, Alex, what say we all go look around their place while they're gone?" Jim suggested calmly, not exhibiting an increasing sense of alarm at this disturbing disclosure.

Jamal Khatibi was Etzion's Chief Financial Officer. He and his wife, Zara, were Christian Arabs originally from Israel's Negev region. Educated in England, Jamal was the son of a wealthy desert sheik. A powerfully-built, if somewhat rotund, man in his late 40's, he had worked initially for Etzion Enterpises in Israel. After transferring to the American plant in Houston, he had assumed responsibility for the monetary operations of the corporation and eventually became a U.S. citizen.

On entering the Khatibi's log cabin, the five men split up and began to search the premises for anything suspicious. But after an hour, their efforts had yielded nothing and the place appeared to be clean as a whistle. As the four were about to leave, Ivan spotted the very tip of an alligator clip, protruding from the back of a clock radio in the bedroom of the Khatibi's 17 year old son, Jamie.

"Aha!" exclaimed Ivan, "What's this? An antenna lead? Hmm . . . "

Further investigation revealed a previously unseen thin copper wire running up the back of a curtain. Ivan followed the wire under the window sash to the window screen where it had been clipped to the screen's frame. Tightly folded bits of cardboard had been wedged under the window screen, holding it away from the steel window frame to electrically insulate it from the building. Removal of the back of the radio cabinet revealed the chassis of a miniature radio transmitter.

"So, this is how it's being done," announced an infuriated Ivan, "Looks like a low-power home-made crystal-controlled ham band rig. This thing looks very familiar to me but I can't quite place where I've seen one of these before. The transmitter's final amplifier stage enables the window screen to act as an antenna, by tuning through what the old-time ham radio operators called a 'pi network.' It's a very old but effective way to make odd-shaped pieces of ferrous-metal infrastructure resonate as a radio antenna. You can actually load up almost anything made of ferrous material. This one guy I knew loaded up a steel bed spring! Hey, let's take a further look around in here," he quipped.

On completely disassembling the radio cabinet, Ivan snorted, "Yup, just as I thought. There's an endless tape mechanism feeding this transmitter. Undoubtedly, it contains the Morse code messages I heard. Fortunately, the transmitter is pretty low power and that antenna setup has a limited range even on 20 meters. Besides, we are in the worst of the sun-spot cycle which also helps limit the range and intelligibility of shortwave broadcasts. Let's hope no bad guys heard this thing in action," he grinned.

Meanwhile, Jim rummaged through the night stands and dresser drawers again and eventually found a copy of the Quran, with Jamie's name engraved on the front cover, hidden in a jewelry box.

"Looks like Jamie is a Muslim. We'll have to ask the Khatibis some very pointed questions," sighed Jim, obviously dismayed, "Who would've thought we'd have a traitor in our midst? Ivan, analyze that tape and pinpoint the frequency the transmitter is on. You are all witnesses to this whole thing," he declared sternly.

"Witnesses? Why witnesses? Are we going to conduct a trial? I mean we have no lawyers, a judge or legal setup?" croaked Arie, somewhat shocked.

"Being the owner of this place, Grandfather will have the last word on this. I'm going to defer to his judgment and authority as to how we should proceed. It's 'Age before beauty,' boys," said Jim, reluctantly.

An hour later, the Khatibi family returned and walked into the cabin laughing and happy after their outing.

Jamie was startled as he walked into his bedroom and found five men sitting in his chairs and on his bed.

"Wha . . . . what are you guys all doing here?" he asked, astonished.

"We were going to ask you the same thing, Jamie. What have YOU been doing here? We found the radio transmitter and your Quran. You want to tell us what you've been up to?" snarled Jim.

"I . . . . uh . . . well . . .uh . . . General . . . I," Jamie stammered as his countenance fell and his face flushed, crimson red.

"What's going on in here? What are you all doing here?" demanded Jamal as he walked into the room, obviously shocked, alarmed and a little angry at this intrusion on his privacy.

"Jamal, we found a hidden radio transmitter in the clock-radio on Jamie's night stand and a Quran with his name on it. The transmitter's been broadcasting the coordinates of this place on the long range 20 meter shortwave band for the whole world to hear for some time now. And I suspect whoever put it there informed our enemies of many of our planned moves along the way here from Houston. We don't know yet how much damage it's already done," announced Jim, tersely.

Jamal looked angrily at his son, "Is this so? What have you done? And why?"

Jamie hung his head and was silent.

"How *could* you do such a thing?" demanded Jamal, getting right in Jamie's face, "You answer me NOW!" thundered his father.

"I . . . . uh . . . Allahu akbar!" Jamie shouted defiantly, raising a clenched fist over his head.

"Allahu akbar, indeed!" roared Jamal, "So that's it! That's why you have been acting differently over this past year. You have converted to Islam! How could you turn your back on Jesus and damn your soul to hell? How could you shame us this way? Get out of my sight and out of my house, you ungrateful little whelp," shouted Jamal as he back-handed Jamie across the mouth, sending him crashing into a wall. Picking himself up off the floor with a bloody nose and mouth, the boy stood glaring defiantly at his father and his inquisitors.

"Easy, Jamal, easy! We'll put Jamie in the old brig and I'm afraid we'll have to search the house further to be sure we've found everything and to determine that the rest of you were not involved," said Jim apologetically.

"I understand perfectly," came Jamal's obviously chagrined response. "You have my full cooperation to do whatever is necessary to investigate this terrible thing. By all means go over every bit of this property, including our personal belongings, with a fine-toothed comb, Jim. We'll all leave the house and remain in the Lodge while you and your people take your time. I want this house—and my name—cleared. I have never been so embarrassed in my entire life. You were kind enough to take us in many years ago and I have sought to serve you faithfully and honorably in every way I could. I hope you know how very much we love Jesus and you and how deeply we love America," replied Jamal, with tears welling up in his eyes.

"Yes, as far as I know, you've always been faithful," was Jim's immediate sincere response, "I'm sure you are a good and decent man, Jamal, but I hope you understand that we must be sure we have gotten to the bottom of this," said Jim, on the verge of tears himself.

"Eli, see to it that the old brig is cleaned up and Jamie is locked up tight for his protection as well as ours. Have an armed guard detailed to keep an eye on him 24/7," ordered Jim, brusquely.

"Yes, Sir. The place seemed to be in reasonably good shape when I last looked at it, except for a little dust, some cobwebs and some small critters we'll have to evict. We'll cuff Jamie to something solid and get the place ready by this evening," replied Eli.

"Ivan, Uri, you guys go over this place and scan everything from top to bottom. In the meantime, we will consult with Grandfather to decide how we should proceed with Jamie. We can't just turn him loose or slap him on the wrist either. Treason is a very serious matter. Some would say it's automatically a capital offense," Jim observed.

"Since there remains no system of law and order in this country at the present time, I guess *we* are the governing authority. So, we'll have to determine how to proceed the best we can according to the Bible and common-sense law," mused Jim, in a lowered tone.

A very somber group left the Khatibi cabin and walked to the Lodge along with the rest of the Khatibi family.

"Now what do we do?" asked Jim haltingly of his confidants. Then, in a more affirmative tone, he continued, "I hate the thought that we might have to execute someone so young, but we cannot excuse treason for any reason. If we were to make an exception for this one, we would have to wink at something else next time."

"Aye!" echoed Alex, "Tis indeed a fine kettle o' fish we have here." The others nodded in agreement as they walked along, each totally lost in his own thoughts.

"General Black, I would like to tell you all a bit about my background, if I may," said Jamal softly, breaking the deafening silence. "I need to share some things now, which I have never related to anyone else before except my wife. I realize now that my silence was a grave mistake, especially in light of these developments with my son. I was so afraid people would think of me as a raving lunatic, but Jesus is taking me to task for my silence."

"Jamal, if you don't mind," interrupted Jim, "I'd like everyone to hear this next Sunday morning. It might help both you and Jamie a bit later."

"Yes! Yes of course. I agree," replied Jamal quickly, appearing somewhat relieved.

Arriving at the Lodge, Jim promptly informed Grandfather of the situation and asked for his perspective on the problem.

After carefully considering everything Jim had detailed for him, Grandfather said, "Alright. Here is what we must do: Since I was not there and because I am the patriarch of this place, I will sit as the presiding judge. Have every willing adult put his or her name into a hat and we will select a jury of twelve by a chance drawing. We'll appoint someone to represent Jamie for the defense and someone in the group who discovered this thing will act as prosecutor. The prosecutor and the defense will cull the jury and replace any rejects by an additional drawing if necessary. Then, we'll go to trial and let the chips fall where they may. No political correctness, just common sense. If Jamie is adjudged guilty by the jury, we will have no choice but to sentence him to death, because his actions have endangered the lives of every person here. If we do less than that, we will potentially invite further future issues from him and others."

On the following Sunday morning, Jamal Khatibi walked slowly to the podium of the media center and fidgeted nervously with a sheaf of notes, occasionally looking back at his wife, Zara. Mopping his brow with a handkerchief, he glanced furtively at his still-defiant son sitting in the front row. He then turned to the audience and began to speak in slow, measured tones.

"I am going to share some things with you, my friends, which I have never related to anyone else before, except my wife. I realize that my silence has been a grave mistake. I was afraid people would think that I was crazy but Jesus has forcefully commanded me to end my silence.

"I have been a Christian for many years now, but I was born into a Muslim family in Israel's Negev Desert. I would like to help you understand why I became a Christian. I hope you will pardon my language but, frankly,

I literally had the hell scared out of me," Jamal said, looking nervously at his wife, who nodded reassuringly.

"I was a devout Muslim who prayed five times a day facing Mecca. I had been visiting the Al Aqsa Mosque on the Temple Mount, listening to the imams rail against the Jews, the Christians and America. I was seriously considering joining Islamic Jihad in their fight against Israel, but God had other plans for me.

"Zara and I had only been married a year at that time and I was working at a construction job in East Jerusalem very near the Hadassah Medical Center. I was what you might call 'grossly obese' at that time. One afternoon, in the heat of the day, I felt a strange tightness in my chest and had difficulty breathing, before finally collapsing. My co-workers rushed me to Hadassah and then ran to find Zara."

"As I was carried into the Hadassah emergency room and placed on an examination table, my heart stopped. Suddenly, I found myself standing beside the gurney looking down at my body as the doctors fought to revive me. Almost immediately, I heard a maniacal laugh from the foot of the gurney. Turning, I saw leering at me an unbelievably ugly being, with large spirally twisted horns and a frightening countenance.

"He laughed again, bowed sarcastically and in a gravelly voice snarled, 'Welcome to Paradise, Mr. Khatibi.' Immediately, he grabbed me and threw me into a cell with rough stone walls and steel barred door. There were creatures on the walls that looked like Komodo Dragons and huge spider-like beings walking across the floor. Two ten foot tall demons entered the cell and began to beat me unmercifully. You see, in Hell, you do have a body, but it has no blood. Although it will never die, it can be hurt. One of the demons dug his sharp talons into my chest and tore out strips of my flesh. The pain was like a hot iron. All the strength went out of my body and I collapsed on the floor, unable to rise. The heat was unbearable and I became terribly thirsty, but there was no water anywhere. The stones beneath me were like live coals of fire. I could hear the screams and moans of millions in torment. Somehow, I knew that there was no escape . . .for all eternity. I was overcome by paralyzing fear and utter hopelessness. Hell is a place of unbearable regret. Terror overwhelmed me. One of the demons jerked me to my feet, threw me out of the cell, clamped me in chains and placed me with some other men who were busily rolling a huge, red-hot boulder toward a chasm. The pain was indescribable and penetrated my entire being like liquid fire," he said, stopping to shakily take a sip of water from a glass on the lectern.

"I asked the man beside me how he came to be there. He said, 'I was a suicide bomber. These others were my brothers in Islamic Jihad who were killed in an Israeli air strike. We were taught from childhood that we would go to paradise if we died as martyrs. There we would have 72 mansions, each with 72 beds and 72 virgins to serve our every whim for all eternity—sort of a celestial bordello. As you can plainly see that vision of the afterlife was not quite accurate and now we are doomed to burn here for all eternity in this horrible prison—some paradise! The other man beside him avoided eye contact with me, so I asked the man who had been talking with me who his neighbor was. The man sneered and said 'This lying cur dog was my imam' and he kicked the man in the shins."

Jamal cleared his throat and continued, "By this time, I was so frightened I was petrified. I remembered one of my co-workers, a Christian Arab, mentioning that the blood that was shed on the cross by Jesus, the Christian Messiah, two thousand years ago was the only thing that could save a person from Hell. At that point, I had nothing to lose, so I cried out with a loud voice, 'Jesus, if You are there, if You can hear me, if You can help me, I call on Your Name and plead Your blood to save me from this awful place and I will serve You forever.'

"The demons and all the men around me began to laugh viciously, but suddenly a voice from high above thundered something I did not understand. Then, the creature with the spiral horns and all the other demons shuddered and hid their faces as a great angel approached me. My chains simply fell off, as the bright angel gently grasped my arm.

"Immediately, I was back in the emergency room in Hadassah Medical Center. The angel smiled at me and comforted me, saying, 'Jamal, the LORD heard your request and you have passed from death to life. You will live and serve Him forever, just as you have said.'

"I could see and hear the doctors and nurses conversing rapidly in Hebrew, while they worked feverishly to revive me. The next thing I knew, I was back in my body and woke up screaming with terrible chest pain. As soon as I was quiet again, the head doctor came around the side of the gurney, looked into my face, smiled and said, 'Welcome back, Mr. Khatibi. For a while there, we thought we had lost you.'

I said, 'Doctor, you have no idea how glad I am to be back. I was in Hell.' The doctor said 'Yes, I suspected as much. You sounded like all the demons down there were after you a few minutes ago as you were regaining consciousness.'"

"At that point," Jamal continued, "He walked out of the room into the waiting area and told my wife 'Mrs. Khatibi, good news! We nearly lost him. He died on the table and it was touch and go, but he is back and conscious now. We had to insert a stent in his heart. I think we have him stabilized now. I believe he'll be alright. We will transfer him to Intensive Care, where we can monitor him for a while. He's very lucky to be alive.'

"I tell you, if I'd been strong enough to lift myself up, I would have grabbed that Jewish doctor by the lapels and kissed him." As nervous laughter swept the dead silent room, Jamal continued, "When I was finally strong enough to sit up and talk coherently, I told my wife everything that had happened to me in the Nether Regions. She turned pale at what I related to her and began to weep. I said, 'I am never going back to that horrible place again, Zara, and I certainly don't want you to go there either. We are going to visit that Messianic Christian Assembly down the road from our apartment. We must find out more about this Jesus of Nazareth, because He really is the Savior of the world. He saved me from Hell when I cried out to Him, and I will never forget Him. I promised to serve Him forever and I am going to keep my promise.'

"As they say, the rest is history. Within two week's time, in that little church, we both received Jesus Christ as our Lord and Savior and were baptized. Both of our families disowned us and we received a number of death threats. But, what could they do to us, threaten us with Heaven?

"Soon afterward, we had an opportunity to go to England where I was able to obtain an advanced degree in business and accounting. That prepared me to work for my friend, Jim Black.

"Well, I have said a lot in a short time. I hope this has been helpful. I guess that's about all I have to say." concluded Jamal, retrieving his notes and turning to sit down.

Jamie shouted from his seat "You are a demented fool, father. I do not believe any of it. Allahu akbar!"

The room was deathly silent as Jamal smiled sadly at Jamie, and then took his seat. One could have heard a pin drop. Suddenly, the place erupted in cheers and loud applause, as the congregation jumped to their feet and gave an astonished and embarrassed Jamal Khatibi a long, standing ovation.

"Thank you Jamal, that was absolutely fantastic! I wish I'd known all this before," smiled Jim.

"Folks, we'll break for coffee and fellowship now! Be back here at 10:00am for our regular service," announced Jim.

Looking a bit pale, Jamie Khatibi arose from his front row seat and walked unsteadily toward the rear of the auditorium accompanied by his jailer escort.

"May I use the rest room?" he asked the guard as they walked down the aisle toward the back of the auditorium.

The guard swung open the door to the men's rest room to satisfy himself that the room was unoccupied.

"Go ahead, Jamie, but don't dawdle."

Jamie entered the rest room, headed for a toilet stall. Glancing at the mirror over the sink, the young man suddenly froze in his tracks. An anguished, soul-piercing cry escaped his lips.

"Yiiiiiieeeeeee!! My God! Help me!" screamed the boy.

The guard rushed into the rest room, his hand on the butt of his sidearm, followed by Jim, Jamal and a host of others.

"What in the world is going on in here?" demanded Jim.

Jamie was white as a sheet and his breath came in short gasps as he stood, pointing at the mirror in stark terror.

They all turned to look in the direction Jamie had pointed and chills went up the back of every man present. There, in the mirror, stood a skeleton garbed in Jamie's clothing.

"What is happening here? I've never seen anything like this!" whispered Jim to Jamal, both visibly shaken by the sight before them.

Jamie collapsed at his father's feet in tears, wrapping his arms around Jamal's legs.

"Oh, Jesus forgive me. I am such a fool. Oh Lord Jesus, save me! Please cleanse me and take me back! I'll serve You, Lord, for the rest of my life. Oh dad, I was so wrong. I had no idea I have been such a total fool. In the assembly, as I listened to you talk, I felt God speaking to me but I was too proud to let on. But when I saw my reflection just now, there was no doubt I was in much deeper trouble than I could ever imagine. General Black, I am so sorry for what I've done to you. Can you ever forgive me? I promise I'll straighten up and help you any way I can," wailed the repentant boy.

"Yes. Yes, of course I'll forgive you. We're all okay in spite of what you did and I know Jesus has also forgiven you," said Jim, "We'll let you go home if your parents agree. What do you think, Jamal?"

Jamal appeared dubious as he thought for a moment. "How shall I know whether you are sincere, Jamie? You're not going to repent and then stab me in the back again, are you?"

"Dad, please. I know what it looks like, but I promise I'm for real," the boy sobbed.

At length, Jamal said, "Well . . . okay, maybe there is a way to tell. Stand up, son! Let's have a look at you in the mirror again," he said as he raised the skinny boy, trembling, to his feet.

The men once again beheld Jamie's image in the mirror. There was no longer a skeleton in blue jeans and T-shirt, but a normal, healthy young man in full flesh. Jamie dissolved in a flood of tears.

"Thank God, thank God! You have sincerely repented and He has forgiven you," wept Jamal and Jamie with their arms around each other, "Welcome back, son. Let's go home."

Jamie turned to Jim and said, "General Black, I want you to know how I got involved in all this. It was partly my fault. I was drawn into Islam by my school friends and I began attending a local mosque on the sly. One night, as I was walking home, a limo pulled up to the curb and a middle-eastern-looking man in a business suit and sunglasses got out and grabbed my arm. He told me they had been watching me and they needed my help. He told me that you and your company were plotting against Islam which made me very angry. They convinced me to help them. They gave me money and, later on, some equipment, part of which was the radio you found. It was I who alerted them when you flew to pick up Senator Dalton and I also told them about your fuel stop in Kansas on the way to the Lair. And, of course, you already know that I transmitted the coordinates of the Eagle's Lair after we arrived."

"Well, that explains a whole lot of things, Jamie. But tell me, do you know who those people really were?" asked Jim, stifling a sense of alarm.

"They said they were from the CIA, that's as much as I ever knew about them," the young man replied.

"Okay, Jamie. Go on home with your family—and behave yourself," instructed the general.

"I understand, Sir. I've changed—you'll see!" Jamie said, a slight smile returning to his tear-stained face.

Beckoning to his group of confidants, Jim retired to his office. "If what Jamie is telling us is true, which I have no reason to doubt," Jim began, "And, if those guys who involved him actually were CIA, that confirms to me America has been betrayed by a whole conglomerate of seemingly disparate interests at the highest levels, both inside and outside, of our government None of this really surprises me. The whole Washington establishment was rotten to the core. For a long time before this happened, America's borders have been totally, and intentionally, left open to illegal immigration, allowing all sorts of terrorists to come in. U.S. Border Patrol agents were even penalized for enforcing the law. There has been a movement among the fat cats behind the scenes to do away with national sovereignties and turn the whole of the North American Continent into one huge Mex-ameri-canada, secretly ruled by unknowns in the shadows— undoubtedly the New World Order—which in turn is without doubt run by Kaiser Bill and the fanatics in the French Prieure de Sion, which Alex spoke of earlier.

"Well, gentlemen, now that we've solved the world's problems, let's get a cup of coffee and go to church," grinned Jim.

THE DISCOVERY

Winter was beginning to soften a bit in the mountains of central Montana. The first of May was approaching and some of the snow pack was beginning to melt. Many of the folks were starting to move around outside more freely. Quite a number were exploring the airport grounds, the lake and the surrounding mountains and forests.

Some of Etzion's Airframe and Power Plant (A&P) mechanics were busy checking over and servicing the airplanes in Hangar Number 1. During a break one day, two of them—John Hunnicut and George Mendes— entered Hangar Number 2 to look over the C5-B. As they were conversing, John leaned up against the side wall of the hangar to rest—and something moved.

Knocked off balance, John turned around to see that a sliding door had opened and behind it lay what appeared to be a steel bulkhead with a wheel-like locking device. Printed on the door were the words 'PRESSURIZED CHAMBER—ROTATE HAND WHEEL SLOWLY UNTIL PRESSURE BEGINS TO RELEASE. STAND CLEAR AND ALLOW PRESSURE TO EQUALIZE BEFORE FURTHER UNLATCHING DOOR.'

"What on earth is this?" John muttered under his breath.

"Better go get General Black. I wouldn't touch that thing with a ten-foot fork!" exclaimed George.

Jim was deep in conversation with Eli, Alex and several other men around the fireplace of the Lodge's great room as the two mechanics walked in.

"Uh, excuse us General, we just stumbled onto something you've gotta take a look at in Hangar Number Two," announced John, nervously crumpling his cap.

Mildly annoyed at the interruption, Jim asked, "What is it that's got you two so lathered up?"

"A door, Sir. You gotta to come check it out," stammered George Mendes, apologetically.

"Okay, Okay, I'll look at it. But I don't understand. What's the big deal with a door that I have to look at it personally?" Jim chided, irritated.

"This isn't a regular door, Sir. It's steel and looks like a ship's bulkhead in the end wall of Hangar Number Two. Printing on the door says it's under pressure. We sure aren't going to mess with it ourselves," explained George Mendes.

A bulkhead? Under pressure? This I've got to see!!

Jim and his companions followed the two mechanics through a service door into the interior of the cavernous Hangar Number Two, past the aluminum hulk of the C5-B. As they passed the giant transport, Jim looked up and was surprised to see emblazoned on the fuselage "The United States of America".

"Hey, Hunnicut, when did you guys paint THAT on this thing?" asked Jim.

"We didn't. It was already there when she arrived from Israel. The fuselage had a layer of rime ice when she came in so we didn't see it at the time. Wonder where this aircraft really came from anyhow," wondered Hunnicut.

As they approached the mysterious door on the far side wall, Jim's curiosity began to arouse.

"Sorry I doubted you boys. How did you happen to find this door?" Jim wanted to know.

"Leaned up against the wall to rest and the thing just slid sideways—had my back on it and it almost tipped me over. Didn't like the looks of the whole deal, so we thought you oughta handle it. What on earth could this thing be, General?" queried John.

"Well, John, I have no idea what it might be. I guess there's only one way to find out. We'll never know by just standing here staring at it. Everybody stand clear," ordered Jim as he stood to the side of the door, leaned over and began to slowly turn the hand wheel on the door.

There was a sudden rush of gasses from a louvered vent at the bottom of the door. The escaping gasses smelled of some sort of aromatic solvents. The pressure finally equalized a half-hour later at which point Jim rotated the wheel until the door unlatched and swung inward by itself.

"Give me a big flashlight," Jim called to one of the mechanics.

Shining the flashlight through the doorway revealed some sort of machinery beyond, but that was all Jim could make out.

"Well, I don't see any big eyes in there looking back at me, so here goes," he said as he thrust a hand inside the doorway searching for what he hoped would be a light switch. Presently, he grasped a switch handle and flipped it up. With a faint hum, the interior began to slowly illuminate. Jim stuck his head in first, then stepped inside and disappeared briefly. A few minutes later, he emerged with an incredulous look on his face.

"Boys, I don't believe what I've just seen. Go in there and take a look around, I think you'll be very surprised at what's in there," announced Jim mysteriously.

As the group entered the chamber, there were "ooohs" and "aahs" all around.

Before them stood two pristine World War II era B-29 Superfortresses, the same type of aircraft that delivered the atomic bombs to Hiroshima and Nagasaki, Japan. These appeared to have just rolled off the assembly line. Both bombers bore nose art typical of WWII. One was dubbed 'The City of New Orleans.' The other was named 'The City of Chicago.' The vertical stabilizers on both B-29s bore a huge "A," an American flag and an eagle with a fist-full of arrows. Behind the two bombers, sat a P-51 Mustang with nose art proclaiming it to be 'Triple Trouble.'

"Well I'll be hornswoggled," drawled Eli, "I've never seen anything so beautiful. But what on earth are these antiques doing here in a sealed chamber?"

Jim and Grandfather exchanged glances. "Grandfather, do you suppose this is what Jesus meant for me to discover here that He wouldn't tell you about? And, if so, what is the significance of these three old airplanes?" Jim asked as his eyes met the old man's gaze.

"I don't know, but outside of Alex and his friends, these are certainly the first hidden things we've stumbled upon in the months we've been here. There has to be an explanation and I know He will let us know what it is," assured Grandfather.

"Wonder how we're ever going to get these old girls out of here, anyway?"

Grandfather produced the remote control with the three buttons and looked at it thoughtfully.

"Hmm, I wonder . . . . ," he murmured as he pushed the button marked '3.'

The group was startled by the rumbling of rollers and whine of gears and electric motors as a previously hidden hangar door began to open.

"Well, that answers that! Apparently, opening that bulkhead door activated the circuits associated with this hangar's big doors," reasoned Grandfather.

Meanwhile, Eli and the mechanics were rapidly exploring the interiors of the fighter, the two bombers and the storage rooms behind. They emerged totally amazed at the condition of the aircraft and everything else in the previously sealed hangar.

"Sir, these ships are fully equipped and seem to be 100 percent preserved. Normally, tires are the first thing to deteriorate on a dormant airplane, but even the tires seem fresh and new as the day they were made. We'll have to check these old crates over, but they appear to be eminently airworthy and fully equipped for a bomb mission. These engines are the latest improved Pratt & Whitney R-4360 'Wasp Major' engines. Even so, WWII era engines had a much shorter lifespan than modern aircraft engines and these are the series of engines one old A&P mechanic described as an engine that was normal when you shut it down, but that would malfunction when you started it again. But the engine clocks show only 3 hours on both ships. That means at least 22 good hours of flight time before the top 5 jugs on each engine would have to be replaced, and 72 hours of flight time before engine replacement. The store rooms have a treasure trove of spare engines and critical parts," concluded Eli.

"I'm a major enthusiast of B-29s, man! I've loved 'em since I was a kid. I'll run the serial numbers past the official records on my laptop computer, but I'd bet these ships were among the last ones built by Boeing's Renton, Washington, plant before the assembly line was shut down for good. It's just amazing they'd show up here! And what kind of technology has preserved them this way?" marveled Eli.

Jim quickly broke in saying, "Let's close this place back up for awhile and think about all this. There has to be a message here. I was supposed to find something hidden on this base, according to Grandfather and, as he said, these are the first really hidden things we've stumbled onto since we've been here," mused Jim.

Unknown to Jim and his companions, an answer to their questions was about to appear.

☆ 12 ☆

THE CAVALRY ARRIVES

Be careful how you welcome strangers, for in so doing some people have entertained angels without knowing it. [13]

Several weeks went by and the last snow of the winter was melting rapidly, revealing green grass and flowers in the meadows. The pines, cedars and spruces all began to put forth new growth.

One windless, sunny day as Alex, Eli and a group of other men were out exploring some of the older buildings on the base, a teenager came running up to Jim all out of breath. "Sir, Ivan says your phone is off so he sent me out here to let you know there is an AC-130 gunship requesting permission to land. Pilot says he's U.S. Air Force and has something he needs to talk to you about."

"Hmm . . . that's the first contact we've had with anyone on the outside in months. He found us so it must be someone we need to talk to."

Jim switched on his phone and called Ivan, the communications technician.

"Tell that AC-130 to come on in, Ivan," ordered Jim.

Within a few minutes, a 4-engine C-130 Specter gunship came in low over the trees and made a high-speed pass down the runway. Painted on the tail were the stars and stripes and an eagle with a fist full of arrows. Pulling up in a steep climbing turn over the far rim of the canyon, the craft made a tight turn, lowered flaps and gear and touched down softly.

"That guy flies like a Navy carrier pilot," laughed Eli.

As the aircraft taxied up in front of the Lodge and cut the engines, two men in Air Force uniforms emerged and approached the group that had been watching their arrival with great interest. The two walked up to Jim and saluted crisply.

"General Black, I'm Colonel Wohno and this is Major Maag. We have some news and some equipment for you, Sir," the colonel declared.

"Now wait a minute," said Jim, more than a little taken aback, "How do you know my name? I have been retired for quite a few years and I don't think we've ever met. How did you find us and what is it you want here?" Jim demanded, beginning to bristle as his stomach tightened.

"You are more widely known than you realize, General Black. We have been ordered to deliver some equipment and instructions to you. You recently found two airworthy B-29s, did you not?" inquired the Colonel.

"Well . . .Yes, but . . . but how did *you* know that? No one has been out of this compound or communicated with anyone on the outside, since we arrived here, as far as I know. And what have the bombers to do with you . . .me . . .us?," stammered Jim, wide-eyed, fighting an increasingly strong sense of alarm.

"We have a very sophisticated intelligence network, Sir. We came to tell you that the liberation of America from the toils of the invading armies is not far off. Your services will be required in the process," said the colonel in an irritatingly even tone.

"Oh, I see. And what might those 'services' entail?" Jim demanded edgily.

How do they know all this? These guys are really spooking me and raising the hackles up on the back of my neck. Wonder exactly who they are and what are they up to?!

"General, you have the two airworthy B-29s, the trained pilots, the equipment and the expert personnel to prepare them for your mission, which will be, basically, to launch cruise missiles, armed with neutron and nuclear warheads, simultaneously on the oriental enclave in Los Angeles and the United Nations complex in New York City. You will deliver a thermo-nuclear weapon, targeted upon the invasion fleets that are anchored off both coasts. The neutron weapons will not destroy or contaminate real estate, but they will destroy enemy personnel in the immediate area. Soon, representatives of the invading nations will meet at the now-abandoned U.N. building in New York City. Your attack will end their euphoria over toppling the United States and send a chilling message to the World Order," the colonel announced flatly.

"Muslims have been dancing in the streets all over the world rejoicing that what they term 'The Great Satan' has been defeated and Israel is a juicy, ripe fruit ready to be plucked. They think the American Eagle has been declawed and his wings clipped, so rest assured that jaws will drop all around the world when news of these missile strikes gets out. They'll all be in shock and awe wondering what crawled out of its hole and dared to bite the Kaiser and Allah's soldiers in the behind! But this will only be the beginning of the invader's problems," grinned Colonel Wohno. "You should also know that the remnants of the nuclear-powered American fleet, which has been in hiding, will follow with their own multiple strikes on the invasion fleets," he concluded.

"Colonel, I have just one question," enjoined Jim, "You people obviously possess far more sophisticated aircraft than these beautiful old B-29s. Why is it necessary to use antique equipment to deliver modern weapons? Why not deliver these weapons with modern aircraft?"

"Well, Sir, there's really nothing mysterious about it. Without locating B-52s, B-1s, B-2s or some similar craft, which are mostly unavailable at the moment, we would have to resort to kicking our bombs off the cargo ramp of a C-130. That is neither sophisticated nor accurate. But delivery of the weapons by venerable WWII aircraft, which symbolize the air superiority of the greatest U.S. war victory in history, will be broadly publicized when this is all over. This will begin to raise the spirits of and restore patriotism to the American people like nothing else could. It's as simple as that, Sir," concluded Colonel Wohno.

"Okay, what comes after our cruiser strikes?" Jim inquired.

"Don't be concerned about that right at the moment, General. Just do what you've been asked, then relax and watch the fun begin. But the time is not quite yet. You will be advised when this will occur and given your final instructions at that time. What I have just told you will come to pass. And now, we really must be going. And I must ask you for a solid answer: Will you cooperate in what we are asking of you?" inquired the colonel, gazing steadily into Jim's eyes.

Crazy as all this sounds, these guys appear to be on the level and, odd as it seems, I actually trust them—why, I really don't understand. But they seem to know things no average mortal could possibly know.

Jim and Grandfather exchanged glances and Grandfather nodded his head.

"Yes . . . . Yes, of course, Colonel, we will cooperate. But who is it that sent you?" queried Jim.

"We are not at liberty to discuss such details with you right now, Sir. Everything will be explained in due time, General. Be completely confident that there is nothing nefarious about our mission or our commander. Tell me, is there anything that your enclave here currently lacks, General Black?" asked Major Maag, quietly.

"No, Major, I believe we have all we need right now. But is there some way for us to contact you if we do need something?" Jim asked.

"We'll be flying in here on a regular basis, with your permission, Sir, but here is a satellite phone number should a critical need arise," Colonel Wohno explained, "Now we must return to our duties serving the Americans who are currently facing the enemy 600 miles south of here. Oh, by the way, we need to off-load four missiles into one of your storage areas. Don't worry, they are perfectly harmless in their present state. Do you have any preference where we place them?"

"Yes, we'll put them in Hangar Number Three," responded Jim, "Eli, go help them stow those things in Storage Room One in the back of the hangar. It's the largest."

"Yes, Sir, I'll be happy to," said Eli.

"Colonel Wohno, can you tell me in what way you are aiding the defenders down south?"

"Food, water, medical supplies, guns, ammunition, blankets, tents, fuel—you name it, we haul it. We also evacuate anyone who requires more medical attention than they can get locally. And we frequently employ our on-board weapons systems to even the odds when things get out of hand. As you can see, this is a gunship and our weaponry is very effective against troops and armor," he said.

"Would it be possible for some of us to accompany you to that area some time? I'd like to see firsthand what is going on down there?!" Jim asked.

"I can't make any promises, but that may be possible. We'll have to clear it with headquarters first. Now, if you'll excuse us, Sir, we really must go as soon as we unload these weapons," responded Colonel Wohno.

The missiles were unloaded and stored within an hour. Bidding Jim and his associates farewell, Wohno's AC-130 was off the runway and out of sight in mere minutes.

Jim turned to Eli and Arie, "Did you guys get a close look at those missiles yet?"

Eli was grinning from ear to ear, "No problemo, Boss. Guess what, man, those cruisers are identical to the ones we build in Israel."

"Okay, that's a relief, but how can we launch cruise missiles from B-29s, the birds are too long for the bomb bays?" Jim asked, puzzled by this latest turn of events.

"I brought up at least five sets of controls from the Houston plant to keep 'em from falling into the wrong hands" interrupted Eli, "I don't see why we can't make external mounts and hookups for the '29s to launch those things. Sure, it'll create a certain amount of drag but I really don't see any major problem with doing that. All it'll take is a little time and effort. We'll get started on them right away."

This is all so absolutely incredible—it's almost more than I can believe!!" mused Jim as he walked toward the Lodge and his supper.

☆ **13** ☆

THE TEST FLIGHT

Eli and Arie spent almost two solid weeks working over the B-29's with the help of the A&P mechanics and the electronics people on staff. Many days they worked late into the night.

Finally, Eli and Arie entered Jim's office in the Lodge and announced, "Boss, the '29s are each set up to carry two cruise missiles externally on the fuselage. The control systems have been installed and tested, the missiles have been tested and are fully responsive. They're ready to be mounted whenever they're needed. What's next on the agenda?"

"We need to choose the flight crews and familiarize them with the aircraft," was Jim's quick reply.

"We brought up three of our most sophisticated flight simulators from Houston and I have the profiles of the B-29 ready to go on them," Eli said.

"I think I'll fly the New York mission. How would you like to fly the Los Angeles mission, Eli?" Jim asked trying to conceal his excitement.

"Whooee! I'd love it," came Eli's instant answer.

"I think Arie should be my co-pilot," announced Jim, more calmly.

149

"Okay. Let's get on the simulators. Then, we better crank up the engines and flap around the patch a few times to be sure we're really competent and to certify that the planes really are as airworthy as we think they are," said Eli, regaining his composure.

After ten days and some thirty sessions each on the flight simulators, the three pilots were convinced they were as ready as they would ever be. The big day had come at last—flight time.

"Let's go kick the tires and light the fires," drawled Eli excitedly.

After the mechanics pulled 'The City of New Orleans' out of the hangar, the men climbed aboard and were greeted by the sweet, pungent smell of high-octane aviation gasoline.

"Ya' know, nothin' smells sweeter than av-gas, Boss" remarked Eli with a wide grin.

"Amen to that, Eli! It smells a whole lot better than jet fuel" echoed Jim, lightheartedly.

Jim settled into the pilot's seat and Eli into the copilot's chair. Arie was ensconced in the flight engineer's seat. As the three went through the prestart checklist, a ground crew of volunteers began walking each of the big four-blade propellers through several revolutions to prime the engines.

When Jim was satisfied the engines were ready, he asked Arie for generator start. Somewhere in the rear section of the fuselage, a small gasoline generator whirred to life.

"Okaaaay, we have power on the bus!" announced Arie from the flight engineer's seat.

"Clear the props," Jim shouted out the window.

From somewhere below on the tarmac came the reply, "Clear!!"

"Starting Number Three," intoned Jim.

The starter motor on the right inboard engine emitted its steely scream as the propeller began to turn. Everybody held their breath as they counted each revolution of the propeller.

"Come on, baby. Come on!," muttered Jim under his breath, "B-29 engines have a reputation for being hard to start—looks like that's correct."

"Come on, come . . . Whoom!! Number three erupted in a cacophony of sound and a characteristic cloud of blue oil smoke. Everybody cheered and watched expectantly as the other three engines similarly coughed and rumbled to life.

"Normal oil pressure and cylinder head temps on all four engines, partner. We're ready to roll" Arie announced.

As Jim released the brakes and nudged the throttles to get the old bomber moving, her four 18-cylinder Pratt and Whitney radial engines galloped and loped at idle like a flock of NASCAR stockers.

Jim taxied the old warrior out to the main runway, lined up on the centerline, set the brakes and ran through the pre-takeoff checklist.

Eli spoke up, "Uh, Jim, I forgot to mention that it's best to launch B-29s from a rolling start rather than from a stand-still; we really should check the magnetos and other vitals during takeoff roll, otherwise the top engine jugs tend to get too hot."

"OK, we'll do that from now on. How are the engines doing, Arie?" Jim asked, concerned, over his shoulder.

"They're a little warm but not in the red zone. We're Okay," Arie answered quickly.

"Okay, we're good to go. Fasten your safety belts. Gimme takeoff flaps, Eli. Here we go, boys. Hang onto your seats!" Jim shouted as he released the brakes and advanced the throttles smoothly to full power.

For the first time in decades, the Montana forests reverberated to the thunder of the B-29's big radial engines. As airspeed reached takeoff velocity, Jim pulled back smoothly on the control quadrant and the 'City of New Orleans' rotated smoothly off the runway clearing the rim of the canyon with room to spare.

"Yee-haa, she's flying!" yelled Eli triumphantly over the silken drone of the engines.

"She flies like a dream, guys," exulted Jim, moving the throttles to cruise power and raising the landing gear, "I've always wanted to fly one of these babies—what a hoot! Let's get the engine temps settled down and then all three of us will do several touch-and-go landings."

Two hours later, Jim taxied up to Hangar Number Three, moved the throttles to idle-cutoff, then turned off the avionics and master switch. The elated flight crew exited the ship and stood talking quietly under the craft's nose greenhouse, listening to the *crak!* . . *pop!* ..*tink!* of the ancient engines as they cooled above their heads. The mechanics brought a fuel truck along side, topped off the tanks, hooked up a tow cart to the nose gear and rolled the 'City of New Orleans' back into the hangar.

"Tomorrow, weather permitting, we'll fly the 'City of Chicago' and get her checked out too. Then we'll be ready when the go-ahead comes," announced Jim, "Be here at 9:00am ready to go flying, gentlemen!"

No one voiced the thought, but all three had the feeling that they were about to become vital cogs in the gears and levers of history.

14

THE COMBAT ZONE

Far to the south of Montana, loyal American military personnel, who had refused the Pentagon's order to surrender, were fighting a war of attrition in a number of locations. The largest enclave was backed into a tight perimeter on two sides with a low mountain range in between. The patriots fought the invaders with every resource at their command and the help of every able-bodied civilian there. Many an American hunter brought his high-powered hunting rifle to bear with devastating results. Nevertheless, the means and will to resist were running dangerously low.

"General, Colonel Wohno is on the horn, Sir. Says he will be landing in about 20 minutes and wants to know if you and some of our people still want to take a ride with them down to the southern combat zone he mentioned a while back," announced Ivan.

"Ivan, gimme the mike," replied Jim.

"Colonel, we would very much like to accompany you to the combat zone. How long will we be gone and what equipment should we have with us?" inquired Jim.

"You will be gone not more than 48 hours—in fact we will try to have you back by this evening if conditions permit. As our guests, you won't actually need anything in the way of equipment. However, it would be best to dress in military fatigues and boots. If you wish to bring weapons, by all means do. It would be a good idea to also bring sleeping bags, and canteens just in case we have to stay longer," responded the colonel.

"I take it your headquarters has approved this jaunt?" asked Jim, obviously pleased.

"Yes, Sir! Encouraged it, actually!" the colonel answered with a broad smile.

"Great! There'll probably be about six of us, if that is okay," Jim responded excitedly.

"Absolutely! But I must warn you again that the conditions there are not for the faint of heart. Their situation is really deplorable—but, you asked to see it and so you shall," the colonel said flatly.

"When should we be ready?" Jim asked immediately.

"We'd like to leave in about two hours, if possible," came the reply.

"All right, we'll be ready. See you soon," said Jim, handing the mike back to the communications technician.

"Listen up, everybody," announced Jim walking into the great room of the Lodge, "Colonel Wohno has offered to take six of us to get a first-hand look at the southern combat zone, where there is a large group of U.S. military and civilian fighters faced off against the invaders. If you have a strong stomach, and the urge to go, draw an M-4 with 200 rounds of ammo, fatigues, boots and a sleeping bag from the commissary. Be back here in an hour and remember, only six can go. Eli, you will determine who should go and who shouldn't."

Jim went over to Alex privately, and said, "Alex, I'd really like you to go along if you want to go."

"Aye, wouldn't miss it for the world. But I'll just wear my hunting clothes and boots. I doubt there's anything in your commissary that'll fit me anyway. I wear size 20 boots! An' I'll bring 'Ol Betsy wi' plenty o' ammo— might come in handy, y' know," grinned Alex.

As they were talking, Wohno's gunship came in low over the trees with a 'whoooosh' and touched down. He taxied the plane up to the Lodge and cut the engines. Wohno, Maag and several other individuals exited the craft and entered the Lodge.

"Welcome, gentlemen," greeted Jim, "can we offer you something to eat or drink?"

"Coffee, if you have it, Sir," answered Maag brusquely.

"We'll be ready to go shortly. Is there anything else we need to know about the combat area?" inquired Jim crisply.

"At the moment, American positions are under attack on two fronts and four of our other aircraft have engaged the enemy. I must warn you all, again, that the place is not very pretty—if you are disturbed by some fairly horrific scenes, it is not the place for you!" warned Wohno.

Jim scanned the faces of the half-dozen men who had already come from the commissary with their clothing and equipment, saying, "You heard the colonel. Are you all sure you're ready for this?"

"Sir, three of us are U.S. Marine Corps combat vets. We've pretty much seen it all," answered a tall young man with a burr haircut. The others nodded agreement as they stacked their gear along the wall.

"Colonel, we appear to be ready when you are," said Jim, turning to face Colonel Wohno.

"All right, let's mount up," exclaimed the colonel, "We have work to do."

Entering the AC-130, they were amazed at the amount of equipment crammed into the fuselage. A number of monitors and control stations were manned by the young men who operated the onboard weapons.

"We have extra seats in several areas of the ship where your men can strap in. Find a seat and get in it. Tal, give them a hand," ordered Wohno.

The huge Black Airman with Master Sergeant's stripes arose from his seat at a console, sized up Alex out of the corner of his eye—and smiled, approvingly.

"Follow me, gentlemen," said Tal as he headed down the aisle, showing each man his seat. "When we reach cruise altitude about 15 minutes after takeoff, the seat belt lights will extinguish and you will be free to leave your seats and move around the cabin to observe our operations. Just don't touch anything," he warned.

After the seat belt lights went out, Jim, Alex and Eli walked up and down the aisle looking at the various weapon system monitors.

"Looks like this ship is really an aerial firebase," Jim remarked to one of the gunners.

"Yes, Sir, this is a modified AC130 Specter Gunship. We have 105mm howitzers, 40mm cannon, 30mm chain guns, .50 cal quad machinegun mounts and .30 caliber miniguns. All weapons mounts have precision targeting capability. When we aim at something and push the fire button, the very first round hits the target. In about two hours, you'll get to see us in action," the young man explained.

The time passed quickly. Soon, Colonel Wohno's voice came over the address system, "We are approaching the eastern portion of the combat area. There are infantry and tanks in the open dead ahead. Prepare to engage!"

In a flurry of engagements, the aircraft shuddered under the recoil of the howitzer, the pounding of the 40mm cannon and the scream of the chain guns, as tank after tank was left burning. Meanwhile, the.50 cal machineguns and .30 caliber miniguns riddled vehicles and infantry, as they strafed the battlefield below.

Then, as suddenly as it had begun, it was over.

"Cease fire. Secure your weapons," ordered Maag. "The enemy appears to have had enough fun for today. The seat belt light is lit. Prepare to land."

The big ship banked sharply to the right and Jim could hear the whine of landing gear and flap motors and the craft felt as though someone had thrown an anchor out behind it. The landing gear touched down on a very bumpy landing strip and the propellers immediately shifted into reverse pitch, which abruptly threw everyone forward into their seat belts. Finally, the aircraft came to a halt and the propellers coasted to a stop, as the cargo ramp came down.

"All right, visitors may deplane while we unload our cargo. I would suggest you lock and load your weapons and be on the alert for trouble, gentlemen."

advised Colonel Wohno. "We will introduce you to the local commander and let you get a good look at this area. If all goes as planned, we will take off again within an hour or two at the most. Some of my men will accompany you. They know their way around so do as they tell you," he continued.

Jim observed the looks of uncertainty on the faces of some of his companions and said, "All right, guys, you heard the man. Lock and load! Let's get a look at this place—it's what we came for."

As they walked down the ramp at the rear of the aircraft, the man in the front of the group stopped dead in his tracks and exclaimed, "Ugh!! What is that horrible smell?"

"Rotting corpses," their escort explained. "The enemy on this front, are basically barbarians. Quite often, they leave their dead on the battle field to cause unpleasantness and in the hopes of spreading disease to the defenders. The defenders try to bulldoze enemy corpses as much as possible but often times they come under tank, mortar or artillery fire, so many of the dead go unburied. Bubonic plague is endemic to this area, therefore picking up the dead by hand is out of the question. And besides, the antibiotics necessary to stem such a plague are not currently available. On the western front, the invaders at least have the decency to pick up their dead," their guide explained.

The little party stepped out into a scene of utter devastation. The land looked as though it had been plowed. Whatever vestiges of trees remained were mostly stumps, and a few shattered trunks and leafless branches. Here and there, groups of tattered tents huddled in the lee of sandbag revetments and the few men who were moving about appeared exhausted and depressed.

The defender's position occupied a flat area that stood about 25 feet above the surrounding plains. A deep creek bed ran along the east and north sides while the west and south sides backed up against a low mountain range.

About one hundred yards to the east of the grass airstrip, there was a line of sandbagged bunkers. Their escort motioned for them to proceed in that direction. Stepping into the largest of the bunkers, they were greeted by a man wearing camouflage with the eagles of a 'bird colonel' on his lapels.

"General Black, I presume. I'm Colonel Rawlins Johnson, U.S. Army Special Forces. I'm more-or-less the commander of this rag-tag outfit," the man said with a crisp salute, and offered his hand to Jim.

"Colonel Johnson, I presume you are aware that we are from the Eagle's Lair in Montana. We have been praying for you folks and we asked to come along with Wohno to see first-hand what kind of circumstances you were in," responded Jim warmly, returning the salute.

"Yes, Colonel Wohno has told me so much about you, Jim. I'm glad for your sake you're not stuck in this rat hole. This is a fairly defensible position and we've retreated about as far as we can. We were very low on supplies and manpower but with the good colonel's help, we've decided this is gonna be the start of Kaiser Bill's 'Waterloo'—or we're going to know the reason why!" Johnson stated emphatically.

"We're made up of several battalions of heavy artillery, a couple tank outfits, a battalion of Special Operations 'Snake Eaters' and a number of Army, Navy, Coast Guard, National Guard and Marine Corps people from back east we picked up along the way out. We've got about twenty thousand trained military people here and I guess probably another ten thousand civilians who've picked up the gauntlet and are fighting with us. I don't know the stats on the western front. We don't get much news from that side of the mountains. All I know is the commanding officer over there is a general whose name escapes me—a major general, I think," he continued matter-of-factly.

"The enemy seems to be fighting in a 'hit or miss' manner. They'll attack with tanks and infantry; we'll hit 'em hard and they'll retreat to their redoubt east of here. Then, we won't see them again for several days or a week until they decide to try it again. The folks over there don't seem to be Europeans, and I don't know just what they are trying to accomplish. They appear to be conducting a campaign of containment and attrition, rather than trying to take us on and go for broke! They haven't come out of any of our engagements so far with the upper hand, thanks to Wohno's people. As you have already seen, the enemy leaves a stinking mess out in front of our positions. We are very thankful indeed that we are upwind from the kill zone most of the time. The buzzards are healthy and well fed around here, though," he quipped sarcastically.

"All of the kids, most of the women, except for a few doctors and some nurses, have been evacuated since living conditions here are very primitive so we just make do with what we have. Were it not for Colonel Wohno's people, we wouldn't survive here for long. Medical care is only slightly better than it was in the middle of the nineteenth century so we have to depend on God and Wohno's Air Force people to evacuate our seriously ill and wounded," the colonel said soberly.

"Where do they take the evacuees?" Jim asked, trying to process the dire situation at hand.

"Don't know exactly. It's apparently an island somewhere, I understand. But, we never see them again, once they leave," he said absently. "By the way, General, if you'd like to look at our 'front yard,' step over here," Johnson announced, quickly recovering himself.

Jim stepped up to an observation port to view the battlefield. The debris of war was everywhere. A number of burning tanks and several enemy corpses were visible just beyond the bunkers, mute testimony to the effectiveness of the gunships' airborne artillery.

"Colonel Johnson, if I may, I'd like to ask you what you make of Colonel Wohno," Jim asked, abruptly changing the conversation. "Where is he based and where is he obtaining the supplies he brings in here? Frankly, he is a puzzle to us," Jim continued, "He and his gunship just showed up one day unexpectedly at our redoubt. Furthermore, he seems to be more or less in charge of a lot of things under the orders of a mysterious commander, whoever he is," confided Jim in a lowered tone, as he quickly surveyed the immediate surroundings, satisfied their conversation was not being monitored.

"Well, Jim, I don't know any more about Wohno and his associates than you do," Johnson said flatly, "He and his airborne artillery just showed up here one day as well, in the middle of a firefight and saved our bacon. He then began hauling in supplies by the plane-load and he's never quit! Frankly, I'm mystified myself . . . . but I'm sure not going to look a gift-horse in the mouth," responded Johnson with obvious gratitude.

"Colonel Johnson, Sir," interrupted a Marine Gunnery Sergeant, "we just picked up four enemy strays, who were apparently part of that last attack force, but went into hiding when their outfit withdrew. They were on our side of the wall when we first saw them, but we don't know how they got in. We checked for tunnels all along Sector 4 but there doesn't seem to be any. They've indicated they want to surrender and they seem to be very apprehensive about something. They keep looking around as if they expect the devil to jump out at them any minute!" snickered the sergeant.

"Get our interpreter in here and bring 'em in, Gunny. Let's see what they have to say," ordered Colonel Johnson warily.

As the four ragged combatants walked in with a trooper's rifle at their backs, they kept glancing around nervously as if they were looking for something.

"Do any of you speak English?" demanded Colonel Johnson.

One of the group just shook his head, "No."

The interpreter, a Captain Walker, strode into the room, very relaxed, and smiled at each of the prisoners.

"See if you can communicate with them, Captain," Johnson ordered wearily.

Walker spoke to them in Arabic and their faces lit up.

"Ask them what they want," Johnson demanded.

"They want to surrender, Sir, but they ask that we not turn them over to 'the giants,'" Walker answered, quite incredulously.

"Giants? What are they talking about?" Johnson demanded.

"Your guess is as good as mine, Colonel," came Walker's somewhat uncertain response.

"Hmmm . . . . Well, ask them why, when they attack, they never get closer than about 100 yards from our positions," barked Johnson.

Conversing with the men at length, the captain finally laughed and said, "I asked them about that, Sir. They said, 'Are you crazy? Nobody in their right mind would get too close to the giants. Those swords of theirs are murder!'"

Johnson and Jim exchanged uncertain glances.

"Makes you wonder what these guys have been smoking, eh Jim? Sergeant, put 'em in the stockade for tonight. We'll feed 'em and send 'em back tomorrow morning," grinned Johnson, intending to close the whole episode.

"Wait a minute, I have a hunch about this," exclaimed Jim, "Captain, ask them when and where they see these giants."

After a very animated conversation, Captain Walker said, "They say that they see them all over the place—along our revetments and on the roof of our command post. Apparently, some of their friends have been killed by them when they got too close to our positions. They say these giants are nearly ten feet tall, dressed in armor and carry huge swords. They explained that they are all terrified every time their commander has ordered them to attack us. He threatens to kill anyone whose refuses to attack, but of course he himself never joins them. They said they are tired of being threatened by both sides and since they believe we Americans and our allies are more merciful than their own people, they are requesting asylum."

"Ask them how they got in here," Colonel Johnson asked suspiciously.

Following another rather lengthy exchange, the Captain said, "They hoped they could throw themselves on the mercy of the giants, but they did not expect the giants to act as they did. When these guys approached the walls with a white flag, they said the giants smiled at them and opened a gate in the wall for them to enter."

"Well! This is really amazing!" mused Colonel Johnson, "Sector 4 extends from here to the southern end of our compound. There aren't any gates in Sector 4!" Rubbing his chin thoughtfully, he continued, "Looks like we have some mighty strange things going on around here, General. That explains why they always come just so far, retreat and then don't show up again for several days. I guess we won't be sending these guys back. We'll keep them here, if they behave."

"Colonel Johnson, are you aware that there is an observer out there about 1500 yards who is glassing your position?" asked Alex nonchalantly, peering through 'Ol Betsy's telescopic sight.

"Yeah, we've tried to get him for quite a while now—even tried taking him out with a 105mm howitzer, but he always manages to disappear before the rounds land," responded Johnson, with a twinge of irritation in his voice.

"Och, I'd be glad to punch a wee hole in that guy, if ya' don't mind, laddie!" snorted Alex, adjusting the scope.

"This is Alex MacIntosh, our most distinguished rifleman," said Jim.

"Yeah, and also our largest," quipped Eli with a grin.

"Be my guest, Alex! If you think you can take him out, by all means do. He's been calling in artillery fire on us with impunity for quite some time now." replied the colonel, his attention riveted on the big Scot.

Resting his Sharps buffalo rifle across two sand bags, Alex read the mirage and wind, carefully adjusted the sight, engaged the set-trigger, took careful aim and broke the shot amidst a cloud of white gun smoke.

"I've killed plenty o' big game at long range with 'Ol Betsy, here. The man's a bit smaller, but I think I can take him anyway. These big .50 caliber lead bullets are very resistant to wind drift, ya' know!" Alex stated with confidence.

Colonel Johnson peered through his Battery Commander's scope at the enemy observer, almost a mile away, who was brazenly sitting atop a mound of rocks looking through his binoculars. Several seconds later, Johnson erupted in a cheer, "You got him, Alex! Great shot! Man, we have professionally trained snipers here but I wish I had a shot like you around here all the same!" he exclaimed, slapping Alex's broad shoulders in grateful appreciation.

"Don't get any ideas, Colonel Johnson," chided a grinning Colonel Wohno as he strode into the room. "I'm under strict orders to return all these people to Montana when we leave in a few minutes. We put the ammo and other supplies where we usually do and we'll be back tomorrow with more. Also, we have some heavy transports coming in tomorrow morning, so we should have you in pretty good shape for supplies by week's end."

"Thanks! You're literally a life-saver, Wohno. We wouldn't survive long without you," said Colonel Johnson with unfeigned gratitude.

"We are happy to be of service to you, Sir! Okay, all Montanans back to the aircraft. We've wrapped up our business here and we'll be taking off in about fifteen minutes. I'm personally responsible for each of your men, General Black, so make sure they're all present and accounted for. Stragglers are not permitted," instructed Wohno, turning on his heel and disappearing in the direction of the airplane.

"I'll make sure of that, Colonel," Jim called after him.

"Colonel Johnson, I'm sorry to have to leave you now, but I'm sure we'll meet again soon. In the meantime, I wish you and your people Godspeed— here, there or in the air," said Jim as he shook the colonel's hand and bade him farewell.

15

THE PRISON CAMP

As Jim boarded the C-130, Colonel Wohno approached and sat down opposite him.

"General Black, we have a mission for you when we return to the Lair—if you and your men are willing to help us," he said in a low, even tone.

"And what might the mission entail?" asked Jim warily.

"There is a death camp about two hundred miles from the Eagle's Lair. It is run mostly by Syrian, Hezbollah and Iranian troops. They have been shipping in captured American civilians and military, especially Christians and Jews, and executing them in Sarin gas chambers just like the NAZIs," explained the Colonel, without emotion.

Blinding anger arose in Jim as he replied, "What? Consider it done, Colonel."

Wohno then briefly outlined the mission to Jim. "We require the assistance of your low-flying aircraft which have the firepower to significantly neutralize the enemy troops there and allow us to liberate the prisoners. The B-25s and P-47s with their heavy firepower are especially well suited for the job. We will be bringing in a company of American Special Operations troops from Colonel Johnson's command here, to clean up what's left of the opposition after your people finish their job. We will handle the evacuation and further care of the prisoners ourselves.

"The enemy," he continued, "will be conducting a mass assembly ceremony outside the compound. You will attack at precisely that moment. They will be unaware of your presence until it is too late for them to escape. Our gunships will lend our strategic fire power overhead a few seconds after you strike, if needed. The Spec Ops troops will drop in by helicopter, secure the compound and assist us in evacuating the prisoners, while your people return to the Eagle's Lair," concluded Wohno.

"As I just said, consider it done! We'll give those monsters something to think about. I doubt we'll have any trouble getting volunteer pilots and crews among my people," retorted Jim, vehemently.

Obviously pleased with Jim's response, Colonel Wohno answered, "Very good, Sir. The mission will be scheduled early in the morning, the day after tomorrow."

"Colonel, we will require resupply of our .50 cal ammo to ensure that our aircraft are adequately armed," said Jim.

"Certainly, no problem! We'll load 500,000 rounds or so on our cargo plane and bring it to the Lair tomorrow. How is your fuel supply?" he asked.

Jim thought for a moment and said, "I think we have at least 90,000 gallons left."

"Okay. We'll also bring in a tanker and top off all your aircraft and storage tanks. And incidentally, General, there's more where that came from if you need it," remarked Wohno, softening a bit.

Man!! Supplied with ammo and fuel, just like that.

Jim looked intently into Colonel Wohno's eyes and said sternly, "Colonel, I'm very curious. I'd like to know exactly where your base of operations is and where you get all your supplies and information."

Wohno grinned, "General Black, don't ask me questions like that. I am not authorized to divulge that kind of information at this time. Just rest in the fact that all your needs will be met, and then some, and your questions will be fully answered, all in good time, Sir."

With that, he stood abruptly, turned on his heel and strode quickly in the direction of the cockpit. "Alright! Attention everyone! Buckle up for takeoff. This grass strip is a little bumpy, so find a seat and strap in tight," shouted Wohno.

The takeoff was indeed rough and Jim winced with every bump and gopher hole that reverberated through the superstructure, until the big 4-engine ship mercifully rotated off and began its ascent.

Man, this thing is like a chiropractic clinic with wings!

That evening at the Lair, Jim assembled all the pilots to explain the situation and ask for volunteers.

"Will we volunteer?" shouted one the pilots, "You've gotta be kidding, General. I'm as angry as you are at the gall of these people. How about, it guys? Are you with us?"

The whole assembly erupted in cheers. "Yeah! Hoo-rah! We're gonna kick some booty," yelled several of the pilots and all were agreed on the mission.

"Okay, naturally I'll fly the 'Black Knight.' Are you B-25 pilots sure you're up to a combat mission like this?" queried Jim, half-jokingly.

"Yes, Sir! We flew A-10 Warthogs in Iraq. In principle, the '25s are not that much different to us. We'll be fine, General Black," came their strongly affirmative answer.

"Alright, I'm satisfied we're all familiar with our aircraft. Eli, I suppose you'll be flying that P-47 'Jug' of yours?" Jim asked jovially.

"You betcha, Boss! Love that flying tank!" he shot back.

"Fine, it's all settled then. See you all in the morning at 9:00am," Jim said as he dismissed the men.

Colonel Wohno arrived, as promised, early the next morning with several aerial tankers which dumped thousands of gallons of aviation gasoline of various octane ratings into the Lair's storage tanks. The C-130's crew unloaded many palettes of .50 cal machine gun belts. The remainder of the day was spent by Jim's technicians and mechanics checking, and rechecking, the aircraft and loading the machineguns on all the war birds with fresh supplies of ammunition.

At supper that night, John Hunnicut announced, "Everything is ready, General. Each aircraft is fueled and armed with as much ammo as it can carry."

Turning to Colonel Wohno, Jim asked, "When do we go, Colonel?"

"As I previously outlined, the enemy will be assembling in an open area outside the camp enclosure around 9:00am tomorrow morning. Takeoff from here should be no later than 8:00am, preferably a little earlier. We'll be here tomorrow morning by 6:00am for final instructions. At that time, we'll go over maps and aerial photos of the area, and the plan of attack. Sleep well tonight, men. See you all in the morning," the colonel called over his shoulder, as he walked toward his aircraft.

Morning came all too quickly for Jim. Awaking early and unable to sleep further, he rolled out of bed at 5:00am, shaved and donned his flight suit. Walking out to Hangar Number one, he checked all of the 'Black Knight's' fluid levels and gave the ship one last inspection for his own satisfaction before walking back to the Lodge to join the rest of the pilots for breakfast .

Promptly at 6:00am, Colonel Wohno's plane swooped in over the tree tops and touched down several minutes later. Both the colonel and Major Maag walked into the Lodge with a roll of maps and photos.

"Gentlemen, gather around, please, and I'll brief you on what we will be doing today," announced the colonel, placing the materials on the large library table in the middle of the great room.

As the men assembled around the table, the colonel pointed out the position of the prison camp, situated in a valley hemmed in by low hills.

"Since America theoretically has no air forces in operation, they're not anticipating an air attack, so their camp is not protected by antiaircraft missiles or guns. The enemy will be gathered here in this open field, on the west side of the enclosure. You will approach at tree-top level over this line of hills from the south. We will guide you from a point five miles to the south on to ensure that you are approaching the ridge and the target properly. Surface winds will be 35 knots out of the North and the enemy will not hear your aircraft until it is too late to escape. Your approach to the target area will be on a course heading of 345 degrees true, and must center on a very tall dead pine which, as you can see in these photos, stands out prominently from the surrounding forest on this barren ridge. I recommend you approach in fairly tight formation, placing the tremendous firepower of the two B-25s in the center with one P-47 on either side, followed toward the outside by one P-51 on each side to mop up the enemy's more fleet of foot. One P-51 and the P-38 will bring up the rear to fire on any targets of opportunity. The B-25 tail-gunners can also fire parting shots on enemy stragglers as they pass by. Be prepared to engage the target immediately and begin firing as you clear the ridge since, as you can see here, the target area is only a half mile from the ridge. After your initial strafing run, we will move in with our gunship for tactical support, followed by the choppers and the Spec Ops people, which are currently in place thirty miles south of the target area. Unless you receive an order from us to make another strafing run, you can head for home as soon as you clear the immediate target area. Any questions? Okay, we'll take off at 7:30am. Let's break a leg, gentlemen," smiled Colonel Wohno.

"Boys, each of you should thoroughly pre-flight your aircraft," ordered Jim. "You B-25 crews be sure to check over all your guns. You tail-gunners, make certain your weapons are ready, too. We have some time before we take off. Let's crank up these birds, taxi out to the test area on the tarmac one at a time, and test our shootin' irons so we know they're all working correctly and shooting exactly where we think they do! Don't forget to turn off your arming switches before returning to the parking area. I'd hate to have an accidental discharge before this excursion." he concluded.

The B-25s were the first to crank up and taxi out to the test area. The thunder from their fourteen .50 cal guns rattled the windows of the Lodge as a barrage of red-hot tracers flew down-range to the sighting targets. On turning around for the return to the parking ramp, the tail-gunners checked their guns as well. The P-38 followed suit. Although the rest of the flight were 'tail-draggers' and couldn't level on the targets, they simply taxied into position, fired a few rounds and returned to the parking ramp.

"Yup, we're ready to go, Chief," drawled Eli, excitedly.

"Alright, men, it's nearly 7:30. Let's mount up and be on our way. B-25s first," Jim ordered.

As the first aircraft taxied onto the runway, the radios crackled to life, "Attention, all aircraft! This is Colonel Wohno. After takeoff, we'll fly a heading of 76 degrees. That will bring us to a point between five and ten miles south of the target area. From there, you'll turn left, on my command, to a heading of 345, that's 3-4-5, degrees. Any necessary course corrections will be issued from there. Good hunting, boys! Wohno out."

The flight to the target area seemed all too brief. Even so, the rhythmic din of the engines had a mesmerizing effect on the pilots. Nevertheless, everyone bolted to attention when the radio crackled, "Attention! All aircraft turn left on my count . . . 5 . . .4. . .3 . . .2 . . .1 . . .Turn! That's it. You're on course. Arming switches on."

The 'Black Knight' took the right-hand P-51 position, as the formation lined up with the two B-25s in the center, the two P-47s on their wingtips and the two P-51s on the outside. The lone P-38 Lightning and one more mustang flew half a mile behind.

"Ridge coming up, boys," shouted Jim, "Y'all look alive now! Be ready to roll those noses down and rake these guys good! Here we go! Bonzai!"

As the ridge and the dead pine flashed by, the B-25s' noses dipped sharply and their gun sights lined up on a gathering of what appeared to be about 1,000 men.

"Fire!!" yelled Jim. The ancient airframes creaked and groaned under the hammering of the heavy .50 cal guns. Under the fiery hail of bullets, the field below erupted in a thick cloud of dust partially obscuring the pandemonium and bloodshed taking place within the ranks of the enemy. Some of them tried to run for cover toward the outside of the field and many were cut down by the P-47s and P-51s.

The tail-gunners in the B-25s saw what looked like yellow hail, as a torrent of brass cartridge casings from the machine guns flew beneath them in the bombers' slipstreams. As their aircraft passed over the target area, the tail gunners strafed what was left of the enemy ranks below. Within seconds, both the P-38 Lightning and the trailing Mustang finished the job the first wave had started.

"Hey, Colonel Wohno. How's about we come around and take down the main gate of the camp for you and strafe any targets of opportunity?" called one of the B-25 pilots.

"Fine," Wohno returned, "but aside from the gates, fire only on the buildings farthest to the east in the compound. The rest are all occupied by prisoners."

The B-25s banked sharply left in formation only 200 feet off the deck, came around and lined up on the main gate of the camp. One of the pilots said, "I'm gonna whack the main gate pylon with the 75mm. You go on and hit the east buildings and I'll follow."

"Roger that. Good luck!!"

The inmates of the camp had been observing with excitement the bloodletting and general mayhem among their captors. They cheered wildly on hearing the report of the 75mm howitzer, and the soft ripple of the round in flight, before it connected with the main gate supports collapsing the entire structure in ruins in a matter of seconds.

The B25s made several strafing runs on the farthest east buildings. The pilots were gratified to see several violent explosions in several of them from the tremendous torrent of fire from their guns.

"Woo-Hoo!! Don't know what *that* was, but something sure went 'boom'," crowed a voice over the open channel.

"You took out their power plant and the ovens, gentlemen," calmly explained Colonel Wohno.

"Ovens? You mean . . . . people ovens? Like in the Nazi death camps?" the voice asked incredulously.

"Yes. They were hoping to eventually outdo Hitler's SS," continued Wohno, flatly, "Go home now, boys. We can handle it from here on. The helicopters will be landing with the Spec Ops people in a few seconds. There aren't enough of the enemy still able to navigate to be a problem the paratroops can't handle. This day, about five thousand Americans will be freed because of you men. You've all done a fine job. We're very pleased," came his heartfelt commendation.

"Okay, boys," called Jim, "Colonel Wohno just gave us our walking papers. Secure your weapons and let's head for home. We've done what we came here to do—and then some."

There was considerable whooping and hollering over the radios on the way back to the Lair. Every man in the flight was elated at what they had accomplished—and gratified to have administered some payback to the despoilers of their country. They each prayed silent prayers for their countrymen being liberated at that very moment from the fate of a gruesome death at the hands of the wannabe SS Storm Troopers.

As the aircraft all taxied into Hangar Number One and shut down their engines, the rest of the refugee band at the Lair came running into the hangar, where there was a tumultuous celebration while the crews emerged from their cockpits and cabins.

"Hey, everyone!! We've got an elk and buffalo barbecue ready at the Lodge. Is anybody hungry?" yelled Alex.

The festive group picked up Alex bodily, all four hundred plus pounds of him, and carried him back to the Lodge to partake of his celebratory spread.

As Uri was about to shut down the radio shack, Colonel Wohno called. "I need to speak with General Black immediately," he demanded.

"General Black, Colonel Wohno is on the horn. Says he urgently needs to talk to you." Uri reported.

"What can I do for you, Colonel?" Jim asked politely.

"There has been a change in the situation at the southern combat zone. The Spec Ops people and their helicopters need a place to stop for a while. Would it be agreeable to you if they came to the Lair?" he asked.

"Well, we don't have much bunk space left here. Don't know how we'd accommodate them. We may be able to resurrect some of the old barracks latrines, but I don't even know if the old troop's quarters are livable," Jim answered hesitantly.

"The weather is pretty good right now. We'll be able to accommodate them in tents for a few days. We can take care of all those alterations and we'll be bringing in mess facilities and food supplies as well. Tomorrow morning our men will help do whatever else needs to be done," Wohno assured Jim.

"Okay, Colonel. They're certainly most welcome as far as we are concerned," Jim replied, relieved.

As the group joyously prepared to eat Alex' feast, the distant sound of helicopters diverted their attention. Over the rim of the canyon came a flight of helicopters with American flags emblazoned on their fuselages, followed by three flat black Apache Longbow gunships.

Colonel Johnson stepped out of the lead aircraft as it settled onto the tarmac, and approached Jim, who was standing on the front porch. "General Black, I'm sorry to barge in on you on such short notice. Colonel Wohno called us in mid-air that we would be delayed in returning to our area in the southern zone and that we should come here. We don't know exactly what is going on and he doesn't always give us a reason. Since his outfit seems to call the shots, I usually just say 'Yes, Sir' when he gives an order."

"Colonel Johnson, I'm sorry we have a shortage of accommodations for your troops," Jim said apologetically. "We're pretty full here and I'm not sure if we can resurrect the old barracks to make them habitable. We'll do the best we can for you. In the meantime you and your men can clean up a little in our Lodge's guest baths. Wohno says he'll provide mess and other facilities so I'm sure you'll be well taken care of. You can all camp over by the lake for now, if that is agreeable to you," Jim offered.

"Yes Sir, we'll be fine. Thanks for your hospitality! This place beats our place down south all hollow anyway. At least we don't get shot at here," Johnson replied graciously.

"By the way, Colonel," Jim asked, "where did you pick up the Apache gunships? I never saw them in your unit before."

"That was the strangest thing, Jim. Those boys had been on a training mission when the nuke attacks on our cities started. When they saw one of the mushroom clouds and couldn't contact their headquarters, they were able to refuel somewhere and diverted up into Montana here and finally landed. They've been hiding out for months in the forest where there were two large steel shop buildings they could get their choppers into for cover. They've been living off the land but had no communication with anybody.

They didn't know what the situation was and they decided to stay put, until they saw somebody who looked friendly. We just happened to fly over their location on our way up to the prison camp. As soon as they spotted us, they radioed us asking who we were and if they could join us," he explained.

"Naturally, we are very excited to pick up the Apaches," he continued, "As you know, because of their enormous firepower, our enemies all over the world call them 'The Angel of Death.' We didn't use them at the prison camp because there was no need. Your old war birds had already decimated the enemy staff, so all we had to do was go in and pick up the pieces. By the way, when we went into that camp I couldn't shake the feeling I'd been there before. As we were about to leave, one of my men directed my attention to the sign that had been above the gate. It read 'Arbeit Macht Frei.' Sent chills up my back."

"So what does that mean?" asked Jim.

"It's German. It means 'Work Makes Free.' It was on the sign above the main gate at the Nazi Dachau death camp in Poland during WWII," replied the colonel with a grimace, "I saw that sign myself when I visited Dachau some years ago. These swine were apparently intending to build more of these camps all over the U.S. No telling how many Americans they had already murdered here."

"Where are the death camp prisoners now?" Jim asked, concerned.

"Wohno's fleet landed and picked them all up. Don't know where they went, so I can't say. I'm not sure I want to know."

"Well, Colonel, you and your boys are invited to our big celebration here. I'm sure we'll have plenty of food for everyone. It's getting late in the day so you go ahead and set up your camp. Your people are welcome to use the public showers and rest rooms tonight," Jim said, gesturing toward the Lodge.

16

LOOKOUT BELOW

"All rise! Order in the courtroom, here come da judge! Wohno and Maag presiding," announced Ivan with a wink.

The four-engine gunship made a short approach without flying the normal traffic pattern. Although the engines were shut down several hundred yards out on the tarmac, the aircraft continued to roll, finally coming to a stop, amid the squeal of brakes, in front of Hangar Number One. Wohno and Maag hurriedly emerged and approached Jim, who was sitting in front of the doors with a group of the men.

"Crunch time, General Black," announced Colonel Wohno hurriedly, "You have 48 hours to prepare for your primary mission. This is the 'Big One' you've all been anticipating. As you may be aware, two of the cruise missiles you received previously have neutron warheads and two have 200 kiloton atomic warheads."

"Yes, we wondered about that," Jim answered, looking intently at Colonel Wohno.

"You'll mount one of each onto both B-29s. Your mission will be to simultaneously deliver the neutron weapons to the U.N. building and the main Chinese installation in Los Angeles. The conventional nukes will be targeted on the enemy fleets presently at anchor off both coasts. The flagships will be vaporized and all the other ships within close proximity will be thoroughly irradiated.

"Here is a list of coordinates for all your targets," Wohno announced.

"Time the departure of your B-29s so that they arrive off both coasts opposite their targets and the weapons detonate as close to the same time as possible. Is that a problem?" inquired Wohno with a slight smile.

"Nah! Sounds like a real blast to me, Colonel, sir," retorted Eli, grinning like a fox.

"Alright, Eli, alright, no comments from the peanut gallery!" laughed Jim, "Yes, we can do that, Colonel. The cruise missiles have a range of about 1000 miles. We can launch a little closer than that to the targets if necessary and still be well outside the blast zone," observed Jim.

"Good!" Wohno said, "The optimal time for weapon impact at the U.N. site will be day after tomorrow at 4:00pm Eastern Time. The U.N. target is the time-critical part of the mission. Weapons impact on the West Coast targets at 1:00pm, Pacific Time, is not as critical. Your aircrews won't have to 'get up with the chickens' to fly either mission. We will be in contact with you a little later, to check on the status of your preparations. In the meantime, we're going to return to the southern zone. If you need anything, let us know immediately," concluded Wohno, with a slight nod as he turned smartly on his heel and headed back to his waiting aircraft.

As Wohno's plane lifted off the runway, Jim turned to Eli and the rest of his staff and said, "Gentlemen, you heard the man. Let's get those missiles loaded and these aircraft ready to roll. Make certain the fuel tanks are topped off. I will pilot 'The City of New Orleans,' myself, and deliver the East Coast weapons. Arie, you will be my copilot and flight engineer. Eli will fly the 'City of Chicago,' to the West Coast. "Here are the coordinate lists for the primary and secondary targets for both aircraft, as well as emergency airfields. Get these punched into the onboard navigation computers right away, so they will coordinate with the satellites. That way, if the targets happen to move, the satellites will be able to track them and shift the impact coordinates in the missiles' guidance systems accordingly."

"Any questions? All right, let's shake a leg," Jim said with great anticipation.

Six hours later, just as Wohno's gunship whooshed in overhead, Eli reported to Jim that both ships were ready to go.

"Have everyone on the flight crews report to the multimedia center in fifteen minutes, Eli," Jim ordered.

As the flight crews assembled, Wohno and Maag walked in as Jim stepped to the microphone. "Gentlemen, our satellite sensors tell us that winds aloft at 30,000 feet over most of the U.S. are minimal. If these conditions persist tomorrow, I will take off at 8:15am, and, assuming a cruise speed of 225 miles per hour, should reach my launch zone on time. We'll be in the air about eleven hours round-trip. Eli will take off at 11:30am and will have a much shorter trip. We will plan to launch our missiles about 500 miles from our closest targets. Each ship is loaded with approximately 8,000 gallons of gas which should get us back home unrefueled. If not, we can gas up at our emergency airstrips. Don't take any unnecessary chances with your fuel tanks—I'd kind of like to keep you guys around, as well as these beautiful old birds, when this is all over.

"The transponders on the B-29s are programmable and we will impersonate the invader's propeller-driven cargo aircraft. Maintain radio silence at all times. Any necessary communication should take place only over our secure satellite channels but keep even that chatter to a minimum. B-29 engines are rather fragile compared to modern aircraft engines so let's baby them and not try to push the envelope beyond a 225 mph cruise. We can't let an engine failure ruin your whole day," laughed Jim.

"Allow me to interject some things at this point, General Black," interrupted Wohno, stepping to the microphone. "Gentlemen, I can assure you, on good authority, that the winds aloft will remain calm and no one will detect the presence of your aircraft anywhere along your flight paths. You will all return safely."

Jim made inquiring eye contact with Wohno, but neither one said anything.

Hmmm. . . . He's never been wrong before. This guy has got to have some kind of major connections. Better just shut up and trust him on this one.

Collecting himself in his thoughts and clearing his throat, Jim croaked, "Okay, does anyone have any questions?"

The wide-eyed crews shook their heads "No" in unison.

"Thanks, Colonel. I believe we are all ready to roll tomorrow morning," Jim exclaimed.

"Yes, I believe you *are* ready, General Black. We'll be here at 7:30am to see you off tomorrow morning. Get some sleep tonight. Tomorrow will be a long day," advised Wohno.

Jim spent a restless night repeatedly rehearsing the upcoming mission in his mind. Rolling out of bed at 6:20am, he ate a light breakfast and was just pulling on his flight suit just as Eli walked in, at 6:30am, similarly attired.

"What're you doing up so early, Eli? You're not due for hours yet," questioned Jim.

"Ah, who can sleep? I can't wait to get this show on the road, Jim," Eli answered bluntly.

The two were interrupted by the roar of turbo-props overhead.

"Well, there are Wohno and Maag right on cue," observed Jim, admiring the colonel's penchant for punctuality.

As their aircraft came to a stop on the tarmac, Colonel Wohno and Major Maag exited quickly and strode into the flight shack.

"Well, old friend, let's go preflight our birds, kick the tires, be ready to light the fires and make sure everyone else is ready to go, shall we?" Jim said lightheartedly, slapping Eli on the back.

The two men, together with Jim's crew, Colonel Wohno and Major Maag in tow, walked out to Hangar Number Three and proceeded with their preflight inspections.

"Will you look at that ground fog this morning?" sighed Jim, "Hope we can see the runway center stripe."

"You won't have any problem with that," Wohno confidently assured him.

At 8:05am, everyone shook hands and Eli said, "Well, Jim, as our friends in the Luftwaffe would say, '*Hals und beine bruch*'—break a leg, Ol' Man!

Jim bear-hugged Eli, as Arie and the crew climbed aboard to take their stations. A number of volunteers were already walking the propellers through their arcs.

At 8:10am, engine number three began to crank and all four engines were soon up and running. With the entire company of exiles watching from the tarmac outside the hangar, 'The City of New Orleans' came rolling onto the ramp, her engines galloping and loping at idle. She appeared to be floating up to her belly in ground fog, with bright sunshine on her back. The eagle with a fist-full of arrows and the Stars and Stripes on her rudder shone brightly in the morning sun. Over the hangar's PA system came the strains of a familiar tune with new lyrics: "'Good mornin' America, how are ya?' I said 'Don't ya know me? I'm your native son?' I'm the plane they call 'The City of New Orleans' and I'll have flown three thousand miles when my day is done . . . '" Needless to say, there was not a dry eye in the band of refugees.

As the venerable B-29 taxied out, the ground fog was dissipating a bit over the runway. Jim gunned each engine to check the magnetos then rolled the nose wheel onto the center line of the runway and slowly firewalled the throttles as Arie monitored the engines' vital signs during the takeoff roll. The forests rang to the thunder of the big engines as she lifted off the runway and disappeared over the rim of the canyon.

"Okay, everybody, "drawled Eli, "Show's over for a while. Let's go watch the satellite monitors."

Colonel Wohno turned and bade the company farewell. "We'll keep an eye on your boys—from a respectable distance, of course—just to make sure there's no trouble."

"But how . . . . . ?" asked Eli.

"Don't ask. Just trust us," was Wohno's mysteriously ominous answer.

"OK, man! They're in your hands, Colonel," Eli said blandly, turning to hide tears and shrugging as he turned his attention to the satellite monitors.

The AC-130 rocketed off the runway and flew in the direction of the departed B-29.

Thirty-five minutes later, Jim brought the 'City of New Orleans' level at 30,000 feet, set the trim, adjusted the engine cowl flaps and power settings. Outside, the air temperature hovered at -65 degrees Fahrenheit and Jim thanked God for the pressurized, heated cabin.

If this was a B-17 or B-24, we'd be dressed in wool-lined sheepskin and still freezing our tails off right now. Those poor souls who flew those things in WWII were men indeed.

"Sir, I think we have company behind us," announced the tail-gunner. "Looks like a C-130."

Jim smiled. *Must be Wohno! It's good to know someone is watching over us.*

The hours seemed to drag by. Lost in the hypnotic drone of the engines, Jim was startled when the navigator announced that they were within 600 miles of their targets.

"OK, Mr. Bombardier," announced Jim jovially over the intercom, "Let me know what you need and when. Get your birds ready to fly."

"Yes, Sir. We'll be ready to launch at 500 miles from Ground Zero."

Suddenly, the reality of the situation struck Jim as he noticed the palms of his hands were perspiring. Twenty minutes later, the navigator announced, "OK, we're 500 miles from our targets and ready to launch, Sir."

The bombardier reported, "We are go for launch."

"You may fire when ready, Gridley," said Jim with a grin.

The 'City of New Orleans' lofted slightly as the weight of the first missile left her airframe.

"One away, Sir," announced the bombardier.

Thirty seconds later, came the announcement, "Two away, Sir."

A few moments later, the bombardier announced "We have engine start on both missiles, the birds are flying strong and on course, Sir."

"Okay. Keep tabs on 'em. Boys, our job is done here and we're going home," announced Jim as he banked the old warrior sharply into a 180 degree turn and headed west. In the distance, he saw Wohno's ship slip into a cloud bank and he smiled again.

"What's our fuel look like, Arie?" Jim asked casually.

"We have about 5,000 gallons left. Should be plenty to get us back home and then some. We're looking good, Jim! All engine vitals are A-Ok. The Pratt & Whitneys are running like Swiss watches."

An hour later, the bombardier came over the intercom. "Sir, I have the birds on their nose TV. The neutron missile is now snaking its way between the sky scrapers of New York City and I can see the U.N. building dead ahead. Here we go . . . . impact! Bulls eye! Okay, the nuke is hot on the trail of the naval target—just cleared the waterfront. We're coming up on the naval armada and . . . . yup, there's their flagship. Well . . . there was their flagship. What's left of their flotilla is going to glow in the dark tonight. Mission accomplished! We did well, General!" crowed the bombardier, obviously elated with their success.

Jim picked up his secure satellite phone and called Eli. "We just plastered our targets. How's it going with you?"

"Ditto here, Jim. The west coast gang is sporting a nuclear suntan. Their shore installation is *kaput* and their fleet is gonna glow tonight. We're headed home."

"Great! Looks like Wohno and Maag made good on their promises. We'll see you soon. Bon voyage!"

"Uh . . . Jim. . . . I'm afraid we have a problem," announced Arie warily, "Number Two's oil pressure is dropping and Number Four has elevated cylinder-head temps on six jugs."

"Keep a sharp eye on everything, Arie," cautioned Jim, "B-29s are famous for engine troubles."

Another hour elapsed before Arie yelled, "Jim, we gotta shut down Number Two—NOW! Its oil pressure is dropping into the basement!"

Jim intoned, "Feathering Number Two," and pulled Number Two's throttle to idle-cutoff and feathered the prop as he adjusted the power settings on the three remaining engines. "Well, boys, pray hard, we're still 900 miles from home."

For the next two hours, Arie watched the gauges and held his breath.

"Oy, vey! We have a fire in Number Four," said Arie, his voice cracking with strain.

Jim shut down Number Four engine as Arie activated the fire extinguishers.

"Hit it again, Arie, she's still burning," Jim yelled, "If that fire gets through the firewall, we're in big trouble."

Arie operated the fire equipment twice more, then checked his gauges.

"Okay, Jim, the temp in the engine nacelle is back to -65°F. Whew! Thank God, thank God, the fire is out!" announced the very relieved Israeli.

"Okay, let's everybody just pray Number One and Number Three hold together for the next 400 miles," advised Jim.

Everyone was on pins and needles for the next hour praying and hoping the old warrior would get them home. Suddenly, Number One engine began to run erratically.

"Boys, looks like Number One is going to die on us. I can't control the RPM. Governor must be going bad. I'm going to have to shut it down. We're still an hour from home and now we're steadily losing altitude. Lord, please get us home in one piece," prayed Jim.

As Number One's propeller coasted to a stop and feathered, Jim began a running battle with Satan, binding him and commanding him to get his hands off God's property. Number Three was putting out almost 125 per cent of rated horsepower—Jim feared the old engine couldn't stand that for very long.

After what seemed an eternity, and with only a thousand feet of altitude remaining between the landing gear and the runway, 'The City of New Orleans' locked into the instrument approach beacons at the Eagle's Lair and skimmed in just above the tree tops on the canyon rim. Jim managed to get the gear down and locked as he set her down softly and rolled out.

He breathed a prayer of thanksgiving as he moved the remaining throttle to idle-cutoff and switched off the master and avionics.

Jim and his compatriots exited the ship and walked around the nose, looking up in awe at Number Three as she was singing and cracking from the heat.

"This old girl earned her salt today, boys!" said Jim.

Jim, Arie and the rest of the crew slowly made their way, somewhat unsteadily, to the Lodge where Eli and his crew were already celebrating.

"Yee-haw, Boss, we did it!" crowed Eli, as the returning warriors entered the building.

"Well, it certainly would appear that way, thank God. But we'll have to wait for the other shoe to drop. The 'City of New Orleans' came close to not making it back at all—we literally came in on a wing and a prayer with just one engine running. Let's see what happens next," cautioned Jim, "We should know something by tomorrow. Incidentally, the A&P boys have their work cut out for them—my mount will need to have all four engines replaced and I want her airworthy ASAP just in case she's needed for something else."

"Like what?" asked Eli warily.

"I'm not really sure. Wohno didn't elaborate on anything after we delivered the missiles. So, we'll just have to wait on them to tell us what comes next. We can watch the satellite monitors, but that's about as far as it goes for right now, so I'd just suggest everybody chill out for a while," cautioned Jim.

Retiring to the library with his Bible, planning to do some meditating, Jim was interrupted by John Glass.

"General Black, I'm sorry to disturb you, Sir, after your grueling mission, but my friends and I have a gut feeling that we need to go do some serious skulking over east of here, towards the mountains where you destroyed the prison camp," John said soberly.

"Are you sure, John? I mean, you're certainly free to do that, but I'd hate to have you out there tromping around the boonies for nothing," Jim returned, with a heightened sense of curiosity.

"Rest easy, Sir, we're old hands at back-country scouting. Actually, General, we feel like we've lain around here so long that we're all starting to get just a bit rusty. Frankly, we think you could use some boots on the ground out there. Those satellites are great, but even they can't tell you everything," responded the big Sioux.

"Well, okay John, we'll provision your party. Say, we have extra maps and several sets of military pack radios, which have about a two hundred mile range. There are also some extra satellite phones in the communications center which work with our birds. You'll be able to stay in close contact with Ivan and Uri while you're out there," offered Jim.

"Thank you, Sir!! We'll get our animals ready this evening and leave tomorrow morning at first light," John responded excitedly.

After Glass and his friends scurried off to check on their horses and equipment, Jim began to relax with his Bible. He was almost dozing off when he was rudely awakened by Uri and Arie whooping and hollering, as they burst into the quiet library.

"Hey, what has got you two so fired up?" demanded Jim, groggy and more than a little irritated at this intrusion on his solitude.

"Boss, you won't believe this but the invasion fleets have even more problems right now," laughed Uri, barely able to contain himself.

"So what is going on, boys?" Jim asked, now fully awake and giving them his undivided attention.

"Okay! When Kaiser Bill's satellites were knocked out by that solar storm a while back, he couldn't keep track of our nuclear-powered navy. I just spoke to a couple of our battle group commanders who said they've been constantly on the move hiding out from the old boy's scouts. Apparently they've been pretty successful because right now, what's left of both our Atlantic and Pacific fleets are turning a whole lot of enemy naval assets into fish habitat. Bill's buddies never saw them coming" whooped Arie.

"That is great news indeed," grinned Jim, "Now, if you guys don't mind, I'd really like to take a nap in peace," he winked, signaling them to leave.

"Oops! Sorry, Boss, next time we'll knock" said Uri apologetically, "Come on Arie, let's get back to our monitors."

17

THE WORM TURNS

Several days had passed since the Sioux scouting party had departed and Jim was just starting to unwind, when Ivan breathlessly burst into his office in the Lodge.

"General, John Glass just radioed me from over east of here somewhere. We've got big trouble headed our way. You better talk to him," he said.

What now? Boy, will I be glad when I can finally unwind for more than a day!!

Within moments, Jim picked up the mike in the radio shack and said rather testily, "John, this is General Black. What's going on out there anyway?"

"Sir, we encountered an enemy convoy last night, headed in your direction. We infiltrated the camp after dark where they had bivouacked and eavesdropped on their officers talking in the command post. It sounded like they know your location and are on the way to take you out. If I were you, I'd at least post a lookout up on the East Ridge and prepare to possibly evacuate the Lair."

"Nuts!" was Jim's instant reply, "We can't evacuate! Just where would we go?" Regaining his composure, Jim asked, "Exactly what are we facing, John? Give me some exact details."

185

"There are about four hundred men and approximately forty vehicles. They're currently camped near White Sulphur Springs, Montana, on Highway 12, which puts them approximately 120 miles from you. They have six main battle tanks on transporters which are lucky to make 20 mph in the mountains, so that might buy you some time. "

"Okay, let us know when they start to move again. Thanks for the 'heads up', John. Black out," Jim said, hanging up the mike and hurrying out of the control room.

Jim summoned all the pilots and staff to the great room. As he laid out maps of the area east of the Lair on the library table, he began, "Gentlemen, we have a problem!" Clearing his throat, he continued in a very serious tone, "Our Sioux scouts have just reported to me that there is something like a battalion of invaders just east of here, supported by tanks, apparently on their way here. If they are able to locate us, we are in real trouble. Has anyone heard from Wohno recently?" he asked, looking at Uri and Ivan.

"Nope, not a thing, General, I tried to call him several hours ago, even before this came up. Seems like he's occupied elsewhere right now," responded Ivan.

"Well, unless Colonel Wohno's people show up with their gunships, the only major weapons we have here are our old war birds, and the Spec Ops people with their choppers. We may very well be on our own. I'm starting to suspect the reason that Colonel Johnson's group was diverted to the Lair, a while back, was no accident. Now, the enemy is not going to drive their tanks very far without having a huge store of fuel on tap. Because of the mountainous terrain between Highway 12 and the Lair," said Jim, pointing to the spot on the map, "The only logical, practical route in here will be to turn off Highway 12 and come up this gravel road to the north and east of the Lair. The road comes through a long mountain pass about ten miles east of here."

"I figure a convoy of forty trucks will stretch from one end of the pass to the other. If we can time it just right, we can close both ends of the pass simultaneously and seal up the convoy and their troops in a box canyon. At the very least, the Apache gunships can target the front and rear trucks to totally hem them in. Then, it'll be like shooting fish in a barrel. What do you all think?" Jim asked.

"Sounds like a plan to me," agreed Eli, his eyes dancing at the thought of the coming enagement.

"Say, by the way General, I just remembered something we forgot to tell you," volunteered one of the mechanics. "Some time ago, the boys and I were out bumming around the grounds when we stumbled across an old bomb dump over on the other side of the base. The door was locked tight and none of our keys fit so we never found out what was in it. It's hidden in a thicket of aspens which have grown up over and around the mound. It might be nothing, but then again with all the unexpected things we've found on this ol' airbase there just might be something useful in there."

"Hmm . . . . bomb dump, huh?" he said rubbing his chin, "Well, let's just have a real quick look. We don't have much time, so lead the way, gents," Jim declared, intrigued by this interesting disclosure.

I've seen 'bomb dumps' on WWII U.S. Army Air Corps bases before and they generally had heavy reinforced concrete walls, ceilings and floors with several feet of earth bermed up over and around the structure just in case something set off the munitions.

On reaching the old dump site, the men cleared a path through the trees, while the mechanics drilled the locks on the rusty steel doors and opened them with pry bars. Once inside the musty old structure, the entourage gazed in amazement at what lay before them. Eli and Jim walked up and down inside the old vault taking stock of its contents.

"I count at least two hundred five-hundred-pound bombs, along with a stock of both quick and time-delay fuses. Everything looks good. They've all been very well preserved in here. This old base is just full of surprises. The five-hundred-pounders are the B-25's stock-in-trade. They can drop 'em one at a time or a whole bomb bay load at once," exulted Jim.

"How do we know all this stuff is any good, Jim?" queried Eli, cautiously.

"We don't! There's no way to test it on this short notice. But munitions, quite like small arms ammo, quite often is good for nearly a century. This looks good so we'll just have to trust the stuff to go 'boom' when it hits," concluded Jim, with a reassuring grin and pat on the back.

"Eli, have the armorers load the B-25s with maximum loads of these 500 pound bombs with quick fuses, 75mm howitzer shells and all the machinegun belts they can stuff in that bird. Also, load the 'City of Chicago's bomb bay full of these five-hundred-pounders with quick fuses. Stock the fighters with ammo and get everything gassed up. We're going to give our playmates out there something to think about. Wohno is conspicuously absent right now and I have a feeling he knows something we don't about all this," concluded Jim, wryly.

Returning to the Lodge, the men gathered once again around the map-laden library table, as Jim laid out his plan. "All aircraft will launch as soon as the convoy is within five miles of the east end of the mountain pass. Then, we'll lay low, just below the skyline, and wait for them to enter the pass. By striking the mountainsides all along the length of the pass with five hundred pound bombs, we'll bury at least the leading and trailing trucks in an avalanche and effectively hem in the entire convoy. The B-29 will destroy as much of the convoy as possible by laying down a bomb pattern the length of the road. The B-25s will then follow up by dropping whatever they have left in their bays on the convoy and then join with the fighters to strafe whatever is still moving. Any remaining light armored vehicles can be engaged by the P-38's 20mm cannon. If we encounter any other real tough targets, the Apaches can take them out with their 30mm chain guns. At that point, Colonel Johnson's Spec Ops people will chopper in and mop up. That should do it! What do you all think? All present nodded in agreement, including Colonel Johnson.

"It's the only thing we can do, General. We don't have a lot of options" said one of the B-25 pilots.

"Okay, Arie, can you handle a B-29 with just a skeleton crew?" Jim asked hesitantly.

"Sure, Jim. With that 29's updated weapons systems, as Eli would say, 'I can flick a fly off a mule's ear.' That bombardier we used on the east coast mission is really good, so I'll use him. But what are you planning to do yourself, Jim? I'm a little concerned about you getting shot at," said Arie, concern for Jim's safety registering on his face.

"I'll fly the 'Black Knight' and Eli will take the P-47 T-Bolt he's been flying. The others will follow suit. You know the drill for laying down the bombs on the convoy so I'll leave that in your very capable hands, Arie.

Get your ship off the runway first. Achieve altitude west of the Lair. Wait until you hear my order to attack before you make your bomb run. At 10,000 feet, you should be out of the range of any heavy machineguns and anti-aircraft guns," Jim instructed.

"Sounds good, partner," Arie replied confidently.

"Okay, everybody get as much rest as possible now and be ready to move out as soon as we hear from Ivan," said Jim.

Around 2:00pm that afternoon, Eli having informed Jim that all aircraft were loaded and ready for action, then positioned himself alongside Arie at the satellite monitors. Throughout the rest of the day and well into the evening, they watched the convoy as it sat in a roadside park, with nothing moving.

Early the next morning, John Glass radioed Jim. "The enemy convoy is just now preparing to move. We're on our way back to you."

"Wonder why they sat still so long, John? I thought they'd be on top of us by last evening," remarked Jim.

"Well, Sir, we were sneaking out of their camp and on our way out, we were accidentally blocked by their sentries. We had no choice but to take them out. I think that is what unnerved the whole outfit," John explained with a guffaw.

"Why would that have upset trained soldiers?" Jim asked bluntly.

"I guess finding your men dead with Sioux war arrows sticking in them is a bit unusual, General. I think they feared they were about to be attacked by thousands of wild Plains Indians and suffer the fate of General George Custer! So, they decided to hunker down and stay put for a while. I don't think most of those guys have ever seen combat before." John answered drily.

"You've got to be kidding," Jim hooted in disbelief, "You actually shot them with arrows?" he asked, flabbergasted.

"Yes Sir! Remember, I told you we are trained in the use of the Sioux's ancient weapons? Arrows don't make much noise, ya know!"quipped the scout.

"Well, I'm sure glad you guys are on our side!" laughed Jim, "Hey, thanks for the help. We have a little surprise of our own planned for our new guests, so get back as soon as you can. See you guys later," was Jim's final remark.

Some hours later, from his post at the monitors, Eli crowed, "Well! well! well! Jim, you were right. Here's our invasion force. They've just turned off the blacktop onto the gravel road. They're about twenty miles east of the pass. Whooeee! Here's something I can't believe: Except for our immediate area, this whole region for hundreds of miles around is just socked in tight by weather. Those guys are not going to get any air support and we shouldn't have any problem at all operating our little air force!"

"Ivan," Jim ordered, "I want you to man the satellite monitors for us and give us radio progress reports. Our code name will be 'Falcon 1'. When the enemy's lead vehicle is nearing the western end of the pass, say 'Falcon 1, Backfire!' Then, we will commence our attack from south to north. Any questions, boys? Okay, saddle up, let's go light the fires! And God speed to all!" shouted Jim as he slipped into his flight suit.

The mission looked like something out of an old WWII movie as they started their engines and roared off the 200' wide runway, with the 'City of Chicago' in the lead and the fighters close behind in pairs. Clawing for altitude, Arie expertly guided his ship to the west, while the fighters and the B-25s headed southeast, hugging the terrain to stay as much out of sight as possible until the trap was sprung.

As the enemy truck convoy neared the western end of the long mountain pass, Ivan radioed, "Falcon 1, Backfire!" The B-25s came boiling over the hills and attacked both ends of the pass simultaneously. The 500 pound bombs worked exactly as Jim had hoped they would, bringing down thousands of tons of rocks, trees and earth, totally burying the lead and trailing vehicles of the convoy. Moments later, the 'City of Chicago' roared in overhead laying down a precise pattern of bombs along the centerline of the road, which decimated most of the remaining vehicles. Four of the six tanks received direct hits and another was destroyed by a 500 pounder from a B-25. The sole remaining tank was tipped off its transporter upside down on its turret by the impact of a 500 pound bomb.

As the B-25s and fighters raked the convoy with machinegun fire, one of the B-25 pilots radioed, "We just took several rounds through the fuselage from a vehicle backed into that south dry wash."

The offending vehicle, an armored half-track with a twin 23mm automatic gun mount, had managed to maneuver into a side draw and was firing on Jim's little air force. Pulling the 'Black Knight' around, Jim attacked the vehicle, braving heavy fire from its guns. As he banked sharply into a climbing turn and passed over the vehicle, Jim heard *chunk, chunk, chunk, chunk* and the 'Black Knight' shuddered as shell holes appeared in the left wing and the Rolls-Royce Merlin engine began releasing a stream of engine coolant past the canopy.

"Black to flight! Mayday! Mayday! Mayday! I just took a direct hit in the engine! I'm heading for home, boys! Get that P38 or one of the Apaches around there and shut that half-track down," he ordered sternly.

Jim again pulled the 'Knight' into a climbing turn to gain as much altitude as possible while he could before leveling off at about four thousand feet above the forest.

"I'm right behind you, Jim," Eli radioed, reassuringly, "You're leaking coolant pretty badly. You must have taken a major hit in the water jacket."

Jim was several miles from home with the runway at the Lair in view when the engine temperature gauge pegged in the red zone and the engine began to falter.

"It's no good, Eli," Jim radioed calmly. "I'm not going to make it. If this engine seizes or catches fire, things are going to go south in a hurry. I can't take a chance on crashing inside the Lair and starting a forest fire or hitting a building. And I'm sure not going to attempt a belly landing."

Jim spotted a large expanse of rolling grassland about a mile to the north. Kicking full right rudder and full right ailerons, he managed to turn the crippled fighter onto a northerly heading.

"I'm gonna bail out, Eli. Break right so you don't run over me," Jim ordered abruptly.

Jim slid the canopy back and unlatched his harness.

"Goodbye, old girl!" he said, fondly patting the instrument panel as though the sleek fighter were a beloved pet.

Rolling the 'Black Knight' over onto her back, he expected to free fall from the cockpit, but was horrified to discover that something was holding him back, suspended about two feet off the seat. Being completely out of reach of the controls and unable to extricate himself, he was being violently buffeted in the slipstream.

Must be a strap or something fouled in the seat. Can't reach or feel anything holding me. Lord, help me!

For several seconds, Jim struggled, hanging suspended half in and half out of the cockpit. Suddenly, the engine seized, the propeller snapped to a dead stop and he was enfolded in a deathly silence. There was not a sound except for the rush of air past the airframe. It seemed as though he was in a vacuum and time stood still. Finally, something snapped and he fell free of the cockpit. As the Knight's rudder flashed past, he pulled the rip-cord and the parachute blossomed above his head with an authoritative tug. Jim breathed a sigh of relief and a fervent prayer of thanks. Moments later, the doomed fighter expired in a huge ball of flames as it struck the ground.

Eli was immediately on the radio to Ivan and the rest of the flight team yelling, "The 'Black Knight' just went down two miles east and a mile north of the eastern end of runway three-zero. General Black is out, his chute has opened and he appears to be okay. I'll fly cover for him."

Jim had the wind knocked out of him as he hit the ground hard, bouncing over several low hillocks as the wind dragged his chute. Recovering, he was finally able to stand, unhitch his chute and take stock of his situation as Eli's P-47 roared by overhead, and began to circle the downed pilot.

Keying his helmet mike, Jim said, "Ivan, how soon can you get a Humvee out here to pick me up?"

"Not for a while, Chief. There are some huge trees down to the east where the access road cuts through the rim of the canyon. Our guys say they can't get through, but they'll get a bulldozer up there and clear out the jam as soon as possible. Sorry, Sir!"

"Eli, how are Johnson's people doing on the convoy?" Jim asked, diverting attention from his personal predicament and focusing on the mission's progress.

"They're engaged in firefights with a bunch of survivors. Don't know how long it'll take to break them loose, Jim," he answered.

"Well, I'm not going to stand around out here hobnobbing with coyotes and prairie dogs, so I'm going to start walking toward the rim of the canyon," Jim announced, a bit irritated, "If nothing else, I'll meet the boys on the other side of the ridge. Eli, how's your fuel holding up? Are you gonna be able to cover me?" he asked.

"Got several hours of fuel left, my friend, but I'll get someone to relieve me if I run dry. The aerial shooting is mostly over to the east of here and I'll let the rest of the boys land and refuel. We'll keep an eye on you, Jim," came the comforting reply.

An hour or so later, Jim reached the escarpment leading to the nearly vertical wall of the canyon which surrounded the Eagle's Lair. He clambered through thick underbrush to the top of the canyon wall. Then, straightening up on level ground and walking about fifty feet into the trees, Jim was greeted by a deep-throated growl in the brush to his left. Freezing in his tracks, he slowly turned to face a pack of eight of the largest timber wolves he had ever seen. The closest wolf, with ears laid back, teeth bared and hackles up, made two stiff-legged bounds toward Jim. There was no question what he had in mind. Jim instinctively reached for his handgun, but the weapon was not in its holster.

Drat! Must have lost it when I bailed out. What a time to lose my sidearm. Oh Lord, please help me. These pups must weigh over 200 pounds apiece and they look like they mean business.

"Eli, I got wolf trouble, man! They're planning on having me for lunch," Jim spoke into his headset in a low, measured tone.

"Yeah, I see them, but I can't fire too close or I might hit you," Eli answered, "I'll fire into the trees on your right and we'll see if that scares them off."

The P-47's guns riddled the pines several hundred feet to the west. The wolves yipped, jumped and milled around apprehensively as Eli fired but seemed otherwise generally unimpressed.

"Sorry, Jim, those pooches are just too sticky," Eli responded apologetically.

Jim deftly drew his razor-sharp survival knife and faced the head wolf. "Okay, Bud. You get too close and I'll slice you from ear to ear," Jim threatened, looking the wolf in the eye.

Immediately, Jim noticed the entire wolf pack unexplainably shifting their focus upward as though they were now concentrating on something above his head. The wolves' all laid their ears back, ducked their heads, raised their hackles and bared their teeth, like misbehaving but defiant puppies expecting to be swatted with a newspaper.

Jim kept one eye on his immediate adversary while glancing quickly first one way and then the other, using his peripheral vision to identify what had captured the wolves' attention, but saw nothing.

Now what is it that's behind me? A bear? Or a maybe big cat? Whatever it is, it can't be much worse than what's in front of me. I'll just trust You, Lord, and keep my eye on these really bad boys.

Suddenly, a loud voice behind him with a positive air of authority shouted "Jim, duck!" As Jim instinctively followed orders, the menacing wolf reared up on his hind legs like a dog begging for table scraps. From somewhere over the top of Jim's head, something sliced through the air with a *"swoosh"* at tremendous velocity, punctuated by a metallic *"ting."*

Jim was sprayed with blood as the wolf's head was severed from his body and went rolling down an incline. The rest of the shocked pack instantly turned tail and disappeared into the forest, yelping like whipped pups. Jim could only gaze open-mouthed at the quivering body of his late adversary. Turning about cautiously to see what, or whom, had saved him, Jim was dazzled by the brightness of the being there before him. Standing silently not ten feet away, shining like the sun, was a flaxen-haired warrior, who appeared to be a good two feet taller than Alex. The warrior smiled and sheathed his broadsword which was in the process of cleansing itself of blood in a small cloud of smoke. Jim's deliverer was dressed from head to foot in golden armor and helmet, and wore a white cloth over-garment embrioderd with an intricate pattern of red crosses.

"Wh . . . . who . . . who are you?," stammered Jim, in breathless, wide-eyed disbelief.

"I am Michael who speaks for the Great I AM," his benefactor announced calmly.

"What? Y . . . you are Michael?" was all Jim could manage to say.

"That's my name," he said cheerily.

"The Archangel?" Jim croaked in an almost reverent tone.

"You got it," grinned the great angel.

Jim's knees began to buckle beneath him.

"Do not bend the knee to me, my friend—I am your fellow-servant. Worship only God." said Michael kindly, reaching out and steadying Jim on his feet.

Still in a daze, Jim croaked, "How do I rate the protection of the highest of all angels?"

"Why should this amaze you? I am called 'Archangel' and 'the Great Prince of Israel' and so I am. You are a Christian *goyim*—a Gentile—but you have been grafted into the olive tree of Israel. As such, you are no less a citizen of Israel than a natural-born Jew who is an ethnic descendant of Abraham. You, yourself, are a military man who knows how to unquestioningly follow orders. The inhabitants of heaven are all servants of God and of each other. I am but a soldier of the Great God Jehovah. Although I am the Captain of the myriads of the Lord's Army, I do instantly whatever I hear from the Throne—tasks both great and small. I minister to everyone from heads of state in royal palaces to infant children in the worst slums of the world at various times. I have been temporarily given personal charge concerning you and I have not failed in my mission. Every human being born into the earth has at least one full-time guardian, but your regular guardians requested aid, so you have become my special assignment at this moment.

"Aside from dealing with the wolf, I have appeared to you to tell you that, just today, Satan has tried to kill you three times. I deflected the path of the cannon shells that struck your airplane. Those guns were aimed by a demon guiding the hands of the enemy gunner and the projectiles were meant for you. He will not do that again! Another demon held you in your seat as you were trying to bail out. He truly regretted his decision to interfere, as I severed one of his arms when I cut the strap that held you. And, that wolf I just killed was no ordinary canine. He was inhabited by a high-ranking demon, commanding a group of lesser demons, which were embodied in the wolf pack. Look at the wolf's head over there," the golden giant said to Jim, "Go ahead! Command the evil spirit in the wolf to come out and be gone."

Screwing up his courage, Jim called out with all the authority he could muster, "Foul spirit, you must go. Come out now, in Jesus' name, go from here and never return!" Something appearing like a black vapor emerged from the wolf's head, snarled, spit like a cat, cursed and instantly disappeared into the forest like a shadow.

"Do you see the great authority God has given to those who believe in Him? Go now, O man of God, honored one. This demon and his cohorts will bother you no more. I must now return to my primary duty station in Israel. But remember, there is always at least one powerful guardian under my command near you at all times who commands more than a legion of angels. They are at his instant beck and call as am I. Don't forget, too, that God's man is invincible until God welcomes him home. I must go now! Your friends approach." With that, Michael disappeared leaving Jim bedazzled.

Honored one? Man of God? Me? What is so special about me?

Just then, Eli's P-47 whooshed by overhead again. Eli radioed, "Hey Jim, who was that big guy down there with you just now?"

"He's . . . uh . . . an old friend, Eli," Jim stammered, "Listen . . . I'm okay. He . . .uh . . relieved that pushy wolf of his head and the rest took off pronto. "

As Jim collected himself, Colonel Wohno stepped through the trees, glanced at the dead wolf and grinned, "Well, General Black, it would seem that your guardians are on the job today."

"Well, yeah, a big guy named Michael killed that wolf," Jim sighed in relief.

"Ah, yes. Michael, the Great Prince of Israel, the highest of all angels. He'll take good care of you," Wohno remarked approvingly.

"Huh! Archangels as personal body guards? I never would have believed that one," exclaimed Jim. "I'm totally amazed but very thankful," Jim exhaled.

"Yes, you have several guardians most of the time, actually," was the colonel's unpretentious answer.

"Several . . . . ? But . . . . how . . do . . you. . . ?" Jim stuttered, his head still spinning from this latest encounter.

"Come, come, Sir, I have a Humvee waiting at the bottom of the hill," Wohno gestured officiously. "Let's get you home for supper and some well-deserved rest. I'm sorry for the loss of your airplane but airplanes are replaceable—you are not."

"Irreplaceable? Huh! I was actually starting to think I have a target on my back," grinned Jim, but Colonel Wohno appeared not to hear.

Half an hour later, as Jim walked into the Lodge to the cheers of the entire community, Eli drew him aside. "Jim, what's the deal? I saw a big guy with blonde hair standing down there beside you wearing some kind of tin suit. But as I passed over you that last time, he was gone. You said he was an 'old friend.' So who is that guy, anyway?" he demanded through tightly pursed lips, his eyes narrowed and staring piercingly at his commander.

"Ever hear of Michael?" queried Jim, with a toss of his head.

"Michael? Michael who?" demanded Eli suspiciously.

"The archangel!" grinned Jim, coyly.

"No way!" Eli guffawed.

"Yes, way! Back away, man, you're wilting my carnation," Jim laughed.

"Why'd you say he was 'an old friend'? I wasn't aware that you were in the habit of hobnobbing with archangels" smirked Eli.

"Well . . . I'm not . . .but you've got to admit he's old. And as my guardian, he's definitely a good friend," rebounded Jim.

"Hmph . . . you're a sly dog, General Black! But I will say, somebody up there likes you a lot to assign the most powerful angel in God's army to you," Eli grinned, slapping his employer on the back.

That evening, there was much celebration at the Eagle's Lair. The cooks prepared a splendid feast to which Colonel Wohno, Major Maag and the crew of their AC-130, as well as Colonel Johnson's men, were invited. As the meal concluded, Colonel Wohno arose to address the assembly. "Ladies and gentlemen, the road has not been easy for any of you but this was nothing compared to the suffering of your fellow citizens who were not blessed to be invited to such a place as the Eagle's Lair. Nearly seventy million of them have perished. The captivity and judgment of America is nearing its end and shortly you will see the culmination of God's plans for your great and beloved land. Very soon, you will witness a spectacle that will both awe and encourage you, reassuring all that God has His hand upon you and your nation. We must leave you folks now, but we will be back shortly. Thank you for your hospitality and good evening."

☆ 18 ☆

THE VISITOR

Several days went by and the whole crew was beginning to relax. The mechanics and other technicians were busy cleaning up and servicing the aircraft and the entire company of refugees seemed to be at ease.

Then, in the wee hours of the morning one Sunday, Jim was jarred awake by the ringing of the steeple bell in the vacant old chapel building. As he lay there wide awake, he wondered what idiot could be ringing the bell in the old church at that hour of the morning, waking everybody up.

Later that morning, in a funk from lack of sleep, Jim made up his mind to ferret out the culprits during the usual Sunday morning communal breakfast with the other residents. As Jim stormed into the dining area with blood in his eye, Uri tried to catch his attention. "General, there's something I need to talk to you about immediately," he insisted.

Jim brushed the little Russian aside with "Not now, Uri, there's something I have to do first." Seeing the look in his employer's eye, Uri knew better than to ask again.

Most of the other residents were already seated and eating breakfast as Jim stood behind his chair at the head of the table as Maryann seated herself with her plate of food.

"May I have everyone's attention, please?" announced Jim in an official tone.

Maryann looked up from her seat surprised. "Now what is going on, Honey?" she asked. Jim ignored her question and looked angrily about him at the seated families.

"I want to know which of you kids were out running around the place in the wee hours last night," thundered Jim.

The children and teens looked first at each other startled and then back to their parents with obvious foreboding. The youth had universally treated their host with a great deal of respect but it was obvious they were now fearful of both the general and his loaded question.

One of the parents spoke up. "What seems to be the problem, General? Our kids were home in bed all night."

"Folks, early this morning sometime around 2:00am, someone repeatedly rang the bell in the old church building over a long period of time. It woke me up, as I'm sure it must have done to others, and I want to know who did it. I'm not going to tolerate such pranks around here," he snapped.

"General, there was something that shook this whole place last night. We found bottles and picture frames tipped over or fallen off the walls in our cabin this morning," a middle-aged father explained. "Didn't you notice anything unusual when you got up this morning, Sir?"

"Well. . uh. . . did we see anything amiss this morning, Honey." Jim asked Maryann, taken aback.

Regarding her now blushing husband evenly with an uncustomary wifely stare, Maryann snapped, "I found several things tipped over but nothing too serious. Jim, what is your problem, anyway?" Maryann asked testily, irritated and embarrassed by the rudeness of her husband.

All this time, Uri was unsuccessfully making hand signals to Jim to pay attention to him, but he finally spoke up. "That's what I wanted to talk to you about, General Black," interrupted Uri, "I'm pretty sure the bell wasn't rung by a human hand. I'm afraid it was something far more serious."

Somewhat crest-fallen, Jim turned to Uri and said, "Okay, Uri, my mistake. I always seem to be last to know about anything. What is going on around here, anyway?"

"Well, I heard the bell too and went over to investigate this morning. Whatever rang that bell popped a number of pieces of siding off that old building. Something really wracked the steeple. Arie and I have been checking into it," concluded the technician, almost apologetically, hoping to avert his employer's anger without inciting unnecessary concerns among the rest of the group.

At that moment, Arie walked in from the equipment room with an uncharacteristic frown on his face. "I think I have the answer to the general's question, and I fear it's not good news," announced the Israeli. "We have been eavesdropping on the international info services, consulting our satellites and some of our experimental seismic instrumentation. The culprit in all this seems to be the New Madrid Fault Line under the Mississippi River south of St. Louis. The fault shifted last night which resulted in a quake of about 9.0 on the Richter, and then there were several 7.0 aftershocks as well. It was those tremors that rang our old church bell, Jim. The last time this fault moved was around 1812, and it rang church bells as far away as Boston, Massachusetts. Right now, the Mississippi River is backing up into Iowa—New Orleans is going to get it when that ponded water finally moves downstream. An additional, even greater, danger is that there are several major dams within 200 miles of the epicenter. If they were to collapse, the resulting catastrophe will be monumentally increased. We've known it could erupt again at any time but I never imagined we would be affected to this extent by the shocks up in this area," concluded Arie.

Red-faced, Jim turned to the congregation, "I apologize in sack cloth and ashes, my friends. I am so sorry to have unfairly accused you youngsters without fully knowing the situation." said Jim remorsefully.

"Jim, I think I speak for all of us when I say that you are forgiven. You've had enough pressure the last few months to unsettle anyone," said Senator Dalton, smiling kindly. "Right now, we need to pray for those poor souls still around that area and on south. I can just imagine that if a wall of water were to come down the Mississippi, it would absolutely finish the annihilation of New Orleans which Hurricane Katrina started some years ago," he concluded with a pained expression on his otherwise gentle face.

"Ah, but this isn't the end of the story," continued Arie, "There's something else far more sinister for us brewing less than 300 miles away virtually right in our own backyard. The scanners on our American satellite indicate there is an ever-growing possibility of a catastrophic eruption of a super volcano in Yellowstone Park! Apparently, there are something like six of these 'hot-spots' worldwide. The scientists have debated for years as to whether or not this is possibly one of the volcanoes that killed the dinosaurs. I've heard that in recent years, the park trails have been quietly closed as the ground had become so hot it would melt the hikers shoes and, besides, the surface of the land has been rising for some time. If that thing blows, it's pretty much all over. America, and potentially most of the globe, will be in a natural 'nuclear winter' for months. For sure, we here at the Eagle's Lair better hope the winds are out of the north and they stay that way until it's all over. But unfortunately, there may not be much left of the rest of the country anyway. Furthermore, we have to consider California's San Andreas Fault on the Ring of Fire. Before the invasion, geologists were all fearful of a long overdue major temblor that would level Los Angeles. We all need to spend some time on our knees tonight, my friends," concluded Arie, unabashed concern in his voice.

"By the way, Jim, I have something else you should see that I found playing around with the video cameras on the satellite. Look at this!" said Arie, pointing to several locations on the screen.

Jim recoiled at what he saw: Huge concentration camps obviously full of people. "What in the world is going on with these places, I wonder? Looks like a wholesale imprisonment system adjoining what used to be a major U.S. defense installation!"

"That is a good question, my friend. Is it Kaiser Bill's boys or El Presidente's? We won't know until we can get a good boots-on-the-ground look at it. And I've found several others, too. So, we need to file that away for future reference," concluded Arie.

The remainder of the Sunday morning meal was considerably subdued as everyone communed with their God and their own hearts.

Several days later, in the wee hours of the morning, Jim awakened at 3:00am, after a restless night and sat up on the edge of the bed. He looked at Maryann breathing softly beside him and wondered how he was ever going to get back to sleep. Presently, he became aware of a faint glow in the darkness, which appeared low in one corner of the room.

What is this? Wonder where that light is coming from?

Jim got up and slipped into his robe to investigate. Presently, the glow grew brighter until it gradually filled the room. Excitedly, Jim tried to awaken Maryann, but she remained sound asleep. Then, out of the brilliance, the King of the Universe appeared.

All strength immediately left Jim's body as he began to fall to the floor. But a hand touched his shoulder and strength flooded back into his being.

"Arise and walk with Me, my son. Your maid will not awaken."

Shaken, Jim looked Jesus full in the face. His eyes seemed to penetrate Jim's very soul, yet there was no embarrassment or fear. Jim felt bathed in more love and acceptance than he had ever imagined possible. He noticed the Lord's beautiful appearance. The glory of God shone from His face. His robes sparkled like diamonds. The nail wounds in His wrists and feet were huge and the glory of God shone out from them.

"Lord, I never ever expected to actually see You this side of the veil. I am a sinful man and totally unworthy to be in Your Presence," confessed Jim, barely able to speak.

"I don't know that you are. I've washed it all away, Jim. My blood has made you eminently worthy. You are completely forgiven! I know your heart, my child. Like David, you are indeed a man after My own heart and I am well pleased with you, as your grandfather has told you. I have come to discuss My plans with you," He said gently.

"The sins of American society and the corruption in American government had reached such a point that I had no choice but to bring judgment—you see, I love America and have destined her for greatness in My kingdom. But America's people have now been decimated and their cries have come up before My throne. I will return to earth in the very near future to set up My kingdom in Jerusalem. My saints will rule the earth with Me, including you. Until then, I have appointed you as My viceroy over not only this nation but the entire northern half of the western hemisphere from the equator to the arctic circle. You are to lead these nations as they rebuild under My authority," He instructed.

"But . . . But Lord," stammered Jim, "Certainly there must be others far more qualified than I. I am not equipped for a job such as that. I'm not a politician, and certainly no public speaker. I am not even a good Christian! I have commanded air wings but I have no experience whatsoever governing anything larger than my company," was his incredulous response.

"Jim, listen to Me. I just told you that you are forgiven. All your sins—past, present and future—have been washed away. My blood has cleansed you and when the Father looks at you He sees Me. My strength is made perfect in weakness. The fact that you are not a politician or a public speaker is a plus rather than a minus. Your argument is essentially the same as Moses' excuses for not obeying Me. They didn't fly in the Arabian Desert four thousand years ago and they won't fly in Montana today. It's not about you—it's about Me. You see, it all rests on My power and ability, not yours. I will be with you and will empower and lead you in all things," He said, affectionately.

"But . . . Lord . . . ."

"No 'buts,' Jim. You said you'd cooperate. I know you meant what you said to My servants and I am counting on you. Like Moses, you are My man, My chosen one. This is My plan for your life, My son. My gifting and calling is irreversible."

"Your servants? …. You mean . . . Wohno . . . and . . . .Maag?" Jim exclaimed, as his mind began to grasp what the Lord was trying to tell him.

"Exactly! Do whatever they tell you as though I were speaking to you Myself —they are My servants, and yours, and they hear directly from Me. From this moment on, you will hear My voice clearly for yourself and I will visit you on a regular basis to give you your marching orders," declared the Lord of Hosts.

"So . . . that's who they are—angels! I wondered but never knew for sure. How could I have been so dense? Well .. uh, Yessir!. . . certainly, Lord, I'm glad to serve You to the best of my ability. I'm both humbled and honored" said Jim, recovering his composure quickly and snapping to attention.

"You will see monumental miracles, Jim, just as Moses did in the desert—even far greater ones than that. Those who say that manifestations of My power died with the death of the last of the Apostles will have ample opportunity to repent."

"But . . . where? . . . do I start, Lord?" Jim asked, still uncertain about his commission.

"The chastening of America has been accomplished. All of the purveyors of evil among you assume that they have been successful due to the 'rightness' of their cause. They think I am one of them—but now I will lay out My case against their evil doings and bring swift judgment upon all of them. As you will remember, in Old Testament times I allowed tyrannical, evil nations to discipline Israel, but I never once intended to destroy her. My chastening was only for a season and always for Israel's benefit, so that I could bestow mercy on them and restore them, In so doing, I demonstrated to their neighbors that I alone am God, and that Israel is My chosen people. Later, I punished the very people who disciplined My beloved Israel. What I did for Israel, I have done again—this time for my beloved America which is also a nation dedicated and set apart for My glory.

"I want you to understand some of the mystery concerning the connection between Israel and America as a covenant people. There is great significance in numbers that emerge in My Word—the number thirteen, for instance. Although Jacob, who was later named Israel, had twelve sons, there were actually thirteen tribal areas numbered in Israel after the Exodus from Egypt. Joseph's tribe was split into the two half-tribes of Manasseh and Ephraim. There were thirteen disciples, thirteen apostles and there were thirteen original American colonies all founded by covenant with Me for the purpose of religious and political freedom and the spreading the Gospel around the world. I am a faithful, covenant God; I do everything by covenant. Contrary to the unholy ruminations of some theologians, no covenant I have ever made with mankind has ever been annulled or broken, that is why I said to My disciples "Do not think that, as Messiah, I came to do away with the Law, the Prophets or the Writings. I did not come to destroy any of them but to fulfill what they foretold. For truly I tell you, till the heavens and the earth pass away, nothing that I have said, not the tiniest letter, not even a dot, will be deleted from the scripture until all is accomplished. My words shall never pass away."

"Some say I am unfair or unpredictable. Others think I am only a God of love and forgiveness forgetting that I am also a God of wrath and judgment. All men die and I take no pleasure in the death of any human being, however the death of each of My saints is precious to Me because I await their arrival in Heaven with great anticipation. I love every child who is conceived in the womb. I died on the cross so that everyone who truly calls upon My Name might join Me in My Father's heavenly kingdom. Children who die, even those who are aborted or die before birth, before reaching an age where they can make a decision to reject or accept Me automatically return to heaven and the Father's bosom. The covenant in My blood provides for the salvation of all mankind. The terms of salvation are very simple. Everyone who believes in his heart and who confesses with his mouth his belief that I am the Messiah Who shed His blood for the remission of sins, was raised from the dead, and that I am Lord, will be saved. What remains a great mystery is that many are not interested and some even hate Me without a reason. Truly, mankind does not break My laws, but, truthfully, My laws break rebellious men. I send no one to hell. There is no excuse for anyone ending up in Hell—but those who reject My freely offered salvation send themselves to that terrible place the Father had originally reserved for the Devil and his angels. I wish I could change it but I cannot—the terms of mankind's destiny are fixed.

"Some see Me only as the 'Warm and Fuzzy" savior and forget that I am also a God of wrath and judgment. Very soon now, I will send legions of angels to bring a terrible plague upon all My enemies. I know who they are. I also know My own sheep and My sheep know Me. As My Word says in Zechariah 14, so shall it be in America . . . 'And this shall be the plague with which the LORD will smite all the peoples that wage war against Me: their flesh shall rot while they are still on their feet, their eyes shall instantly rot in their sockets, and their tongues shall rot in their mouths.'"[14]

"About that plague, Lord, I always thought it described nuclear war," Jim said, with a bit of uncertainty.

"No, Jim! Remember in 2 Kings 19:35, how a single angel was sent to the camp of the Assyrian invaders and destroyed 185,000 of their soldiers in a single night. Well, he didn't even work up a sweat. The slaughter of My enemies will occur in both America and Israel simultaneously. America shall be cleansed and returned to her Christian roots. Governance shall only be vested in those who belong to Me. This 'City on a Hill' shall once again be a true beacon of My righteousness and grace to the world. America must be prepared to come to the rescue of Israel in the near future. Look for all these things, Jim; they will come to pass very soon now. You will see it with your own eyes," warned the Lord.

"Your grandfather will also reveal something else important about you very soon now that will amaze you. Listen to him, for he is also My chosen servant. Now I must leave you. Trust Me, My son, and rest in My peace. And I'll be seeing you in My kingdom a little later, Jim," said Jesus, as He raised His hand in blessing.

Then, He was gone as suddenly as He had appeared.

Shaken to the core of his being, Jim tried to arouse Maryann, but she sleepily mumbled something, turned over and began to snore.

Feeling the need to talk to someone, Jim made his way to Grandfather's room. But the old man was snoring so loudly it seemed the windows rattled and the curtains swayed.

Better let them all sleep until morning.

Jim stepped out the front doors of the Lodge into the moonlight and gazed up at the stars for a long time. Later, he returned to the Lodge and spent the rest of the night praying, reflecting upon Jesus' words and reading his Bible in the library.

What a responsibility He has placed on my shoulders . . . yet my heart is light as a feather . . it's really wild. I think I know how Moses must have felt after the burning bush episode.

REVELATIONS

Grandfather knocked on Jim's door early the next morning, "Jim," he said once inside the room, "the Lord appeared to me last night in a dream and instructed me to have you read this without delay," the old man announced, handing Jim a small booklet. "When you're finished, we'll need to sit down and talk together," the elder Black Hawk concluded.

Jim turned the book over in his hands, reading the title, "George Washington's Vision."

"What is this, anyway? Is this some sort of joke? What has this to do with me?" demanded Jim.

"Oh, this is no joke, my son. It's dead serious. This is a very old document, Jim. Since the late 1700's, the liberals and secular progressives have tried hard to discredit it, but its authenticity has been verified by a number of prominent patriots. 'The proof of the pudding is in the eating,' as they say. So, just chill out and read it. I think you'll find it most interesting," the elderly patriarch said, leaving Jim staring after him with his mouth open.

An half-hour or so later, Jim emerged from his quarters and walked briskly to his Grandfather's room.

"Grandfather, this is very interesting . . .but . . . . well . . . why do I have the sinking feeling there is more to this for me than I can even guess at? You mind cluing me in?" Jim asked, not sure he wanted to know the answer.

"Yes, that's what I intend to do, but you'd better sit down first, my son. I have some important revelations for you which I have kept secret for many years. The Lord said last night that it is time for me to tell you the whole truth about your background."

"This sounds serious," Jim laughed nervously trying to fight the tightening of his gut and a growing sense of alarm.

Settling into an easy chair, he asked uncertainly, "The truth? About what?"

Choosing his words carefully, the elder Black Hawk began, "You, my son, are not related to me by blood. Neither were you related to your parents by blood. In fact, you have no Native American blood in you at all. You are very much of Anglo-Saxon heritage. You were adopted by my son and his wife."

"What? . . . .Adopted? . . . . .From where? From whom?" Jim interrupted as he jumped to his feet, his head beginning to spin.

"Your dad and mom told me that they had taken you as a favor to an old friend of theirs from Harvard. who was your real blood uncle. Your uncle's brother and sister-in-law had been murdered leaving you an orphan as a babe of three months. Your uncle was your only living relative but he was young, unmarried and unable to care for you. Furthermore, he was concerned about your safety since he suspected the murders were possibly politically motivated. But the main thing you must understand here is that . . . well . . . you are not gonna believe this," fretted the old man.

"Just lay it on me, Grandfather, and we'll see," Jim demanded, by now totally overwhelmed by the events of the past 24 hours.

"Okay! Here goes! You are the direct blood descendant of George Washington," he said, barely above a whisper.

Jim tried to grasp this last bit of information, but his head was spinning at the weight of the revelation. He stood motionless, staring out the window.

Finally, he said, "Now wait just a minute. This has got to be bogus. George and Martha never had any biological children."

"Yes you're right! George and Martha didn't have any children of their own together—but George had one. It was never public knowledge and he didn't even know about it, himself, until 1799, only weeks before his death. Now don't think it was the result of some casual hanky-panky, because it was very much above-board," explained Grandfather gravely.

"Now, how could that be?" Jim wondered aloud.

"Here is the story: In the eighteenth century, arranged marriages were still very common and people tended to marry quite young. George was a lad in his teens when he journeyed on business from Virginia to North Carolina where he met and fell in love with the beautiful daughter of a very wealthy importer. The rub was that the girl's father took a dislike to George and forbade her to see him. In those days, daddy's word was pretty much law. The girl's mother, however, liked George and was most sympathetic to her daughter's wishes. She favored their marriage but had to defer to her husband's authority.

"When the girl's father departed for England on a business trip, the romance continued quietly. Several months passed and one day a message came from the British Admiralty informing the girl's mother that her husband's ship had been lost at sea with all hands. With this revelation, the girl's mother soon gave her approval and George and the girl were married.

"Two weeks after their marriage, the girl's father suddenly reappeared. It seems the Admiralty had confused his ship with one of a similar name which actually had gone down in a violent storm in the Irish Sea. The girl's father was furious to learn of his daughter's marriage, because he had promised her hand in marriage to his new English business partner, a Mr. Samuel Sherman. Being a man of considerable wealth and influence, the father prevailed upon a local judge to annul his daughter's marriage. George returned to Virginia, broken-hearted. The importer immediately moved his entire family to New Orleans to set up a new business as he awaited the arrival of his new business partner. The girl did not realize she was pregnant until she was living in New Orleans. Her father adamantly refused to send her back to George. By the time her intended husband arrived from England, she was seven months pregnant. He was a very honorable man who had no objection at all to marrying her. And so, they were wed.

"The baby boy that was born to her was named Anthony Sherman. Young Anthony remained unaware of his heritage until he reached his late teens when his mother told him of his real background. Curious about his father, Anthony left home at 19 and traveled to Virginia, where his ability as a business man soon became well known. Being a patriotic fellow, in 1776 he became an officer in the Continental Army, keeping his true identity to himself," the old man paused.

"Oh yeah! That's right! One of the main characters in that story about Washington's vision was a Colonel Anthony Sherman," interjected Jim, stroking his chin thoughtfully.

"That's correct, Jim. It was during a command staff meeting with General Washington that Colonel Anthony caught the General's eye and was invited to dine at Washington's table. The two took an immediate shine to each other spending more and more time together forming an inseparable bond. General Washington made Anthony his chief *aide-de-camp*, often confiding more in him than the more senior officers, to the consternation of the general staff. Washington remained completely unaware of Anthony's true identity, however, until just a month before the ex-President's death in 1799. At that point, Anthony Sherman dropped off the radar, but he left a long list of distinguished descendants behind him of which you, my son, are the most important in this hour. I have a genealogy of your family tree which I will give you. I truly believe that, like Hadassah the little Jewish girl, who became Queen Esther of the Persians, you may have come to the 'kingdom' for just such a time as this," concluded Grandfather.

"And if I perish, I perish! Right?" murmured Jim, with a grin.

"Jim, the Lord appears to have some mighty special plans for you. I wouldn't be too worried, if I were you," Grandfather assured him.

"Oh, I'm not so much 'worried' as I am amazed and bewildered," Jim said, humbly.

☆ 20 ☆

THE FRENCH CONNECTION

"General, there is an F/A-18 fighter with an American transponder on short final to Runway 30. Can't seem to raise him by radio. He's just coming straight in uninvited! Looks like he's in trouble of some kind," Ivan commented matter-of-factly.

"Okay, people, grab your weapons and let's go check this guy out as soon as he lands," yelled Jim.

The intruder touched down, rolled out and came to a stop at the end of the runway. Eli, Jim and several others ran to Jim's Humvee. Eli slid into the driver's seat. Another small group crowded into one of the other Humvees. As Alex started to climb aboard Jim's vehicle, Eli grinned, "Careful how you get in there, Alex! Don't capsize us, Boy!"

Alex shot back, "Och, no comments from the peanut gallery, you skinny little pipsqueak!" as he threw his massive frame into a seat with a sly grin.

"All right, all right, you two! Just pay attention to your driving!" grinned Jim, trying his best to hold a straight face and look serious.

As they approached the motionless aircraft, a figure emerged from the cockpit and climbed quickly down the hand-holds to the concrete. Shedding flight suit and helmet, the man stood erect, staring as the vehicles approached. Nearing their quarry, Alex gave a loud cry of recognition and shouted excitedly, "Good heavens! Don't anyone shoot! I know this man!"

Jim keyed his radio mike and said, "Everyone, hold your fire. Alex seems to know our visitor. Do not fire."

As they drew closer, Alex grabbed the public address mike from Jim and his booming voice rang out, "Henri! Henri is that you?"

"Alex? Alexander MacIntosh? Do my eyes deceive me? Is that really you?" cried the newcomer in disbelief.

Alex vaulted out of the Humvee's top gunner's position and picked the man up off the ground like a rag doll. The two men embraced and held each other for a long time, weeping openly.

"Mon Dieu, mon Dieu! Merci! Merci beaucoup!," cried the man with a mild French accent, "Oh Alex, *mon ami*, I cannot tell you how glad I am to see you. I thought we'd never meet again in this life, my huge friend. Now, here we both are in the middle of a nightmare!"

"Aye, you're right about the nightmare, Henri. Man, am I glad to see you, my friend! But what're you doing in America and why're you wearing the uniform of an E.U. officer? And how did you come to drop in here, of all places?" Alex inquired, looking closely at his old friend.

Meanwhile, the two vehicles full of armed men watched with guarded interest as events unfolded.

Exasperated, Jim finally chided, "Uh . . . Alex, would you mind introducing us to your friend here?"

"Och, sorry lads! This man is Henri Montsegur of Lyons, France, Professor of European History at the Sorbonne—or at least he used to be. If you'll remember, I told you we were colleagues some years ago before I disappeared, perforce, from France without saying goodbye to my old compatriot here."

"Get the mechanics out here with a tow tractor and get this plane under cover, Eli," ordered Jim good-naturedly, "What say we all adjourn to the Lodge? There's no point in standing out here jawing in the middle of the runway. Let's let Henri get cleaned up, something to eat and rest a bit before we begin grilling him."

Once at the Lodge, Henri was given a fresh change of clothing, assigned a room and pointed toward a hot shower. An hour or so later, the little Frenchman emerged a much calmer man, wearing civilian clothes and very much in need of a cup of coffee. Almost the whole population of the Eagle's Lair gathered around the newcomer, to hear what news he might bear from the outside.

"And now, Lad, catch us up on all the news and your history," Alex said, leaning back in his chair with his fingers laced behind his head.

Henri began slowly, "I know you're all wondering who this crazy Frenchman is. Before I received my PhD at Oxford, I served in the French Air Force as a fighter pilot and rose to the rank of major. When our new E.U. Caesar, 'Kaiser Bill', came to power, his organization of goons began looking for bodies to fill his quota of officers. Eventually, my name came up and I was summoned before an induction review board, where I informed them that I was a university professor and really had no interest in serving in that madman's Gestapo. Of course, I didn't dare use those exact terms, but that's what I was thinking. After due consideration, they made me an offer I couldn't refuse: Sign up or be shot as a traitor. Naturally, I had no desire to stop a bullet so I 'volunteered' hoping I could accomplish something—anything—by keeping my nose clean and working quietly behind the scenes.

"When Bill decided to invade America, I was shipped over here and stationed as a supply officer at a converted civilian airbase in Minnesota. From the very first, I had the uneasy feeling we were intruding on holy ground and, although I was a Christian among pagans, I was still be to be numbered among the transgressors.

"Things were pretty quiet in our area until several days ago. We had received word that two entire divisions of Alliance troops in New Mexico, Arizona and southern California had just been wiped out by Bubonic Plague. That, plus a surprise nuclear attack on the Alliance's naval fleets off the Atlantic and Pacific coasts and the U.N. building in New York City, was devastating beyond belief to the whole command structure. Emergency orders to begin withdrawal from America were posted. The High Command feared the spread of the Plague as well as the possibility that more nuclear attacks were in the offing. Nearly every member Alliance nation's ambassadors, and even some heads of state, were gathered at the U.N. when the weapons struck. Virtually all were either killed outright or are currently in critical condition suffering from severe radiation sickness. Unfortunately, Kaiser Bill was not among them."

"Yeah, we know all about the strikes. We're the spoil-sports who dropped the weapons from our old B-29s," volunteered Eli, with glee.

"Ah, so you fellows are the culprits!" Henri laughed, "Nice shooting!"

"But plague? In the Southwest? Are you sure?" inquired Eli incredulously.

"Absolutely! It was confirmed by Kaiser Bill's top medical people" assured the little Frenchman,"You'll remember that we Frenchmen became intimately acquainted with the Black Death back in the 14ᵗʰ century and we don't wish to go there again" grinned Henri.

"Well, I was doing some paper work in my office this morning when a radio operator in the next room, who is an acquaintance of mine, became very excited. He was receiving reports from our other bases that Alliance troops were suddenly dying like flies of some terrible plague, a wasting disease which acted like ebola, only it killed within moments. The other bases said the flesh of those afflicted just fell off their bones where they stood. Frankly, I was dubious! Who had ever heard of such a thing? Not even ebola or the Black Death worked that quickly," he said casually, rolling his eyes. "I walked outside the building to get a bottle of pop from a vending machine and noted that there was a thin overcast. But as I looked a few moments later, the sky suddenly grew brilliantly light. That's when I saw them descend from the sky, a chill went up my back, and my knees began to knock," Henri recalled with a shudder

"Wait a minute, wait a minute," interrupted Jim, with unconcealed alarm, "Who is 'them'? Who are you talking about?" he demanded, trying to get a handle on what he was hearing.

"The destroyers— some sort of alien or supernatural beings armed with huge swords. Probably angels, I'd guess. They came down among the personnel on our base and wherever they moved, men were being cut down in droves," responded Henri, as he fought to control his emotions.

"No one actually seemed to be able to see them except me! The men knew 'something' was among them but didn't know what to do. They were absolutely terror stricken as was I," his voice quivering as he relived the whole fantastic event.

"There were three captured USAF F/A-18 fighters sitting on the tarmac with full drop-tanks under the wings. One of the pilots who was authorized to fly them had informally familiarized me with the aircraft during our downtime. You see, my last service with the French Airforce had me flying the Dassault delta wing fighter, which is sort of an antique by now. I had been thinking of commandeering one of those F-18s for some time anyway and flying to a 'City of Refuge' rumored to exist out here somewhere in the western U.S. or Canada; I knew that Kaiser Bill's people had the coordinates of such a place because our radioman had picked them up on the ham bands. A 'repository of troublemakers' they called it. I managed to acquire the coordinates 'on the sly' and plotted a course out here, but I had only a general idea where it was. The F-18s we have don't have working GPS equipment, so I couldn't punch the coordinates into the navigation computers. I could only fly by dead reckoning and the seat of my pants," he said, smiling sheepishly at the raptly attentive audience gathered around him.

"Without really thinking, I quickly donned my absent friend's G-suit and flight helmet and made a mad dash for one of the F-18s, hoping no one would recognize me and that the engines would fire without a start cart. As I climbed into the cockpit, a ground crewmen standing near the nose of the airplane just seemed to melt like a slug, you know, like when you pour salt on it! His eyes fell out of their sockets and his flesh literally melted off his bones and ran down his legs. His skeleton just stood there momentarily inside his clothes, before it collapsed in a heap. It was so macabre, I couldn't stand to look at it or the others who were suffering similar fates all around me. It was like a bad grade-C horror movie. I literally had to suppress the urge to vomit," he shuddered involuntarily at the thought of the horror he had witnessed.

"I was so terrified," he continued, "that the only thing I could think of was putting as much distance between myself and that place as fast as I could! I never stopped to consider that if those beings, whatever they were, meant to kill me, I would probably have already been dead or starting to melt. I certainly could not have outrun them even at supersonic speed.

But I closed the canopy, lit off the engines, dropped takeoff flaps and firewalled the throttles into afterburner. Man! The power of those F-18s is truly amazing! You Yanks make some great airplanes! I took off diagonally right across the tarmac in about 2,000 feet without benefit of the runway. I rotated off near the edge of the grass. As soon as the craft was cleaned up and I had built up sufficient air speed, I pointed the nose straight up, leveled off at 42,000 feet and headed due west. All I was hoping for was to find a safe place to hide," the little Frenchman continued, beginning to relax a bit.

"Everything was going along swimmingly, until I approached the eastern foothills of the Rocky Mountains. At that point, the engines began to run rough, then erratically and finally my right engine flamed out altogether. I flew on the left engine for about twenty minutes until it too flamed out. I tried frantically to restart the engines five times. I was rapidly losing altitude and the mountains were getting closer and closer so I was ready to blow the canopy and eject when something stopped me. As I looked, the clouds parted and I saw your runway dead ahead. I figured landing at any airfield was better than parachuting into those trees. For some odd reason, I felt compelled to try another engine restart and, *voila*, both engines lit off producing about 60 percent power. That gave me just enough thrust and auxiliary power to operate the landing gear and flaps to make a normal landing. And here I am!" Henri concluded, leaning against the chair cushions, looking positively drained.

Alex smiled broadly, "Well, my friend, you've certainly found your 'City of Refuge' here among us. For a fact, you didn't arrive here by accident. I'd venture to say there was an angel sitting on your wingtip all the way here and he knew exactly how to set your course and control your engines just right," he beamed triumphantly.

"Listen," Jim broke in quickly, "Henri's description of the deaths of Kaiser Bill's people is confirmation of something the Lord spoke to me about just a few days ago. He told me the invading armies would be decimated by a plague exactly as Henri has described it," he said in amazement.

Arie concurred emphatically, "Yes. It's the very curse which the Prophet Zechariah predicted would happen in the last days, near the Lord's return, to all who war against the Him and His people."

"Now that you mention a prophet, I'll tell you all something else," intimated the little Frenchman, "The Church of Jesus Christ has flourished under the Alliance's persecution. I have been hearing here and there that there are miracle church meetings going on all over the U.S.—the Church is the strength of your nation, my friends, never forget that. On the sly, I managed to attend several church services in the town I was stationed in and I was flabbergasted. I saw miracles of all kinds take place—blind eyes opened, cancers fall off, deaf ears unstopped, people walk out of wheelchairs, several persons raised from the dead and others too numerous to mention. And I was near tears when they sang, 'Rally Round the Flag' and 'The Battle Hymn of the Republic.' One night, some of Bill's thugs came to the church I happened to be attending, intending to break up the service and drag people off to prison, but they all ended up joining the congregation in prayer at the altar rail. I've never seen the power of God in operation like that—not ever. You Americans are most assuredly a people of faith, the like of which I've never seen before."

"Wow! That's really music to our ears to know the Church is alive and well. Before the invasion, people were pretty ho-hum about Christianity. Apparently, Americans are starting to rally. Henri, we are so glad you've dropped in here. Welcome, my friend!" Jim said warmly, extending his hand to their new-found friend.

☆ 21 ☆

THE MANAGEMENT LOWERS THE BOOM

Behold, Your enemies make a tumult; They have taken crafty counsel against Your people, And consulted together against Your sheltered ones. They have said, "Come, and let us cut them off from *being* a nation, that the name of Israel may be remembered no more." They form a confederacy against You: Who said, "Let us take for ourselves The pastures of God for a possession."[15]

For months, Israel had endured the constant pounding of mortars, rockets, artillery and sniper fire along all its borders, especially around Jerusalem itself. It was patently obvious that the Russian and Muslim allies were busily preparing a coordinated *blitzkrieg* to drive to the very heart of Israel. Everyone in Israel knew it was coming and feared that each day would be "The Day."

Although facing the approaching battle with great dread, Israel's Commanding General, Zechariah Ziv, was still sleeping soundly at 5:00am oblivious to the turmoil around the millennia-old stone-walled tower that served as his quarters, when he was rudely awakened by an unfamiliar but authoritative voice.

"Zechariah!" The voice boomed insistently, "Zechariah! Wake up!"

In his somewhat dazed condition, the voice seemed to Zechariah to be coming from somewhere near the massive door. Swinging his feet out of bed and donning his eyeglasses, he wondered who could be calling his name at this hour, as he had given strict orders not to be disturbed until 6:00am. Assuming it was an aide with some urgent news, he shouted into the darkness, irritated at this intrusion on his rest, "I'm awake! I'm up! Who is it and what do you want?"

Suddenly, the ancient vaulted tower room was ablaze with a dazzling white light. Abruptly, a gigantic flaxen-haired figure in golden armor appeared in the midst of the light with drawn sword in hand. Completely startled and awed, Ziv slid off his bunk and sank to his knees on the hard stone floor.

"Get up, Zechariah," the intruder said, gently helping the old warrior to his feet, "You must not worship me for I am but a fellow-servant—worship only God."

"Wh . . . . . who . . . who in the world are you, Sir?" stammered Ziv, barely able to talk and stifling sheer terror.

"Fear not! I am Michael, the Great Prince of Israel, who stands in the presence of the Great God, Jehovah. God, Himself, has come down to defend His Holy City and His people, Israel. He has sent me to you, O mighty man of God, to tell you not to fear the coming battle. The vast armies encircling Israel will be destroyed within the hour. Several legions of the heavenly host are here awaiting the signal to commence their assignment. Stand still and see the salvation of God. I will return to you again, very soon."

Then, the great angel was gone as suddenly as he had arrived, leaving Zechariah stunned yet exhilarated.

'Mighty Man of God' he calls me!! Me? Lord, You can't mean me! I'm honored by that and I do try to do my best, but I fall so far short. I am hardly what I'd call 'a man of God!'

Abruptly, a still, small voice answered in his mind, "That is your opinion, Zechariah; it is not Mine! Believe what My servant has spoken to you, for it is one hundred percent true from My point of view which is the only point of view that matters here!"

Receiving no further reply, Ziv arose cautiously to shave. Donning his uniform and boots, he stepped out of his billet into the cold morning air. At the same moment, his personal aide-de-camp, Colonel Abrahamson, stepped out of the next bunker. He was dressed, except for his shirt, and had Günter, his German shepherd, on a leash.

"Good morning, General. Looks like it will be a beautiful day," Abrahamson chirped cheerily to his commander.

"Yes, indeed! And a day of certain victory for us," Ziv replied with an air of positive exuberance.

Günter, growling and whining with his nose to the ground, was darting back and forth straining at his leash. Reaching down, Ziv gently patted the agitated dog on the head and scratched his ears. Günter, promptly laid down on the paving stones, panting and shivering, but relatively quiet once more.

"Poor Günter! I've never seen you so unglued, boy," Ziv spoke soothingly to the disquieted dog as he stroked his coat.

"I don't know what it is with him this morning, Sir. He woke me up a bit ago and was acting very strangely. He was whining, barking and pacing like he was crazy. He finally got hold of my arm and tried to drag me out of bed," Ziv's mystified aide explained.

"Well, Abrahamson, I think I know exactly what is bothering poor Günter and I also know today is a day of certain victory for Israel," he replied again.

Colonel Abrahamson regarded his superior with a quizzical expression. "Sir?"

"What I mean, Abrahamson, is this: I am no longer concerned about the outcome of this conflict. Let's drive up to Jerusalem in a few minutes. I want to see this operation with my own eyes."

"May I ask what has changed the General's outlook?" the colonel asked carefully, remembering Ziv's pessimistic outlook the day before and trying to figure out exactly the reason for the sudden change of outlook.

"Yes, Abrahamson, an angel!" was the general's matter-of-fact reply.

"An angel? Wha . . who? What . . . ?" Abrahamson stammered.

"Michael!" Ziv returned flatly.

"The Archangel?" the junior officer asked in total disbelief.

"Exactly!" Ziv replied bluntly.

"Why, no angel has been seen for centuries, that I am aware of. And I don't remember that Michael has ever been seen in either the Tanakh or the New Testament . . . Are you sure?" The words were no sooner out of his mouth than the colonel immensely regretted his bone-headed question. Regardless of which military organization one belongs to, it is never advisable for a subordinate to cross-examine someone wearing several stars. But it was now far too late—the incredulous words had been spoken and could not be recalled.

Ziv turned and regarded his subordinate with a mixture of amusement and anger. "You know, you're a real piece of work, Abrahamson! Are you nuts? Are you a *masuganakopf* or something? When a guy ten feet tall dressed in fiery armor walks into my quarters through stone walls 6 feet thick, and locked 6" thick solid oak doors and tells me he's the Archangel Michael, I'm not about to antagonize him by demanding to see his color ID badge. Besides, this guy carries a sword a good seven feet long, and I'd wager it's sharp enough to shave with. He woke me up at 5:00am in my quarters. Scared me half to death! Says he has thousands of warrior angels under his command just waiting for the signal to do a number on the assorted riffraff out there. Günter, here, must have sensed his presence. Dogs are very sensitive to the supernatural, you know," Ziv chided the younger man.

"General . . . Sir . . . I apologize for my remarks. I was way out of line. I . . . I didn't mean . .," stammered Abrahamson nervously.

"Forget it, Abrahamson," smiled Ziv, his tone softening, "I'm no stuffed shirt brass hat! I'm as incredulous as you are at all of this. Don't worry, you'll make general yet some day, my friend—in fact, I will see to it! But this impending spectacle should be most interesting. Get dressed and let's go observe this exchange of unpleasantries firsthand," the general said in a jovial tone.

As their armored staff vehicle stopped at the main Israeli command post in Jerusalem, they were greeted by the local IDF commander, General Aphar[16] "Dusty" Akiva.

"What is the situation, Aphar? Has there been any significant activity on the other side?" inquired Ziv.

"Sir, intel reports massive troop and armor movements in the West Bank area just to the east of Jerusalem. We are expecting a concerted attack within the hour. You really shouldn't be here, Zechariah, we can't afford to lose you," General Akiva said anxiously with a genuine concern for his superior.

"I'm not worried, Aphar, I have it on good authority that we are going to see the 'Russian Bear' and the 'Crescent Moon Society' humbled in dramatic fashion today," Ziv grinned mischievously.

Giving Ziv a quizzical look, General Akiva knitted his brow, shooting Colonel Abrahamson an enquiring glance when Ziv's back was turned, encircling his ear with a finger tip, questioning Ziv's mental state. Abrahamson merely shrugged and smiled diplomatically.

"Yes, I tell you, Akiva, this is going to be a battle of biblical proportions," continued Ziv opening his Hebrew Bible, "Do you remember how the King of Syria sent cavalry to capture Elisha, the Prophet in Second Kings, you know . . uh . . . Melech Bet?" He asked.

"Well, Sir, I'm not exactly what you'd call Observant. I've never really studied the Tanakh that closely. What does this Melech Bet passage say, anyway?" General Akiva asked, a slight blush surging across his tanned face.

"Well, 'Dusty', this situation today is quite similar to the one in the Melech Bet passage, which reads, 'The King of Syria sent horses and chariots and a great army to Dothan where Elisha lived, and they came by night and surrounded the city. And when the servant of the man of God arose early and went out, behold there was an army surrounding the city with horses and chariots. And Elisha's servant said to him, 'Alas, my master! What shall we do?' So Elisha answered, 'Do not fear, for those who are with us are more than those who are with them.' And Elisha prayed, and said, 'LORD, I pray, open his eyes that he may see.' Then the LORD opened the eyes of the young man, and he saw that the mountain was full of horses and chariots of fire all around Elisha.' [17] I believe that, as Elisha was, so are we at this moment, Akiva," crowed the Israeli commander-in-chief.

"I certainly hope you are right, Zechariah. If not, we may be overwhelmed when that mob attacks," Akiva observed darkly.

"'Dusty,' I received a visit, not more than an hour ago, from the great angel who is the guardian of Israel. I've never been so astounded and frightened, in my life. He told me that there are literally thousands of unseen warrior angels all around us under orders to slaughter the enemies of Israel when they attack. I came here to see it for myself," crowed Ziv.

"You . . . . you have seen the Archangel Michael?" Akiva stammered in disbelief.

"I thought you were biblically illiterate, Aphar," chided Ziv with a twinkle in his eye. "Yes, that is who he said he was. Big guy! At least ten feet tall! Hefted the biggest sword I've ever seen!" he remarked, ignoring his subordinate's dumbfounded expression.

"This is unprecedented," marveled General Akiva.

"Well, I've never seen an angel before myself. It's an awesome experience—like coming in contact with a live high-voltage electric wire. Raises the hair right up on the nap of your neck," Zechariah remarked, shuddering slightly as he relived the vivid experience.

"Incoming! Hit the dirt!" shouted Abrahamson.

Diving to relative safety under their adjacent staff vehicle, a mortar round struck where they had all been standing only seconds before. Within moments, hundreds of shells began landing all along the Israeli positions, accompanied by artillery, tank and small arms fire.

"'Hit the dirt' the man says, as we're standing on solid rock," snickered Ziv.

"Looks like it's getting under way," Ziv remarked matter-of-factly above the din of continuous explosions.

Down the ancient cobblestone streets came the enemy by the multiplied thousands, accompanied by Russian and Arab tanks. Israeli gunners began firing a barrage of artillery, mortar, anti-tank and small arms fire into the approaching hordes, but the masses of invaders climbed over the corpses of their fallen comrades and continued to advance. Closer and closer the crowd of enemy soldiers came.

Then, as the three Israeli officers watched through their binoculars, something utterly astounding occurred: A gigantic figure in golden armor with a drawn broadsword in his hand appeared out in front of the Israeli positions and a host of bright beings, similarly armed, appeared with him. It was obvious that the approaching enemy also saw them, because many turned and tried to retreat the way they had just come. Confusion reigned supreme as they bucked the advancing tide of their comrades who had not yet seen the angelic destroyers. Some of those who fled fired their weapons into the crowd of their comrades attempting to clear a pathway for their own escape.

Then, in what appeared like the swath of a great scythe cutting through grain, the enemy soldiers began to literally disintegrate. Their eyes fell out of their sockets, their bodies melted and slid out of their clothing like ice on a hot stove. The three Israeli officers watched slack-jawed as the slaughter continued unabated. Within minutes, the enemy advance had turned into a rout. Amidst derelict tanks, the streets were covered with thousands of the rag-clad skeletons of Israel's enemies. As those still alive disappeared down streets and alleys, General Ziv began contacting commanders on the other fronts. Sure enough, the same thing was happening everywhere. The very enemy that had been so poised, proud and confident was now fleeing in stark terror. Of those who were fortunate enough to escape the destroyers, many ran for miles on sheer adrenalin before collapsing from exhaustion. Many Israeli command posts reported seeing enemy units firing wildly on each other.

"Abrahamson," chuckled Ziv, "let's go back to headquarters. I do believe Israel has been visited by her God. Carry on, Akiva. I'm going to get myself a bottle of wine, a hunk of cheese and a loaf of fresh bread to chow down on. Then, I may just sleep for a week—I hope. This will give our enemies a great deal to think about. But I fear this is only the first of many battles before our Mashiach returns. You watch, these idiots will rush back for more punishment before the dust settles on this one," he chortled, turning to leave.

As General Ziv walked to the door of his staff vehicle, he leaped into the air, clicked his heels together and was overheard singing, "Oooooh, whenever they got His Irish up, Yahweh lowered the boom . . . !"

☆ 22 ☆

LAST HOORAH

"General Black, it appears that we have more company coming our way," Arie announced, entering the Lodge accompanied by Ivan, Eli, Alex and the Sioux scouts who had only just returned from their expedition to the east.

"Oh, swell. What is it this time?" Jim snapped sarcastically, steeling himself for the answer.

"Sir, about three hours ago, we spotted a scouting party on the trail a few miles east of here on our way back to the Lair. We took out several of them, but the rest got away. We captured one of their wounded who told us of their mission. The Alliance is sending a force of about two thousand troops from back east somewhere to take us out—probably airborne. Unfortunately, he died before he could tell us anymore than that," related John Glass.

"Jim, I've just located them by satellite," confirmed Arie, "They're on the way right now. I'm estimating their ETA to be less than an hour. The overcast is clearing and this time, my friends, I'm afraid they will have air support, as well as armor. If they have the coordinates of the Lair, they may drop ordnance whether they can see us or not. What do you think we should do, Jim?" he asked anxiously.

"If we had some place to run to," Jim returned, "I'd say call everyone together, get them in the airplanes and move out of here, but, there's no place to go that I know of. Before we go off half-cocked, we need to talk to Wohno. Give the good colonel a call and tell him we have a problem," he instructed.

"I'll get right on it, Chief," said Ivan.

"In the meantime, I want lookouts posted on the east rim of the canyon with sniper rifles and radios. Tell 'em to whistle if they see anything," Jim ordered brusquely.

"Yes, Sir. We'll take care of it." promised John Glass as he hurried out the door.

"Eli, alert everyone as to what's going on. See to it everyone has a weapon who feels confident carrying one, and plenty of ammo. Notify Colonel Johnson to get his Spec Ops people ready for action. Get our aircraft people busy checking the armaments on the war birds and make sure they're fueled. We're going to have a fight on our hands any time now," Jim said in rapid succession.

"Roger, Chief. Right away," Eli snapped to attention.

"The enemy will undoubtedly approach us on the eastern flank, if that is where they had their scouts," Jim said, thinking out loud. "Let's all get our hides up on the east ridge as fast as our feet can carry us. Alex, please get me an M-4 and at least 1,000 rounds of ammo out of the armory. Then, let's move out smartly, gentlemen," he ordered.

"Aye, it'll take me just a few minutes. I'll be right back, Sir," Alex responded over his shoulder as he ran out of the room.

Several minutes later the bearded giant returned with an M-4 and several of the ammo canisters Jim had requested. He was also carrying a large weapon case in one hand and three sizable ammo cans of his own in the other.

"What do you have there, Alex?" Jim asked bemused.

"I've brought my .50 caliber Barrett sniper rifle and 1,000 rounds of ammo. My .50-170 Sharps is my favorite, but she's low velocity, high trajectory, slow to fire and puts out clouds of smoke that'll give away our position. This Barrett is fast, smokeless and deadly—I can whack a target first shot nearly two miles away with this artillery piece," Alex grinned in anticipation.

"Cool!" Jim smiled, "We need all the help we can get. Okay, let's mount up, gentlemen, and go see what we're facing."

Fifteen minutes later, the armed party arrived on the east rim of the canyon, near the spot where Jim had encountered the wolves. As the men spread out along the ridge to find cover and advantageous fields of fire, Jim and Colonel Johnson surveyed the expanse of open country to the east with binoculars.

"Nothing yet," Jim observed calmly, "Hope we're in the right place, Johnson."

"We'll know shortly, Jim," Johnson replied tersely.

At that moment, Jim's radio crackled with Ivan's voice. "General, I just heard from Colonel Wohno. He is on his way. He says the attack will come from the east and that it will be airborne troops who will be air-dropping tanks and artillery. He also says not to worry; everything is under control and to keep your aircraft on the ground."

"Well, that's a relief to finally hear from him," Jim said wryly, "Notify the pilots to stand down, but be ready at a moment's notice."

"Och, Jim, I think I hear heavy aircraft to the east. Sounds like our company is about to arrive," Alex said, loading the Barrett's magazine and checking the sights.

Several minutes later, transport planes appeared east of the canyon, dropping a cloud of paratroopers on the open prairie. A second wave of aircraft dropped heavy equipment—several main battle tanks and artillery pieces.

Alex lined up on a tank commander as he mounted the turret of his vehicle. Moments later, the Barrett's .50 caliber 750 grain armor-piercing bullet sliced through the tanker's 'bullet-proof' vest like a knife through hot butter, blowing away his right arm and a quarter of his rib cage. "Gotcha!" chuckled Alex. Soon, the big Scot was pouring a deadly cadence of fire upon the enemy troops, each shot downing another man. Oil smoke was rolling out of the Barrett's action and stock as Alex paused occasionally to allow the big rifle to cool.

As the enemy began advancing within range of their .30 caliber sniper rifles, Colonel Johnson's Spec Ops men also began picking off troopers left and right.

When the enemy had advanced to within six hundred yards, Jim became seriously concerned. Tank and artillery rounds were churning up the tree-line and shattering boulders all around them while small arms fire was denuding the trees, forcing the defenders to fall back taking cover behind every large boulder they could find.

"Where is Wohno, anyway? We can't hold off this outfit much longer," Jim yelled, firing his M-4 continually, "I'm almost out."

"Aye, I'm down to just a few rounds myself," yelled Alex.

Suddenly, the enemy advance slowed, then halted and the incoming fire stopped abruptly. In the deafening silence, Jim peered around the boulder he was hiding behind and beheld an awesome sight. Enemy troops were standing staring in the direction of Jim's little band of brothers, eyes wide with fright. Many threw down their weapons and turned to run. None got very far.

Michael, the golden giant, was standing in front of Jim's boulder with drawn sword, smiling at Jim. Raising his sword, he moved toward the enemy with the cry "Onward, for the glory of God" joined by a host of fierce winged warriors who began appearing out of thin air.

Enemy soldiers began to die on their feet, melting like slugs, leaving their skeletons inside their clothing. Within minutes it was over and the prairie was littered with uniform-clad skeletons, derelict tanks and other vehicles.

In the ensuing silence, standing up and gingerly peeking over his rock, Jim yelled triumphantly, "Cease fire. Lock your weapons. I think we have just seen the glory of the coming of the Lord."

As the sum total of the Eagle's Lair defenders came out of their defensive positions and gathered around Jim, they determined that no one had been wounded or killed. As they stood there, Colonel Wohno's gunship swooped in overhead and landed on the runway below them.

"Let's get down off this ridge and let the whole camp know what has happened," said Jim joyfully.

Once back at the Lodge, the whole company of refugees was summoned into the media center and Jim related what had taken place, especially describing the arrival of the angelic visitors, with Colonel Wohno and Major Maag standing beside him.

Turning to Jim, Colonel Wohno said, "General Black, you, and Colonel Johnson and several others, have wondered where we have taken all those whom we have evacuated from a number of places across the U.S. over the last year or so. If you'd like to take a ride with us, we'll show you the place. We can't take everyone, but we can take you, Jim, and Maryann, Alex, Arie, Sarah and Colonel Johnson plus a couple others."

"You bet we would, Colonel. How far is it?" Jim asked excitedly.

"It's quite some distance. You will be gone for several days, but I promise you will enjoy it. The shooting is all over and everything will be just fine here until you return. There will be excellent accommodations at the other end," Wohno declared reassuringly, searching Jim's face.

"When do we leave?" asked Jim.

"Within the hour," replied Wohno.

☆ **23** ☆

THE EAGLES GATHER

As the four-engine gunship climbed to cruise altitude, Jim, Arie, Colonel Johnson and Alex crowded into the craft's 'business office' where they could observe the expanse of landscape passing below. The beauty of the countryside below them was marred here and there by burned out towns, cities and farmsteads.

Returning at length to their seats, they tried to nap, ignoring the thrum of the engines. After what seemed like hours, the turbo-props changed pitch as the nose dipped. Within a few minutes, they were alerted by the whine of gear and flaps coming down.

"Why are we landing, Colonel?" Jim asked curiously.

"We are pausing to refuel, General. You should recognize this place, Sir," replied Wohno.

As the propellers coasted to a stop, the little party emerged from the ship to stretch their legs as Wohno's crewmen set about servicing the airplane. Looking around, Jim did indeed recognize the place.

"Hey!" Jim cried, "This is Etzion's Nevada emergency fuel stop. How long have you been using our place, Wohno?" he asked good-naturedly.

"Oh, for quite some time now, General. But don't be concerned," Wohno replied, "we service your fuel tanks on a regular basis—you won't be out anything."

"Oh, I'm not worried, just surprised," Jim answered, grateful his facility had been available for good use.

Jim and Maryann walked along the taxi strip breathing the perfume of the desert air. "Ahh! The desert smells wonderful, doesn't it Hon?"observed Jim.

"Yes, it's certainly a change from the Montana pine forests. After all those months freezing to death in the North Land, I welcome the chance to defrost here," she replied ruefully.

At length, Colonel Wohno beckoned to the pair, "We've taken on a full load of fuel and we're ready to be off. We're roughly a third of the way to our destination," he said, motioning for them to board the aircraft.

An hour after lift-off, Jim again went forward to the cockpit and observed the instrument panel over the pilot's shoulder. The heading on the gyro-compass read 244 degrees. As the California coastline passed beneath the belly of the ship, it was obvious they were headed for a destination somewhere out in the Pacific Ocean.

Curious, Jim tapped the pilot on the shoulder and asked, "Where are we headed, Captain?"

"An island we call 'Aurora', 750 miles off the coast of Baja California and about 900 miles southwest of San Diego," was the pleasant reply, "I think you'll like it. We'll let you know when the island comes into view so you can all see it from the air, Sir," he offered graciously.

Jim returned to his seat next to Maryann, pulled out a reduced set of air-navigation sectional charts and searched for an island in the approximate area that the Captain had described. There was nothing but uninhabitable seamounts and open ocean. Scowling, he returned the maps to the pouch and sat thinking with a vacant expression on his face. Maryann, poked him in the ribs and said, "What's the problem, sourpuss?"

"I dunno, Honey, this whole thing just gets weirder and weirder. Captain says we're going to a place that doesn't even exist on the map," he answered, scowling and stroking his chin thoughtfully.

"Well," she laughed, "what's so strange about that? The Eagle's Lair isn't on the map either. So what else is new?" she asked wide-eyed, feigning surprise.

"Yeah, you're right, Hon. Why am I always blind to the obvious?" Jim asked with a far-away look on his face as he turned to stare out the window.

"Maybe it's because you've had a lot on your mind lately, General," she said smiling lovingly and squeezing his hand.

"Ahh, well . . . . " Jim sighed audibly and let his voice trail off.

Several hours later, the co-pilot shouted, "General Black, 'Aurora' is in sight; you and your friends might want to come up and have a look at it," as he came down from the cockpit, passing Jim's seat as he moved toward the rear of the ship. Jim motioned to Maryann, Arie, Alex and Colonel Johnson to accompany him to the cockpit.

Alex was a tight fit in the limited space of the cockpit, but the view of the island dead ahead was breathtaking. There was a low coastal area just above sea level that contained an airstrip. Behind the coastal area, cliffs and mountains rose thousands of feet with a high valley in between the mountain ranges. The mountain peaks were shrouded in rain clouds and waterfalls could be seen at various elevations around the island, splashing into azure lakes below. Tropical vegetation ringed the lower levels and it appeared that more temperate vegetation grew at the higher elevations.

"Wow, what an idyllic place! I never knew there was an island like this off Mexico," marveled Jim.

"Sir, this island does not appear on navigation charts for the same reason that the Eagle's Lair is normally hidden," explained the Captain, "This is another 'City of Refuge', or 'Island of Refuge', if you will. We're about to land, folks, so you should all return to your seats now and strap in tight. We often experience considerable turbulence from thunderstorms around the island this time of day."

Minutes later, the aircraft was abruptly subjected to violent buffeting as it passed through a flock of scudding thunderstorms on final approach. The turbulence was so severe that several in the party lost their lunch and Jim wondered if he would have bruises where the seat belts cut into his lap.

But as the pitch of the engines changed, and the gear and flaps whined into action, there was a rush of sweetly-scented tropical air throughout the cabin. The aircraft touched down, turned onto a taxiway and rolled to a stop on the tarmac. As the doors opened, the greatly relieved travelers disembarked into a tropical paradise.

"Man, I think I've died and gone to heaven," marveled Jim, as he gawked at the surroundings like a *tourista*.

"Heaven is so much better than this, you can't even imagine," replied Colonel Wohno drily as he joined them on the pavement, "Here comes a tram to pick you all up. It will take you to our guest accommodations, where you'll eat your evening meal and meet some of the folks already here. Tomorrow, we'll take you all on a tour of the island," he said graciously, ushering them into the open-air vehicle.

As the group entered the commons building hall, which adjoined their accommodations, they discovered that a large group of island inhabitants were obviously already enjoying themselves and partaking of refreshments and music. Someone in the crowd shouted, "Hey everybody, there's General Black and that big mountain man we've been hearing so much about. Dr. MacIntosh, tell us about your encounter with the invaders."

"Ah, well, if I must, I must," Alex grinned slyly and winked at Jim.

As Alex was concluding his tale an hour later, a Scottish brogue behind his back caught his attention. "Alex, I must speak wi' ya," the owner of the voice said quietly. "Aye, and who might you be, Sir?" inquired Alex turning about, as the rest of the audience walked away.

"I am Angus MacLeod of Kilmartin, in Argyllshire, Scotland. My father was Aaron MacLeod, the rector of the church in the Kilmartin Valley that you visited some years ago," he began slowly, focusing intently on Alex.

"Aye, I remember him well. How is he?" Alex asked with a broad grin.

"He passed away several months before I arrived here in the U.S.," replied the Scot somewhat distantly.

"Och, I'm sorry to hear that. I wish I'd been able to talk freely and more at length with him that day when I was run out of town by some of your local hoodlums," Alex responded with regret and sympathy for the other man's loss.

"Well, Dr. MacIntosh, before he died, he verbally imparted some confidential information to me, which I committed to rote memory. He made me promise to find you and transmit the whole thing to you in person. It was information of a very sensitive nature so I was on my way to visit with you face-to-face when the invasion occurred and I ended up here. I think it might be best if we talked privately if you don't mind," he said lowering his voice mysteriously to a bare whisper.

"Ye . . . uh, yes. Of. . .of course," Alex croaked, "Let's . . . uh . . . let's find a quiet place where we can sit down and talk," he said looking around furtively, "I rather thought there was more to be learned than your father had shared with me that evening."

As they walked into an unoccupied room and closed the door, Alex said, "I am just blown away. How did you ever find me? When did you come here, anyway?" his weathered face visibly registering a mixture of intrigue and concern.

"Well, Sir, I was on my way to Denver to rent a car by which to drive up to Montana hoping to locate you when all this unpleasantness struck and my flight was forced to land in Rapid City, South Dakota. My father knew approximately where you lived and had somehow heard of the Eagle's Lair. Knowing its approximate location, we suspected you might be in the vicinity. So, when my captors at Rapid City proved a bit too busy, I managed to sneak away and hide until nightfall. When the opportunity presented itself, I . . . uh . . shall we say . . .'liberated' . . .a private aircraft at the Rapid City airport and flew directly to the Eagle's Lair hoping to find you. You were apparently, not yet known to General Black, so I flew on against his better advice. I was captured by Hezbollah at Great Falls, Montana, and incarcerated in their death camp, which was later liberated by the General's little air force. I was then brought here by Colonel Wohno's people to recover from a minor gunshot wound I had sustained during the raid. I tell you, it was quite a sight to see vintage American WWII combat aircraft come boiling over the hill with guns blazing. The fighters came in so low, I actually saw some of my captors struck by propeller blades as they ran for cover. Now, that's what I call 'close air support'! And I shall never forget the sound of the artillery shell fired by one of those B-25s which took down the main gate of the camp or how those gunships destroyed the death ovens on the other side of the camp," he said, instantly reliving those events with a mixture of awe, gratitude, and terror in his eyes.

"Well, lad, come, come, what is it you have to tell me?" Alex said, patting him on the shoulder, intrigued by his new friend's remarks.

"Dr. MacIntosh, my father told me that he had operated for many years as a double agent 'working both sides of the street' in the Prieure de Sion, as you Americans would say. You see there are two main opposing factions within the Prieure—the side Kaiser Bill is on and the side your family is on. Father dared not tell you all he knew at the time of your visit for fear of his life. The walls may have had 'ears,' you know. He was always suspect and had been called on the carpet for interrogation by both sides on many occasions. He always managed to smooth talk his way out of trouble, however. I do not know exactly how he came by all the information I am about to impart to you or what his exact function might have been in the rarified atmosphere of worldwide intrigue, but all that is academic at this point, I suppose," Angus continued.

"What I wanted to tell you first, Alex, is that you are the descendant of Jean and Guillaume de Gisors, both of whom lived in France during the 12th and 13th centuries," the little Scot intimated.

"Aye, I'm thoroughly acquainted with that whole crew, and I have always known I was somehow tied to them by blood in some way, but I've never really been sure of exactly how, my friend," responded Alex.

"Well, then, know that Jean was the descendent of Godfroi de Buillon who bore the title 'King of Jerusalem.' Godfroi organized the first Crusade against the Holy Land, and captured Jerusalem from the Saracen Muslims in 1099. Jean was the grandfather of Guillaume and both men were Grand Masters of the Prieure de Sion—the Order of Zion. Godfroi and the de Gisors were said to be descendants of the Merovingian kings and therefore descendants of the so-called 'Grail Family,' the reputed bloodline of Jesus and Mary Magdalene, if you believe in that sort of thing. In other words, you, Sir, are reputed to be of the royal bloodline of Jesus of Nazareth!" he explained with trepidation.

"Och," roared Alex, "I fully repudiate that 'royal bloodline' bit o' malarkey. Jesus of Nazareth never married nor did He ever have sex or earthly children by any woman."

"Well, your ancestor, Chretien de Gisors, believed it. He was a giant of a man like you and a favorite nephew of Guillaume's. Chretien was a Knight Templar while Guillaume, as I said, was Grand Master of the Prieure, which allegedly betrayed the Templars. Apparently, Guillaume forewarned Chretien and some of his brothers in arms at Bezu in southern France, of the coming purge on that fateful day in 1307 when King Philippe of France conspired with the corrupt Pope to annihilate the Templars, arrest most of their membership and seize their vast assets. Chretien, aware of the king's plot, escaped to the seaport of La Rochelle just ahead of the king's henchmen, carrying some sort of Templar treasure. There, he boarded a Templar galley lying at anchor in the harbor, joined by others of his brethren also bearing Templar treasures. Their galleys hurriedly set sail and split up in a dozen different directions. Chretien's ship sailed around the western shore of Ireland, stopping at Galway, before heading for Scotland where she landed near Loch Sween. She was later scuttled off the east coast of the Isle of Jura, as soon as the cargo and passengers were offloaded. Chretien already owned a fortified manor house in what is today Argyllshire on Loch Awe, near Kilmartin. There, he and some of his compatriots took up permanent residence. Obviously, the de Gisors name was well known and would have raised eyebrows in certain quarters, so Chretien assumed the name of Gregor Campbell. Chretien subsequently married the daughter of a highland chieftain named MacDougal. Being the accomplished warrior that he was, Chretien joined the ranks of Scottish King Robert the Bruce to help the outnumbered Scots defeat the English at the Battle of Bannockburn in 1314. Can you imagine the terror instilled in the enemy by the sight of a man standing 7'-6," wearing the tunic and armor of a Knight Templar, riding a huge charger and wielding an enormous broadsword, coming at you over the hill? Chilling!! Positively chilling!!

"Well, fast-forwarding to the 20th century, your father's name is William Campbell. Your mother is an Irish woman of noble lineage named Maeve Dunlavy. Your mum's last name is a corruption of the name 'Duns Levi'—

Gaelic for the 'House of Levi'—for you see, she is descended from the Levite priests who accompanied Jeremiah the Prophet to Ireland over twenty five centuries ago" exclaimed Alex's companion excitedly.

"Whoa! Wait! Wait a minute! You keep speaking of my parents in the present tense. Are you implying that they are still alive?" croaked a red-faced Alex in disbelief.

"Indeed, Alex, your parents are very much alive! They live in a heavily guarded, walled compound in a high valley in a remote area of Costa Rica. Your adoptive parents were spirited out of Glasgow, Montana, only minutes ahead of Burgoyne's torpedoes and are also living in the compound with your birth parents. But let me continue.

"Colonel Wohno gave me a recording of the teaching sessions you conducted at the Lair. It will be significant for you to know that your mum and dad who were in their teens at the time, were married like the kings and queens of Scotland while standing upon the *Lia Fail* stone, also known as the Hebrew *Stone of Destiny*—this gives you an idea of what important persons they, and you, are," concluded Angus.

"But . . . . but how could that have happened? The *Lia Fail* has resided in England's Coronation Chair in Westminster Abbey since 1296," asked an incredulous Alex, his eyes narrowing in disbelief.

"Och, Laddie, obviously you haven't heard that the Stone of Destiny was stolen from Westminster—removed from the chair—during Christmas eve of 1950, by certain unidentified Scottish patriots. The theft, actually carried out by Prieure people, was never 'solved' despite the 'best efforts' of Scotland Yard. Unfortunately, during the heist, one of the operatives dropped the stone and broke it, but they repaired it as best they could. The stone was eventually returned to British authorities surreptitiously some time later in the dark of night," Grinned the little Scot.

"Your mum is nearly seven feet tall and your father is well over seven and a half feet. You are a dead-ringer for him, which is the reason why most of the older townsfolk around Argyllshire acted as though they'd seen a ghost when you showed up. For those in the know, the other side of the Prieure had warned people not to confide in you. Your mum's sister, Marie, married a Frenchman by the name of William Burgoyne—our very own 'Kaiser Bill.' Burgoyne's family is an inferior branch of the de Gisors family.

Furthermore, it eventually came to light that they had put out a contract on you and your parents, inasmuch as your branch of the family has the proven hereditary right to what is now Burgoyne's position. Of course, they stood to benefit greatly by eliminating the competition. Either your father, or you, should rightfully have been not only Grand Master of the Prieure but Emperor of the EU instead of Burgoyne. If that had occurred, we would not now be in this worldwide mess," Angus said breathlessly.

Alex, wiping tears from his face and shaken to the very core of his being, was quiet for some time, lost in thought. Finally, he said, "Well, this answers much of the malaise of my life. But I have no organization, no power and I certainly have no desire to sit where William sits. I have met him and from the sheer evil I saw in his eyes, I suspect that he is the person spoken of in the Revelation of St. John as the Antichrist," he said, almost in a wail.

"I think you are most probably correct! By the way, Alex, I heard through the grapevine that a group of Burgoyne's people disappeared in the Montana forests right around the time your wife and brother-in-law were murdered," grinned MacLeod, with a knowing wink.

"Och, I wonder how that news got out!" grinned Alex, "Aye, that lot of them fed the forest critters that winter," laughed Alex heartily. "Bless you for coming to me, Angus. Let me pray about all this. And, please, let's keep all this just between the two of us for a while."

"As you wish, Sir," agreed Angus reassuringly.

"Come, Lad, let's join the rest of the folks in the Great Room," Alex smiled as he arose, a bit unsteadily, to his feet.

That evening, while the Eagle's Lair party was eating, a group of strangers walked into the hall. As Jim scanned the faces of the newcomers, he spotted a familiar face.

"Steve Nelson!" cried Jim jumping up from his chair, "Am I ever surprised to see you."

As the two embraced, Jim queried, "When did you come here, my friend?"

"Aw, Jim, am I glad to see you! Guess you all just came in from the Eagle's Lair? We were brought here not long after you all left for Montana. The Marines scooped us up right under the noses of the invaders and brought us out here. Man, what a place this is! Check out my suntan! I've been oinking out on fresh fruits and veggies—lost 20 pounds."

"Well, if you don't know it by now," Jim said emphatically, "I can tell you these folks aren't 'Marines'! They are something else altogether. The Lord has appeared to me and we've also been visited up at the Lair by Michael the Archangel and some of his associates. We saw what God does to those who hate Him and Israel. Man, what an experience! Listen, George, we'll have time to talk later. I'd love to fill you in on a lot of things that have happened, as well as some others that are coming up. 'Vacation' may be about over for all of us."

Steve slapped Jim on the back, with a quizzical look on his face, and began mingling with the others.

The next morning, during their grand bus tour of the island, Steve settled into a seat next to Jim and proceeded to pump him for information.

"Okay, Steve, here's the deal. All my life I have thought of myself as someone other than who I really am. I'm not a Native American, as I've always assumed. Apparently, I was adopted as a baby . . .and. . I now understand that I am a direct descendant of George Washington! Somehow, this fact seems to qualify me, in the Lord's view, and He has appointed me to be the overseer of North America as it rebuilds and gets back on its feet. I don't know what you'd call me—certainly not 'President Black,' since I'm not elected! What happens after we rebuild is up to Him, but I can tell you one thing . . . I have no desire to be 'King' of America'! It just goes against my grain!" Jim stated vehemently.

"All I know is this: The enemies, foreign and domestic, that came up against our country, as well as those who were about to flatten Israel, have all been decimated by the swords of angels to the extent that if they would try it again, I'd have to say they were smoking peyote or something. Our country is in terrible shape right now. We've lost about seventy million of our people. But we have been assured that we will have the wherewithal, as a nation, to rebuild under the shelter of the Almighty. And I intend to get it done. I'm not going to put up with 'Political Correctness,' just the Constitution, the whole Constitution and nothing but the Constitution!

If horse sense is good enough for horses, it's good enough for me. We're gonna get this country back on the right track just as soon as possible, and I'm going to demand some incontrovertibly explicit language changes on certain provisions of the Bill of Rights—especially the First Amendment right to a free press and freedom of religion, not freedom from religion, and the Second Amendment right of individuals to keep and bear arms, just for starters," Jim said emphatically.

Back at the commons building on the stage of the Great Room, Jim gathered his principal people around him for a forum meeting. Jim described to them the conditions surrounding his appointment as the overseer of the 'Northern Tier.' There were remarks of approval from most, but some grumbled.

"I'm with you all the way Jim," chuckled Steve Nelson, "I can't wait to get started. But I'll sure miss the good life on this island," he laughed heartily.

"This island will be accessible to all of you for a very long time, my friends—for as long as you need it," interjected Colonel Wohno.

Jim asked, "Okay, Colonel, where do we go from here?"

"Well, I . . ." began Wohno.

Before Wohno could complete the sentence, Michael stepped abruptly into their midst as all fell back at the brilliance of his appearance, awed by his size and weakened by the power of God that radiated from this mightiest of angels. The golden giant observed, "You have all seen the final deliverance of your nation from the enemy that has overtaken and raped her. The men destroyed east of the Eagle's Lair were the last to die. Their destruction was reserved so you at the Lair could see it with your own eyes. All the rest died within an hour of that event or have withdrawn from American soil—none will return to America. Know that the same death was visited upon the armies that have been drawn up around the borders of Israel awaiting the chance to annihilate God's people and seize their lands. But the end is not yet—this is but the beginning of the judgments of God on His enemies.

"General Black, as you well know, God has chosen you to oversee all of America, Canada, Mexico and Central America in the process of rebuilding.

I say this publicly for the benefit of all who are within the sound of my voice here this day so that all will understand that you have been chosen and are to be obeyed in all things, just as if it were the Lord Himself issuing the orders," Michael said emphatically, as he turned and made explicit eye contact with those who had grumbled about Jim's appointment. Those who were the object of Michael's pointed stare, blanched, trembled in fear and tried to hide behind the others.

Turning, at length, to a huge Black angel standing beside him, Michael said, "Tal, the flag please."

"Och, Tal! Haven't I seen you before? I thought you were Air Force!" shouted Alex, incredulously.

Tal merely smiled as he produced an American flag from a case slung across his back, upon which fluttered a golden banner with the word 'Union' emblazoned upon it. Michael took off his own helmet and removed a golden crown from its interior which also bore the word 'Union' and hung it upon the flagstaff crying aloud, "While the stars remain and the heavens send down dew upon the earth, so long shall your Union last. Let every child of this Republic learn to live for his God, his land and the Union," as all the people knelt and said, 'Amen.'

General Black, you are now in charge of everything. As the Lord's viceroy, your word is law in all things until He Himself returns. Do you understand and accept this commission?" Michael asked solemnly.

"Yes, Michael, with God's help I will accomplish all that He requires of me," promised Jim reverently.

"Please kneel, General," said Michael.

As Jim complied, wondering what was about to happen, Michael retrieved a small flask from his belt, stepped before Jim, opened the flask, and poured sweet-smelling oil over Jim's head saying, "With this oil, I anoint you, James Black, as God's Viceroy and Acting President of the United States of America. Serve God, and bless the people!"

"I must leave now," announced the great angel, "Know that America, as well as the entirety of the North American land mass, will be shielded from the destroyers of the earth and shall have everything needed to rebuild. General Black, the serious enemies of God here are no more. There will still be those who do not agree with you but no one shall be able to stand before you all the days of your life. Your people will find natural resources in unexpected places, which have been preserved and hidden for this day and hour. My soldiers and I are always available to aid you. You have only to call on us!" With that, the angels departed as suddenly as they had arrived.

"But . . . But, now that I think about it, this essentially makes me a dictator. I'm not really happy with that, Colonel Wohno," Jim complained uncomfortably, "That's not the American way! We went to war with England twice to be able to choose our own leaders democratically—dictators need not apply."

"God understands all that, General Black, but eventually, even America will come under the kingship of Jesus at His return to earth. When He gives an order, do you think anyone will be able to countermand Him? Do you think anyone will dare argue with the King of kings? He will one day return and set up His throne in Jerusalem to rule His world. The Bible says, 'As I live, says the LORD, Every knee shall bow to Me.'[18] Revelation also reads, "Out of His mouth goes a sharp sword, that with it He should strike the nations. And He Himself will rule them with a rod of iron. He Himself treads the winepress of the fierceness and wrath of Almighty God."[19] The LORD knows that you are trustworthy. Understand that He has approved and installed you as His viceroy, so do not wince at wielding the righteous power He has given you for good. There is much that must be corrected in North America and you are just the man to do it. Just take care that you are faithful in all things," concluded Wohno.

"We will return you to the Eagle's Lair when you are ready," explained Colonel Wohno, "Houston was never touched as far as its infrastructure is concerned—no nuclear weapons were detonated there and most of the houses, as well as your company plant, are intact just as you left them. You may pick up your Citation and other aircraft and return your people to Houston to resume their lives there. The C5-B already displays the designation of 'The United States of America.' Your technicians at the Eagles Lair are even now busy lettering the fuselage of your Citation with the same designation—when you board any aircraft, from a Piper Cub to the Presidential 747, it automatically becomes 'Air Force One.' When all is restored to your satisfaction in Houston, and your lives have been put back into a semblance of order, you and your advisors, my friend, will choose the location for a new capitol complex. God-appointed delegates will come to you by revelation and reconstruction plans will be laid with the aid of these anointed patriots. Revelation from the Lord will come to all of you. The wisdom and authority of Heaven shall be revealed to all," assured Wohno.

"But, Colonel, our founding documents are gone! The Declaration of Independence, the Constitution, the Bill of Rights. We have copies, but that's just not the same as the real thing!" Jim lamented.

"Ah, not to worry, Sir. Patriots in positions of high authority within the former government at the Pentagon, with the highest-level security clearances, were alerted to the coming attacks. Just an hour before the attacks began, they raided the National Archives and the Capitol, spiriting the original documents and other artifacts out of Washington to a secure location. Never fear, these people will produce these materials safe and sound, as soon as the new government is organized. We will see to that," said Colonel Wohno.

"Oh, thank God!" Jim breathed with a sigh of relief.

"All right, Colonel Wohno, I believe we're ready to get started. Get us back to the Eagle's Lair tomorrow morning. For the time being, the government will reside there. Later, I'm thinking we may move it to central Kansas or Missouri—someplace away from both of the 'left' coasts."

☆ **24** ☆

AIR FORCE ONE

As Colonel Wohno's aircraft scuffed down on the Lair's runway, Jim's heart leaped in anticipation of the task ahead.

Soon after landing, the returnees entered the auditorium of the Media Center and Jim addressed his companions, "I will need the help of every one of you who will be available. Arie, Alex, Colonel Johnson, what are your plans at this time?"

"My men and I are available to assume whatever duties you assign us, Sir," replied Colonel Johnson with obvious enthusiasm.

Alex chimed in, "Och, Laddie, as soon as I get my family situation straightened, I will be 100 percent at your disposal! But Mr. MacLeod here has informed me that I am the 'heir apparent' to the hegemony now occupied by Kaiser Bill. I have no interest in that; but, more importantly, he has revealed to me the wonderful news that my parents and step-parents are still alive and living together. I assumed they were all dead years ago. I cannot wait to see them," he announced, grinning from ear to ear.

"That is marvelous news, Alex. Do you know exactly where they live, Angus?" Jim asked the other Scot.

"Aye, that I do, General. They reside in a fortified, walled village, called 'Tiaglen,' high in the mountains of Cost Rica, southeast of San Jose."

"Alex, now that I am in charge of everything from Costa Rica north, I will be visiting Central America in a few days to begin getting certain things realigned there. When I have completed my work there, we will all accompany you and Mr. MacLeod to Costa Rica with some of our Sioux friends. I'd love to meet your family myself," Jim beamed.

"That is more than generous of you, Jim," Alex responded gratefully, "I can't tell you what that means to me," the depth of the big man's gratitude resounding in his voice.

"It's the very least I can do for you, my friend. We can't have you going it alone in a strange country," Jim said with genuine concern.

"Arie, what about you? Will you return to Israel at this time?" Jim asked, turning his attention to his Israeli partner.

"Not just yet, I'm trying to reach General Ziv right now. Until I know more, we'll just stick around and help you any way we can, Jim," Arie said evenly.

"Excuse me, General," announced Ivan abruptly, "But we are receiving radio transmissions from a number of aircraft on their way here bringing delegates of the new government—several former governors and U.S. senators are among them. Looks like the word is spreading, courtesy of 'Wohno and Company'!" he quipped with a twinkle in his eye.

"Great! Show them into the Lodge as soon as they land," Jim said, elated, "See if you can raise some of our other military commanders and get them in here too."

"I think some of them are also on the way, General," Ivan assured him.

"I know we've lost a ton of high-caliber people in this country, and we need to contact as many as are left. I particularly want to see petroleum engineers, power scientists and military commanders from all the various service branches, for starters. I want oil exploration started immediately on the outer continental shelves, everywhere in the ANWAR, all over the rest of Alaska, North Dakota, Montana and Idaho—wherever the scientists suspect we have untapped oil reserves. During WWII, Hitler had the technology to convert coal to oil and gas and we certainly have far more sophisticated technology available today, so we need to make conversion plant proposals our highest priority. I also want plans developed immediately to build at least four dozen nuclear power plants!" instructed Jim.

"What about the environmentalists? They'll have a fit!" snorted Eli.

"I will not tolerate any foolishness! The environmental extremists will just have to understand that their day is over and Political Correctness is now a thing of the past. There will be no protests—period—only common sense. We need every barrel of oil, every kilowatt of power, every board-foot of lumber we can muster just as soon as possible!" Jim pronounced testily, his voice calming and the fire in his eyes abating somewhat.

"Uh . . . General, there's a call for you on a secure channel. Don't know who it is or how he got our number but he says his name is John something or other," Uri announced, sounding somewhat irritated.

As Jim picked up the phone, the person on the other end responded, "Hello? General Black? This is John Mason."

"Well, General Mason, you old horse-thief! How are you anyway?" chortled Jim, as his somber mood evaporated, "Haven't seen you in a coon's age. Where have you been hanging out? Heard a while back you got star number three before the invasion. So, how did you find me, man," cried Jim excitedly.

"Well, you see there was this AC-130 gunship, piloted by an Air Force colonel and a major. They gave me your satellite phone number and told me you had been appointed by the 'Big Guy Upstairs' to be Acting President. Congratulations, Sir! You always were a straight-arrow kinda guy!" responded General Mason with obvious admiration.

"Thanks . . . . I think," Jim grinned a bit cynically, "But say no more, John, I know that pair you're talking about very well and I'm not surprised they sought you out," Jim concluded, recovering his usual good humor.

"Yep, well, I guess it's been about ten years since you and I served together at the Pentagon," the general resumed, "I injured a knee several years ago to the extent that they pulled me out of the Pentagon and put me 'out to pasture' teaching at the Air Force Academy. I own a remote log cabin and, as you can imagine, I've been living out there in the boonies while the foreign riffraff were tearing up the country. I sort of drifted back into town when they pulled out. But, to get down to brass tacks, Jim," his demeanor shifting perceptibly, "I'm the acting mayor here in Colorado Springs right now and we have something here that probably belongs to your office, Sir, so . . . we'd kinda like to return it," Mason replied.

"Now, let's see, 'Something that belongs to my office?' I'm sorry but I just don't follow you, John. What're you getting at?" responded Jim, clearly intrigued.

"Well, we've got a situation here I'd rather not discuss over the phone. Is there any chance you could stop by here sometime in the very near future? It's really important for several reasons," declared Mason sounding vaguely mysterious.

"Well, I'm scheduled to fly to Houston this afternoon. Guess I could drop in for a bit on my way down. Meet me at the airport at about 3:00pm," said Jim, curious as to what Mason might be alluding to.

"Copy that! See you soon, Jim!" Mason concluded, signing off.

As Jim's biz-jet taxied up to the gate at the Colorado Springs airport several hours later, he could see his old compatriot togged out in full dress blue Air Force uniform, three silver stars shining in the sunlight on each shoulder, perched on the seat of a motor scooter.

"That's a mighty snazzy staff car you have there, General," laughed Jim heartily as he deplaned.

"Well, Jim, you know all about 'RHIP,' 'rank has its privilege,'" quipped the general as they shook hands and embraced.

Wasting no time getting to the point, Jim asked, "Now, what's so all-fired important that you dragged my aching old carcass down here, John?"

"Well, it's like this, my friend: On the night the bombs went off all over the country, our tower turned off our runway lights at midnight. In the wee hours of the morning, the tower received a distress call from an aircraft declaring an in-flight emergency. They repeatedly refused to identify themselves but insisted upon their need to land immediately. Reluctantly, the tower turned on the runway lights and gave permission to land; an obviously large aircraft landed and taxied up near the gates, where it was dark. Our head security officer, Ed Acosta, happened to be on duty and went to investigate. He found Air Force One, VC-25A 30000, doors wide open, sitting on the tarmac, deserted. He saw the President and his party breaking into two brand new SUVs the Airport Authority had just acquired. Knowing the President's reputation, and noticing that the Secret Service people with the President were carrying submachine guns, he decided caution was the better part of valor. Acosta decided to just stay out of sight and follow the vehicles at a respectable distance to see what they were up to. They made a beeline for the Cheyenne Mountain Directorate. We later learned that 'El Presidente' had ordered the place to be rewired enabling him to personally launch any, or all, of the Nuclear ICBMs still in their silos, as well as take complete command of most of our other strategic weapons in the U.S. arsenal. Man, I don't know what that guy had in mind but I'm glad we never found out," continued the general, further stimulating Jim's growing sense of apprehension.

"So, they're holed up in that fortress, are they?" Jim fretted, "We'll never get them out until they get hungry and that'll be a very long time," lamented Jim, knowing the reputation of the invulnerability of the Cheyenne Mountain installation.

"Not to worry, Jim, they're not in Cheyenne Mountain," replied Mason, grinning and looking askance at Jim.

"But . . you said. I thought . . . " Jim stammered, trying to interpret where the general was going.

Beckoning to a man who had walked up and stood a short distance behind him, General Mason introduced him. "Jim, this is Ed Acosta. I'll let him finish the story in his own words. Come over here, Ed, and tell General Black what you saw that night!"

"Well, Sir," began Acosta, "It's like this: They were on their way but . . . they never made it. We'd had an unusually early cold snap out here that night and there was freezing precipitation all over the area. It was late at night, visibility was very bad and the roads were covered in black ice. The President's drivers were pushing the SUVs way too fast for those road conditions. At an intersection, an 18-wheel tanker truck, loaded with 10,000 gallons of jet fuel, slid through a red light on the ice and T-boned the lead vehicle that was carrying the President and his family. The trailing SUV lost control and collided with the wreckage. The tanker exploded and . . . . well . . . Sir . . . as you know . . . jet fuel burns much hotter than gasoline. By the time the fire was out, there was nothing left except three badly melted vehicles. They found nothing in the ashes but small fragments of bone here and there. Everything and everyone in that conflagration was literally cremated. We found a badly melted gold belt buckle, bearing the Presidential Seal, which we recovered from the ashes at the scene," concluded the officer, "As they say in 'Ye olde flag shoppe,' '*Sic semper tyrannis*,' thus always to tyrants.' It was a fitting end for a very bad man," he observed, with a slight smile.

"Now, do you want to hear something really ironic? That 10,000 gallons of jet fuel, which incinerated the Presidential motorcade, was the first of five loads ordered by his administration to refuel Air Force One! We found out about that the next day, when the owner of the fuel company called the Airport Authority office demanding to know how he was going to be paid for the fuel and who would be held responsible for the destruction of his truck," interjected General Mason, obviously amused at this point.

"But there was something else, Sir," Acosta intimated lowering his voice, "Something I haven't told you or anyone else yet, General Mason, because I was afraid you'd think I was nuts," Ed said looking around apprehensively.

"Well, out with it man!" Jim chided good-naturedly, "Don't worry about either one of us. We've seen all sorts of weird things the past year or so. I'm getting used to weird!" he grinned.

"Well, Sir, as I was standing beside my cruiser that night watching the fire a short distance away, out of the corner of my eye I saw some movement to my right. I looked and there was a small group of men—really big guys—standing not fifty feet from the street on a small rise. I turned to look directly at them but I couldn't tell how tall they were at first. After they were gone, I paced off the distance and realized the biggest one had to have been close to . . . uh . . . ten feet tall!" said Acosta in embarrassed tones.

"Did they say or do anything?" Jim asked, intent on what the officer was trying to tell them.

"Yes, Sir, they sure did! One of them—a big blonde guy dressed in what looked like . . .uh . . .medieval armor, raised a sword and shouted, 'Evil has slain the wicked. Vengeance belongs to the Lord. This night, our God is avenged of His deadly enemies. Up! Let us be going!'" Acosta related trying to emulate the voice and body movements he had witnessed.

"Then, you know what they did?" he said in disbelief, "They . . .they . . . took off . . . straight up like 4th of July rockets and disappeared in the clouds. Never saw anything like that in all my life except maybe in the movies! Do you guys think maybe I'm a little nuts?" Acosta asked, fearing the answer.

"No, not at all, my friend!" Jim reassured him, "I have met that very same blonde gentleman myself, the very one you saw, Ed. So relax, you are definitely not nuts. It just so happens that he is Michael, the Archangel. And what, may I ask, ever became of Air Force One? Where did she end up?" Jim asked, changing the subject.

"That's why I wanted you to come down here, Jim. The airport staff cranked her up and ran her into a brand new empty hangar down the flight line. She's been in there ever since, so she should be in pristine condition. But we do need to get her out of there—the city needs the hangar space now. Do you have some place you can stash her or do you intend to fly her yourself?" Mason inquired, looking expectantly at Jim.

"That Boeing 747 is a wonderful airplane but it really takes a lot of fuel— 50,000 gallons to fill her up. So, I'm not going to use her on a regular basis. My little Citation will suffice for everyday travel in-country. But I do want to have her available for international travel if that becomes necessary. Let's go take a look at her, John," Jim said, turning abruptly on his heel in the direction of the new hangar.

Air Force One was, indeed, in good shape and Jim marveled at the opulence of the airplane. Calling Eli on his satellite phone, Jim instructed his lieutenant, "Eli, get those Israeli transport pilots and that flight engineer ready to come down here to Colorado Springs, stat."

"What's in Colorado Springs, Chief?" inquired Eli, in his usual comic relief.

"Eli, we have just located a certain elderly 747—precisely, 'El Presidente's' airplane—down here in Colorado Springs in a new hangar. I'm changing my plans temporarily and I'll be returning to the Lair shortly. I want those Israeli pilots to ferry Air Force One down to our plant in Houston, where we'll stash her in one of our empty hangars temporarily. I want our A&P people down there to go through her with a fine-tooth comb, before we go flapping around the world in her," Jim directed.

"Wahl ah'l be cow-kicked—Air Force One in Colorado Springs! What a place to find that ol' thang!" drawled Eli. "I'll have those Hebrew boys ready to fly by the time you get back, Boss!"

"While you're at it, have Alex, Uri, Arie and whoever else wants to come along ready to fly to Houston. They can either go with me in my Citation or languish in the lap of luxury on Air Force One" laughed Jim in return.

"Roger that, Boss. See you in a bit. I'll get the pilots to do some fast familiarization on our flight simulators," concluded Eli, more seriously.

☆ **25** ☆

THE ROYAL FAMILY

Slightly past 6:00am, Elijah Walton was rudely awakened from a deep sleep. He had 'crashed' on the sofa in his office at the Houston headquarters of Etzion Defense Enterprises, International, following a late-night arrival from Montana aboard Air Force One.

"Hunh . . . wha . . . who are ya' and whadaya want, anyhow?" Eli snapped. Realizing he had grabbed the wrong phone in his groggy state of mind, he threw aside the receiver and picked up another one instead.

"Yeah, what?" he snarled, still half asleep.

"Mr. Walton, this is Charley down at the main gate. Hey, I'm sorry to bother you so early, Sir, but we have someone here you may want to check out," explained the unruffled voice at the other end.

"Ohhh . . . Charley . . . . I am sooo sorry I barked at you, man. When I woke up just now, I didn't know which end was up. Okay, I'm really awake now. Wha' did ya' say you've got?" Walton stuttered, trying to clear his head.

"Don't apologize, Boss, I've been there an' done that! Anyway, we have this guy out here at the gate who says he's from Scotland, and from the burr on his tongue, I'd say that much is definitely true! Says he heard through the grapevine that there may be some sort of a 'giant' here by the name of

Alexander MacIntosh. Says he needs to talk to him immediately. You know anyone of that description?" queried the sentry cautiously.

"I . . .uh . . . yeah . . . I sure 'nuf do know a 'giant' named Alex MacIntosh. Listen, bring that guy up here to my office immediately," ordered Eli.

Ten minutes later, the burley gate-guard arrived at Eli's temporary abode with a stranger in tow. Tucking in his shirttails, zipping up his trousers and brushing what was left of his hair to the side, Eli greeted the two as they entered his office.

"And who might you be, Sir, and how do you happen to know Alex MacIntosh?" inquired Eli a bit suspiciously.

"I am Fergus MacTavish, Mr. Walton. Alexander probably doesn't know me, but I am a servant of his family. I have lived in Brownsville, Texas, for many years where I have carried out my duties supplying their compound in Costa Rica and passing communications by shortwave radio. I had to lay low during the invasion and time my radio transmissions carefully. After the invaders left—melted, actually—I lost radio contact with the compound, so I decided to move a bit farther north to get away from the border riffraff. My automobile was destroyed by the invaders and all I have left to get around with is this miserable motor scooter. The other day, I ran into a man drinking beer at a convenience store as I journeyed north on this contraption. The fellow mentioned he'd recently been on an island somewhere in the Pacific where he'd seen a gigantic Scotsman in the company of a General Black, who, he understood, runs a defense plant somewhere here in Houston. Well, my antennae immediately went up and I proceeded to pump the lad for all the information I could get out of him. Today, as I was passing your compound, I had a sneaking suspicion this might be the place so I dropped in. Your establishment just somehow looked to be right. I take it you are acquainted with Alexander?" said MacTavish, finally pausing to breath as his companions tried to process all he had just related.

Eli finally said, "Well, your sneaking suspicion is correct, my friend. This is indeed General Black's emporium and Alex just happened to come with us to Houston last night. He is undoubtedly still asleep somewhere here on the premises."

Turning to the guard, Eli said, "Charley, go bug Uri. I think he and Alex were together last night after we landed. Tell Alex he's got company and to get his considerable hide down here to my office *mucho pronto*!" grinned Eli mischievously, imagining Alex' reaction to being rudely awakened.

"Yes, Sir! Now that you mention it, I do remember seeing a big guy with Uri last night. That must be Alex. I think I know where they ended up. I'll go see if I can roust them out," the guard returned Eli's grin and scurried out of the office.

Fifteen minutes later, three very rumpled individuals, Uri, Angus MacLeod and Alex, walked through the door.

"Fergus! Baby! How's Mrs. MacTavish's little boy?" cried Angus, "I'm so surprised to see you here. How did you ever find us?" he asked, utterly astounded.

"Och, Angus, who in the world is this guy anyway?" inquired Alex gruffly, visibly irritated at the intrusion on his 'beauty sleep,' as he referred to it.

"This man is Fergus MacTavish! He's sort of a go-between connecting our organization in Argyllshire with your family's compound in Costa Rica. He handles shipments of all kinds to the compound—things that can't be conveniently obtained in Costa Rica. Things like haggis and their favorite Scotch whisky. He does all their radio relays, as well," replied Angus, beaming.

"Prince Alexander, I am so honored to finally meet you, Sir. You are even taller than I'd imagined you'd be, but of a truth, a spittin' image o' your father! And a fine specimen of a man you are, at that!" added Fergus, "Ah, but I am afraid your family may be in grave danger, Alex. Two days ago, I engaged in an unsettling radio transmission with the compound that left me in a bit of turmoil. The man I usually dealt with was not available. The one I did speak with acted rather evasive, and I sensed something was not quite right. Then the radio went dead. Try as I might, I was never able to reestablish contact again. Frantic, I contacted Argyllshire but they said that, due to the world situation, they were unable to lend any assistance or shed light on what might be wrong. I prayed to God to somehow get me in touch with someone who could help me. Thank heaven, He led me here." exclaimed MacTavish, almost on the verge of tears.

Without another word, Eli picked up the phone and called the Black residence. Jim groggily answered the phone. "What's up, Eli?" the Boss wanted to know.

"Jim, we have a problem! What else? We've just received word that Alex's family in Cost Rica may be in some kind of trouble. Got any ideas how we can help 'em?" drawled the skinny Texan, grinning from ear to ear.

"I'll be right down. Needed to get up and going anyhow. Are you in your office?" Jim asked, instantly awake, his mind racing.

"Yup," Eli fired tersely.

Fifteen minutes later, a Humvee pulled up to Eli's office building and Jim Black emerged sporting camouflage fatigues, combat boots and three day's growth of beard.

"So, what's going on, boys?" Jim wanted to know as he breezed into the office.

"Jim, this is Fergus MacTavish who handles stuff for the compound where Alex's family lives in Cost Rica. He says he suspects the royals may be in some sort of danger. Is this something you would care to address at this time, Sir?" Eli proffered with a sly wink.

"Now, you know better than to ask me something like that, Eli!" Jim chided drily, winking back at Eli, "Whenever there's something nasty going on, my first reaction is always to go for the perpetrator's jugular. What are 'we' planning? Or do I want to know?" Jim grinned with a twinkle in his eye.

"Jim, I'm thinking we should get on down there to Costa Rica *poste haste* and check this thing out with our Sioux Spec Ops guys. Fergus here says there's a grass air strip about two miles from the compound over a low range of hills. The hills should shield us from the view of the compound. It's near a small village where he has contacts who should be able to provide transportation to the compound. We could fly 'The Black Cat,' that old C-47 we have out there that once was a 'Puff the Magic Dragon' in Nam. She was equipped as an AC-47D gunship mounting three of those 6-barrel electric Gatling guns. The guns were mounted to fire from the pilot's seat out the port side as a 'target suppressor.' She could circle a target and lay down eighteen thousand .30 caliber rounds per minute to subdue just about any enemy position. The rails, mounting hardware and wiring are still in place and we just happen to have stored four cherry miniguns back in our armory. And we have an equally cherry pilot, Charlie Volks, to fly her. What do you think, Chief?" concluded Eli smugly.

"I think you just might have something there, Eli," Jim grinned, "That ol' 'Gooney Bird' will give us the range and load capacity to get all of our party and gear where we want to go, and, the firepower to back us up to boot. The C-47's one of the best back-country cargo airplanes ever built. We'll fly directly to San Jose, refuel and proceed to the compound site. How long will it take to mount and stoke those miniguns?" Jim asked.

"With all the boys in the shop helping, I'd say maybe three hours," answered Eli.

"Okay, let's haul it, man! Alert Charlie Volks, get the ship togged out, serviced and fueled. I'll notify our scouts, grab my equipment and be back in an hour or so," said Jim excitedly.

"Aye, I'll be ready myself. I'm taking all my artillery along on this one," Alex declared darkly.

"Jim, I'm just wondering whether you should be going along on this kind of mission, though. I mean, you're no longer just any ol' private citizen, ya know. You could get hurt on a deal like this!" Eli reminded his friend, trying to be the voice of reason in an emotion-charged moment.

"Are you kidding, Eli? I wouldn't miss this for the world!" snorted Jim, "I want very much to meet Alex's family and besides, this is the best excuse I have for a wild-eyed junket down south," he said flippantly as he hurried out of the office door to prepare for the trip.

Jim entered the impromptu bunk quarters where the members of the 'Sioux Warrior Society' were just emerging from their overnight hibernation.

"Gentlemen, I have a mission for you if you're up for it. Would you boys be interested in participating in a possible assault on a walled compound?" inquired Jim with a grin and a hint of intrigue in his voice..

Instantly 'all business,' John Glass asked, "So, what's the bottom line here, General?"

"Alex's family lives in a walled compound in Costa Rica," Jim began, "We have reason to believe that they may be in some trouble there, possibly with some of Kaiser Bill's goons, and we're going down to go check it out in a couple hours. We'll be flying down in one of my old C-47s with three miniguns pointing out the window just in case we have social trouble when we arrive. What do you think?" said Jim.

"Okay, what do you guys think?" John asked his fellow warriors with excitement flashing in his dark eyes, "Are my Sioux brothers ready for some excitement?" queried John Glass.

"Are you kidding, man? Alex is like a brother. He's big and tough but he's a large target, too. We can't let him and Jim and the rest go wandering around down there under-manned and under-gunned. I'm sure enough going!" replied George Standing Bear, passionately.

"We're all going!" whooped the rest.

"Okay, looks like you definitely have your raiding party, SIR! We brought all our gear and our best skulking duds along from Montana. This oughta be interesting!" grinned Glass, rubbing his hands together in anticipation of the mission ahead.

"Alright, boys, report to the 'The Black Cat' in about an hour; she's parked down on the tarmac by Hangar One. Eli's making sure the bird is ready to boogey right now. I'm going back to the house for my equipment. It's wheels up in three hours or less, boys!" cried Jim as he hurried out the door, as excited as his men about the upcoming action, but also gravely concerned for the safety of Alex' family.

After eight hours in the air, 'The Black Cat' touched down in Costa Rica at the Juan Santamaria Airport near San Jose, Costa Rica. Jim and his party emerged on the tarmac to stretch cramped legs and aching bodies, while Charlie Volks supervised the refueling of the aircraft. Surprisingly, nothing much seemed to have changed in Costa Rica since Jim's last visit several years earlier. Several groups of Ticos obviously noted the miniguns poking out the windows but, much to Jim's relief, no one said anything or approached the aircraft.

Half an hour after departing San Jose, the old transport touched down on a grass strip near a small village some miles inland from the Caribbean coastline. As everyone deplaned, the soldiers went about organizing their equipment while Fergus went into town to locate his contact. Half an hour later, an ancient rattletrap bus, complete with Tico driver, came lumbering up to the airstrip.

"This fellow says he can get us to within half a mile of the compound unseen for a mere $100 bucks, so I paid him," announced Fergus. Then, looking apprehensively at the sky, Fergus said urgently, "It's getting late in the afternoon. We better get moving, gentlemen," advised the little Scot.

After jolting over a very rocky road for thirty minutes, with dust rolling in the open windows, the party gladly left the old bus behind and set off on foot toward the compound. Skirting open areas, taking cover in the forest, they approached Tiaglen compound. Jim and John scrutinized the facility with binoculars, taking note of several sentries on the walls, but could not determine if they were friend or foe.

"Fergus, do you know any of the guard staff here?" Jim asked quietly.

"No, that's just it. They're not dressed in uniforms so I don't know if those guys up there on the wall are friendly or not. Either way, when our scouts enter the place, they'll open up on us and we won't know whether to shoot back. What should we do?" Fergus fretted.

"Whoa! Wait a minute! Look . . . near the gate . . . there's a couple of vehicles I never noticed before just sitting there. Let's move in closer and have a look," John Glass suggested, searching for anything that would help them determine the prevailing situation in the compound.

Peering through the bushes near the main gate, Jim chortled, "Well, well, well! Whadaya know?! Kaiser Bill's insignia. Those guys on the wall must be some of Bill's torpedoes! John, let's prepare for an assault. I think we can safely assume that the place is occupied by the enemy."

"Okay, are you guys ready?" Glass whispered into his headset.

"Ready, John," came Standing Bear's whispered reply.

Glass and his Native American commandos, dressed in their native costume complete with moccasins and war paint, slipped silently through the bushes with their bows and arrows. Five minutes later, the sentry standing at the main gate failed to hear the faint hiss of the deadly missile that ended his life. He fell backward into the bushes with a Sioux war arrow protruding from his skull.

Jim and the rest of the group watched in silence from the underbrush as the six 'Masters of Mayhem' deftly scaled the wall and disappeared from view inside the compound. Within minutes, several bodies plummeted to the ground from positions atop the wall. Ten more minutes passed with no further sounds from the compound. Then the main gates opened and John Glass silently motioned for the others to move in.

"Guess it's all clear, boys," Jim whispered, motioning for his people to advance.

Entering the compound, they observed John and his men dragging ten bodies to the side and stacking them like cordwood. The company of rescuers quickly reconnoitered the compound which had obviously been thoroughly ransacked by the intruders. There was no sign of Alex's family.

"Alex, come up here on the wall! Quick!" yelled one of the Sioux.

Alex ran up the stairs to the wall with his big .50 caliber rifle.

"What now?" puffed Alex, red-faced.

The snap of a bullet past Alex's ear answered his question. Scanning the forest, Alex finally spotted a small group of men in the underbrush using a ravine for cover.

"Aye! There's the blighters! Down there, in that ravine!" he whispered, "Why don't you guys go take them out, otherwise we'll be trading shots with them all day?" said Alex angrily.

"Yeah, I see 'em, Alex. Give us a bit. We'll see what we can do," answered John tersely, motioning for his compatriots to follow him.

A few minutes later, several bursts of automatic weapons fire were heard followed by rapid single rifle shots. A helicopter could be heard spooling up behind a stand of trees. As Alex observed the action, a soldier in an unfamiliar uniform emerged from the forest, turned and fired several parting shots at his pursuers. Alex's big rifle dusted him off on both sides. In a few minutes, the six Sioux emerged from the forest laughing and joking as they returned to the compound.

"We blew them all away except for two guys who booked it out on the other side of the trees. They cranked up a chopper that had been sitting there and took off before we could get a clear shot at them. They're probably half way to the Caribbean by now," laughed one of the Sioux raiders.

"I'm not so sure about that. I think I hear a chopper not far away. So . . . let's not assume too much too soon," warned Alex cautiously.

A few moments later, through an open space in the forest, the men observed an elderly helicopter gunship turn on approach to the compound. Quickly, Alex assumed a prone position, read mirage and wind, adjusted the telescopic sight on the big .50 caliber rifle and took careful aim.

"Lord, guide my hand," he prayed aloud, without taking his eye off the target.

The powerful rifle bucked amidst ear-splitting muzzle blasts as the big Scot fired two careful shots in rapid succession, then proceeded to empty the magazine at the approaching chopper. He reloaded and peered through the scope again to observe the results.

Moments later, almost a mile away, the approaching helicopter leveled off and the pilot was calmly flipping on his weapons switches, entertaining thoughts of 'sweet revenge,' when the windshield exploded in his face. The copilot's head snapped left in time to observe that half of his companion's head was no longer there. A moment later, the right windshield exploded as he suffered an equally unpleasant fate.

From their vantage point on the compound wall, the raiding party watched as the chopper began to yaw, pitch and skid before it finally pirouetted and spun in, spiraling downwards to the forest floor and exploding. When no other threats had emerged, the men began to relax a bit.

"Awesome shooting, Alex," said Sam Red Eagle, with great admiration.

"Very likely divine intervention I'd say, my friend! I'm good, but I'm not that good," Alex laughed, releasing the pent-up tension he was feeling. "Well, lads, I hope that just about closes the book on this nasty bunch. Now we must learn what has become of my family," concluded Alex darkly, looking down at the smoking weapon in his ham-sized hands.

"Well, I do believe I know where they are. At least . . . I know where they should be. Follow me, gentlemen," announced Fergus, obviously relieved that the gunfire had ceased.

Fergus led Alex and the rest of the party into the ransacked compound library. Stepping immediately to an entire wall of bookcases behind a massive walnut desk, he reached into the now-empty bookshelves, touching an area of the rich wall paneling behind it with the flat of his hand, fingers pointed vertically, and spoke several words in Gaelic. A voice promptly responded from an unseen speaker with a decidedly Celtic brogue.

"Password please!" the voice demanded calmly in English.

Fergus retrieved a plastic card from his wallet and repeated a long and complicated series of passwords. Finally, the voice demanded one further instruction extracted specifically from Fergus' rote memory.

"One moment please!" said the unseen gatekeeper almost mechanically.

Suddenly, a large area of paneling began to swing away from the wall. It proved to be attached to a massive metal door similar to that of a bank vault. Two armed men promptly emerged with automatic weapons at the ready, followed by a bald, wizened little man wearing large spectacles.

"Fergus, you are a sight for sore eyes," cried the grey-haired little man, "We thought you'd never come and . . . . Oh, my! . . . you brought along Crown Prince Alexander at last! I am deeply honored to meet you, Sir," he said, bowing before Alex in a sign of abject honor and obeisance.

Looking more than a little embarrassed, a blushing Alex said, "Och, man, ya needn't bow ta me. I came ta see me family, that's all. Where are they anyway?" clearly uncomfortable with the little man's actions.

"They are deep in the mountain, Sir. As you may have surmised, I am their personal valet. Please, give us a bit of time. The royals are all still asleep in their quarters and, as you can imagine, they are a bit infirm since they are somewhat advanced in years," explained the little man with great decorum, "I will notify them of your arrival and present them to you as soon as possible."

"Och, certainly! We'll wait in the courtyard until they are ready to join us," answered Alex, genuinely relieved to learn of their safety.

"What is going on out here?" cried a very tall, slender, grey-haired woman with a marked regal bearing. Oh, my!" she cried, rushing into the room with tears spilling down her face. She threw her arms around Alex's neck and smothered him with kisses. "Alexander! Oh, Alexander, my son, my dear son! You've come at last! I've prayed all these years to lay eyes on you before I die, and now you're really, actually here!" she sobbed uncontrollably.

"Mu . . . . Mum? Are you my mum?" stammered a startled Alex in utter bewilderment.

"Yes, Alexander, I am indeed your mum," the woman sniffed, wiping her tears and trying to regain her composure. "It's been 48 years. You were but a wee *bairn* when we were parted," she began to cry again, "Your father will be absolutely elated to see you. He is not at all well, but he will be as overjoyed as I at your arrival. We wondered if you were even alive. Your adoptive parents, Betty and Harold MacIntosh, are also here. They will be out shortly, and they, too, will be so happy to see you. If you will please excuse me, I must retire to our quarters to get myself and your father dressed. We will join you very soon. Come along Fenwick, we must hurry now," she ordered the little man gently.

"Yes, Madam," he replied meekly.

"Fenwick? . . . Fenwick? . . . Hmm! Guess the name fits!" snickered one of the Sioux under his breath.

"Gentlemen," Fergus broke in quietly, "I am so thankful the planners built this place with a hidey-hole in case of emergencies like this. I was pretty sure that the royals would retreat to these underground quarters if given half a chance. Once inside and sealed up, there was no way for the criminal element to find or harm your family, Alex," he explained. "The bulkhead and blast doors here are very similar to those in Colorado at Cheyenne Mountain, only far smaller of course. They are non-magnetic and designed to withstand a near miss by a nuclear weapon. There are survival stocks of food and other necessities in there sufficient for at least twelve months inside," observed Fergus proudly.

"That's fine," observed Jim, "but Alex's family can't remain here. We need to get them to a secure place in America where no one can get to them. I'd say we should put them up temporarily at the Eagle's Lair where we can protect them and minister to their needs. We haven't any blast doors at our facility but then, Sir, I can assure you that no one of Kaiser Bill's ilk will ever get in there either," declared Jim with certainty.

"Aye, I'd certainly agree with that," chimed Alex confidently.

Jim reached for his satellite phone and quickly dialed the Houston office. His long, tall Texan CEO answered. "Eli, we've rescued Alex's family from the Kaiser's goons and everyone is okay but we need to get them to the Lair, stat. Send Baruch and Samuelson down to Santamaria Airport in San Jose, Costa Rica, with my biz-jet, ASAP and don't spare the jet fuel," ordered Jim brusquely.

"Copy that, Chief! The ship is ready and so's the crew. They should be there in a little over three hours," responded Eli reassuringly.

"Okay, tell them to call me as soon as they have Santamaria in sight. We'll make it up as we go from there," concluded Jim.

At that moment, Fenwick approached the group and announced, "Gentlemen, may I present Mr. and Mrs. Campbell and Mr. and Mrs. MacIntosh."

With tears in his eyes, Alex exclaimed, "Well, praise God! It's not every day a man receives two mums and two dads at the same time," as he tenderly greeted and embraced each of the four elderly Scots.

"Alex, I really hate to interrupt, but we've got to get your people to a safe place immediately. You're going to have to postpone your family reunion. You never know when the rest of the New World Order might show up here. My biz-jet will arrive in San Jose shortly to move your family to the Eagle's Lair until we can establish a safe place for them in a more desirable location where they can be protected from Kaiser Bill. Let's get their personal belongings together and then all head for the 'Black Cat' and Santamaria," advised Jim with grave urgency.

"Aye, you're right, Jim. This is no place for these folks. Fenwick, how long do you think it will take you to get my family packed and ready to go?" asked Alex gently so as not to subject his elderly parents to further unnecessary stress.

"Sir, we are way ahead of the situation. We packed our necessaries during the time we were hiding in the cave. We can depart immediately," answered the bespectacled little man proudly.

"Okay, the bad guys graciously left us their vehicles to use. Let's load up the duffel and head back to our aircraft immediately," Jim grinned happily.

As the old C-47 approached Santamaria airport, the pilot announced, "General, we have radio contact with your Citation on final approach. They're right on time, Sir!"

The 'Black Cat' touched down and rolled out, then taxied into the lineup at the fuel pumps as the Citation pulled into line just ahead of them. Alex and his family, along with their armed guards, were quickly transferred to the biz-jet as Jim waited nervously for the Citation's turn at the pumps.

Just then, a stranger approached the group as Jim was standing near the C-47's wingtip with the Sioux soldiers standing watch at his elbow. Taking notice of the approaching figure, John Glass, said in low tones, "General, that fellow doesn't look like he's on a social call. Wonder who he is and what he wants?"

"Hmm! That man is an old Costa Rican acquaintance of mine. He is one of the big wheels here at the airport. Wonder what's up," exclaimed Jim with growing interest.

"Senor Mendoza, so good to see you! What brings you out in this heat, my friend," greeted Jim cordially, concealing a bit of apprehension.

"Senor Black, I heard you were in-country. I am sorry we have no time to talk because you and your people are in grave danger here! I will expedite the refueling of your aircraft so you can all leave here *mucho pronto*!" explained the manager with urgent concern in his voice and perceptible fear in his eyes.

"Wha... what is going on?" demanded Jim, as his stomach was beginning to tighten and the hair on the back of his neck stood up.

"As you know, we have no standing army here in Costa Rica. Our police personnel are spread especially thin right now. We've been informed that a group of guerillas loyal to Caesar William are on their way here right now in a truck convoy intending to capture or kill you and your entire party. They have no legal standing here, except the force of their arms, but unfortunately we have no way to stop them. Get your aircraft up to the pumps immediately. My men are making room for your airplanes as we speak," instructed Mendoza looking around nervously for signs of trouble.

Jim immediately ordered the pilots to comply with Mendoza's men, then turned to his raiding party and said, "Glass, get three of your boys into the Gooney and unlimber those miniguns so they'll swivel. The orientation of our aircraft is such that the guerillas can only approach on the minigun side. Hold your fire until I tell you. Then point those guns where they'll do the most good and let 'em have it. The rest of you take your rifles, spread out and be ready for action. Be sure your personal communication systems are working so we can all communicate unobserved." ordered Jim brusquely.

Ten minutes later, the Citation was refueled and Jim ordered the pilots to take off immediately. "I'll see you guys either in Montana or Houston. Just get out of here with these precious people. Do what Eli tells you when you get home," yelled Jim into his mike as the biz-jet taxied out, poured the coals to the twin engines and pointed her nose toward 'angels 43.'

Fifteen minutes later, the C-47 had just finished refueling when a convoy of military trucks bearing E.U. insignias came tearing out onto the tarmac.

"All right people, look alive! Our 'company' has arrived," advised Jim, "Gunners be ready for action. Pilot, be ready to take off on a moment's notice."

Jim held his pistol behind his back as the convoy screeched to a stop. A young E.U. officer in camouflage and black beret quickly exited the lead truck and approached Jim with a hand on his side-arm while his soldiers began unloading from the trucks.

"Senor Black? We are here to arrest you and your men in the name of Caesar William for crimes against his majesty, I . . . . "

"Fire," Jim yelled into his throat mike as he swiftly brought his side arm to bear and shot Kaiser Bill's officer dead in his tracks. The C-47's three miniguns opened fire on the trucks in a wall of flame and massive muzzle blast from the three 6-barrel miniguns. In mere seconds, all of

Kaiser Bill's friends were dead on the concrete and the trucks had been reduced to something resembling huge kitchen sieves on flat tires. Blood ran everywhere as the C-47's engines came to life.

"Alright, cease fire! Cease fire! Everybody into the 'Black Cat'! Move it, people. Do it NOW!" shouted Jim.

As the cargo door closed behind the last of the raiding party, Charley Volks firewalled the throttles and dropped takeoff flaps. Running diagonally across the tarmac, he immediately popped the tail-wheel off the concrete and then rotated the old cargo plane off the ground at the edge of the grass, banking quickly toward the north and home.

In the shadows, a huge flaxen-haired warrior stood with a group of his compatriots, smiling and sheathing his sword. He observed, "General Black has done well. Up! Let us go hence!"

Aboard the 'Black Cat', there was a collective sigh of relief. "Well, now, that was exciting," grinned John Glass breaking the tense silence, "Encore, anyone?" he joked, beaming at his fellow raiders with admiration.

"Quiet, Gunney! I, for one, have had just about all the 'excitement' I can stand for a while," groaned Jim, "Hope we didn't puncture any innocent bystanders," he remarked drily.

"I don't think so, General. At least collateral damage should have been minimal. The line of fire was pretty clear behind those trucks," exclaimed the big Sioux.

"Okay, what's done is done. I hate to leave Senor Mendoza's people to clean up our considerable mess. But at least we got Alex's family out of harm's way and, hopefully, on their way to a place where they can live without fear," observed Jim.

Suddenly, the radio crackled to life with Mendoza's voice, "Senor Black, on behalf of the people of Costa Rica, I would like to thank you for eliminating that nest of vermin you just destroyed. Now we will not have to sleep with one eye open anymore. If you are ever down this way again, please call me and we will get together for a cup of Costa Rican coffee. Have a safe trip, my friend! Mendoza out."

Jim immediately grabbed his satellite phone and called Eli in Houston.

"Eli, do we have any fighter outfits in this area of Central America?" inquired Jim.

"Well, let me check around here, Boss. Hmmm . . . . . yup, here we go! I've got four F-22 Raptors that just departed Guatemala not two minutes ago headed for Houston," replied Eli.

"Okay, get 'em turned around back to us. We just took off from Costa Rica and are over that swamp on the border with Nicaragua. We could use some fighter escort. I have a hunch we're in Kaiser Bill's gun sights right now. We just wasted a bunch of his people at Santamaria airport and I'm convinced that he'll have other operatives gunning for us. This old 'Gooney Bird' can't shoot back in an aerial gunfight and she's not much on speed or agility," declared Jim, worried about their current situation.

"Alright, just a sec, Jim . . . . .Yeah, a major Jacobson is the flight leader. He says he has just reversed course and has you on his radar and in his flight computer. Says they've gone supersonic and he'll be with you in about 16 minutes. So, let's hope that's soon enough. Umm . . . . Uh, oh, Jim, I hate to say this, but . . .I think you may be right . . . I just picked up four E.U. aircraft departing Panama City. They seem to be headed in your direction and also appear to be supersonic. Our boys should be able to intercept them though. I mean, what's a little jet fuel, anyway? And those Raptors are one mean airplane," chuckled Eli, hoping to break the tension of the moment and wishing he were flying one of the sleek fighters himself.

"Okay, thanks Eli! Pray for us, man! Black out," Jim replied tersely.

Turning to Charlie Volks, Jim shouted over the drone of the engines, "Keep an eye peeled, Charlie. We may have bogies coming up behind us. There are four of our fighters up ahead coming to escort us. Turn on the sound system so I can hear the radio traffic."

Fifteen minutes went by peacefully. Then Charlie yelled back to his passengers, "We have four bandits approaching from the rear. Everybody buckle in tight. I also have four F-22s not sixty seconds away and closing. Uh oh, we are about to be shot at."

The old transport banked sharply left as the starboard wing took half a dozen cannon shells. The old bird shuddered and shed some pieces of wing skin but continued to fly.

Then a Germanic voice came over the radio in fractured English, "Ja, ve greet you in ze name uf Caesar Villiam. I am flight leader Captain Hans von Weirich. Ve vill shoot you down, President Black, but ve vanted to give you time to make peace mit your Gott, ha, ha, ha! As one of your state governors used to say, 'Hasta la vista, Baby!'"

Just then, Charlie pulled a handle under the instrument panel and there was a thunderous explosion behind the 'Black Cat.'

"What was that?" shouted Jim apprehensively.

"Oh, Captain Hans back there just fired a missile and I blocked it with a 'hairball'," Charlie snickered.

"Hold on! Here we go again! Ol' Hans just slid in behind us," he chirped, "Hey! What in the world is wrong with this thing?" the pilot yelled, furiously pulling the handle several times more with no apparent results.

Captain Hans von Weirich had indeed pulled his aircraft around into direct alignment with the rear of the old C-47. Being somewhat personally penurious, Weirich had decided not to fire any more 'expensive' air-to-air missiles, so he was intending to fire another burst of cannon shells into the defenseless transport's tail assembly. But he was following a bit closer than he should have and just as he was about to push the gun trips on his stick, a huge ball of fire and flashing aluminum foil was released by the 'Black Cat.' Before he could react, it struck his aircraft just below the cockpit, near the area that bore the stenciled warning 'Danger Jet Intake.' There was a muffled 'Shlooomp' sound as the fiery ball of tinfoil was sucked into the engine. Almost instantly, there was an explosion that shook the fighter and a cockpit klaxon sounded as warning lights on the instrument panel lit up like a Christmas tree reading 'Engine Fire,' 'Turbine Failure,' 'Eject, Eject.'

Hans' wingman yelled, "Hans, what's wrong?"

Hans screamed, "Mein Gott im Himmel, ich ben kaput!!"

"Speak English! Hans, Speak English!" shouted the wingman.

"Ja, my aircraft has had it. Ze engine just ingested a bomb and is on fire. I must bail out before it explodes," screamed Hans frantically, as he jettisoned his cockpit canopy and ejected.

273

Hans' wingman then noticed that he and his remaining comrades were unquestionably in the cross-hairs of four rapidly approaching American F-22 Raptors and decided it was time to go home.

The American flight leader radioed, "Unidentified aircraft, this is Major Andrew Jacobson, United States Air Force. I'd advise you to break contact immediately. Or do you wish to engage?"

The C-47 pilot remarked calmly, "Boys, our welcoming party has just peeled off. They've cut the 'mules' loose and they're headed for the shed," he snickered.

At that moment, the old C-47 was greeted by quadruple sonic booms as Volks commented drily, "Looks like the guys in the white hats just arrived at mach speed."

The remaining E.U. aircraft were already headed south supersonic on afterburners.

Jacobson yelled, "Sic 'em, boys," as his aircraft slipped in near the 'Black Cat's port wingtip, while the rest of his flight pursued Kaiser Bill's retreating aircraft.

"Glad we were in the neighborhood," grinned Jacobson, "Guess that bunch decided it was time to hang it up. Funny, they didn't want to engage. Hah! Looks like that bird of yours must be more dangerous than I thought. General Black, where did you dig up that old 'Gooney Bird' anyhow?"

"Well, ya know, Major," began Charlie, answering for Jim, "I was a Warrant Officer and flew her in Nam during the war. She was named the 'Black Cat' then too. Several years after I got out of the service, I just happened to stumble across this old girl just as she was going to be surplused. I bought her and flew her haulin' cargo for a while. Then, General Black happened to see her and wanted to buy her. I said I'd sell her on the condition that I went with her. Well, I've been workin' for the General here for a number of years now, and very glad of it."

"Hey, how in the world did you manage to down ol' Hans and that foo-fighter of his back there? Man, he sure bought the farm!" inquired Jacobson, "I was listening to the Kaiser boys' radio chatter and I gathered something went waaay wrong on their end, but I haven't figured out just what happened yet."

"Well, in Nam, I fitted the 'Cat' here with a home-made gizmo that releases little thermite bombs attached to big balls of tinfoil strips which I call 'Hannoi Hairballs.' Used 'em to mess up the mind of heat-seeking missiles, ya' know. I spent a coupla' years shootin' up the Ho Chi Minh Trail and ruinin' Charlie's whole day. When they brought in them big AC-130s, me an' the 'Cat,' here, got sent back to the minor leagues an' we ended up shootin' up targets of opportunity, supportin' leg outfits an' clearing especially hot LZs for the whirlybirds. Well, anyhow, today I got the missile ol' Hans fired back there, with a 'Hairball,' an' I figured when he slid in behind us he was gonna fire another one. So, I tried to time it just right, but when I pulled the lever the second time, my gizmo must have goofed somehow an' released a good dozen of those 'hairballs' at once. I looked in my rearview mirror an' saw a huge ball of fire an' tinfoil fly back right into ol' Hans' air intakes. Haah! Serves him right!" laughed the grizzled old pilot.

By this time, Major Jacobson was laughing so hard he was doubled over in the cockpit as the deadly Raptor rocked from wingtip to wingtip.

"Ho, man! You are a hoot, Charlie!" gasped the major, "You'd make a great stand-up comedian. Well, right now, that Hans guy is regretting bailing out into one of the worst swamps in the western hemisphere, snakes and all! Herpetological nightmare! Lots of fer-de-lance and bushmasters! Yeah, big mamas!" roared the Major, "If he gets outa' there alive, I wager he'll go to herding goats in the Alps."

Just then, the other three F-22s pulled into formation alongside Jacobson. "Got 'em all, Boss," one of the pilots reported, matter-of-factly.

Jim radioed, "Alright, gentlemen, give this old girl a visual once-over for leaks and damage. If she seems to be okay, we'll all proceed to Mexico City and put down there to refuel and check her innards. Thanks for the help! You guys are a blessing from Heaven!" said Jim, commending his protectors.

Major Jacobson said, "Begging the General's pardon, Sir, but puleeze, give some future consideration to having fighter escort next time you decide to go off the reservation on another mission. You're waaaaay too important to be killed by some of the Kaiser's scuzz bums."

"Ya know, Major, I was just thinking the same thing. I'm too used to being a 'Lone Ranger,' I guess. I will definitely take your suggestion under advisement," laughed Jim good-naturedly, settling back at last for the ride to Mexico.

☆ 26 ☆

JERUSALEM SONRISE

After returning to North America from Costa Rica, Jim and his advisors had decided to build a brand new U.S. Capitol complex in the farm lands of central Kansas. Six years had passed and construction was well under way on the new capitol and the gargantuan task of restoring the general American infrastructure advanced apace. Jim and his staff were pleased with the overall progress being made nationwide. Significantly, a museum on the Capitol grounds was under construction that would enshrine the two venerable B-29s that had been so instrumental in repelling the enemy.

The days grew into weeks, the weeks into months, the months into years. The scars of invasion were gradually healing not only physically but in the minds and spirits of the American people. The U. S. military was a major priority and the several services had rebounded, rearmed and reorganized at a surprising rate.

Jim was kept so busy, in fact, that he, his staff and friends lost all track of time—until the Office of the President received a completely unexpected invitation from General Ziv to visit Israel during Rosh Hashanah, the Jewish New Year—also known as the Feast of Trumpets, the prophetic locus of things eschatological.

Although at first it had seemed to be bad timing to be travelling abroad with so many enemies still at large, Jim welcomed the break. Neither he nor Maryann had been able to relax for many months and the strain was beginning to tell on both of them. All the nations and groups that had participated in the invasion of America, especially the E.U. and Russia, were warned, on pain of dire consequences, not to interfere with their trip. Kaiser Bill had given his assurances. The Russians and their Muslim allies, however, were considerably less enthusiastic in their assurances and Jim was justifiably leery. To lessen the peril of traveling near enemy domains in the Middle East, Jim's advisory staff had insisted his aircraft be escorted by a number of the Navy's most lethal fighter jets. The fighters were launched in relays from four nuclear-powered carrier battle groups, two cruising the eastern Atlantic Ocean and two in the Mediterranean Sea, for just that specific purpose.

With the Israeli flight crew at the controls, the Presidential Boeing 747's 800,000 pound hulk settled onto the runway at Israel's Ben Gurion International Airport south of Tel Aviv. Her eight U.S. Navy F-35 escort fighters peeled off, four to the left and four to the right, in an intricate and beautifully choreographed display of airmanship, as each executed the classic fighter pilot's 360° overhead approach to land in pairs behind her. Onboard, Jim, Maryann, Arie, Sarah, Alex, and the rest of Jim's entourage, prepared to meet Israel's General Ziv, and other members of the leadership of the Israeli government, for the first time.

As Jim's party deplaned and started down the stairway, Arie and Sarah let out a whoop and waved to friends and family who were anxiously standing behind the police lines below in the cheering crowd. Finally reaching the bottom steps, Jim and Maryann were greeted by General Ziv and several other top Israeli officials.

Arie introduced Jim and Maryann saying, "General Zechariah Ziv, may I present the Acting President of the United States, and my business partner, General James Black, and his lovely wife, Maryann, and a distinguished member of our staff, Dr. Alexander MacIntosh."

Acknowledging each member of the illustrious group before him and firmly shaking Jim's outstretched hand, the Israeli general warmly welcomed them, "Ah, General … uh…Mr. President! It is so good to finally meet you both. I've heard so much about you, General Black! Arie is one of our most distinguished reserve officers and anyone he recommends must indeed be an outstanding person!"

Turning his eyes toward Maryann, he said most graciously, "Welcome to Israel, Mrs. Black! It is indeed a pleasure to meet you. I assure you, we have awaited this day with great anticipation!"

Peering up at Alex, Ziv was awed as he grasped the giant's outstretched hand and smiled in welcome. "Dr. MacIntosh, we are honored to have you here, Sir. I trust you will find Israel to your liking."

"All of you, please, come with me! We have a great deal to discuss over lunch!" Ziv declared, motioning them toward waiting limousines and their military escort vehicles.

Before taking their seats in the limo, Jim and Maryann lingered, conversing casually with General Ziv, as Arie ran to embrace his parents, and Sarah fell tearfully into the arms of her own family. After several minutes of impassioned greetings, General Ziv tapped Arie lightly on the shoulder, grieved to intrude on such an emotional moment. Almost apologetically, Ziv said in a low tone, "Arie, . . . my friend, I am truly sorry to interrupt, but we must be going. Please, we have a very tight schedule today. You can take all the time you need to visit with your family a bit later."

As their limousine turned out of the airport terminal surrounded by IDF security vehicles, General Ziv directed his full attention to Jim and Maryann as he said, "I understand you are quite fond of porterhouse steaks, General Black."

"Yes, I love a good steak, General, but they are still a bit scarce in America these days! Our agriculture is only recently recovering from the invasion," Jim responded warmly.

"Well, I have arranged for us to dine at *NG's* in historic Neveh Tzedek. They are reputed to have the best porterhouse steaks in Tel Aviv, if not in all of Israel," Ziv announced proudly. "We will have the restaurant entirely to ourselves today."

"That sounds wonderful, Sir," Jim answered graciously, as he and Maryann both nodded approvingly, and Alex flashed them all a big grin, rubbing his hands in anticipation.

After the ride to the restaurant, and having passed through the security cordon, everyone was comfortably seated at table in *NG's*. General Ziv addressed the American delegation, "General Black, first off, I'd like to thank America as well as you, Arie, and your entire company for your incomparable contributions to Israel's security. We would be in far graver circumstances without the weapons systems you have supplied us, to say nothing of the extraordinary support from your satellite system. And, I am most especially appreciative of your latest shipments of the newest Arrow missiles. They were issued to our field units just yesterday."

"You and your great nation are most welcome, General Ziv," Jim replied graciously. "Israel is the 'apple of God's eye' so it was indeed our honor to be of service, Sir. By the way, we have brought along proposals for two new upgrades, as well as one entirely new weapon. We have tested it, of course, but are less than completely satisfied with its performance without your input. We'd like the IDF to field test this new system, to see if it meets your requirements," Jim added soberly.

"Ah, wonderful! Well, folks, here comes our food! We shall discuss all this further, after lunch, when we will be meeting with the Prime Minister and the leaders of the Knesset," announced Ziv exuberantly.

Twenty minutes later, as the party was nearly finished with their delicious meal and talking jovially, Ziv's chief *aide-de-camp,* General Abrahamson, abruptly entered the restaurant's dining room and whispered something to General Ziv. Ziv frowned and immediately excused himself from his guests and exited the building to a van, bristling with antennas, parked outside at the curb. Moments later, Ziv returned, appearing visibly shaken. Ashen faced, he addressed the group, "My friends, I am afraid we have a major problem. Israel is under surprise attack by a massive air force approaching from the north. I have also been informed that armor and troop transports have been spotted on the roads approaching our borders from the north, east and south. Russian-built aircraft are approaching from the direction of Turkey, with an ETA of twenty minutes. Syrian, Jordanian and Hezbollah armor and infantry units are *en route* and will arrive at our borders within the hour. We are presently being shelled and rocketed all along our borders. General Black, I am so sorry to have brought you, your wife and all your associates into harm's way. The timing of this attack cannot be a mere coincidence. No doubt the Russians, Syrians, Iranians and other Muslim allies plan to not only crush Israel but also destroy the new American government in one fell swoop. Unless you wish to chance trying to reach one of your aircraft carriers in the Mediterranean, I have no choice but to immediately move all of you to our underground central command installation in Jerusalem. Our main command center is located under Mount Zion and is the most secure place in Israel. We must leave momentarily, by helicopter. The arrangements have been made, the bird is *en route* and will arrive in five minutes. Please be ready!" the silver-haired warrior announced with as much dignity as he could muster under the circumstances.

"General Ziv," replied Jim, speaking for the entire delegation, "I believe that trying to reach a carrier battle group by chopper is completely out of the question at this juncture. The enemy might be upon us before we could reach safety. We'll gladly accompany you to your command bunker."

Using a secure channel, Jim immediately established a communications link with the Commander of the U.S. Navy fighter squadron which had escorted Air Force One to Israel, while Arie placed a call to the Capitol in Kansas.

"Commander Matthews, this is General Black. General Ziv has just informed us that Israel is under imminent air assault," reported Jim.

"Aye, Aye, Sir, we were just alerted," replied the Commander solemnly.

"Son, I will not order you to fight under the command of the IAF, so you have my permission to return to your ships, but if you and your men are willing to volunteer to fight alongside Israel, you certainly have my permission to do so. But you must realize that this may essentially be a suicide mission, if you choose to volunteer," Jim warned him soberly.

"Sir, we'll gladly get into the fray. We're aware of the risk and ready for whatever comes, Mr. President! It's an honor to defend Israel! Our planes are fueled and armed and so are we. The local fighter outfit here has arranged to rearm and refuel us. We've got eight of the best airplanes and pilots in the world right here ready to go! We'll make you proud, General! Incidentally, our carrier, the U.S.S. Teddy Roosevelt, is anchored about 75 miles off the coast if you need to contact the fleet. Well, we take off in five, Sir! Keep your head down, and we'll see you soon, after the smoke clears, God willing! Matthews out!" replied the Commander calmly.

"Godspeed, Commander! Give your boys my best! Black out," returned Jim, verbally saluting the intrepid young aviators on the other end.

Arie was talking to Eli, as Jim ended the link with Matthews. Jim unceremoniously grabbed the satellite phone from Arie and began issuing orders. "Eli! Have Uri patch me through to the bridge of the U.S.S. Theodore Roosevelt. For some reason I don't seem to have their number," ordered Jim irritably.

"Copy that, Chief! Hold on a sec."

After a number of switches and transfers, the Roosevelt's radioman on the bridge answered, "Rough Rider!"

"This is General Black, Son, let me speak to the Admiral," the President ordered flatly.

"AYE!, AYE! SIR! He's right here, SIR! *Admiral, it's the President!*" Jim's handset crackled.

"This is Admiral Henson, Mr. President," answered the Battle Group Commander evenly.

"Admiral, what is your current situation?" Jim asked tersely.

"We have just weighed anchor in the Med and are under way at 30 knots, 82 miles off the coast of Israel, Sir. Radar reports a cloud of largely Russkie bogies approaching central Israel from the north over Turkey. We have launched our Marine Corps Vertical Takeoff and Landing F-35s to protect the fleet. We've just turned into the wind to commence launch of our standard Navy aircraft. What are your orders, Sir?" The admiral's voice was steady and calm, belying the gravity of the situation.

"You are not to consider yourself under Israeli command, Admiral, but I am placing your battle group in a position to aid the IDF. Contact IDF Headquarters immediately and find out where and how they need help! If you have any reservations about anything they may ask you to do, contact me by secure satellite link ASAP. My assistant, Uri Asimov, will instruct you about how to do that when we end this conversation. My party will spend the duration of whatever is unfolding in a maximum security facility here in Israel with General Ziv," Jim said matter-of-factly.

"Aye, Aye, Sir! All of my pilots on board have previously volunteered to mix it up with Kaiser bill's boys, the Russkies, or whoever ... whenever . . . wherever . . . the opportunity presented itself. By the way, General, the

U. S. S. Harry Truman's battle group is about 50 miles west of our position right now, closing at flank speed. They have their defense canopy up and should be here shortly," reported Admiral Henson.

"Great! I'll have to sign off now, Admiral. Relay my orders to the Truman's Fleet Commander. If he has any questions, have him contact me. Black out!" concluded Jim, well pleased with the solid performance of the U. S. Navy.

"Aye, Aye, Mr. President! Watch your six! We'll be in touch! Henson out!"

Climbing aboard the Israeli military chopper with General Ziv and the rest of the American delegation, Jim continued issuing orders throughout the flight to an area just west of the Eastern Gate of the Temple Mount.

As they descended to land, Jim admired the awesome beauty of the newly-completed Third Temple, and mentioned it to General Ziv. "Well, it was completed about six years ago, General. Whatever it was that blew the Dome of the Rock and Al Aqsa mosques to smithereens cleared the mount and gave Israel the opportunity to rebuild the Holy Temple again for the third time with the Holy Place located exactly over the original indentations in the bedrock from Solomon's First Temple. But we had a real disaster here three and a half years ago that required cleansing the Temple all over again—a real long drawn out process." exclaimed the Israeli general.

"We never heard about that. What happened, Sir?" inquired Jim.

"Kaiser Bill and a group of his Spec Ops cutthroats arrived unannounced one day and made a surprise invasion of the Temple, of all things. They took it over for a brief period, before IDF commandos ousted them at gunpoint. We wondered why they did it and couldn't figure out what they were doing there in the first place until one of our priests made a revolting discovery: There was a pig carcass bleeding all over the altar. At that point, we told Bill to get his evil hide out of Israel and not return, but by that time, he had more troops in-country than we did, so we found ourselves in a sort of 'Mexican standoff' with him," explained Ziv, obviously enraged by such monstrous behavior.

As soon as the twin-rotor helicopter touched down, General Ziv immediately led his group of visitors to a hidden vaulted doorway, which concealed what was essentially the entrance to a cave. The cave led them hundreds of feet underground beneath the Temple Mount, into an IDF nerve center manned by uniformed military personnel.

"This isn't the main entrance to our installation, but it is the shortest and fastest way into it, since we got rid of the mosques, the *Martyrs Brigade* and the *Wakf* up here," explained Ziv over his shoulder, moving quickly through the ancient caves and passageways toward the command center.

Then, turning his attention to all his companions, he said, "General Black, Colonel Yehudah and Dr. MacIntosh, you are most welcome to join me in the Command Center. My sincere apologies to the rest of you, but our Command Center can only accommodate a certain number of personnel, because of its compact size. Inasmuch as we don't yet have a clear understanding of what is happening out there, be assured that we are many hundreds of feet underground and this is the safest place in all of Israel, right here! You will all be much more comfortable in this area, where you can move about freely and you have access to the necessary facilities over there," he said graciously, pointing in the direction of the restrooms.

"I have instructed my staff," the General continued, speaking calmly to his guests, "to prepare your accommodations. However, this may take longer than usual, as this is typically an all-male military installation, so we are not properly set up for female guests. We will, nonetheless, make you all as comfortable as possible. So, in the meantime, please help yourself to snacks, coffee –whatever we have – and just try to relax, while we find out exactly what our forces are doing … and what the enemy is doing. We shall return shortly. Thank you!"

Motioning for the three men to follow him, he said, "Gentlemen, this way, please! We must go!"

Entering the Command Center, with Arie, Alex and Jim in tow, General Ziv summoned his staff and announced in Hebrew, "We have with us today, General James Black, God's Viceroy and Acting President of the United States, along with a prominent member of his staff, Dr. Alexander MacIntosh, as well as our own Colonel Ariel Ben-Yehudah, as our trusted and honored guests. I know some of you are not fluent English-speakers, but please converse with me and each other in English as much as possible, so that General Black and Dr. MacIntosh may better understand what is going on. Now, follow me into the Situation Room, gentlemen."

As they entered the Situation Room, General Ziv spoke in Hebrew to an Israeli Master Sergeant, "Sergeant, issue each of these men handguns, with two spare ammo clips." Then, turning to the Brigadier in charge of the Center, he ordered firmly, "Alright, General, brief me! What is our current situation?"

"Sir, our situation is somewhat precarious, but not severe at this point. The first wave of attacks, which included approximately 200 enemy aircraft, has been blunted. Parts of Tel Aviv, several of the smaller outlying communities, and many areas in western Jerusalem have been heavily damaged. A number of fires are currently being brought under control. At last count, Sir, our antiaircraft guns and missiles have accounted for about 30 of the 132 Goggian aircraft that have been destroyed. Approximately 14 of their pilots have been captured. The remainder of their aircraft have now retreated. The IAF has lost 17 aircraft and the Americans have lost 5. American F35s have 40 confirmed kills, and our IAF fighters have downed at least 62 enemy aircraft. IAF and U.S. Navy aircraft are currently refueling and rearming. There are armor and infantry units attacking us across a broad perimeter, and, so far, our lines are holding. Reserve infantry and ranger units have been activated and are being transported to their assembly points around all areas of our borders. Reserve armored units are preparing for battle and proceeding to their previously designated rendezvous areas. Our IAF has requested, and received, close ground support and aerial cover from the U.S. Navy's carrier-based aircraft. We will be receiving revised status reports in about 20 minutes, Sir," intoned the Israeli Brigadier.

"Thank you, General," Ziv replied.

Turning to Jim and Alex, Ziv explained, "General Black, my staff has described the enemy aircraft as 'Goggian.' As you may have surmised, we refer to our diverse enemy simply as 'Gog,' as in 'Gog and Magog' in the Bible. At this point the forces attacking us are of various nationalities. We have identified them as primarily Russian, Iranian, Jordanian, and Syrian and there have also been a few Egyptian units as well. Several other Muslim nations, Ethiopia, Lebanon, Sudan, Somalia and Libya, in addition to some rogue Turkish and Iraqi units, have joined forces with the main attack groups in remote areas, just as prophesied by the Nabi ... uh ... Prophet, Ezekiel."[21]

"Since the invasion of America, Kaiser Bill has significantly reduced his presence here in our land in the face of a rising groundswell of outrage in the public sector, following his desecration of the Temple. He has become exceedingly odious to our people—taking a place in their thinking alongside Hitler, Stalin and the potentate of the Ottoman Empire," General Ziv explained to the Americans, "However, the presence of even his remaining forces has been a definite deterrent to Gog. But trying to rid ourselves of him, though, has been something like trying to rid oneself of Satan; he just hangs around," Ziv explained, restraining the intense visceral reaction he always felt discussing this pariah.

"Perhaps the four of us should retire to the mess hall now for a bite to eat and something to drink, while we can!" Ziv said lightly, turning his mind to a more pleasant prospect, "I know we just ate but I suddenly feel the need of a roast beef sandwich. We'll resume our earlier conversation and enjoy as much social relaxation as the enemy will permit us. I'm certain you men can well envision how things may get very tough for all of us very soon. So, let us take advantage of the moment, shall we?" he gestured toward the door.

Turning, Ziv spoke to the Chief Communications Officer in Hebrew, "Colonel, let me know immediately of any changes in the sit-rep."

"Yes, General! We should be getting some new information in about 15-20 minutes," replied the Israeli officer.

General Ziv sat leisurely for some time with Jim, Alex, Arie, and the rest of Jim's group, chatting casually about a variety of things, in which they happily discovered they shared a number of common interests. Jim was just pouring himself another cup of coffee when the Communications Officer dashed breathlessly into the room, saluting his Commander sharply.

"General! We have a new wave of Goggian aircraft on radar, approaching from the north! Field Commanders all report our lines on the northern and northeastern borders are about to be overrun by massive armor and infantry assault! Many of our infantry units in that area are retreating toward Jerusalem." Somewhat less rigidly and halting to exhale and draw in a long breath, he continued, "Some of our front-line units have reported major in-fighting between neighboring enemy factions. Apparently, several rockets got away from a Sunni patrol and landed in a Shiite unit. Presumably, the Shiites assumed IDF troops were executing a flanking maneuver to cover their retreat, and that they were under attack by Israeli armor. Now ... the two Muslim armies ... are ... uh ...locked in heavy combat ... with each other!" the colonel laughed nervously.

In unison, Ziv and his companions immediately laughed, jumped up and sprinted to the Situation Room. Just as they bolted through the door, an entire wall lit up, as an enormous video screen came to life, displaying a panorama of both Israeli and enemy unit positions.

The Communications Officer pointed wildly to the upper right hand portion of the display and yelped, "Look, everybody! The Chinese military is marching through Iran and into Iraq, across the Euphrates River! Look, they cover the land like a swarm of locusts!" The officer went on to explain to the Americans, "We knew a while back, that Turkey had shut down the tailrace of their dam on the Euphrates, so the river is now essentially dry, at least as far west as Baghdad. With a look of wide-eyed terror on his face, he said, "General Ziv, it looks like the entire East and Middle East is coming here!"

"Very good possibility, Colonel. Good of you to deduce that!" the General said, a bit sarcastically. "Get those reserve Merkava units moving! Why are they just sitting there?" Ziv roared, barking orders to his commanders.

"Sir, that's not possible! All the roads and most of the open fields are so clogged now with civilians fleeing, and our own forces retreating everywhere, that the reserve units cannot move freely without endangering our own people! The armored units, with their Merkava tanks, are moving but very slowly to avoid harming civilians! We have almost total gridlock, Sir!" wailed the Colonel, frantically scanning the terrifying display before them.

"General Ziv," broke in another voice from across the room, "We have another problem! We have just picked up a cloud of hundreds of Chinese aircraft headed our way. Coming in over Iran, Sir!" announced a radar operator, as calmly as he could, "And here is another strange, General. Our aircraft have to navigate through and around enormous flocks of buzzards. Several of our fighters have been damaged in collisions with the big birds. No one has ever seen so many buzzards here. Where could they be coming from and how did they get here?"

With a dark cloud of worry and concern spreading across his weathered face, Zechariah muttered under his breath "Great! As though we weren't under enough strain already! We are being attacked by an aluminum-skinned enemy on the one hand and a feathered one on the other." Scanning the picture vividly displayed across the wall, he announced with alarm, "Good heavens! Look! It appears enemy ground units are moving into the outer areas of Jerusalem! At this rate, they will be knocking on our door within the hour!"

At that very moment, Arie was suddenly alerted. Completely ignoring the pandemonium around him, he pressed an ear against the wall. An uncharacteristic look of fear swept across his face. "QUIET everybody!!!" he yelled. The room suddenly became eerily quiet, no one moved. It was as though they were in a vacuum.

"I'm hearing something! I can't make out just what it is ... it sounds ... like a distant ... freight train. But ... I can't place it," Arie said barely above a whisper.

"Yes ... yes ... I, am beginning to hear something too, but ... what???" added Jim quietly, with extreme caution and concern in a barely audible voice.

"Well ... I don't hear a thing!" Muttered Ziv quietly, "Of course, at my age, that's not unusual," he quipped wryly, mustering a grin.

The words were barely out of his mouth when the place began to shake and small shards of rock began dropping from the ceiling.

EARTHQUAKE!!!!!

Grabbing an intercom microphone for the P.A. system, Ziv shouted, "EARTHQUAKE!!!" ATTENTION ALL PERSONNEL: This is General Ziv! Everybody to the surface! NOW!! THIS IS NOT A DRILL! We are having a major earthquake! Everybody OUT! ... NOW!!

Jim took off down the corridor like a frightened deer, pushing his way through a sea of uniformed personnel frantically trying to vacate the bunker. He felt like a salmon, swimming upstream! He finally found the mess hall and began anxiously searching for Maryann. There she was! Grabbing Maryann's hand tightly, the pair sprinted to the top of the passageway, just behind General Ziv and the last of his staff from the

Command Center. Everyone was dodging chunks of rocks and other debris falling from overhead along the ancient catacomb-like installation.

Finally out of the cave and onto the open Temple Mount, the group was greeted by a heavily overcast day. They shielded their eyes until they could adjust to the brightness of the outdoors. From all around them, they could clearly hear the clank and rumble of approaching armored vehicles, as well as the almost deafening report of heavy tank guns, the crackle of small arms fire very close by, and the roar of aircraft overhead. Because of the low clouds, their view was completely obstructed, so they were unable to tell if the planes were 'friend or foe.' They huddled together, adjusting their eyes to the harsh overcast light.

Suddenly, there was a loud blast of sound that resembled a shofar accompanied by a loud voice as if through a powerful public address system. The voice shouted in Hebrew, "Hinneh!! Adonai Elohainu!!"

"Who said that and what does it mean?" Jim asked Arie.

"It means, 'Behold!! The LORD our God!!'" answered Arie, puzzled as to the source of the voice.

Jim shouted, "Arie, you don't suppose this is the fulfillment of 1 Thessalonians 4:16 do you?"

Arie replied, "I don't remember that passage, what does it say?"

"In my Bible, it reads, 'For the Lord Himself will descend from heaven with a shout, with the voice of an archangel, and with the trumpet of God.'"[20]

"You've gotta be kidding, man! You think?"

As the two partners stared at each other dumfounded, there was a brilliant, almost incandescent, flash of light in the sky above them. It seemed to come from the east, somewhere beyond the ancient wall, and spread toward the west through the clouds like chain lightening.

"Wha ... What was THAT!?" shrieked Maryann, frightened half to death. How she wished— especially at a time like this—she had the cool, calm, collected strength of her husband. She rationalized his ability to remain so calm was due to his military background. Well, now she felt more than a little embarrassed and ashamed to have reacted in such a childish way.

"I ... I have ... no ... idea, Maryann!" General Ziv stammered, as shocked as the others by the unusual spectacle. "I've NEVER seen or heard anything like THAT before!!"

As they all stood motionless, wondering what to do next, they were violently jolted by the intense vibration and roar of more than two dozen Russian-built fighter planes swooping in low toward them from the west over the nearby buildings. Despite the heavy, foggy overcast, the aircraft were so close their distinctive markings were clearly visible. The enemy jets opened fire with cannon and rockets at an unseen target to the east beyond the walls, in the general direction of the Mount of Olives. Instantly, there was a brilliant flash of blue-white light, accompanied this time by a loud crackling sound like high-voltage electricity, that disintegrated the attacking aircraft, reducing them to small confetti-like particles, which tinkled to the ground near the Eastern Wall, like a torrential downpour of ball bearings. Everyone stood, mouth agape, in terrified amazement, utterly immobilized for the moment.

"WOW! Now, it's my turn to wonder," exclaimed General Ziv, yelling at the top of his lungs over all the cacophony of sounds around them. "WHAT took out those Migs?" he asked, scratching his head, addressing no one in particular. "We don't have anything like THAT in our arsenal that I know of!!" "And," he muttered to himself, still shaking on the inside, "believe me, I have seen everything we have!" For the first time in his life, Zechariah, the seasoned old war-horse, was truly frightened and shaken to the very marrow of his bones. He fought violently within himself to keep fear from commandeering his faculties.

As everyone recovered from the initial shock of the blast, they began expressing their anxiety among themselves. The previously stunned gathering was abuzz in emotionally charged high-pitched voices. They became so engrossed in themselves that their physical surroundings seemed to momentarily disappear into obscurity.

Then, through their highly animated exchanges, an authoritative voice rang out which silenced them instantly. "QUIET!! EVERYONE! LISTEN!!" Arie shouted above the hysteria. "I ... don't hear any more explosions ... or ... gunfire!" he announced boldly, scanning the landscape for anything that would provide a clue as to what was happening.

"You're right, Arie! Everything has gone dead silent. It's almost eerie! What in the world is going on?" Jim wondered aloud, snapping back to full attention.

"Great Day!" the Communications Officer cried in disbelief. "Am I mistaken, or is that really the Eastern Gate ... over there!?" he asked in English, pointing to the east.

"Well ... yes, no doubt that has to be ... what they commonly call ... the 'Messiah Gate'," General Ziv stammered, "but ... I've never seen it look like ... THAT! ... before, either!! Why ... it's no longer blocked up!" Then, for his visitors' benefit, he explained in total disbelief, "You see ... it has been sealed for centuries. It was shut up long ago by the Ottoman Turks and has remained sealed through the years!"

Hardly able to process in his mind what his eyes were seeing, Ziv muttered to himself in a barely audible voice, "Oh, My! ... uh ... you don't suppose ... Hmm?"

As the now quieted collection of visitors and military personnel stood wondering and staring at this new development, a large crowd quickly began to form, assembling around the now-opened Eastern Gate. Prominent among the crowd of Israelis were a large number of the Hassidim, the prominent holiness sect of the Jews, readily identifiable by their dreadlocks and flat-brimmed black felt hats. A few Israeli soldiers, and even some Muslim Palestinian combatants, still carrying their AK-47 rifles, began to mingle peaceably with the rapidly growing crowd of Jews.

Looking around wildly, Ziv demanded, "Where are all these people coming from? And WHY? What are they all looking at through the gate?" Then, speaking directly to Jim, Alex and Arie he said, quickly recovering his acumen, "Let's get a bit closer. I must find out what is going on down there! A crowd of this size, under these conditions is extremely dangerous. They can quickly become an unmanageable mob, and, at this moment, I have absolutely NO way to contact our field commanders for help. Come, Gentlemen! Follow me!" Succinctly giving orders to his highest ranking officers for managing those in their care, Ziv led the four men across the normally open expanse of the Temple Mount.

Finally, looking across the open top of the Temple Mount, they were able to see much more clearly as the wind cleared away the smoke from the explosions. With General Ziv in the lead, the group of men began to realize that the earthquake which had driven them above ground had apparently also completely rearranged the area around the Mount of Olives. Moreover, there was definitely something exceptional taking place on the Mount of Olives, itself. Exactly what was happening was completely indiscernible from their current vantage point, due to the erratic movements of the crowd. Even from their distant location, as they watched intently, an electrifying charge seemed to surge through the atmosphere.

Spellbound by the scene unfolding before them, someone in the crowd said barely above a whisper, "He's coming!" Then, the mantra was picked up and repeated over and over, as more voices joined until it became as one voice, "He's coming! **He's coming!**"

Jim turned to Arie with grave concern for the clearly mounting tension of the situation, "What is that they're saying! Who's coming? I don't understand!"

Arie, just as dumbfounded as his friend, replied over the noise of the surging sea of people around them, "They keep saying 'He's coming!' but I can't see who the 'He' is that they're talking about. Do you see anything from where you're standing?" "NO!" both Jim and Alex hollered in unison.

Then from somewhere in front of them, the delegation from the bunker heard someone shout, "Look! ... Look there at the Mount of Olives! ...It has split in two!" Another male voice intoned, "HE IS COMING, JUST AS ZECHARIAH SAID HE WOULD!"

With a look of total shock on his face, Arie turned to Jim and Alex and mechanically translated that last remark, his mind numb at the prospect of what he'd just heard. This last remark, which the largely Jewish crowd began to chant, immediately brought to Jim's recollection the words of the Prophet Zechariah:

> And in that day, His feet will stand on the Mount of Olives, Which faces Jerusalem on the east. And the Mount of Olives shall be split in two, from east to west, Making a very large valley; Half of the mountain shall move toward the north And half of it toward the south[21]

Now, it was Jim's turn to stand in utter amazement, immobilized by even the remote possibility that he was, at that very moment, standing at Ground Zero of the greatest event in human history. One which had been foretold countless times over the centuries by a widely divergent number of people. He mulled everything over in his mind, as he nervously scanned the crowd for a sign ... any sign that would make sense of it all:

Could this really be happening? No! Perhaps this is just mob hysteria? But ... look around ... look at their faces ... there's something extraordinary about their expressions. They're not afraid! ... no! ... they're... they're excited ... overjoyed ... like little children on Christmas morning ... who can't wait to open their gifts! Look! ... Okay! ... Everyone has an extraordinary look of contentment ... expectation ... HOPE! In the midst of war??? Wha ... What is happening? ... What in the world is HAPPENING???

"Oh, my LORD!" the words slipped out of his mouth without even realizing it. Immediately Arie and Alex and General Ziv turned to look in the direction where Jim was staring.

Above the heads of the onlookers, a blonde head moved toward them towering at least four feet above the mass of humanity that was swirling around them like a school of fish, pressing closer and closer toward the Eastern Gate. "Michael! That has to be Michael, the Archangel! He's coming through this crowd! There! Over there!" Jim exclaimed excitedly to his companions as he pointed excitedly at the enormous angel who had saved his bacon before. Jim tried unsuccessfully to find something ... anything ... to stand on, so he could look over the heads of the crowd. But there was nothing anywhere.

Jim was finally barely able to see that as Michael cleared the Eastern Gate, the crowd seemed to part behind him as four widely spaced men in white robes followed him who were obviously carrying something between them. Jim wondered what it could be. Then he heard some of the Hasidim and other Jews in the crowd gasp, "The Ark . . . the Ark of the Covenant is coming. Look, it is coming . . . it hasn't been seen since the destruction of the First Temple." As the four men crossed an opening in the crowd near him, Jim could see an ornate golden box with twin golden angels facing each other on the top lid. The box was being carried by the four men on two long poles through golden rings on the Ark itself, just as he had read in the Bible.

"Wow, what a marvel that the Ark should be revealed now, after all those centuries," Jim thought to himself, "I've got to get a better look at it when this is all over."

At that moment, an incandescent, blue-white light suddenly appeared behind the Ark and reflected off the inside top surface of the arch of the Eastern Gate. Jim could see a glowing figure seated on what appeared to be a snow-white horse. Instantly Jim knew! Every fiber of his being felt as though electricity was surging throughout his body. He was completely sensitized at every level with knowing …with understanding … with the same sensation he'd seen on these faces around him: JESUS was coming through that Gate! It had to be HIM.

Then, in a dream-like state, they all watched as time seemed to stand still   in fact nothing took preeminence over this moment. Despite the sensation of suspended animation, everything and everyone seemed to move about in slow motion, without a sound of any kind.

Many of the Hassidim began to swarm around Him, and managed to stop Jesus as He passed through the Eastern Gate. Jesus dismounted as one of their chief Rabbis approached Him reverently and asked, "Begging Your pardon, Sir! Please! We must know: What is Your Name and is this your First Visit … . . . . or your Second?" as he stared at the ground, not daring to so much as lift his eyes to meet the Savior's gaze. His heart pounded wildly as he struggled to stand to receive the Master's answer.

Jesus smiled and gently lifted the hem of His robe, displaying His sandaled feet, and then pushed up the sleeves of his garment revealing His hands and arms. Never taking his eyes off the Rabbi, He answered compassionately, "My Name is Yeshua and this is My Second Visit. Behold My hands and feet."

At once the Rabbi exclaimed in Hebrew, "Baruch haba beshem, ADONAI"

Alex translated the Rabbi's words aloud, "Blessed is He Who comes in the Name of the LORD! Aye 'tis a wonderful thing to hear and actually see after twenty centuries. Today, we have seen the fulfillment of Jesus' prophecy in Mathew:

'O Jerusalem, Jerusalem, you who killed the prophets and stoned those whom I sent to you! How often I wanted to gather your children together, as a mother hen gathers her chicks under *her* wings, but you refused! So your house is left desolate for I say to you, you shall not see Me again until you say, 'Blessed is He who comes in the name of the LORD!'" [22]

The devout in the Jewish crowd were instantly plunged into mourning. The Hassidim who had gathered around at a respectful distance took one look at Jesus' hands and feet and began to wail, "Oy ve! Oy ve oy! Woe upon woe! There, in His wrists and feet, are the holes made by the Roman nails! We have pored over the scriptures letter by letter for centuries and yet we were blind to the truth. How could we have missed it?" Some fainted, while others stood crying out and mourning aloud, tossing dust in the air above their heads.

"All these centuries, we have failed to recognize You, LORD," cried the Rabbi, "You are, beyond all doubt, the *Meshiach*! Can You ever forgive us, LORD?"

Jesus replied tenderly, "You are all My blood brothers and sisters through Abraham, Isaac, Jacob—through My mother, Mary. You have already been forgiven, but because you have finally seen Me with your eyes, do you *now* believe in Me? Blessed are those who have *not* seen Me, and yet have believed." [23]

Turning about, Jesus touched a Palestinian who had thrown down his rifle and was on his knees weeping and reaching out to Jesus.

Approaching Alex, Jesus reached down and gently touched the big Scot, who was spread-eagled face-down on the ancient paving stones. Like a father gently speaking to his small child, He said, "Get up, My son." Alex struggled, with the help of his friends, to regain his balance as the LORD continued speaking. "Alexander, you have been faithful in a little. I will make you a ruler over much. You and your wife, Mary, will inherit what your cousin had wrongfully acquired. You shall be My chosen ruler over all of Europe, Ireland, Scotland and England," Jesus said in a quietly reassuring voice.

"Och, LORD, please!! I look forward to seeing my beloved Mary again but Ya' certainly must know I am totally unworthy to do what Ya' just said! I am a sinful man and I have spilled human blood," Alex replied with tears streaming down his ruddy, weathered face, scarcely able to look the LORD in the eyes.

Then tenderly, Jesus reached out and touched his face and replied, "My sacrifice on the cross has made you worthy, My son. Fear not, you are forgiven and a man greatly beloved. Enter into the Joy of your LORD!"

Staring intently at Alex and the rest of his companions, Arie's analytical mind suddenly came alive as he noticed something that flabbergasted him: All his companions now suddenly appeared young—about 30 years of age. His mind reeled as he looked at his own arms and hands which were now young-looking, no longer bearing age-spots or the large scar he had sustained on his right arm from a soccer injury many years before. Fishing a small mirror out of his pocket, he examined his own face. He had not looked this young in years.

My God! All of us seem to be suddenly young again. I never thought this would happen this side of the veil. Or maybe this IS the other side of the veil that I've been waiting for.

As He circulated among Jim's other companions, Jesus stopped to speak personally to each one in turn. He blessed them all with a loving touch and a "Well done!"

Stopping in front of a now-very-young looking General Ziv, He hesitated momentarily, gazing down at the man on his knees before Him. "Zechariah Zebulon Ziv! My friend indeed! Arise, My son! You shall be My Prime Minister of this ... our beloved Israel!" said Jesus in a distinctly authoritative and kindly tone. He just stood there smiling for several moments—which seemed like an eternity to Zechariah. Then, He slowly turned his attention to the man's left.

"Ariel Ben-Yehudah! I see you have discovered your new body! You, My son, shall be Chief Minister of My court, along with your wonderful wife, Sarah." Jesus smiled knowingly. "Both of you, come, enter into My Joy!"

Ever since the flash of Light, behind Michael at the gate, Jim had been lost in the Spirit, *My God! My God! It's happened at last! This really IS the Second Coming of Jesus, our Messiah! Oh, Hallelujah! Our LORD has come to set up His Kingdom on the earth at last!*

Michael suddenly stepped in front of Jim, exclaiming, "LORD, he is over here!" The voice of the great angel reverberated through Jim's very being, instantly shaking him from his reverie. As the most important Person in his life stepped before him again, all the strength left Jim's legs and he fell to his knees. He would have fallen on his face had not an enormously powerful hand reached out and caught him, lifting him like a small child and setting him solidly on his feet again.

Jesus, dressed in shining white robes which sparkled like diamonds even in the subdued sunlight, stood before Jim with a look of pure love on His face. He spoke in a tone that was at once loving, gentle, compassionate, authoritative, and absolute. "Well done, My friend, My good and faithful servant. Enter now into the Joy of your LORD. You shall be the ruler of the entire Western Hemisphere. And, your beautiful wife shall stand by your side, as the perfect companion I have designed her to be," He concluded.

Gazing over the gathered worshippers, Jesus smiled and said, "Follow Me, all of you."

"LORD, what about the vast armies and air forces that are headed here or have already arrived?" asked General Ziv, utterly awed by the Man before him.

Hesitating only momentarily, Jesus answered quietly, "They will all collide, in My Presence in the Valley of Megiddo, or Jehoshaphat—just as the Prophet Joel foretold:

> "For behold! In those days, when I bring back the captives of Judah and Jerusalem, I will also gather all nations and bring them down to the Valley of Jehoshaphat; and I will enter into judgment with them there on account of My people, My heritage Israel, whom they have scattered among the nations; they have also divided up My land. They have cast lots for My people ... Let the nations be wakened, and come up to the Valley of Jehoshaphat, for there I will sit to judge all the surrounding nations for the winepress is full, the vats overflow, for their wickedness is great. Multitudes in the valley of decision! For the Day of the LORD is near in the valley of decision. The LORD will roar from Zion and utter His voice from Jerusalem; the heavens and earth will shake; but the LORD will be a shelter for His people, and the strength of the children of Israel. So you shall know that I am the LORD your

God, dwelling in Zion, My holy mountain. Then Jerusalem shall be holy and no aliens shall ever pass through her again."[24]

"Some of you were recently discussing the unusually large numbers of vultures and other wild beasts that have gathered in Israel. I have summoned them from all across the globe; they will soon feed upon the carcasses of My enemies as it is written in the Prophet Ezekiel:

> "As for you, Son of Man, says the Lord GOD, 'Speak to every sort of bird and to every beast of the field: "Assemble yourselves and come; gather together from everywhere to My sacrificial feast which I am preparing for you—a great sacrificial meal on the mountains of Israel—that you may eat the flesh and drink the blood of the mighty, the blood of the princes of the earth—of rams and lambs, goats and bulls, all of them fatlings of Bashan. You shall eat fat till you are full, and drink blood till you are drunk. You shall be filled at My table with horses and riders, with all the mighty men of war," says the Lord GOD. I will set My glory among the nations; all the nations shall see My judgment which I have executed, and My hand which I have laid on them. So the house of Israel shall know that I am the LORD their God from that day forward. [25]

You will all join Me in the greatest battle in all of history," He said to the group He had just blessed, "I will enter into judgment with Satan's minions there in the valley of Megiddo as I lead My army of saints and angels to lay 80 percent of them in the dust of the earth. I shall leave just enough of them alive to limp home and warn their own people that I have come and they had best repent for I will rule them with a rod of iron!

"General Black, my servants are, at this moment, apprising your naval commanders and aviators of the situation and advising key people within your Capitol in America that the threat has ended but one more battle remains. You may join your people as soon as the coming battle in the Valley of Megiddo is over. But for now, come! Let us be going, and prepare to complete the task before us" Jesus said with finality as He turned, mounted His horse, and spurred the great white stallion toward the Temple.

The Hasidic Rabbi stood gazing at the departing Savior and declared, "It is happening as it was prophesied by the Prophet Zechariah: "In that day the LORD will defend the inhabitants of Jerusalem; the one who is feeble among them in that day shall be as strong as David, and the house of David shall be like God, like the Angel of the LORD before them. It shall be in that day that I will destroy all the nations that have come against Jerusalem. And I will pour out upon the house of David and on the inhabitants of Jerusalem the Spirit of grace and supplication, then they will look on Me whom they have pierced. Yes, they will mourn for Me as one mourns for his only son, and grieve for Me as one grieves for a firstborn. And the land shall mourn, especially the family of the house of David. In that day a fountain shall be opened for the house of David and for the inhabitants of Jerusalem, for sin and for uncleanness. [26]

Amen!

EPILOG

The author's intention has been to provide a fictional adventure to bless the reader that is both entertaining and instructive. The sequence and timing of events in the Second Advent of Jesus Christ to earth is unknown. Many a scholar and preacher has prognosticated on the subject, but no one really knows for sure when, or exactly how, this world-shaking event will happen, except God the Father. So, put away your books and charts, concentrate on the Bible and living for God so you'll be ready for your death or His Second Advent, whichever occurs first.

In the Gospel of John, Jesus promises believers, "In My Father's house are many mansions; if *it were* not *so,* I would have told you. I go to prepare a place for you. And if I go and prepare a place for you, I will come again and receive you to Myself; that where I am, *there* you may be also." [27] The consequence of this statement for every person means that the risen Christ will personally return to welcome His children into His Heavenly Kingdom, whether it happens at His Second Coming or when the believer dies. Either way, on a personal basis, Jesus is coming back for His family.

If you were to die before meeting Him personally and having your sins, past, present and future swept away, you will awaken in the depths of Hell to live for all eternity, in a place so horrible that you would not want to send your worst enemy there for five seconds. Hell is so pitch black you cannot see anything around you, but there are demons and other creatures there that can see you and torture you forever. The heat is unbearable and there is no water there to quench your thirst. It is a place of terror and terrible regret. Can you imagine being utterly, totally alone for trillions of years with no one to talk to or love or be loved by, where there is no rest or respite from the pain 24 hours a day? Hell was not originally created for people, but only for the Devil and his angels. God does not vindictively send people to Hell—they send themselves there by misunderstanding, pride, arrogance or stubbornness that causes them to refuse Jesus' free offer of salvation.

God loves you so much that He sent His Son, Jesus, or *Yeshua*, to earth to make a totally free way, by His death on a Roman cross, for anyone who believes that He is the Savior of the world, who invites Him to forgive their sins and come into their life, publicly confessing Him to be their Lord and Savior, to spend eternity with Him in Heaven, the wonderful Kingdom of God.

If you do not know this Jesus as both personal Lord and Savior, wouldn't it be wise to establish a right relationship with Him right now? Jesus says in Revelation, "Behold, I stand at the door [of your heart] and knock. If anyone hears My voice and opens the door [of his or her heart], I will come in to him and [fellowship] with him, and he with Me.

I would like introduce you to the greatest FRIEND you will ever have. If you are sincere and you'll believe these words in your heart as you say the following prayer, you will be born again from above:

Jesus, I believe that You are the Son of God Who died on the cross for my sins. I ask You to come into my heart, forgive all my sins, cleanse me, fill me with Your Holy Spirit and make me a new person in You right now. Jesus, I want to thank You for loving me so much that You were willing to die for me. I accept all that Your shed blood bought for me on the cross, and I receive You now as my personal Savior and Lord of my life. In Your Name I pray. Amen

The Apostle Paul writes, ". . . if you confess with your mouth the Lord Jesus and believe in your heart that God has raised Him from the dead, you will be saved. For with the heart one believes unto righteousness, and with the mouth confession is made unto salvation. For the Scripture says, 'Whoever believes on Him will not be put to shame.'"[28]

If you've just prayed this prayer sincerely from your heart, you are now a "new creature in Christ," as the New Testament says: " . . . . if anyone *is* in Christ, *he is* a new creation; old things have passed away; behold, all things have become new."[29] This simply means that although you don't look any different (and may not feel any different), it doesn't depend on feelings; the fact remains that your entire being—body, soul and spirit— has just gone through what might best be described as a "quantum shift" and you are now a brand new creation, something that has never existed before, ever, in time or eternity.

You may or may not feel any differently, although many do, but feelings are fickle and are not a reliable gauge by which to measure what has happened to you. You may have a sense of peace and joy you have never experienced before but regardless of how you feel, know that when you prayed that prayer, Jesus came into your heart for He is true to His word, and the angels in heaven rejoiced that a new son or daughter of God has been born into the Kingdom of God; never question that fact.

Find a good church that believes in, preaches and practices the Word of God and attend faithfully. Get yourself a good Bible in an easy to understand translation and start reading in the New Testament first, specifically the Gospel of John. When you are a little more experienced, I recommend you study closely the Book of Romans for it is probably the most organized and coherent explanation of the Christian faith and the position of the believer (You) in God's Kingdom.

Shalom, my friend! I'll see you in Heaven.

END NOTES

1. Excerpted from NKJV Psalm 104:3, NKJV Revelation 22:10,12, NKJV Hebrews 12:1

2. Daniel 12:4 Author's idiomatic translation from the original Hebrew

3. NKJV Revelation 1:17-18

4. NKJV Psalm 83:2-8

5. NKJV Genesis 17:7-22

6. Genesis 16:12 Author's idiomatic original Hebrew translation

7. Refers to 1 Samuel 15:7-23 Author's idiomatic translation of the original Hebrew text

8. NKJV Isaiah 17:1

9. Excerpted from NKJV Obadiah 1:6-15

10. Ezekiel 38:1-23 Author's idiomatic translation of the original Hebrew text

11. Excerpted from Ezekiel 39:1-29 Author's idiomatic translation of the original Hebrew text

12. Excerpted from NKJV Matthew 24:14-22

13. Hebrews 13:2 Author's idiomatic translation of the original Greek text

14. Zechariah 14:12 Author's idiomatic translation from the original Hebrew by the Author

15. Excerpted from NKJV Psalm 83:2-12

16. The word "Aphar" means "Dust" in Hebrew.

17. 2 Kings 6:14 The author's idiomatic Hebrew translation

18. NKJV Romans 14:11

19. NKJV Revelation 19:15

20. NKJV 1 Thessalonians 4:16a

21. NKJV Zechariah 14:4

22. Mathew 25:37-39 Author's translation of the Koine Greek

23. NKJV John 20:29

24. Excerpted from Joel 3: 1-17 Author's translation from the original Hebrew.

25. Ezekiel 39:17-22 Author's translation from the original Hebrew.

26. Zechariah 12:8-10, 13:1 Author's translation from the original Hebrew

27. NKJV John 14:2-3

28. NKJV Romans 10: 9-11

29. NKJV 2 Cor. 12:17